Journey to Landaran

The Spirit Mage Saga
Book One

JUDY GOODWIN

Diamond Print Press

DEDICATION

This book is dedicated to my partner and supporter, who allowed me to follow my dreams.

CONTENTS

PROLOGUE

New Life

Night fell over the city of Landaran as Korva Liam dragged her old body up the tower to her magic-working room. Long velvet skirts hampered her way on the stone steps, and she had to pause to disentangle her cane. She cursed as the movement sent pain through her arthritic hands. Upon reaching the top, she struggled to get the key to turn in the heavy iron lock. On groaning hinges, she pushed the door open.

The room was small and circular, with a cot to the left, and a book stand on side opposite the door. Upon the stand was a large volume opened to a detailed genealogy chart that spanned several generations. She crossed to the book and ran her finger down the page, halting as she came upon a name: Arlene Dell. Beside the name was a scribbled note, "Married to Darrant Dernholt, expecting baby by mid-December."

Late November, more like it, Korva thought, shivering. And here she was up in this drafty tower with no fire and a window whose shutters never seemed to close properly. She was crazy to be trying this tonight, when there was chance of snow. But she had to see the birth. Only then, at the first moment of life, would she be able to See the magic potential with accuracy. After that she would have to wait until puberty.

Korva tapped a finger on the *Book of the Magic Line,* a book she herself had created over the span of her life, nearly two hundred thirty years long now. The book listed the names and relationships of her descendants. She tried to bring to mind the face of Arlene Dernholt, a great-seven-times-over granddaughter who, as she recalled, lived with a sheep herder in the Morgaine mountains of the Doane, far to the north and west.

The picture came to her mind with difficulty. The last time she had visited Arlene, the woman had been fourteen, and sadly, while rich in potential, no Talent had materialized in her. Hopefully her child would carry the Life Talent. Korva was tired, so very tired of being the only one of her line able to defend; named the so-called 'Great Protector'. Death called to her, but she could not go just yet. She would have to continue taking her yearly sacrifice to extend her life until her replacement could be found.

"Arlene, Arlene..." Muttering the name helped; into her mind came the vision of a young woman with straight dark brown hair framing a heart-shaped face and large green eyes. She was a diminutive woman, like many in Korva's line, and had seemed timid in Korva's view, but then, her own ornery traits couldn't breed true every time.

Once she'd managed to make a clear image of the one she wanted to visit in her mind, Korva stretched herself across the little bed. She pulled the thick fur coverlet over herself to make sure she was comfortable. She despised coming back to herself to find a crick in her neck or a limb fallen asleep. Just as she got herself perfectly settled, a gust of icy wind blew open the shutters of the room's only window, sending them slamming against the gray stone walls. Korva groaned.

"I'm not closing you now that I'm finally warm and comfortable. You'll just have to go close yourself," she growled at the shutters, and amazingly they did close, with a bang.

Must be life in them yet! Korva thought, chuckling. Life forces within wood rarely responded to her Talent, and in a piece that old— well, at least she wouldn't freeze now. Time to enter the trance.

She closed her eyes, focusing on her life energy, her consciousness. Carefully she separated it from her physical body, disconnecting each energy point: eye, ear, brain, heart, gut, womanhood. When she felt each point was detached, she thought upwards, and soon shed the cumbersome weight of her decrepit body.

Sensing the conical roof just above her, Korva opened her "eyes." She floated over her body, her ethereal form a sinuous ghost, glowing softly in the dark room. So tiny, she thought, looking at the frail thing below her: pale skin covered with wrinkles, flesh sagging off the bones and white hair falling like a river down the shoulders and across the covers. That hair had once been a glorious gold, but now, well, there wasn't much left of her former beauty.

Concentrating on her destination, she rose through the roof and flew out over the walled city, heading north towards the peaks of the Morgaine Range. To the east stretched the foreboding red waters of the Krimean Sea, the main barrier between her people and the Enemy—her father. *May he die and rot in the Underworld.*

She could not stand looking in that direction, so she turned away and passed over the city and up the rocky foothills, up to the higher peaks, already covered in a thick blanket of snow. Faster than any bird, she flew over the range, noting settlements here and there nestled in the valleys and along the rivers and lakes. In a mountain valley before a towering crooked peak, she found her destination, a village of perhaps fifty low buildings, many of them with large pastures of sheep. Hamstead.

Korva swept downwards, checking for a house whose lights were still burning at this wee hour. One cottage on the outskirts of the village was lit, resting beside an old thatched roof barn. Memory stirred. She remembered this humble abode—it was the same Arlene had grown up in, her grandfather's house. Poor dear Bevan; he'd been such a crusader, but he was dead now. So many descendants, dead and buried. It was frightening to dwell too long on it.

She landed at the front door and drew near the window, just to make sure it was the right house. It would never do to spy on strangers. She recognized Bevan's son—Arlene's father, Ethan Dell. He paced the small bedroom as a midwife bent over to wipe the forehead of a woman in the bed, her knees drawn up under the blankets.

She looks like she's going to pop! Korva thought, noting the size of Arlene's belly. After seeing several generations of births, Korva knew an unusual birth when she saw one. If it was required, she would use her Life magic to aid. She dared not help, however, unless she absolutely had to. Her father would be watching for any unusual use of her Talent. And she would let a Talented child die before she let it fall into *his* hands.

Korva used one of Arlene's contractions as a diversion to slip inside where she didn't have to put up with gusts of wind going through her body. Since she had no body she couldn't really feel heat or cold, but the mind didn't always remember that. She tried to keep in the background. Arlene's potential for the Life Talent was high enough that she could sometimes see magic at work, including those traveling out of body.

Once Korva had found a comfortable spot, she waited. The labor drew on and Ethan left to pace outside while the father-to-be took up a place by the fire, nervously untwining a bit of rope. The midwife stayed by Arlene's side, mopping her brow and soothing her when the pains came. She did not seem overly concerned. Korva looked around for Arlene's mother, then remembered the woman had died a year earlier—she remembered writing the entry into her book. So many dead. But life went on. New life came to replace those lost, as it was doing now.

The birth began in earnest and the midwife removed the covers to check for the head. She ordered the two men to fetch the hot water. Korva floated up to the bedside as Arlene grunted and groaned, allowing the young woman to see her, to know she was with family; if not her mother, then at least a greater-than-great grandmother.

"Grandess!," Arlene whispered, reaching out a hand to her, amazed. Korva felt the hand pass through her. Arlene's eyes widened as she realized she was gazing at a spirit. "Are you dead?" she gasped.

"No, I'm alive, just too old to travel in body here. Now push, child. It's almost finished. Push hard for me," Korva urged, smiling on the woman with a tenderness she rarely let show. Arlene screwed shut her eyes and did push, on and on, for nearly a candlemark, before at last the baby came out, howling with indignity.

Korva leaned over the midwife's shoulder as the woman cleaned the babe, frowning as she determined its sex. A boy. Boys were dangerous, too often she had lost her Talented boys to the call of her father. This one would definitely be Talented, of that she was certain. The glow of magical ability surrounded him in a hearty orange glow to her Sense, showing great strength, though in which of the three spheres, Life, Fire, or Storm, Korva could not determine. Amazing that such a glow should come from such a small infant— this one was quite tiny, perhaps only five pounds, with a head full of dark hair and a turned up little nose. It looked healthy. And loud.

After the umbilical was cut, the midwife showed the baby to its proud father as it cried lustily. Korva chuckled. With vocals like that, the child promised to be a lifetime of trouble for his parents. She wished him luck.

Things seemed to be settling down now as the first light of day broke through the room's only window, throwing beams of light across Arlene's happy face. Korva prepared to leave, to make arrangements for when the child's powers appeared in truth, some eight to fourteen years from now. Then Arlene doubled over in pain.

The afterbirth, Korva thought at first, as did the midwife, until she went over to check. From her vantage point, Korva saw little, but the midwife gasped and began frantically waving Arlene's father over to help. "Twins!" She said breathlessly by way of explanation.

Korva returned to Arlene's side and they began the whole ordeal again, Korva urging Arlene to be strong, don't think about the pain, push, push. But Arlene was tired, and this baby did not seem as eager to leave the womb. After a couple of hours when Arlene moaned that she did not have the strength to push any more, Korva resorted to her Talent. With a wave of dizziness, she sent strength from herself into Arlene's battered body.

Korva could feel her thoughts grow sluggish as the energy left her, threatening to dissolve her ties of spirit holding her together. She fought to stay focused. The gods grant that she had not given too much of herself to be able to return to her body, that this effort not be in vain for the sake of the child and Arlene. And that this interference had not been noticed from afar.

With renewed vigor, Arlene sat up in the bed, screaming in pain and frustration, pushing with all of her might. Finally the head appeared, and the birth came swiftly after. This second child was even smaller than the first, and fragile-looking. Korva immediately noticed that it was a girl, light-haired and silent. That changed after the midwife gave it a smart slap on the back and it began to wail, but even its wail sounded weak. A faint glow, violet, surrounded it, suggesting magic potential, but nothing definite. Korva swallowed with disappointment. This one looked too weak to be of any help to her.

Korva had to leave; Father could come in spirit form and look in on them at any second. She couldn't give away these newest additions to her line. After giving a swift kiss to Arlene along with her blessings, Korva limped out of the cottage and drifted up to a safe altitude, flying back as quickly as her tired spirit could manage.

Over the mountains, back to the tower she floated. As she passed over the city she felt something foul which could have been her father's probings, or perhaps only the whiff of a late sleeper's nightmare. There was always such a thin line between reality and the dreamworld while in spirit form. But she managed to make it back to her body, settling down into it to open her real eyes and feel the ache in her legs as well as the beginnings of a shock fever from having used too much power. She had enough energy to send a mental call to her aides to come fetch her. Then she sank into exhausted slumber.

At the edge of unconsciousness, she thought she heard her father chuckle.

1

Fowl Play and Fevered Signs

"Tavish, if you don't watch out, you're going to fall!" Aidah called to her brother as he leapt across the chasm cutting into the slope of the mountain. Her warning went unheeded. Tavish landed with perfect balance onto a narrow ledge.

"I never fall," he boasted, then waved for her to jump across. He caught her as she made a similar leap, staying close to the rocky cliff side. She stuck out her tongue at him, dusting herself off. Then together they scrambled up a treacherous rise to an outcropping on the mountainside, overlooking the valley.

They were far up in the arms of Crooked Peak, looking down on the village of Hamstead. The red sloped rooftops looked tiny from up here, and they could see their own cottage out beyond the edge of town with its pasture and garden. The pasture appeared empty today; Father had taken the sheep to get the last few bits of grass before snow covered the ground. This was the last time they'd be able to climb this peak until spring, high up where the wyrrets made their nests.

"Quite a view, eh Sis?" Tavish said, his breath making a puff in the air. He grinned at the excitement of their venture, gray eyes tinged with mischievous green. Small-boned and lithe, he'd chosen his clothing carefully for today's climb; warm, but not encumbering, with sheepskin leggings and a vest of bear fur. His straight light brown hair was tightly held beneath a woolen cap, making his ears stick out impishly.

"Tavish, if Father knew we were up here…let's just grab one and get back as quickly as possible, okay?" Aidah urged, tucking in her own blond hair back into her kerchief and checking to make sure her clothes didn't hinder her. She preferred dresses, but today she wore her brother's shirt and leggings which didn't really fit her, being loose in the shoulder and tight in the hips. They were both turning fourteen next week, and her body was developing into something more womanly.

"Hey, I promised you a wyrret for your birthday. You worry too much. It'll be easy. Sneak up and snatch. Just like cake," Tavish said, referring to their favorite pastime—stealing tarts and pastries from the baker by climbing over the roof to snatch them from the windowsill. Perhaps their climbing skills were not always honestly used, but Aidah did try to pay back for their mischief by leaving large tips whenever they bought from the baker. Today she would compensate for the stealing of a wyrret by leaving the bundle of food she'd hidden in her pouch.

Tavish hummed to himself as he pulled out a length of rope secured to a metal rake which had been fashioned into a crude grapnel. With an easy grace, he slung the rope and caught the makeshift grapnel on a rock fifty feet above them, pulled on it to test its strength, then nimbly climbed up the rope using mostly his hands. Aidah waited until he clambered off, then shimmied up the rope herself.

They were above the tree line now, and snow piled in the shadowed crevices between rocks and against the cliffs, starkly outlining each jagged rise. To go up much further would be dangerous even on a mildly cold day like today; already her lungs burned at the thin air. But this was far enough for their needs. Tavish crouched under an overhang, looking through a spy glass he had also made with a piece of leather and two crude lenses at a distant object up in the clouds.

"Look here. I've spotted the father," he whispered, waving her over. She crouched by him, looking through the eyepiece while he held it steady.

The small wyrret flew high up in the clouds. Rare, magical creatures created long ago as playthings for the rich, wyrrets eventually outsmarted their creators and adapted to the wild. Mages had taken the blue bird and the ferret and combined them. Their cunning and speed proved to be a great asset in avoiding predators such as hawks, eagles, and giant rocs.

Aidah adjusted Tavish's hold on the spy glass so that she could see the nest hidden in a short recess in the mountain perhaps a couple hundred yards up from them. She saw the mother, her fur in the midst of changing from brown to white for the winter, arching her wings to keep her young warm.

The father landed on the nest with a flutter of wings, whiskers twitching as he checked his mate, his large brown eyes intent on her. Then he took to the air again, playing in the wind, his white wings with soft blue flight feathers and white fur making him nearly disappear against the sky and clouds. Like their non-magical ferret cousins, wyrrets loved to play, but they could be fierce protectors of their cubs. This would take some doing.

"The nest is above an open ledge. It should be easy to reach, but the little father isn't going to like us standing there, and there isn't much cover if he decides to buzz us. Do you have a plan?" she asked. The glee in Tavish's eyes answered her even before he spoke. She felt also a tickle in her head like a giggle of laughter accompanied by a slight dizziness; she shook her head to dispel it. Twice in the last week her head had felt funny like that. Probably just nerves.

"I always have a plan," Tavish said, grinning "I'm going to create a small fire on the mountainside to distract both and to keep them from diving at us." He thrust out his chest and grinned wolfishly. As a full strength Firestarter and future Sun Mage, he had the Talent to affect light and heat. When it had first appeared four years ago it had been a nightmare for him to control, but since then he'd been trained a bit by a visiting Sun Mage, and now he tried to show off his powers whenever possible. It was especially annoying for an un-Talented sibling like herself, but Aidah would forgive him if he could get her a wyrret.

After taking back the spy glass, Tavish lead Aidah up the next rise, an especially treacherous one with biting winds threatening to blow them off balance. Aidah looked down and realized how naked they were here, with no trees for cover, only the overhanging rock from the ledge above.

The wyrrets must have guessed their intention, for they became agitated, flying in tight circles around the nest, squeaking in fear. Aidah opened her mouth to ask Tavish to start his magic. Then a shadow blocked out the sun.

The wyrrets squealed and took off away from the nest,

abandoning their babies as the shadow gave an ear-splitting shriek, the volume of its voice sending trickles of snow running down the cliff at Aidah's back. Light returned as the creature crossed the sun and was illuminated in frightening detail, russet feathers and enormous scaled talons. With a rush of wind which drove Tavish and Aidah into the cliff, the giant roc flapped its wings and took off after its prey.

"Tavish, do something! Save them!" Aidah screamed as the giant bird swooped past them after the wyrrets, its beak opened wide. The roc chased them down around the mountain, out of sight.

The wyrrets would hardly make a mouthful, but the enmity between rocs and wyrrets was far greater than a simple need for food. The small creatures were notorious for annoying the huge birds, stealing their nest sites and diving at their young to steal food right out of their mouths.

Aidah glanced at her brother and found him struggling just to hold onto the cliff.. It seemed the wind and falling snow had made him lose his foothold. She hurried to help him to a more secure part of the ledge.

"What a monster!" he gasped once he was steady. "Is it gone?" He clutched at the rocky face of the cliff, hugging it to keep from the edge.

Crouching to keep her center of gravity, Aidah peered over the edge, but the slope of the mountain prevented her from seeing anything but sky and mountain. "Should we continue? I'd feel awful if our actions today killed those poor things. Did we attract the roc?" Her heart pounded against her ribcage and that strange dizziness overcame her again. She heard Tavish muttering to himself, but when she looked up at him his mouth was shut. He was grimacing.

"Damn bird. If it would just fly up here, I'd show it a thing or two. How dare it attack our prey! And if it finds that nest ..." His eyes widened. "Hurry! We've got to get to the nest to protect the babies." He didn't say what they both feared; that the parents had already both been swallowed.

Carefully they scaled the cliff leading up to the nest on an outcropping of rock. Tavish, his arm muscles contracting, pulled himself over the top then he helped pull Aidah up alongside him. Together they crept into the enormous nest of thorn brush and thistle, softened with molted roc feathers. The outcropping provided just enough room for the huge nest, undoubtedly stolen from its former occupant. Aidah stepped over a long fir branch which made up the base of the nest, trying to make her way into the center where she heard the frightened mewling of the wyrret cubs.

Just as she spotted the brown-furred little fellows stumbling clumsily over each other, there came again that awful screech from behind. Aidah whirled and screamed at the roc to scare it off.

Her movement was too sudden. The branch she stood on snapped, and she fell back, tumbling down the nest towards the brink of the ledge. Tavish reached out and caught hold of her shirt as her legs slipped over the edge.

"Grab my arm! Pull yourself up," he commanded as the fabric in his hand began to tear.

Aidah tried to grab for his arm, but her body was turned awkwardly. At least her predicament seemed to have one benefit. The roc, startled by her fall, wheeled away.

She didn't have time to see if there were any other flying creatures down there, such as a few frightened wyrret parents. The shirt tore. Aidah scrambled to get hold of something, anything,. She felt herself falling, and then Tavish's fingers clamped hard around her wrist, his short nails pinching into her skin.

"Sis, don't move; I'm not secure here. Just stay still and let me pull you up." Aidah looked up at her brother holding her with one hand, trying to get a foothold or any kind of handhold on the cliff to brace himself in order to pull her back up. The fact she was looking up at him alarmed her—she was truly hanging off the cliff, her shoulders rubbing the hard granite of the edge, her lower body dangling.

Tavish found a rock to hold onto and pulled, but while the cords in his neck jutted out and his arm trembled with effort, he couldn't pull her up at all before his feet began to slip. She very carefully grasped his arm with her other hand, but still he was not quite strong or secure enough. Aidah's heart pounded through her rib cage, as fear began to sink in. If she fell, it would be a messy death. Death wasn't something she ever really thought about, yet here it suddenly was, glaring at her. The two of them struggled, trying to get her up, but it was useless. She swallowed back a moan as tears burned in her eyes.

"Gods, if I knew a spell to fix this!" Tavish gasped.

His words seemed to trigger something within her. Strength, that was what he needed. If only she could somehow lend him strength…

A blinding pain tore at the base of her skull, and she could suddenly hear Tavish muttering to himself, although his lips were firmly pressed shut. She didn't have time to listen to what he was saying, however, before a pressure wave suddenly went through her body, traveling from the soles of her feet up through her torso and out through her hands where she gripped Tavish's arm. As the wave passed, strength left her, darkening her vision. She opened her mouth to scream, thinking perhaps she was dying.

With a cry, Tavish pulled hard at her, and she found herself on the cliff again, in Tavish's arms lying at the very back of the ledge. Apparently he had pulled so hard he'd sent both of them back several paces. Even now he looked ready to do it again—there was no trace of fatigue. She, on the other hand, felt pale and sickly. The world was spinning, and she was afraid her knees wouldn't hold her up. Trembling, she tried to get up and fell back against her brother.

He set her down and stood, brushing snow and dirt from his trousers. "Wow, where did that come from, I wonder? I feel like a fresh ox! I think I could move a mountain right now! Did you do something, Sis?" He paced around stretching out his arms and legs, as if unable to stand still.

The world was graying out to Aidah and she found it difficult to follow what Tavish was saying. Her head was pounding with one of the worst headaches she'd ever had. "I don't…think so. Maybe your magic helped you. Can we go home? I'm not feeling so well…" The world suddenly tilted and fell into blackness.

"Aidah? Aidah, talk to me, are you ok?" Tavish gripped his sister's shoulders, gently shaking her as she slumped over, her eyes rolling back. At least he tried to be gentle—the strength and vigor flowing inside was hard to control.

That strength concerned him—he was positive he hadn't done it; couldn't do it, in fact. His power was over light and heat only, not life energies like strength. Perhaps the fear had caused it. He'd heard about men performing amazing feats when terrified, and he'd definitely been terrified, seeing his sister so close to falling. If something happened to her, he didn't know what he would do.

The only response he got to shaking Aidah was a groan. Her head lolled back against her shoulder, and one blue-gray eye opened, but there was no conscious thought there. Her cheeks were flushed; she looked fevered, and in the chill up here that could be deadly. He had to get her down somehow. At least he had the strength right now to make it possible.

He lifted her up, and set her on his back, piggy-back style. It was difficult to keep her upper body straight against him—he hoped she would wake up soon so she could hold on. Otherwise they might very well be stuck up here.

But perhaps with some rope...

"Well bugger me if we don't use that oversize shirt of yours to some good, Sis. 'Specially since I stretched it a bit more trying to keep you from falling," Tavish said, more to comfort himself than for Aidah's benefit. He pushed her arms back into the shirt and used the sleeves to attach her to his waist, tying a few good knots in the material to be sure it held. She moaned weakly, coming to.

"Just a few minutes now, and we'll be back to safety. Don't worry, I won't let you fall," he continued, and took off his overtunic to use as a second tie, securing her legs round his hips. That done, he slowly and carefully started climbing down the cliff.

"Tavish, wh-what's happening? I feel so weak..." Aidah mumbled at his ear, her wispy long bangs brushing at the nape of his neck.

"Shh, be still, Sis. Hold onto your questions til I'm in a better spot to answer 'em," Tavish said, his fingers gripping the cold icy rocks of the cliff. He inched his way down the sheer face of the mountain, down to the ledge where they'd first seen the wyrret, then untied Aidah and rested a moment. Great burst of strength or not, that hadn't been easy.

He checked Aidah to see if she was awake and coherent. She was awake, but fevered, and still very weak—even her breathing was slow and labored. To get down his rope, he used the same method as the cliff, tying her to his waist and making his way very slowly down. Then the way became easier and she was able to help somewhat, walking with her arms around him for support, as in a dream. They had to stop every few minutes for her to rest.

At the base of the mountain Aidah's remaining strength gave out, and again Tavish was forced to carry her through the forested valley and into the rocky meadows where thorny hedges and high stone walls divided one pasture from another. He wove his way quickly through holes in the hedges, over low spots of the walls—the land was familiar, molded by himself and others his age for easy travel away from the eyes of the village grown-ups.

As he went, Tavish tried to keep back the cold fingers of fear which kept trying to squeeze back the air in his lungs. She looked so pale, so very pale, though her heart beat strong through the fabric at his back. What could have possibly happened up there—a curse on them from some mountain god, for trespassing on his domain? A poisoning of the air, like what occurred sometimes in the silver mines?

He couldn't figure out how she had been hit and himself spared—somehow that was the worst part of the strange ailment. Perhaps they would have been worse off, both still suffering on the mountaintop, but to feel so strong while she was so weak…what would he do if he lost her? He began walking faster.

At the edge of his home pasture he spotted their mother hanging out linens to dry on the clothesline, her long dark brown hair tied back in a kerchief, framing her heart-shaped face so like his sister's and his. "Mama, Aidah's sick!" he called to her, hoping she wouldn't ask questions, at least not until Sis was feeling better. He let Aidah lean against the rail post of the fence surrounding their vegetable garden, trying to ignore the soreness in his arms and back.

His mother took one look at them, dropped her basket of linens and ran over, calling, "Papa, Aidah's sick! Come quickly!"

Tavish gratefully relinquished his burden over to his mother's open arms, following in the wake of her long woolen skirts as she went to the door of the cottage where she met Grandpapa to share the weight of Aidah's unconscious body. In short order they had Aidah situated in her bed by the window, her head propped up on several pillows, the blankets pulled up to her chin.

"Mama, is that you? Am I home?" Aidah whispered, blinking slowly, looking angelic with her pale skin and heart-shaped face. Each breath wheezed in her chest.

"Yes, honey. Just rest—I'll have the healer here shortly," Tavish's mother, Arlene, said in a soft cooing voice, gently petting Aidah's damp hair. She turned to Tavish, giving him a hard questioning stare. "Tavish?"

"Yes, I'll go! Be right back, Mama!" Tavish offered, before she could begin asking questions. He sprinted out the door and was off running before she could blink.

Slowly strength was returning, but Aidah's body could not seem to decide if it was hot or cold, and the pain in her head had not lessened one whit. She was snuggled in her cot against the window which was open to allow a cool breeze across her fevered brow. Mama and Grandpapa Ethan were both standing near, eyeing her worriedly. She frowned. Shouldn't she still be up on the mountain?

"How did I get here? Was it just a dream?" She asked, then remembered she wasn't supposed to say anything about where she had been. Everything still seemed fuzzy, and she kept hearing a sort of whispering in her head, but she remembered the roc and the wyrrets well enough. It had happened.

A canine whimper sounded at the door to her room and Derg the Lupas appeared, his large black eyes full of concern. He came over, padded paws almost silent on the packed earthen floor, and took a sniff at her. "And where do you think you've been all morning, Miss?" he said, his canine accent almost making the words unintelligible.

He must have been worried to let his native accent mar his words; Derg was usually the very model of propriety and polite speech, Aidah thought, petting the short silken fur of his head and graceful neck.

Like the wyrrets, Derg's kind, the Lupas, had been in ancient times the pets of mages, created and designed by Spirit Mages to be companions to the rich. They appeared to be abnormally tall greyhounds, standing three feet high at the shoulder. Their paws had elongated digits able to grasp things, though with difficulty. Unlike the wyrrets who remained animal-like in their intelligence, the Lupas had been granted highly intelligent minds and the power of speech, through the Talent of Life magic.

Derg had always used his mind and voice to teach, praise, and scold his human charges, acting for the family as a sort of mentor and chaperone. How he had come into the family was muddled to Aidah; "Grandess" had given him to them as a pup when they were very small. He kept watch on them, always loving and supportive even if their adventures got them into trouble; however, he did not condone anything genuinely dangerous. Aidah was sure she'd be hearing his scoldings soon enough.

"Young lady, did I not instruct you to remain close to the home today? You informed me that you would be away for just a moment to fetch your basket so we could help the Ostlanders with the harvest, and then what? You disappeared! I searched the town, the pastures, the fields—" Derg paced the room, his long tail punctuating each comment with a lashing stroke, "—and now you are taken ill? And with scents of blue mountain pine on your clothing! Where in the world have you been, and why? You're going to disgrace my family name and send me to an early grave, sneaking off as you do."

"Derg, it's all right, she seems to be recovering now. We can get the details of what happened later. Let her sleep," Arlene spoke in a soothing voice, laying her hand on the Lupas and gently leading him to the door. "Papa, are you coming? She probably doesn't want all of us standing over her. I'm sure she'll call if she needs anything, won't you, Aidie?"

"Yes, Mama—but I'm not really tired. Just weak." Aidah rubbed her temple, willing the voices to go away. Instead, they seemed to become sharper, clearer.

*What could possibly be wrong with her—I'd better go talk to the healer—oh, I hope Tavish returns soon with him…*the words, some in a female voice, some male, kept rambling on in her skull, heavily laced with concern and worry. Aidah rubbed her temple harder. *Go away!* she mentally shouted. The voices finally subsided into silence.

"I'll stay with her, just for a bit," Grandpapa Ethan said in his easy country drawl. His short white hair lay flat against his skull from where he had removed his hat, his deeply tanned face in stark contrast to his white forehead. He looked down on her, sky blue eyes clouded with concern. "She can sleep or we can talk, real quiet-like." He went over to sit in an old rocking chair by the fireplace and took out his pipe to smoke, then seeing the look of ire on Arlene's face, tapped it on the arm of the chair before returning it to his pocket. He smiled sheepishly.

Derg and Arlene left the room, but just as Aidah thought she'd have some quiet for her headache, in the door burst her father.

"What happened? Tavish called me back from the fields before tearing off for town. Said you collapsed all of a sudden. How ya feeling, sweetie?" He went to hug her, then hesitated, wiping at the dirt on his trousers. His light brown hair was in disarray, swept back in a ponytail, and his tunic smelled of sheep and grass. She grinned and hugged him hard.

"I'm feeling better now. Just a little weak. I think I just got a scare, that's all. Tavish and I were trying to get a wyrret and a roc showed up and it startled us." She felt bad for tattling on Tavish, but it'd be worse if she didn't tell the truth right now. Derg was going to tell everyone just what he smelled on them, and wyrret fur was not something one would find in the valley.

"You mean you were—" he seemed ready to scold her, then shook his head in confusion. "But you're fine now. That's important." He scratched his head and looked around, noting Grandpapa for the first time. "Hello Ethan," he said, sighing.

"Hey Darrant. Just watching over her until the healer comes and checks her. She's looking better, but she was unconscious when Tavish brought her in. I think it was more than a scare, but I guess the healer will determine exactly what." Ethan lit his pipe and quietly puffed away, blowing his smoke into the low burning fire in the fireplace.

Her father looked worriedly at her. "You're just feeling weak, is that all?" he asked softly, putting a hand to her brow.

She grimaced. He had to feel the fever in her. She didn't want to worry him; he always worked so hard to make her and Tavish happy. Why oh why had this had to happen today?

"I don't need to see a healer. It was probably just the heights, the air. I'm sure I'll be fine soon," she hurried to reassure them, wondering how much the healer would ask her about the adventure. If her parents knew how close she'd been to falling...

She looked at her father, at his tender brown eyes, skin roughened by years in the sun, carved into lines of laughter and wisdom. He was a simple man, but he knew more about things than most people gave him credit for. How much should she tell him? How much could he guess just by looking at her?

"I don't really want to talk about what happened right now, Papa," she said, another wave of weakness washing over her. She saw in her mind's eye a vision—Tavish, running through the village, his cap flying off to fall at the feet of one of the village bullies, Garl Tanner. The bully snatched up the cap and ran in front of Tavish to block his way toward the healer's. A wave of dizziness blurred the vision, then it faded away altogether. She shook her head, fear gripping her.

"Yes, I definitely think I will sleep," she muttered, trying not to show the chaos which was happening inside. Where had that bit of fancy come from? This was beginning to frighten her, between the funny voices, the dizziness, the pain, and now waking dreams? Perhaps she was sick, after all.

Her father's rough hand gently stroked her brow, as he observed her. "Rest, then, sweetie. Papa's here. Everything's going to be just fine," his low voice lulled her.

With the smell of the pasture from his clothes and the warmth of his hands tucking her in, Aidah closed her eyes and let herself sink again into unconsciousness, this time into slumber. At the brink, a thought came to her.

I hope I'm not going crazy.

2

Talent Uprising

Tavish skidded to a halt in the narrow alley between two shops, his boots scraping against the hard-packed cobblestone. Just across the lane he could see the healer's house next to the bakery. Blocking his way, however, was a tall gangly youth about a year his senior, with long arms, big hands, and a scowl on his pock-marked face. Tavish repressed a shudder. Garl Tanner and he had never gotten along with each other, since Tavish at age ten had accidentally set his hair on fire.

On Garl's right and left were his buddies Brock and Dean. Brock, the rounder one, was holding a woolen cap in his hands and smiling wickedly. Tavish felt at his head and realized his cap must have flown off with the speed of his running. He smiled coaxingly.

"Ok guys, ya got my cap. And you can keep it if you want. I just need to get by real quick. Have to get to the healer's," he said, stooping down a little so that he appeared even smaller than usual, trying as a mouse to quietly slip by.

Garl strode up and grabbed his arms in his big hands. "Not so fast, firebrat. I haven't given you permission to go anywhere. Now, how about you get on your knees and ask permission, then maybe I'll let you go."

Tavish stood straighter, trying to stare Garl in the eye though he was half his height. The strength from the mountain was still with him. He was not going to let Garl intimidate him today, though he was generally easy going about the whole game. "Let me go, Garl. Aidie's sick—she needs a healer. If you don't let me pass, I'll set your arse on fire this time."

Garl sneered. "You can't, or they'll never let you become a Sun Mage. You're trained now, so you can't do it by accident neither."

Tavish grimaced, knowing he was right and that he had two witnesses who would only be too happy to blame him for any trouble. He pleaded once more, imagining Aidah in the bed, looking so weak, so pale, and getting weaker by the minute, "Come on, this is serious. She could be dying."

"What, little wart-nose?, little miss la-di-da head-in-the-clouds? I'll bet she just got caught stealing tarts or something and you have to go rescue her. You're such a sissy, always by her side. You're not getting by me. Go around the building if you want."

Tavish knew he should go around, avoid this hassle and his growing temper, but he wasn't going to let Pock-face say horrid things about Aidie. "Take it back," he warned, holding up one fist. Anger brimmed just under the surface, hardening his face into a scowl.

"Wart-nose, wart-nose, stinky little frog toes!" Garl sang, then stuck out his tongue.

The fires burning within burst; Tavish kept a firm check on his Talent, but let loose his temper. "Maybe I can't burn you, but I can sure as hell beat in that ugly face," he said with a snarl, and charged Garl, tackling him to the ground to punch his face. Brock and Dean ran up to pull him off and soon he was punching at all three, letting them pay for the guilt and fear he felt for his sister's condition, and the frustration of not being able to get to the healer. They fell before his blows, and curiously, nothing they did seemed to stop him; with strength he had never before possessed he threw them off again and again, focusing most of his energy on Garl.

"Stop, please stop! You can pass, just lay off me!" Garl's normal baritone was a high-pitched squeal and the sound of that coming from the big brute stopped Tavish in mid-punch, shocking him back to his senses.

The town bully's face was a mess. Only one eye had escaped the bruising and bloodying blows. That eye now looked at him in stark terror. Tavish realized he was trembling, but from rage or fear, he wasn't sure.

"S-sorry," he stammered, backing away from the trio. He'd gotten into fights lots of times, but he'd never beat anyone so badly before. He felt like he was going to be sick. The strength inside was dwindling, leaving him feeling dizzy and shaking with sudden fatigue. He couldn't believe what he'd just done.

"You . : . you *bully!*" Brock cried, his lower lip trembling. A bruise marked one fat cheek and there were tears in his eyes. He stood in front of Garl, protecting him. "I'm going to tell your father. We weren't doing anything and you attacked us." He looked like he was going to cry. Tavish wasn't going to hang around to see if he did.

"Look, I'm really sorry. It really is an emergency, though. Sorry," Tavish said with a gulp, taking another step back. He glanced once more at Garl's battered face, just starting to feel the pain in his knuckles, a scrape across one elbow where he must have been shoved against the wall. Then he turned and fled towards the healer's.

☼

Abel Evanson, the village healer, held up a candle to Aidah and asked her to stare at it while he checked her eyes, ears, tongue, and flesh tone. She blinked at the wavering light, trying to be still as he poked and prodded her, counting her heartbeats and checking for fever. The fever was all but gone, and strength had returned, but the headache and dizziness—and the voices, though she did not mention them— were still very much present.

Derg, Arlene, Darrant, and Grandpapa Ethan all stood by watching. Tavish sat on his bed in the corner, setting bandages to his hands. Derg paced back and forth from watching over her to watching Tavish, making sure he stayed put. Apparently there had been some trouble in town with Garl. A shiver ran through her, hardening to fear in her gut. She'd seen that. How had she seen that?

"So let me get this straight. The two of you climbed Crooked Peak looking for a wyrret, and a roc scared you, then you suddenly felt ill? And you felt fine previously, nothing wrong this morning, then suddenly you were dizzy and weak? Is there anything else, anything you haven't told me? Other symptoms besides the fever or dizziness?" the healer asked, standing back and looking her over. His voice was soothing like his dark woolen robes, speaking of his worship to Meira. Despite his friendly demeanor, Aidah wasn't going to tell him about the voices and the vision of Tavish or about the other odd things that had been happening lately. He'd probably think she was crazy. They'd lock her up and send her to the mages for examination. She didn't want that.

"Yes, sir, that's all. I felt. Hot, dizzy, weak, and my head hurt. It

27

was probably just nerves, though, don't you think?" She squirmed in the blankets, wishing everyone would just go away, leave her alone. She'd had peace while she was sleeping, except for a strange dream of a man standing over her bed, staring at her. He'd been very handsome, but cold, somehow. At least he hadn't badgered her with questions.

"Perhaps she started to catch cold, but we caught it in time to chase it off," Ethan suggested from his seat by the fire. The pipe was out but unlit, and he rubbed it with both hands.

The healer shook his head. "I don't think so. I have a suspicion, but I'll need to fetch something from my shop. You say you are feeling better now, dear?"

Aidah nodded. "Yes, sir. Just a bit of a headache."

"Mm," the healer said, nodding. To her parents he said, "I don't think it's catching, so it should be all right for her to be up and about. Keep someone with her at all times, and let me know of any developments. I'll be back later to run a few tests on her. Until then, good day, everyone. I have to go set a broken nose." He stared hard at Tavish who looked at his feet with a pained expression.

Darrant led the healer out, speaking in a whisper to him while Arlene came forward to again feel Aidah's forehead and look into her eyes. "Do you want to get up now, or go back to sleep?" she asked.

Aidah looked to where Derg was standing before Tavish, the tip of his tail twitching with ire, and at the doorway where her father had gone. They'd soon be lecturing her and Tavish for their adventure. Best to sleep a bit longer to let the fear fade....

"I still have a little headache. Just a bit more sleep, and I'm sure it will go away," she said in a small voice.

Her mother wasn't fooled. "Your father is going to have to talk to you about that climb, you know that." The stern lines left her face and she smiled. "Go ahead and sleep. I'll close the shutters. Grandpapa can watch over you."

She stood and leaned towards the window, but Aidah stopped her, "No, leave the window open; I like to feel the breeze." She wriggled back into the blankets and propped her head on the pillows, staring out at the blue sky and the high purple and white mountain peaks.

Arlene went to Tavish and crossed her arms. "Once you're done, we'll be waiting in the kitchen to speak to you, young man."

She nodded to Derg standing watch and strode out of the room.

Ethan sat back and held out his pipe towards Tavish, sighing. "I've never seen a kid get in as much trouble as you, boy. How about a light? And the truth, of course. I don't buy that scare story. The two of you have probably scared a few rocs of your own in your time."

Derg snorted, nodding.

Tavish sighed and looked hard at the pipe, and a tiny curl of smoke wafted up from it to curl around Ethan's head. Aidah yawned, watching as Ethan took a slow draw. "Go on boy, let's hear it."

Derg spoke up, "I can fill in a part of it. You were in the nest, for I smelled bits of wyrret fur and roc feathers. Both of you were frightened—I can smell that as well—and physical conflict of some kind occurred. Scraped knees, bits of mountain dirt in the scrapes, and Aidah's ripped shirt all attest to that. I agree it was not a simple scare."

Aidah broke in, wanting them to go away, leave her in peace. "The roc scared me and I lost my balance. I nearly fell off the ledge but Tavish pulled me back up and then I fainted. There! That's everything. Can I go to sleep now?"

Tavish glared at her, but Derg and Ethan hurried over to her, worry on their faces. "Darling, is that true? Are you all right?" Ethan asked.

"You nearly fell? Gods, I knew I shouldn't have let you two out of my sight *for one second!*" Derg said at the same with a growl and a wave of his tail. The canine accent was back.

Though her nerves were growing increasingly raw and there was a buzzing in her head—as if their worry was a physical thing drilling into her—she hurried to put on a calm face and assure them, "I'm fine, I really am. Tavish wouldn't have let anything happen. I think he used his power, in fact, to save me. Don't worry; I won't do anything so stupid ever again."

She saw Derg glancing at Tavish, trying to confirm if that were true, and thought hard at him, wishing he would lead this entourage out into the other room so she could be alone, think about all that was happening.

Tavish stood without looking towards her, setting aside the cloth bandages with which he had been tying his hand. "I think I can explain everything. We might as well go to the kitchen, so I can say it to Pa and Mama as well. Come on, let's leave Aidie alone." He dragged his feet as he went to the door, waving a sort of half-hearted salute to her. If he'd been a Lupas, Aidah was sure he'd have had his tail between his legs.

Derg followed him out, then Ethan took his place by the fire, quietly puffing away, his face calm but somehow not calm. She could almost hear the thoughts whirring inside. She *did* actually hear a voice like his in her head…she pushed it away with another surge of fear. Gods, she hoped she wasn't going crazy.

Out the window, Crooked Peak stared down at her, its head wreathed in clouds, arms reaching out to the line of never-ending mountains. Aidah pushed her head deeper into the soft down pillows, facing the window, hearing behind her the soft creak of Grandpapa in the rocking chair. She closed her eyes and tried to sleep, but questions nagged.

What exactly had happened up there? It had to have been Tavish, making himself strong, taking her strength, it almost seemed like. Except that she knew his Talents were with heat and light only, that he couldn't possibly do such a thing as increasing strength. So what did that leave? Either her or the gods. She didn't know which was worse; that she herself had somehow transferred power, or that the aloof gods on high had decided to intervene in the fate of a small girl on a mountain.

And what of the wyrrets? If she was developing some strange Talent, why hadn't she used it to help them? They were probably dead now, and it was all her fault. If she did have some power, she would use it now just to know they were all right, communicate to them that she was sorry.

She sighed, wishing she could see them just one more time, knowing that her birthday dream would never happen now. She could never have a wyrret pet knowing she had killed its parents. A deeper sigh followed the first.

Aidah was dropping off, her eyes closing out the view of the pastures and mountains, when a blur of movement and a rustle of wings made her open her eyes in amazement. On the post of the fence just outside her window perched an adult male wyrret staring curiously at her. She sat up and gaped.

Behind her the rocking chair gave a loud creak. "What is it, sweetie?" Ethan asked, something close to fear in his voice.

His voice was going to scare the creature away, Aidah thought.

In a hushed whisper she said, "It's nothing, just a wyrret. Don't scare him. He's right on the post there." She pointed.

"A wyrret?" Ethan stood and crossed the room to stand beside the bed, peering out over her shoulder. "Amazing . : . I've never seen one down here in the valley before. Very peculiar." She felt him staring at her.

She continued watching the wyrret, as it balanced on its four feet on the post, white wings partly outstretched. Its dark brown eyes gazed straight at her, as if it were waiting for something, like a treat. It looked so much like the one from the nest, but it couldn't possibly be...could it? As Grandpapa said, wyrrets never came down here, certainly never waited outside young girls' homes. Fear clutched her heart. She grabbed the shutters.

"Go away, little fellow," she whispered, shooing it off with a wave of her hand. Inside she told it, just in case it could hear, *If you are who I think you are, you should be getting back to your nest to protect the babies.*

An image came to her of the female, curled up over the babies in the nest,. She didn't know if the image was coming from the wyrret, her imagination, or some unknown source, but she knew somehow that it was true—both father and mother were alive.

I'm sorry about this morning. Now go home! She told it, fear gripping tighter and tighter at her chest until it choked her. The wyrret took to the air, and she hurriedly closed the shutters and locked them. She glanced at Ethan, standing over her with a troubled expression.

"I'm going to sleep now, Grandpapa. It's all right if you leave for a bit—I'm fine now, truly. But I need some sleep. My head hurts," she announced, watching her grandfather's face, silently willing him out of the room.

She saw his eyes glaze over, his expression grow slack. "All right dear," he mumbled, and turned to leave the room. He closed the door behind him, and Aidah noticed he had left his pipe by the fireside.

Odd, she thought; he never left it lying around. So many strange things happening today, so many ominous things...Aidah buried herself in the blankets and shut her eyes tightly, trying to shut out the world.

Eventually, she willed herself to sleep.

Tavish stood sweating by the great kitchen fireplace and the adjoining stove while Arlene cut up turnips to go in the evening's stew and Darrant stoked the fire. Derg was curled up beneath the rough-cut pine table, his tail softly tapping the earthen floor as he waited for Tavish to begin.

Tavish told the full tale, how they had been trying to get a wyrret for Aidah's birthday, how they'd tried to protect the nest after the roc appeared and how Aidah had slipped, "I had her hand but I couldn't pull her up; I wasn't strong enough. Then this big surge of power came into me and I pulled her up real easy. She started getting weak and dizzy but I kept feeling stronger and stronger. I wouldn't have been able to get her back down here without it. And later when I was running to the healer's, that same strength made me able to fight like I've never fought before. Garl wasn't letting me through, and I had to get to the healer's, I just had to. So I punched him until he let me go. I didn't mean to break his nose. Guess I got too strong for my own good," he said, keeping his gaze squarely on his feet, reliving the sensation of power, of rage and fear and then shame. He swallowed uncomfortably.

"And now? Now how do you feel?" Darrant asked. He gave one last poke at the fire then came to sit at the table.

Tavish shrugged. "Fine. The strength left after the fight. More than anything, I'm just tired."

Tavish watched his father's face and knew the lecture was about to come, that Darrant was mulling over the words he would use, the tone and approach. Derg watched also, waiting for Darrant, the master of the house, to start before he joined in. Darrant opened his mouth but was interrupted by a light rap at the back He rose to answer it and greet Uncle Brenton, Arlene's younger brother, "Hey there, heard about Aidah? Come on in and have a seat."

"Thanks. I came as soon as I heard," Brenton said, stepping forward. He bowed his head to pass through the door, his tall broad frame the complete opposite of his sister's tiny form. Tavish smiled. He had at least one ally here now to fend for him. Brenton knew about adventure and fighting for one's honor. He'd wanted to be a soldier. Grandfather Ethan had kept him from leaving Hamstead for that purpose, but he could at least claim to be a soldier of the village militia and holder of all knowledge of the great warrior Bevan Dell, Tavish's great-grandfather. Bevan had been a powerful Sun Mage, supposedly decended directly from the Great Protector herself, Korva Liam.

Tavish came forward to receive a hearty slap on the back from his uncle, then the three of them sat down at the table, allowing Arlene to begin heating the stew on the fire. Derg, noting the lack of room for him under the table, came to sit on the floor beside Tavish, apparently deep in thought.

Brenton shook his head, grinning. "So you punched in Garl Tanner's nose. About time somebody taught him his place."

Tavish grinned back, but was nipped in the calf by a distraught Derg, "Brenton, violence is no way to handle such a dispute! Tavish could have been hurt. And now Garl has been hurt, and that will only escalate the tension between the two—"

"He was calling Aidah a wart nose," Tavish said with a grumble, flexing his swollen fingers.

"That's no reason to hit him, dear," his mother called from where she was now folding laundry.

Brenton leaned over and whispered, "I still think it was a good move. You shouldn't let a kid like that walk all over you."

Tavish nodded, but he knew he had gone further than he'd intended to in beating up Garl. He looked across the table to where his father sat, quietly keeping out of the discussion. "I went too far, huh Papa?" he asked in a low voice.

His father nodded. "Just learn from the experience, boy. A fight is not always the best way to solve a conflict."

"Now about Aidie," Brenton exclaimed, pushing back a wavy strand of his sandy brown hair, his eyes intent on the table, losing the merry sparkle in their warm brown depths to become hard and calculating, "I talked to Abel and got some of the details. Has any weird stuff been happening around her lately?" He looked from Tavish to Derg to Darrant.

Ethan emerged from the bedroom, looking befuddled. He sat down next to Brenton, staring down at the table. Then he blinked, raising his head to look at them. "Now that's strange—why did I come out here? I'm supposed to be watching Aidah," he said to no one in particular, searching his pockets for something.

"Aidie's got a way of making you do things you'd rather not. Like climb a mountain for a silly wyrret," Tavish said in answer to Brenton's question, pulling off his boots and setting his feet on the table. Arlene threw him a look and he immediately removed his feet from the table but left the boots off.

"Mm, I think you're right. Think I should get back in there?" Ethan drawled, giving up on his search.

"No, stay for a moment," Darrant spoke up, watching Ethan. "Brenton, Tavish was telling us how while Aidah was sick and weak, he was feeling exceptionally strong. Are you thinking what I'm thinking? That a Life Talent may be showing up in her?"

Tavish blinked and stared at Darrant. A Life Talent, that would mean Aidah was a mage, and would need training to eventually become a Spirit Mage. His own training was supposed to be going on right now in Landaran, preparing him to become a Sun Mage, Defender of the Republic. He had delayed that training for a few years, however, hoping that Aidah would show some Talent and be able to attend with him. Talent followed family lines, and while it hadn't shown in his since Bevan Dell, both he and Aidah had the potential. He couldn't admit it to anyone, but the thought of going off alone terrified him.

"You think that's what it is? That she's got Life Magic and it's not under control?" Tavish asked. It would explain a lot, like that strength, and the way she often coerced him to do things he didn't want to. Maybe it even explained his inability to leave her for long periods of time. He shivered.

Brenton sighed, stretching his legs out under the table. "Yeah, that's what I thought. And it's a scary thing, Tavish. Life Talented tend to fall into two categories, angels and devils. It's a hell of a powerful gift to be able to affect all living things according to one's wishes. If she's got it, we have to know, and get it under control as soon as possible. Or we could all become her zombies while she falls to bad influence."

"That could never happen to Aidie. If anyone's an angel, she is," Ethan remarked, chewing at his nails. He glanced at Tavish. "Except for the pie stealing, of course."

Darrant wrung his hands. "I don't want Grandess getting her hands on both of them."

"Why not?" Tavish asked, mystified. He knew just the basics about Grandess Korva; she was a Spirit Mage and the Great Protector of the Realm, and she was supposedly related to him in some way, like a great-great-great-great grandmother or something.

He'd heard they were on the eldest line of her family so she occasionally checked on them. She'd come to see them when he was eleven and in the process of training with Sun Mage Nera who also was related in some way, a 5th cousin once removed, whatever that was. She'd kept her eye on them in other ways as well. Derg had been her present to them when they were four.

Ethan answered for Darrant in a tone which hinted that he knew firsthand of dealings with Grandess, "Grandess is family, and she performs an important job protecting the Republic from Innis's Emperor. The problem is she uses people, like you would use a rope or a hoe or a shovel. Sometimes she uses them until they break."

Arlene made a low noise of agreement. "Like her yearly sacrifices."

Tavish looked in alarm at Brenton. Sacrifices? That did not sound promising.

Brenton hurried to assure him, "That would never happen to you, Tavish, or any other Talented person. She needs every mage she can get for the military. But she is over two hundred fifty years old, they say, and even a Spirit Mage can't live forever. She takes the life force from a human once a year to extend her life. They say her father, the Emperor, takes more—dozens and dozens a year. That's why he appears young while Grandess looks so old."

Tavish swallowed. "And Grandess has the Life Talent, just like Aidah might have?"

His mother nodded, looking pained. "Grandess has been looking for a family member with that Talent for a long time. They're so rare. If Aidah has it, Grandess will take her away." She blinked several times then turned away, rubbing at her eyes. Tavish expelled a breath, trying to dislodge the knot of fear in his chest.

"I hope she doesn't have it, then. Maybe we're all just imagining things. Like she says, it could just be nerves." He tried fiercely to believe in the words, to make them true.

"Why would she want a family member with that Talent?" That was the one thing he didn't get.

Arlene shrugged, looking uncomfortable. "She came and visited me when I was little, because she saw the potential in me. She said something about being old, needing someone from her line as an heir." She rubbed her forehead. "I don't know exactly why. But she specifically was searching for a female heir of her blood. A Spirit

Mage."

Storm Mage, Sun Mage, Spirit Mage, those were the three types of magically Talented, those who controlled lightning and energy, those who controled light and heat, and finally those who controled body and mind, the life force or spirit. Maybe it was a Storm Talent Aidah possessed. Perhaps that shock he'd felt hadn't been strength but lightning, making his body react, making him strong. Maybe she could still come to Landaran with him to train but not be snatched away forever by Grandess.

It was a lovely thought, but unlikely. Storm Talents, like Firestarters, were easy to spot. All one had to do was stick one outside during a storm and watch the lightning strike all around them, harmless to them but lethal to anyone else. His own Talent had burst forth most spectacularly, when he'd gotten mad during a fight with Garl. Suddenly flames had engulfed him, but the fire never touched him. Garl, unfortunately, hadn't been as lucky. They'd kept Tavish locked up in his room with buckets of water nearby until Nera came to help him understand his powers so they couldn't go off without his conscious control. Making fires was easy; all he had to do was gather a bunch of the red waves in the air—waves he could see that nobody else could, waves that emanated from anything warm— gather them all together in a small space and boom! Fire.

Life Magic was a mystery to him. Life Talents could hide themselves, it was said, for they seemed like normal people. Only when people started noting little things like cuts healing much faster than normal, people hypnotized into doing things, unusual health or sickness or strength or weakness—these things hinted at an untrained Life Talent.

It sounded like Aidah.

He sighed, reaching over to pet Derg's silken fur. "I guess we'll know when the healer returns," he muttered, staring at the table and his father's hands across from him, clasped together as if in prayer.

Brenton put a hand on his shoulder, "I guess we will. I'm going to go sit with her a bit, see exactly what Abel is talking about. Come on, Pa. Looks like you left your pipe in there."

Brenton and Ethan went to the bedroom to look in on Aidah while Arlene stirred the stew. Derg lay his head on Tavish's knee, muttering to himself. Tavish gave him an affectionate scratch, which he leaned into heartily. With a great heaving sigh, the Lupas looked up at Tavish.

"I am thankful I am not a human."

3

Dreams of Greatness

Everything in the room looked outlined in sharp detail to Aidah: the pine rocking chair popping out against the dark red brick fireplace, the white linens stark in contrast against the sun-touched flesh of her leg. Her senses seemed unusually sharp, sensitive. The room was ice cold, and it was silent. The voices in her head had ceased.

Standing by the bed was a man, the same man from her earlier dream. Her breath caught in her throat. He wasn't merely handsome, he was beautiful. Long blond hair just touched with sandy brown at the roots flowed down broad shoulders and a well-muscled torso. He was dressed in a black leather jerkin and red hosen and shirt. She looked to his gray eyes the same color as hers, but there the beauty ended. They were cold, hard as granite, staring down at her.

Then he smiled, and the hard features softened somewhat. "Aren't you a pretty sight. What is your name, my dear?"

She was dressed in the clothes from the mountaintop but she felt naked somehow, vulnerable. "Aidah. Aidah Dernholt, sir," she responded uncertainly. Was this real or a dream? Everything seemed to be vivid in color and detail, yet she couldn't hear any noises from the window or from the door leading to the kitchen. Where was the rest of the family?

The man chuckled. "Do not fear. You are not asleep, but neither are you awake. Consider this a trance where your mind is awake but your body rests in slumber. Your Talent has called me here to visit you."

"I don't have a Talent," Aidah snapped, fear clutching at her.

She didn't want a magical Talent—that would mean she'd have to become a mage, fight wars, lead people. She wanted a simple life, a husband and children perhaps, or she could become a seamstress or artist.

The man smiled again. "My name is Rangwar. I'll need to leave soon, but could you please tell me, what is the name of this village you live in?"

"Hamstead," Aidah replied, mystified. The name niggled at her memory, but she couldn't place it. Why was he here, and why was he asking her these questions?

He sighed, then leaned over her and the bed to open the shutters and peer out the window. "Hamstead is too common a name. What makes this place unique—is there a landmark nearby?"

Aidah kept her mouth shut, but her eyes darted to the imposing shape of Crooked Peak looming over the valley, its shadows reaching out to touch the cottage in the slanting afternoon sun.

The man focused immediately on where she was looking. "Ah, perfect. Thank you, Aidah. I'll be seeing you again." He cupped her chin in one strong hand and gazed at her again in a calculating way that made her feel uncomfortable. His gaze almost seared her with heat, as he bent down and kissed her lightly on the lips.

Then he vanished.

☼

Aidah sat up with a gasp. She was awake; the room looked normal again. She heard the sounds of birds from the open window, and murmuring voices from the kitchen. But her heart was still racing. What kind of dream had that been, to be so vivid, so incredibly realistic! And what did that man mean, saying her Talent had called him? Gods, she *was* going crazy!

The door opened and Brenton entered, followed closely by Ethan, the latter going to the fireplace to pick up his pipe where it had been left on the hearth. Brenton approached her bedside, and Aidah groaned inwardly. Not another visitor!

"Something wrong, Aidie? You'd think you were indecent!" Brenton remarked, touching her cheek. Aidah knew they were flushed, but not with fever this time. She could still remember the feel of those lips touching hers. She struggled to compose herself.

"N-nothing, uncle. I had a bad dream, that's all," she replied. She noticed the shutters of the window were open, and kneeled up on the bed to shut them. Had she done that in her sleep, or had he? She refused to even contemplate it.

If Brenton noticed her nervousness, he didn't show it. "I'm sorry to hear that. Do you think you can get up for a while? Everybody's in the kitchen. We'd like to discuss what happened, and whether you've been having any problems lately, anything you want to talk about."

Aidah sighed and pushed away the blankets to stand before her uncle. Morosely she slipped on her boots and went to the kitchen, seating herself next to Tavish. He was afraid for her. How she knew that, she couldn't say—he was in animated conversation with Papa, describing the wyrret pups and the incredible size of the roc, and did not seem other than his normal carefree self. But he felt…concerned, frightened for her.

Imagination again, she chided herself. For the next hour, the adults and Derg grilled them not only on the day's events, but other adventures they'd had in the last month. Some of their questions were kind of funny—was she getting feelings or images about things or people, had she felt sick before, and if so, in what way, and had she noticed people behaving strangely around her, doing things they didn't normally do. She answered no to most of the questions— dizziness, disorientating and headaches were probably just due to getting her first monthly cycle, and yes, she'd noticed people going out of their way to do things for her, but why shouldn't they? She was well-liked. Everybody called her 'Aidie the angel'. As for the truly strange, that she wasn't telling anyone, not even Tavish.

Just when the questions had stopped, when everyone had turned to other subjects and the smell of stew began to pervade the room, a light rap at the door woke everyone. Darrant leapt to his feet to answer and let in the healer. Tavish rose and approached him, shuffling his feet. Guilt seemed to flow from him, so thick Aidah could almost taste it. Funny how his emotions seemed so easy for her to read. It was almost as if she experienced them as he did.

"Um, Mr. Evanson, sir, you said earlier you were going to see Garl? Is he—I mean, did I—"

Abel smiled, his eyes crinkling. "Easy, son. Yes, you broke his nose, but it was a clean break. I reset it and there shouldn't be any lasting harm. Next time though, try to settle things peacefully."

"Yes, sir. And I *am* sorry." Tavish resumed his place by the fire and again Aidah sensed his emotions changing, now turning to her, back into concern and fear. She expelled a breath, trying to shut off the emotions. At least the voices hadn't returned.

Mr. Evanson set his bag on the table and began looking through it, pulling out a bottle with a milky fluid, a hand-written journal, and a velvet pouch. Everyone gathered in to watch, her mama and pa standing close together, their hands touching. That feeling of fear in the room was growing stronger. Brenton was almost on top of the healer, trying to peer into his bag, and even grandpapa, always so easy going, was sitting straight and tense.

"Now, young miss, I'm just going to perform a simple test, see if we can rule out one cause of your collapse today. Don't worry, this won't hurt at all. I just want you to tell me what you see." Abel brought out from the velvet pouch an amulet of silver with a large round crystal set in the center. A light burned within the crystal, a bright green light which glowed with an angry intensity. He held the amulet before her, keeping his hands clear of the crystal.

"All right, Aidie. What color is the crystal?" the healer asked.

This was a test? "It's green," she answered immediately, "It's bright green."

"No it's not," Tavish said in a hiss. "Say it's clear, Aidah. It has no color."

She glared at him. What kind of joke was he pulling? "It's not clear, it's green! The crystal's glowing green, it's as plain as can be!" She looked at the expression of dismay on his face, then turned back to the healer and her parents. The healer gazed at her steadily while her parents looked worried.

"Isn't it green?" she murmured.

"Darrant, Arlene, tell her what it looks like to you," the healer said in a soft voice.

"It's a clear crystal. With the silver around it, it looks maybe a touch bluish, but it's actually clear," Darrant said. His arm was clutched around Arlene.

Arlene spoke up. "I can see perhaps a green tint to it. Is that what you see, Aidie, a clear crystal with a green tint?"

"Looks clear to me," commented Brenton.

Aidah stared at the amulet. Were they testing her truthfulness, saying it was clear when obviously it was green? "It doesn't look tinted green; it *is* green. Glowing green," she declared, staring hard at it. The little light within it flickered, and suddenly she was struck with the image of...

"A spider!" she cried, leaping back from it. The image was clear in her head, a big, black, creepy-looking spider, trapped inside the crystal. But that wasn't what her physical eyes saw. She saw with her eyes only a little green pulsing light, yet the light had the distinct feeling of being a spider. It was as if all the essence of 'spiderness' was held in there. "It's the soul of a spider," she murmured, awed. This time when she looked up she saw stark fear all around as her family stared at her.

The healer took a deep breath and spoke. "Aidah, I've determined the cause of your ailment. You've got a Talent emerging, the Life Talent. Long ago Korva the Protector gave this amulet to the village healer that it be passed generation to generation as a tool to discover Life Talents, who, as you probably have heard, tend to be very good at concealing themselves. You are correct; there is the spirit of a spider held in this crystal. Those not having the Life Talent can't see spirits, so it looks like a clear crystal to us. But I was told spider spirits are green, as are most small creatures to the Life Talents' perception. It's because of your Talent that you've felt dizzy. I suspect you've been receiving thoughts and feelings from people around you, and that can be disorientating, I've been told."

"No," Aidah whispered, snatching her hand back from where she had been about to touch the amulet. She peered from face to face. "No! I can't, I don't want to! Please, isn't there another explanation? Maybe it is a Fire Talent? I did have a fever," she pleaded, hugging herself and shrinking back against the hearth and Tavish's side. Fear was all around now, outside, within, in every heart including hers now. She was losing her mind, she was going crazy! This couldn't be happening.

Her brother grabbed her shoulder, holding her tight. "It's all right, Sis, really. You'll get to come to Landaran with me. They'll have to train both of us, so we'll be together there. It'll just be another exciting adventure."

With his words, the truth seemed to sink in. She would become a Spirit Mage while he became a Sun Mage. It wasn't what she wanted, but he was right; at least she wouldn't be alone. She would have to leave Hamstead, though. And her family.

"Why me?" she whispered, clinging to Tavish, "I didn't ask for it." Another thought struck her.

"Does this mean I have to be locked up in my room until I'm trained, like you were, Tavish?"

He looked to the healer and Aidah followed his gaze. The healer looked troubled, but the fear had settled somewhat. *He was afraid I'd use my Talent in anger when he told me*, she realized with sudden insight. She tried to tell herself she was not reading his mind, but she knew she was. That's what the voices in her head had been. She just hadn't wanted to acknowledge it.

"We need to get you to Landaran as soon as possible, but I'll leave the exact date to your parents. Probably you shouldn't go into town now until you are trained, but you shouldn't have to stay in your room—unless you want to. You may find you want to." He didn't explain that, but put away the amulet and began to gather up his things.

Arlene and Darrant went to Aidah to embrace her. "We'll try to get you and Tavish set up with a caravan departing here in a few weeks. That way we can still celebrate your birthdays," Darrant said.

"You don't think they could stay until spring? I don't want them getting stuck in the snow somewhere," Arlene murmured, her hand on Aidah's shoulder, her other hand on Darrant's arm. Aidah looked to the healer, her uncle, grandpapa and Derg, watching but respectfully staying out of the family circle. Would she really have to leave everyone here?

Darrant shrugged. "Hard to say what is best. Perhaps we should send a letter first to Landaran, let Grandess know they're coming. She might be able to help, send someone here who can teach Aidie or protect them." He nodded to himself. "Yep, I'd say that's the best course of action."

Aidah let out a breath. So she wouldn't have to leave immediately. Her mother declared that supper was ready and invited Brenton and Mr. Evanson to join them, and they spent the rest of the evening making plans for her and Tavish and describing the wondrous city of Landaran by the famous red waters of the Krimean Sea. Aidah became so involved in the descriptions she forgot about the voices or the visions in her head.

She also forgot all about her dream, and the strange man who had said her Talent had called him.

Tavish waited outside the main courier's office for his father, watching the women of the town on their daily errands and the village boys playing in the first big snowfall of the season. He was bored. A little over two weeks had passed since Aidah's Talent had been discovered, and since she was no longer allowed into town or anywhere far from the home, he was left to wander around and get into trouble on his own. It wasn't anywhere near as fun as doing it with her. The boys he did find to hang around with were either afraid of him and his Talent, orr they were into worse trouble than he cared to tangle with.

Poor Aidah, he knew she hated it too—the whole family knew it, in fact, because while her ire didn't exactly show physically, it showed in other ways, like bad dreams shared by everyone in the household or sudden pains and fevers appearing in anyone near her, including herself. All this discouraged him from staying home, so he found himself accompanying Papa on his daily errands and rounds in the pasture. Utterly boring.

Today Papa was attempting to get a message out to Grandess before snow closed off the passes to the valley. By the murmurings inside, it didn't sound like it was going too well. They had sent the first message a week and a half ago, but had heard nothing. Tavish blew a puff of steam to watch it float in the breeze, breaking it into its waves of light with his Talent, turning it into a tiny rainbow. He sighed again, wondering how he was going to endure a few months of this being good all the time.

He stuck out his arm and looked at it. When the Sun Mage Nera had taught him the basics of his Talent, she had mentioned that there was a trick one could do to make themself invisible by bending those wavy lines light was made of, but she'd refused to teach it to him, certain he'd use it for all the wrong reasons. That was true, of course, but if Aidah was going to travel with him to Landaran through rough terrain harboring wolves and bandits, he should try to learn a trick like that for protection. Plus, he could go in and eavesdrop on the adults.

He waited until the street was clear, scooting back into the shadow under the eaves of the roof, then concentrated hard on the light around his arm traveling fast, incredibly fast in every direction. He tried to turn the waves, but they were too fast, zipping around him like snow in a blizzard. He noticed them bouncing off him. That was probably it, he realized, working with the light. He squinted at his arm, telling the light not to touch him, but rather go around. It started to work; gradually he began to see through his arm to the muddy slush of the street. Just as he exulted in that, however, he lost his concentration. His arm popped back into view, and he found himself sweating with exertion. He looked up to find Darrant staring at him.

"Neat trick," his father said, his eyes locked on Tavish's arm.

Tavish shuffled his feet, wondering why he of all people was always caught right in the act. "Um, just something Nera told me I could do with my Talent. I'm practicing it, in case I need it for the journey." That was true enough, anyhow.

A worried look crossed Darrant's face, sending a chill through Tavish. "Son, there is something you must understand about your sister. Grandess has been searching for a Life Talent for a long time, to possibly become the next Great Protector, but she's not the only one who might be interested in Aidie. Many of your mother's line have been killed or kidnapped by the Emperor of Innis, and I'm afraid Aidah may become a target. Remember the name 'Rangwar de Innis.' That's the enemy."

Tavish nodded, standing very straight. He was pretty sure he'd heard the name before, in lessons or something, but it hadn't stuck. The Emperor had always just been known as "The Emperor." He noticed the scroll his father had written for Grandess was still in his hand; apparently he had not been successful in sending it. "You think we'll have trouble on the way to the city?" Something—fear, excitement, tickled at the hairs on the back of his neck.

"Gods above, I hope not. But if trouble does happen and I'm not around, I charge you to be her protector. You're smart, and you have your powers. Don't be afraid to use them. I know you like to make mischief, but I won't forbid you from any experimenting you want to do with your Talent. The more you can do, the better I'll feel about sending the two of you off. Think you can handle the responsibility of being her keeper, boy?"

"Always. Always, Pa, I promise it. I'll flame anybody who tries to take her away." Papa rarely made requests like this; Tavish knew he was dead serious and genuinely worried about them. He tried to impart in his tone and stance that he was just as serious in accepting it. He might be called a troublemaker, but he was serious about a few things—his Talent, for one, his family, and his role as a future Defender of the Realm.

Plus, he loved his sister so much it scared him sometimes.

Darrant relaxed, though he did not smile, "Thank you. I know you'll do fine—I've always been proud of you." He held up the scroll and began walking with Tavish, "The couriers won't take our message; they say there's been word from Storm Mages in the valley that a big snow storm is supposed to hit us in the next few days."

Tavish groaned. More time with an untrained Talent. He remembered all too well his own confinement—being drenched with water after he lost his temper, the cool darkness they'd tried to keep him in so he'd have less light or heat to cause fires with—it had been sheer torture.

"What are you going to do?" They stepped out into the street, and Tavish reached out and touched a single falling snowflake. The skies were gray, but not threatening any serious snowfall. The Storm Mages' forecasts were usually correct, however. He sighed.

"All I can do is watch the weather and keep trying to send a message. I've decided with reports of bandits up and the chance of blizzards, you two aren't going anywhere until spring."

That was what he had figured. They met up with his mother at the bakery holding a wrapped package smelling of cinnamon—Aidah and his birthday cake—and several other brightly wrapped packages. Darrant explained his failure to send the message, taking a few of the packages to carry. Arlene took the news surprisingly well, and put an arm around Tavish as they walked.

"Well, that just means more time with the children. Happy Birthday, Tavish," she said, pulling back before he could peek at the packages.

They walked in silence along the dirt country road down the little hill towards their cottage, and Tavish's gaze was drawn up from the house and barn to the line of peaks overlooking the valley to the east. The four peaks of Falas, Grinar, Ranin and Thoras, named for hunters of ancient legends of the hill people, were wreathed in soft white clouds, with Grinar and Ranin closest to the village, their foothills extending out like fingers to touch the snow-covered pastures. Beyond them, Tavish could just see above the clouds the high peak of Scarath, the scarred remnant of a long dead volcano, and on and on the range of Morgaine mountains, which eventually ended at the Krimean Sea. Across that sea, so far away and yet never far enough, was the Innis Empire. If one did not cross the sea, but followed its shoreline west and south a bit, then one would come to the great City of Landaran, ever watching, ever awaiting the next attack.

Such a big world, and all of it unknown to him, Tavish thought. He looked back to the tiny cottage almost made invisible by the white of the snow and the shadows of the great peaks, in particular Crooked Peak to the north. Ma was right; they had to cherish the time they had together here.

"Happy Birthday, sister," he whispered.

Incarceration was going to drive her insane. Aidah sat on her bed in the small bedroom, staring at the wall, making imaginary pictures out of the looping rings on the wooden boards. Outside a December blizzard screamed in full force, raking at her nerves, making it impossible to concentrate on knitting or drawing or playing cards in the kitchen with Mama and Pa. Across from her, Tavish growled in ire as he attempted for what must have been the hundredth time to get all of himself invisible at once.

"I can still see your clothing, hair, shoes, and teeth," she remarked dryly, shifting a leg that was falling asleep.

"I know, curse it! Now be quiet and let me concentrate." His nerves were as raw as hers, and she could feel them strung tight in his body, creating a headache to pound in his temple. As soon as she felt it, a headache of her own sprung up to pound behind her eyeballs, in time with her pounding heart.

Anger and frustration boiled up in her, and she gritted her teeth to stay silent as he tried again and failed, this time making his whole body half visible, sort of a wraith-like vision through which she saw things behind him. He gave up and came back to full visibility, plopping down on his bed with a snarl.

"You're giving me a headache!" he hissed.

"I'm giving *you* one?!" she shrieked as the wind outside howled and the shutters rattled. Three weeks, for three weeks she had not left this house, barely left this room, trying not to affect anyone with her power, and he had the gall to blame her for his problems? Using too much of his Talent always gave him a headache. He knew that.

She wished she could just pick something up and break it,

smash it into a hundred pieces and get rid of this awful boredom and tension! Or even better, to go outside into the storm, become one with it…she pressed her fingertips to the sides of her forehead to soothe away the pain. In the other room, she heard sounds of her parents in discussion with Grandpapa over a hand of cards. They sounded irritated as well.

Tavish scowled, pacing the room, glaring at her, at the bare walls, at her rack of embroidery currently under work. All of a sudden he strode up, picked up the rack, and smashed it into the wall, crushing the fragile reed frame with a satisfying *crunch*.

Aidah's mouth dropped open. That was exactly what she'd wanted to do, but instead he had! She was affecting him. She stood, meeting the fear in his eyes with forced calm.

"Maybe I should go to the other room for a while."

He had suddenly grown ashen. "Sis, I didn't mean to do that—I don't know what happened—wait!" he called, but she was hurrying to the kitchen where the discussion was turning into a fight, with her parents arguing with Derg and Grandpapa over the validity of their hand of cards before them. As she entered her mama and papa started to argue with each other as well. Tension in the room was at a boiling point.

I've got to get out of here, Aidah thought, nauseous with all the negative emotions, *I'm not just driving myself crazy; I'm driving everyone mad!* She ran to the cloak rack to grab her mittens, cloak and scarf, slid her feet into her boots as Darrant rose to shout at Ethan that they were upsetting her, then she tore out the door and into the snow.

Wind ripped at her clothing, sending snow into her eyes and stealing away every shred of warmth in seconds. She could hear above the roar of the storm her father and Tavish calling frantically for her. She staggered through the thick drifts of snow towards the barn, where hopefully she could have some peace as well as protection from the weather.

She ran across the yard and managed to heave open the barn door against the quickly piling snow, then closed it with a thud. The smell of hay and the bleating of sheep greeted her, and she quickly sat down among the sheep to absorb some of their warmth. The tension and the frustration began to melt away at the soft touch of their fleece as they sniffed at her hair, nuzzled her hands, and tried to wiggle into her lap.

"Now come on, I don't have any food for you today," she said with a chuckle, patting their soft moist noses. She shut her mouth and crouched down as she heard something. It had to be in her head, because the wind's howling should have drowned it out. Tavish and Pap called for her, searching the yard. *Go away! Leave me alone!* She thought at them, not caring if her Talent controlled their actions, hoping it would. No sense in them freezing to death looking for her.

The sounds—or whatever it was—of their voices faded away and she enjoyed a moment of peace amidst the bleating of the sheep inside and the howl of the wind outside. The headache gradually began to fade.

Aidah went to the back of the barn where the family mule was kept in a stall away from the sheep. She sat down just inside the stall door away from where old Muser was sleeping. He snorted at the smell of her, but did not wake.

She sighed. The fear had receded, but the refuge here was only temporary. Eventually she would have to return to the house, to her confinement, knowing every thought, every emotion could be acting on those around her, possibly hurting them. She put her head in her hands and moaned.

What she needed was training, just as Tavish had needed it when they were ten. She chuckled despite her anxiety, remembering the time he'd wanted to go outside to play and hadn't been allowed to. He must have pulled sunlight from outdoors into the house—everyone had been blinded, and several small things near him had caught fire. Other than the incident with her embroidery, she wasn't causing any real destruction in the home, but how long would that last?

There was that man, Rangwar, or whatever he said his name was. He'd said her Talent had called him. He hadn't appeared since, so perhaps it had only been a silly dream, but if her Talent had called him, it meant he had Life Talent too, to come to her. Perhaps he could help...

She hesitated, pulling her thoughts back from that avenue. Maybe this wasn't such a good idea. She had no idea who he was or why he had come the first time. He'd been a little frightening also, but then he'd kissed her...

A nervous flutter went through her, settling in her stomach.

Well, the man had seemed friendly, and what was wrong with a small kiss? She was fourteen now, and a woman. Plus, he'd said she was pretty. All she needed was a bit of information, and if she'd called him, she could probably send him away too. She closed her eyes and got comfortable, sitting back against the wall of the stall.

Rangwar? Rangwar, she called with her mind, not exactly sure how one called with Talent. Of course this whole thing was probably just a figment of her imagination, and this was going to simply prove—

"I am here, Aidah."

Aidah's eyes flew open. She knew she was either asleep or in 'trance,' for everything was again outlined in brilliant detail. The sheep and mule had disappeared. The blizzard outside was just a faraway murmur. Before her stood the man, Rangwar, this time dressed in a black velvet doublet and violet silk shirt with matching hosen. He smiled at her intimately, sending a shiver down her spine, and knelt down to sit beside her, glancing around.

"Interesting place. A barn, yes?"

Aidah nodded, swallowing. "I come here sometimes to be alone. H-how did you find me so fast?"

Rangwar licked his lips. "You called me, as I knew you would. I was waiting for you. Do you know what you are now?"

Aidah shifted as his hand brushed her leg. "You mean my Talent? I know now that I have the Life Talent, and as soon as the passes are clear I'll be going to Landaran to train."

He chuckled, leaning back against the wall with a creak of old timber and stretching out his long legs beside hers. "I doubt that will happen until spring. What are you doing in the meantime? I imagine your powers are manifesting themselves more and more frequently."

"That's why I called you. You're a Spirit Mage, right?" Aidah looked into his eyes, trying to read them, but they were opaque. In fact, all of him was opaque to her senses, she realized—she couldn't read emotions, thoughts, anything.

"Yes, I am. Among other things."

"Do you work for the Realm? For Grandess?"

A blond eyebrow went up. "Grandess? You mean Korva? The *Protector?*" Rangwar said, and Aidah caught a slight sneer to his voice. Her guard went up instantly.

"Yes, the Protector. Did she send you?"

"Yes, of course she did—how else would I know of an obscure Life Talent like you, living in a tiny village in the middle of the Morgaine Range? My dear, your Talent does not shout out its existence to the world. Korva told me about you a long time ago. It was merely a matter of waiting. I do work for the Realm. You can trust me on that," he explained, taking her hand and holding it in his. Aidah felt the strength in his hands and realized beneath his rich clothing, he had the body of a warrior.

She gently pulled back her hand and tried to straighten her clothing, a simple gray homespun dress. "Well, that's good. What I need right now, you can probably guess, is a little training. My family—I keep causing things to happen—they were fighting, and they don't usually, you see—"

"You don't have to explain. I know exactly what you are talking about. What you are doing is absorbing and projecting emotions, increasing them." The opaque mask faltered; Aidah saw evidence of past pain and frustration mirroring her own.

Rangwar took hold of her shoulder and turned her so that she was facing him. His voice became serious, instructing, "Close your eyes. Imagine you are seeing with your gut, sensing emotions in the air like steam, or smoke. Imagine you can see this image through a third eye, here," he touched the middle of her forehead. "When you feel you have a clear image, open your eyes. Tell me what you see."

Aidah concentrated, and could sense it—a large cloud surrounding her of frustration, fear, isolation, and anger at her predicament and her future. The cloud was enormous, stretching out through the barn and into the home, touching everything and everybody. She opened her eyes, focusing on looking through her forehead and saw it clearly, a purple haze edged with dark red and black. Beside her she noticed a much smaller cloud surrounding Rangwar, tight against his body, a solid dark red.

"I see a sort of cloud around me, a huge cloud, purple, with a little red and black. You've got a cloud too—red, and very small. What is that? What am I seeing?"

He smiled, and his cloud rippled. "That is your aura, Aidah, that is how you exert your thoughts, emotions, and will over others. It should be kept close to you unless you want to affect others."

Aidah shook her head. "I don't want that. How do I pull it in?"

"Close your eyes again."

She did so, feeling Rangwar's hand on her shoulder, guiding her.

"Imagine inhaling that cloud, pulling it into your lungs, into your gut. Imagine it returning from every crevice it occupies, drawing inwards. Experience the emotions within it as your own, collect your own thoughts and push out any that are not yours. That cloud is all you, and it belongs inside unless you wish it otherwise. Let me know when you have gathered it all."

Aidah did so, and actually felt as the cloud drew away from Tavish, Darrant, Arlene, Ethan, and Derg. She felt relief immediately, in control of her emotions. When it was as gathered as she could make it, she nodded her head once.

He must have been right by her ear by the sound of his voice, "All right, now continue looking through that third eye and open your eyes. Where is the cloud now?"

She opened her eyes and could see it, floating about her like a bubble of air, "Well, it's all in this room now. It's not as tight as yours, though—goes about two feet out from me."

He nodded. "Your vision for the aura is perfect, even if your control is lacking. Close your eyes, then look out your normal eyes. The cloud should no longer be visible."

Aidah did so, and was relieved to find her vision normal once more.

"So now you can see where your aura is and pull it back if necessary. Keep in mind having it far extended is taxing on your energy, leaving you open to headaches and exhaustion. This lesson will not stop other's thoughts and feelings from being picked up by you, but it should keep you from affecting them and turning your home into a field of battle!" He laughed, apparently finding something about her situation very funny. She scowled.

He sobered immediately. "I am sorry, but you see, this sort of thing happens to all Life Talents before they're trained. It happened to me, it happened to Korva, everyone. One word of warning though, before you go to your 'Grandess'. Beware her, Aidah. She pretends to be good but in fact she is a power hungry, manipulative, cold-hearted old woman who will stop at nothing to get what she wants, no matter who it hurts or what it destroys."

Aidah gasped—it was exactly what she'd feared to hear about the Protector. What future was ahead of her in Landaran? "But you work for her?" she whispered, trying to imagine the function she would serve, the role she would play once she was fully trained.

He frowned, running the hand that had been on her shoulder down her back, sending a shiver up her spine. "I would rather say that I work for the Realm. For the people. I'll tell you more of myself soon, when you're ready." He stared at her, measuring her, then his gaze flicked to the stall door, seeming to see something beyond.

"Your brother has found you. I must go, but all you have to do is call. Any time, any questions, I'll be there." He leaned forward, and Aidah braced herself, seeing his intention immediately. Then he paused, smiling.

"I think you should give me a goodbye kiss this time."

Heat flooded her face, and she swallowed nervously. Was this a bad request, or simply normal between mages? He certainly seemed to enjoy it, seemed to find her interesting, maybe even desirable? And he was so handsome…she leaned forward to give him a light kiss on the cheek but he turned and she found herself instead kissing his mouth. Then she seemed to lose all power as he leaned forward to kiss her harder. A shock went through her as he suddenly stuck his—

She woke up. Tavish and Darrant were standing over her, shaking her.

"What?" she asked, running her tongue over her lips, acutely aware that she was still flushed with color. She could taste him! That had been his tongue, she couldn't believe he had actually put his tongue—

"Thank the gods! I thought you were dead there for a moment! Why didn't you wake up?" Tavish said, gasping. He knelt down and hugged her hard and she felt he was ice cold and trembling with fear. She hugged him back, pushing away the memory of the dream.

"I'm sorry, I just wanted to be alone for a while. I didn't mean for you to be searching everywhere for me."

Tavish sat back on his heels and rolled his eyes. "Well of course I'm going to look for you—you ran out of the house after I smashed your embroidery. I figured you were flaming mad at me."

Aidah grimaced. "Oh yeah. That was actually my fault, and that's why I had to come out here—I had to get control of my Talent. I'm better now."

Her father exclaimed, "But we couldn't wake you—"

She cut him off before he could ask further, "That was because I was in a trance. I was learning a few new tricks. It's all right, really." She considered telling him about the man, verifying Rangwar's identity, but just the thought of him now was enough to make her blush, and Papa would undoubtedly notice that and ask questions. Best to keep silent and research it by her own methods. Uncle Brenton knew all the mages of the realm by name, and his questions would be easier to skirt around.

Despite her assurances, her father looked ready to inquire further. Aidah considered extending her aura, making him accept her explanation, but decided against it. It would be wrong for her to alter his thinking, though she knew she had the power to do so. Maybe that was why everyone said Spirit Mages were either totally good as angels or evil as devils.

Darrant sighed and helped her to stand. "If you say everything is all right, I'll believe you, honey. I have to admit, I feel like a cloud's been lifted from this household. I don't know why everyone was getting so nervy and irritable."

Aidah punched him playfully in the arm. "That was my fault too. It won't happen anymore, though—I fixed it. I'm ready to come back in with everyone."

Her father put an arm around her while Tavish hung close behind. The mule woke up and gave them all a friendly nuzzle as they left the stall.

Outside, the blizzard blew on, unrelenting in its fury.

4

Storm of Fear

Aidah ran through the snow-covered field, the sun on her face and a small shovel in hand, reveling in the rare sunny day. For three weeks the village of Hamstead had not seen the sun, bombarded by storm after storm. Snow piled in six foot drifts against the side of the barn, evidence of the ceaseless pounding of nature. Not in ten years had they had this much snow this early in the season. Leta, Goddess of rain and weather, must be in a frightful mood.

Brenton caught up with her as they passed a half-buried post marking the beginning of the communal pasture, sheep struggling behind him to make a path, Derg at their heels, herding them. They'd broken out the snowshoes today, along with their heavy woolen cloaks and mittens. Aidah stubbornly wore her blue woolen dress, insisting it was warmer than breeches.

"Well, I doubt if anything's left alive, but here goes," Brenton commented, plunging in with his wide shovel to move aside the foot or more of snow covering the field. "I know before the storms there was still good fodder here for the animals, but if this doesn't work we may be stuck using the hay storage for the rest of the winter." He shook his head. "Gonna be a long winter."

Aidah nodded, glancing at the mountains on every side. The sky above was mostly clear, but east she could see dark clouds threatening another storm. To the north in the village there was a flurry of activity as people tried to make the best of the brief respite, patching roofs, selling wares, and doing as they were—exercising the livestock.

Papa, Grandpa, and Tavish were trying once again to get a message out to Grandess and to see if the news carrier from the lowlands had arrived in town during the calm. Mama was taking the opportunity of an empty house to clean and to do laundry.

A fresh breeze whipped at Aidah's hair, sending flakes of snow swirling around her in a tiny dervish. She dug her shovel deep into the snow and threw it with all of her might to her right, working alongside her uncle in alternating rhythm.

They worked in silence a moment before Brenton spoke. "So I haven't seen you for a bit, what with the weather and your confinement. How you been feeling lately? Haven't heard of any problems from your mother."

Aidah grunted as she shoveled another load, feeling the soft fleece of the sheep at the back of her legs as they crowded in, looking for grass, "Well, I haven't blown up the place or started any fires, but it has been tough. You know how much I hate being cooped up and it was really hard trying to keep my feelings from affecting everybody."

Brenton paused for a moment in his work to give her a one-handed hug. "I'm sorry you got stuck with that particular Talent in the family, Aidie. I know you didn't want it. I'm really proud of how you're handling things."

Aidah shrugged, moving aside as she found a bit of grass for the sheep to eat. A stronger gust of wind tried to blow off her woolen cap, and she noticed the dark clouds seemed to be creeping in faster than expected. Almost unnaturally fast, in fact. "Uncle, my Talent can't affect weather patterns, can it? I mean, I'm not the cause of all these storms, right?"

Brenton leaned against his shovel, watching the encroaching clouds. "No, they're not alive, so you can't affect them. And nobody is born with more than one Talent. Huh. That is rather strange, isn't it. And I don't think anyone else in town has a family history of

Talents. I wonder..." He frowned, deep in thought, while Derg trotted up, panting with his efforts to keep the herd in line.

"You're talking about the peculiar weather? I must say, it borders on the unnatural, but in the year 1078, a similar pattern did occur. I'm sure it is simply a natural phenomenon, don't you think, Brenton?" Derg asked between breaths, his dark eyes appraising the sky.

Aidah took note of Derg's tone of concern, seeing now that he was doing his job today a little more earnestly than usual. She could sense his thoughts as easily as any human's. He was agitated, sensing something suspicious about the weather and trying to expend his nervous energy with a little extra exercise. Derg was always worried about something, so perhaps it meant nothing, but he was more attuned to nature than humans.

"What else could it be?" she asked the two of them. The sheep had devoured the little patch of grass, so she set to moving aside more snow.

Brenton came up to help her. "Only other possibility would be a Storm Mage. The Storm Mages of the Realm will sometimes affect the weather for droughts, but they always warn those who will be affected. This sort of thing would have to be the work of an enemy mage. Not a comforting thought—I mean, why attack little mountain villages unless..." he stared at Aidah. "Aidie, nobody strange has tried to talk to you, have they?"

Aidah tried to look calm, though her heart clenched painfully in her chest. "Talk to me? No, how could anyone, what with the storms?" She tried to tell herself that it was physical visitors he meant, physical conversations, but she thought of her dream visitor, wondered once more if he were truly a friend.

Well, she had wanted to ask Brenton, though not exactly in this context. "You know all the names of the Realm mages, don't you, uncle?" She paused at the sharp questioning look he gave her, wondering if she should go on, fearful of what she might hear.

Brenton stopped in mid swing, sending a rain of snow into a

couple of sheep who bleated in protest. "Yes, yes I do. Any particular reason?"

Derg was here; he could probably smell her fear. She had picked the wrong time to bring this up directly. But perhaps indirectly, "Oh, I was just wondering, having heard some kind of bad things about the Protector and other mages. Are all of the mages of the Realm good, or are there some I should watch out for? For when I go to Landaran, of course."

Brenton nodded, relaxing. He resumed shoveling. "Can't think of any to really warn you about—Korva's supposedly a bit cranky, but people say she's got a good heart. Gabriel is the next senior—your fourth cousin—he's quiet from what I gather..." he thought for a moment, tapping his foot. "Can't think of any you might have problems with. Everyone I met when Grandfather used to bring the mages by was very nice and there aren't too many rumors saying otherwise, even with the younger generations."

Derg spoke up after retrieving a few straying ewes, "The mages you need to worry about, Aidah, are the mages of Innis. In particular the Emperor, Rangwar."

Suddenly the cold of the snow was inside her, shooting up from her toes, freezing her heart, chilling her mind. She tried to hide the shock from her face. Too late.

"What? What is it, Aidah? Have you heard that name before? Has he tried to contact you?" Brenton shoved a sheep out of the way in his haste to go to her, take her by the shoulders and look into her eyes. She was shaking; she couldn't seem to help that. But her mind was recovering, setting aside the shock, promising to go over the implications of this as soon as she had moment to herself. In the meantime, she had to keep herself out of trouble.

"I had a dream where he introduced himself to me, right after my Talent appeared. He was offering me assistance, but he frightened me so I told him no. That was all that happened. Nothing's happened since. My Talent would protect me from having those kind of dreams, don't you think?"

Brenton paled, but he shook his head, releasing her. "I hope so, I really do hope so. Hasn't happened since, you say?"

Aidah tried to think of a way to explain the second occurrence, but she couldn't. She had invited him, the enemy, into her mind! She couldn't let anyone know about that. What would they think of her? And she couldn't tell the...the other stuff. She didn't want to think about what it meant, not yet. Life Talents were either angels or devils. Seemed she was teetering right on the edge of an abyss...

"No, nothing since," she stated. She glanced at Derg. Sometimes he could tell when she was lying. Hopefully, oh hopefully she wished, not this time.

He seemed about to say something, then fell silent, staring at the ground. Aidah went around to herd in the sheep which were trying to wander off. A rumble of thunder from above caught all their attention at once.

Aidah searched the skies, noting that now the dark clouds were just about overhead, wondering if they should get the flock back to shelter. A lance of lightning split the sky, followed by a crack of thunder.

Derg's ears were standing straight up. "Now that most definitely is not natural this time of year!" he yelped, leaping over the bank of snow to control the suddenly panicking flock.

Brenton seemed to be in shock, staring at the skies as a strong gust of wind blew white flakes of snow around him. "It's too cold for lightning, it's not possible—" He grabbed Aidah's arm and turned her around towards the house just visible through the coming storm. "We have to get you some place safe. This is because of you, I am certain."

Guilt knotted her throat. He was more right than he knew. She was beginning to suspect the reason Rangwar had been so inquisitive the first meeting, asking for the name of the town, local landmarks. She had fallen foolishly into the trap.

They began guiding the sheep back towards home, and Derg ran up ahead then back to report, "I smell men, Brenton, and not mountain stock either. I'm not sure returning to the house is a good idea. It may be under attack."

A crack of thunder punctuated his statement, and a bolt of lightning struck the silo of a farm near town. Smoke billowed up to join the dark clouds now covering the sky. From far off, a woman screamed.

"Mama! She's alone at the house!" Aidah cried, picturing a hoard of men swarming the house like locusts. Another bolt of lightning streaked down from the sky, hitting the steeple of the main temple in town. Above the rising wind, she heard distant shouts and screams.

"And Ethan's with Darrant and Tavish in the village," Brenton added, brandishing his shovel in frustration. Aidah could see he was torn, but she *knew* where Rangwar would search for her, and she could sense Tavish, see a vision of him as she had when he'd fought Garl. He was running to the temple, helping Mrs. Tanner from a fallen timber, using his magic to combat the flames. She pulled on Brenton's arm.

"Mama's alone. We have to get her out of there. Then we can go join Papa and Tavish."

Brenton looked to Derg, seeking courage, but the Lupas was busy trying to keep the flock from scattering. Brenton groaned and hurried forward to help lead the flock. "It's foolish to go there, but I can't think what to do. We'll try to get the sheep within the yard, shut them in, and take a look at the house. Maybe they haven't reached it yet."

With that he broke into a run, chasing the sheep through the snow drifts highlighted in the blinding whiteness by the flashes of lightning, as the falling snow turned to sleet and hail, pelting at their backs. Aidah followed in his wake, heart pounding, trying to keep focused on her surroundings despite more and more intrusions from what could only be Tavish's mind. From her vantage point she saw numerous bolts of lightning hitting farmlands surrounding the village, but from Tavish's eyes she saw firsthand the destruction they were causing, blasting out buildings, destroying the well so that the fires would be impossible to put out, sending people into a panic running through the streets...she stumbled and fell into a bank of snow, lost in the other vision.

She blinked several times to refocus herself, then leapt up as Derg ran to check on her. "Do not get separated, Aidah, and let us know if you sense anything strange. Between your special senses and my smell, I think we should be able to avoid an ambush."

She nodded and ran alongside him, ignoring the cold, the howl of the wind, the eerie red glow ahead—Aidah gasped as she got a good look at her house through the sleet and flashes of light. Flames licked out from the windows, and smoke billowed out of the chimney in great black clouds. The barn was an inferno—Aidah heard the shrieks of the mule still in his stall, trying to escape. There was a splintering of wood, then she heard hoof beats as the mule broke free and ran, disappearing into the storm.

They reached the home pasture and the gates; Brenton sprang to shut them as soon as the last sheep entered. Aidah was sure they were missing a few but they couldn't worry about that. She ran forward towards the house when Brenton pulled her back, forcing her to kneel down behind a snow covered haystack.

"Stop, Aidie, the fire's spread too far. I can't let you go in there," he explained.

"Mama!" Aidah cried, trying to stand. The sheep ran about in confusion, beyond concern now.

Derg ran up to her."Let me check, Aidah. Keep still—I smell men near, very near. Cover yourself with snow and stay silent. You can't help her if you're captured." He ran off towards the red glow, a sleek dark shape against the snow.

Rangwar was here. She was sure of it, though she didn't know how. Her insides were fluttering, as they had in the dreams. A fever seemed to burn in her cheeks. Slowly, very cautiously, she crawled under a layer of snow to look around the haystack.

There he was, standing just outside the back door, apparently watching for anyone trapped inside to come running out into his embrace…yet he wasn't solid. She could see right through him. What did that mean?

She saw Derg run past his tall figure, apparently blind to him, to enter the house. Aidah waited in anguish for her mother to appear, but for moments nothing happened. She received another vision of Tavish facing a dark-haired man, the Storm Mage, hearing through his ears the man's challenge, experiencing Tavish's fear, his desperate planning. In sudden insight, she called to him, *Come here! The house is on fire! Come and put out the flames here, and don't' let them capture you!*

He heard the message. She felt him receive it with a kind of shock. And as she *felt* that, the ghostly image of Rangwar spun about and looked straight at her. She scrambled back through the snow and flung herself at Brenton, feeling those cold eyes upon her.

"What is it?" he asked in a whisper, throwing an arm around her as she tried to hide against him.

"It's him—he's here!" She hissed into his ear. Then she couldn't speak, for he was there, floating above the ground, a true specter dressed all in black. He came around to hover before them, and again she noticed that only she could see him. Brenton was searching everywhere, looking, oblivious of Rangwar's presence.

He stared at her silently, smiling like a mountain cat who'd caught its prey. Rage suddenly swept through her, that he'd fooled her, that he'd taken advantage of her lack of knowledge, "Get away, Rangwar, go back to your own dreams! I didn't call you, you liar, and I don't want anything to do with you! Leave me and my family alone!"

Brenton stared at her, then at where Rangwar stood, eyes searching but not finding the focus of her anger. He gripped her tighter as if the enemy spirit could lift her right out of his arms. "He's there, Aidah?"

She nodded vigorously. Rangwar didn't speak, he simply continued smiling, but one golden eyebrow twitched. He lifted his head, seeming to listen to something, then crouched down to hold out a hand to her. She shrunk back. The smile faded.

"Aidah, you may either make this painless or unpleasant. Your mother is safe under the care of my men, eagerly awaiting your arrival. I am not a liar. I do work for the Realm—the realm where you belong. The Innis Empire. You should have been born there; it is your true ancestry. Trust me when I say I am saving you from a horrible fate, from the greedy machinations of your 'Grandess' Korva. Now come along."

Aidah kicked a foot at him; it went right through, proving to her that he wasn't here physically, only present in her mind. She tried to wish him away, but without success. So all she could do was talk to him, it seemed.

"I'm not going anywhere with either you or your men. You tell them to let Mama go and leave this place, do you hear? Why would your men start all the fires and attack the town if they're trying to help me?" Aidah looked for Derg to return, show that Rangwar's words were lies, but she heard only the crashes of thunder from the town and crackle of flame from the house. Was Derg captured now too?

Brenton stood with her, holding onto her tightly. "Aidie, let's get to town, get you under the protection of the militia. If he's got Arlene we can organize a party to get her back, but out here we're vulnerable. I can't see him, but I bet he's fixed it so his men can, and he can probably use his powers to let them know where we are. Let's get out of here."

Aidah nodded, and the two ran forward towards the fence, but quick as the wind Rangwar was there in front of them. Aidah skidded to a halt, uncertain what would happen if his spirit got hold of her. Brenton was forced to stop as well, his arms wrapped around her waist, his eyes desperately searching for what only she could see.

"Go away! Leave her alone; she's just a child. She can't hurt you!" Brenton cried, turning around with her, searching for any men who might overhear, Aidah guessed.

"You're frightening her—stop it. I have no intention of

harming her or any of her family. The fires are to confuse Korva when she comes to investigate. Now come along. This village and entire area is surrounded. There is nowhere to flee." Rangwar's voice sounded different this time—louder. Aidah realized she was hearing him both with the physical ear and with her head. Looking to Brenton she saw he had heard as well, though by his eyes he still couldn't pin its source. He was shaking, and his face had gone several shades paler.

Brenton whispered in her ear, "Where is he? Is he right in front of us?"

"Yes, uncle," Aidah whispered back.

Before she had a chance to wonder why he was asking, Brenton let go of her to charge forward waving his arms, passing right through the ghostly image of Rangwar. Rangwar made a face, cringing in discomfort, then again like the wind he was flying up over their heads to land right behind her. She ducked away before he could reach out to her—Brenton had passed through unharmed, but her instincts were telling her not to let him touch her. She trusted her instincts more and more in light of recent events.

Brenton saw her and stopped, motioning for her to join him. She backed up slowly, trying to think how they could escape this phantom, when suddenly the world tilted as she was struck with a vision from Tavish. He was running down the hill towards the house with Papa, Grandpapa, the healer and a couple men from town. She felt his heart pounding, a headache beginning to gnaw at the side of his temple from using his Talent so much in such a short time, and she could see what he saw. The house was in full flame, the door broken in, the barn just a heap of cinders now, and out in front of the house on the road stood about twenty men in gray peasant garb with swords and crossbows. A four-legged form lay in the snow— Derg! Held between two men was Mama, her hair down in disarray, her face white with fright.

A wave of dizziness and nausea passed through Aidah, then she was back where she should be, looking out her own eyes. Rangwar was right before her, Brenton off a little ways, and from the direction of the house, four men—part of the same group holding mama in front—were running up to take hold of her. Brenton ran forward, challenging them, but the ghostly image of Rangwar swept through him and this time Brenton fell, clutching his head. He was quickly grabbed by a couple of men, and Rangwar began to fade in and out, panting with exertion, until he faded away altogether.

Aidah was left to face Rangwar's men alone.

5

A Message Unsent

At the first crack of thunder, Tavish knew something was amiss. He'd been standing near Papa, watching housewives push snow off the roofs with brooms and rakes, wondering at the bulk of wet snow accumulating along the street as people prepared for the next storm. It seemed awfully early in the season for so much white stuff.

The message carrier for the village was addressing Darrant and Grandpapa, "No, I haven't heard of any messages returning from Landaran. With the weather, it's been impossible to go either direction. Now if this break holds for about a day more, we could probably get somebody through, but I—" a crash of thunder which shook the earth below their feet drowned out the rest of his words.

Tavish, Darrant, Ethan, and the message carrier stared wide-eyed at each other in stunned silence. Where had that come from? Out on the street, people stopped to eye the skies, and Tavish noticed where sunlight had bathed the streets only moments before, now a cloud overshadowed them, rapidly growing darker. A lone man, a member of the militia, ran through the street to disappear into the healer's house. People milled about, nervous and silent. Not a bird called, not a broom swept, not a voice ventured to challenge the ominous air. Ethan blinked, took out his pipe, stared at it, bit on the end of it, and turned to Darrant. "Now how fast do you think a storm like that can spring—"

A crash louder than the first shook the ground, shook the walls, and the very air within the little wooden building. A second noise pierced the air, not of thunder but of wood splitting asunder. A woman screamed. Everyone leapt into action.

The healer ran in, shouting, "We are under attack! Militia men, grab your weapons! Bandits north and east of the village—cut across the fields to apprehend them."

"Gods above, they must be using magic!" the messenger cried, leaping away from the little desk where he'd been checking caravan schedules. Tavish followed him out to the street to stare at the blown out roof of a rye silo just up a hill from the center of town.

People scrambled to grab buckets and shovels under direction of the healer. Members of the militia ran to the armory for the weapons, hurrying to defend the town from foe and fire. Darrant and Ethan ran up as another ear splitting crack of thunder echoed around them, and this time Tavish saw lightning striking the steeple of the Temple of Meira to break it nearly in half, sending burning timbers falling down on panicked townspeople. Flames burst into life from the charred remains of the steeple, threatening not only the temple but the entire town, packed close together with its narrow streets.

Tavish had to help. "Papa, have everyone work on dousing the fire at the silo; I'm going to take care of the temple."

Darrant nodded, slapping a hand on his back. "Good idea, boy. Be careful—somebody's guiding those lightning bolts." He and the messenger grabbed buckets and began filling them with wet snow, calling out for everyone to help at the silo, that Tavish would be working his magic on the temple.

People gave him a wide berth as he ran to the destruction in the street before the stone and wood building which had stood for generations. A woman—Brock's mother—was trapped beneath a burning timber. He reached out with his mind and told the heat to depart the log, releasing it into the air in a burst of light— "heat" lightning, as it were. The timber thus cooled, he struggled with Brock and the healer to lift the heavy beam. Brock flinched as Tavish's hand brushed his, but once his mother had been freed, he swallowed and whispered, "Thanks."

Tavish took no time to acknowledge his former foe as the healer lead away the woman, tending to her injuries. His mind locked on the blazing heat now consuming the whole front of the temple, scorching the statue of the Lady Meira and the basin of Her Holy Tears. So much heat could not simply be released into the air—it would cause an explosion which could flatten nearby buildings. What would be nice would be to find the culprit responsible, scorch *him* a bit. As another lightning bolt struck Miller's square and the main town well, Tavish began to pull bits of heat from the flames, exploding them in bursts of color, sent high up into the clouds which caused a light scatter of rain over the Temple. The flames did not grow to consume more, and as the rain began to fall harder, they were slowly extinguished. A chuckle behind him diverted his attention, and he turned around.

He saw a man, a man who was not running. The man was dressed for heavy winter travel with a waterskin and travel pouch across his chest, a long gray cloak, sturdy fur-lined boots and—Tavish gasped—a sword, an actual *sword* at his hip. The only men with weapons were the local militia, and they had spears and maces for the most part. The man carried a bucket but he walked slowly, not running as others were. He stood in the middle of the street, just down from Tavish. Too close.

As their eyes met, the dark-haired man sneered. "So there you are, my young fire Talent."

Fear gripped Tavish's body, but his mind raced. At any second the Storm Mage could call lightning to strike at him. He could disperse the heat but not the power of the shock; it would kill him. Tavish could also call fire from the hot embers of the temple, but doing so might cause the mage to strike. From where the militia had charged up the hillside to the treeline he heard shouts and the sounds of battle. There would be no help from them.

He wondered: did the fellow want him alive or dead?

The man walked up, boots crunching on black embers in the snow, dark eyes appraising him from beneath the hood of his gray cloak. The nostrils of his hawkish nose flared. "My name is Madhar. Give yourself up quietly, or I'll destroy what's left of your village."

Ah, so he was wanted alive. Perhaps an attack would be possible, but he had to be careful. Meanwhile, the fire at the silo had been almost put out, and he could see his father and grandfather leading the greater part of the village over to put out the flames at the well. He hurried to put distance between himself and Madhar as the man tried to reach out for him.

"So what are you after? Stealing Talents for Innis or something? You may find me a little more than you can handle, mage."

He prepared to engulf the two of them in flames, forming protection in his mind for his clothing. As he began to direct the heat, however, a loud voice rang out in his head, and an image flared of another building in flames. He gasped.

"Come here! The house is on fire! Come home and put out the flames and don't let them capture you!"

It was Aidah, and the inferno was his own home! There was no time to play with this annoying Storm Mage. Aidah and Mother were in trouble.

He pulled, and as flames engulfed himself and the mage, he ran around Madhar towards where his father was shoveling slush on fire consuming the structure of the well. He moved quick enough that a small lightning bolt meant for him hit empty space, but the force of the impact sent him flying into his father's arms. Behind him he could hear Madhar crying out with surprise and pain as he dove to escape the flames. With no fuel and with Tavish's concentration broken by his fall, the flames disappeared in a puff of smoke.

Tavish shot to his feet, ignoring curls of smoke wafting up from his clothing and the headache beginning to pound within his skull. "The house is on fire! Aidah sent a call for help, with her mind. And there's an enemy ma—"

"Halt there! The Emperor wants you." Madhar, his face covered with soot, staggered forward, sword drawn.

Blinking from the shock of the blast and Tavish's flying entrance, Darrant stood and moved in front of Tavish, rattled but recovering quickly. He held up his shovel up like a weapon. "Who are you?"

"In the name of Innis, this town has been surrounded, and you are all now prisoners. Give up quietly or face my wrath." A stroke of lightning lent power to the mage's words, narrowly missing the mill up on the hillside by the creek.

"Gods of sky and earth!" Darrant gasped, the full impact of who he was facing falling on him. Tavish thought furiously of a way to get past the mage.

"They won't save you. Surrender or die!" Madhar shouted. Lighting struck behind him, setting the Healer's home ablaze.

That heat was what Tavish had been waiting for. He reached up a hand to shield his father's eyes and pulled the heat to become white light surrounding them. With a cry, Madhar covered his eyes. The light soon faded, but Tavish doubted the mage saw that, or anything else, for that matter.

"Come on, Pa, we have to get to the house!"

As they ran forward, Darrant called to the townspeople, running in fright from the enemy mage or covering their eyes against Tavish's attack. "The Enemy is here! Kill the mage, or he'll destroy the whole town! Ethan, Abel, follow me—my house is under attack."

"They're after Aidah!" Ethan cried, running up to join them, breath wheezing in his lungs. He tossed aside the bucket he'd been carrying to grab a snow shovel. Fires still burned around them and new ones were being lit by continuing spears of lightning, as the mage cried out in fury, but now the strikes were ill-aimed, random.

"The militia is fighting men dressed like bandits, but their weapons are too well made for ruffians—I'm afraid Innis is behind this," Abel said, gesturing with his walking staff up towards the treeline.

Darrant nodded. "We should have seen this coming. I should have done more to protect Aidah, to protect all of us."

Abel grunted in agreement, helping Ethan navigate the icy path. "No time for those worries. Let's see what we can do."

Tavish lead the group down the hill towards home, melting any snow in their way, urging them on. Once past the chaos of the town fires, they saw the flames and smoke pouring out of the little cottage and the burnt shell of the barn. Tavish saw by the glare of the fire a group of twenty or so men gathered by the front door, two of them holding Arlene, another two inspecting a body in the snow—Derg, he realized, heart clenching painfully. He would flame them, all of them—how dare they attack his home, hold his mother, harm poor Derg...

He was gathering up the heat, imagining a great fireball bursting over the foreigners, a shielded bubble for Arlene and Derg, when a gust of wind tore past him, sweeping him off his feet. The fall knocked the air out of him as he struggled to rise, peering up at the tall shape of Madhar coming to land before him, borne by a magical wind.

Tavish stood to face Madhar, wondering how he could possibly get everyone out of this now, with a fully trained Storm Mage before him, and at least twenty armed warriors. Madhar squinted at him, and stepped forward, reaching out. Tavish growled, warning the mage with his eyes and his stance that one step closer and the man would find himself a living torch. Rage fueled his resolve—if he had to kill to escape, he would.

Madhar took the hint and stepped back, regarding them with frustration. With a flick of his wrist he pulled out a handkerchief and wiped blood and soot from his face. His dark brown hair was disheveled and dirty, and he looked bitter.

"I didn't finish introducing myself earlier, little fire Talent. I am Budris Madhar of the Innis Empire, and I don't take kindly to being flamed. You will pay for your actions."

"Leave this place, you ruffian, or it will be you who pay," Abel said, stepping up beside Tavish. Darrant and Ethan joined him on the other side, makeshift weapons held high. The mage smiled and chuckled, unfazed, as one of the men who had been inspecting the fallen form of Derg came forward. Though he was dressed in simple peasant ware, as all the men were, he wore it with a sort of military neatness no bandit would ever attain. With an air of command he strode forward and brushed back the hood of his gray cloak, revealing stone chiseled features and cropped blond hair.

He spoke to the mage, "I believe your orders were to occupy the town and discourage witnesses. We have the Talent's mother and we'll shortly have the girl. I don't think further pyrotechnics are necessary."

Madhar snapped, "My orders were to retrieve the Fire Talent if at all possible, and I intend to do that. I'll gladly refrain from attack, but only if he surrenders."

Just as Tavish was about to make a reply, four men came around from the back of the house, two dragging the unconscious body of Brenton, the other two pulling along a struggling figure wrapped in a gray cloak, kicking at them with booted feet and faded blue skirts. They brought her near where Arlene was being held and pulled back the hood. Aidah glared at them, her blond hair all in disarray, defiant and apparently unhurt.

"His Majesty brought down the fellow there, Sir, but then disappeared. This looks to be the brat he wanted, doesn't it?" one of the men said in a thick foreign accent. The blond who had first spoken to Madhar, nodded, holding a finger to his lips for the men to keep silent.

"Toran, Magovern, keep watch on the uncle—he'll come to eventually. And you two keep a good grip on the girl no matter what she pulls." The leader turned and shot a triumphant look at Madhar. "I guess that about finishes it. His Majesty will be pleased."

Above them the storm rumbled on, sending a mix of rain and snow to hiss and sizzle on the glowing embers of the barn and the still burning roof of the house. Tavish looked at the well-armed party before him and gulped.

"Aidie, we're in a mess this time," he whispered.

6

Sundered and Sought

She stood inches away from her mother, only feet away from her brother and father with their companions, and yet Aidah was helpless. She couldn't even move her arms, held fast in the grasp of two burly men. Her fear and the fear for her family was a choking thing in her throat, making it impossible to speak. In addition, she could feel Tavish's headache, hear his every thought. It seemed the more stressed and emotional he became, the more she was with him, inside of him, almost. She wondered if it went the other way as well.

"You can't just lead us out of here and expect to get away with it. I'm sure Korva's got mages watching over us. You can't think you're actually going to succeed in smuggling us out, do you?" Tavish said standing feet spread apart, chest thrust out. Inside he was nauseous with fear, according to her senses, but he himself seemed unaware of that, maintaining a stance of outrage.

Papa added, "You won't get out of this village, not without a good fight. I'll kill every one of you myself if I have to."

The man who seemed to be the leader, who her captors had reported to when she was brought here, laughed, blond hair catching the glow of a streak of lightning crossing the sky. The man next to him, the Storm Mage who Tavish thought of as 'Madhar', chuckled and said, "You don't seem to understand, Mr. Dernholt. You're under capture as well. And your boy's no match for a fully trained Mage."

Darrant looked furious. It was the first time Aidah recalled him ever looking so angry, the veins standing out in his neck, brown eyes filled with fire as he glared at the leader. "And what makes you think I'll surrender? You've go no hold on me—I know you want my daughter alive."

The leader nodded, smiling. "Of course. That's why we also captured your wife. She's expendable."

Tavish had to restrain Darrant as he surged forward, brandishing his shovel. Arlene cried out, "No, dear! Get help—there's too many of them!"

After pulling Darrant back, Tavish whispered in his ear, which through her link to him Aidah could plainly hear, "Have to think, Papa, have to think. We won't get 'em that way. I've got an idea that might work. Just keep stalling them."

His idea was to become invisible, get Mother under his protection, and flame the place while still invisible. It was a tall order for a half-trained Talent, especially one who as of yet had not been successful with the invisibility spell. He was desperate.

Could she do something with her powers? Aidah focused, looking through her 'third eye', to see where her aura was. It was drawn tightly in, surprisingly enough given her stress. She extended it out over the enemy party and their hostages, not trying to affect them, just sensing things. Derg was only playing dead, she realized—he was awake and alert, assessing the situation. Brenton was in worse shape, slowly coming to in a fog of pain. Her fear and excitement seemed to leak to him and rouse him into to slowly opening one eye. His mind snapped awake, but he remained prone and relaxed as he too assessed the situation.

Well, perhaps she had done something. Now they would be able to assist in an escape attempt. However, Tavish did not realize Derg was alive. If he flamed the place and didn't shield…she should warn him, she thought, but last time she had done that, it had brought Rangwar's attention. If he were still around, capable of appearing again…she shuddered. No, she couldn't risk that again. The only other option was to act before Tavish did.

Emotion, that was part of her Talent, the part she knew most about right now. She heard Darrant challenge Madhar, and Ethan was demanding to see if they'd hurt Brenton. She couldn't listen to them. She had to concentrate, fast, for she felt Tavish preparing his mind for the attack.

She could spread her fear, perhaps make the enemy falter,

mistrust their orders or their superiors. Perhaps make them think she and Tavish were more dangerous than they'd figured. She touched her aura to Rangwar's men, searching for their thoughts, and particularly for their emotions. She wasn't sure how to recreate what she'd done before, but if she wished hard enough, *something* should happen. At least, she hoped it would.

As Madhar started to make a retort against her Papa, Tavish came forward, saying he was surrendering in order to check on Brenton. The two men watching Brenton came forward to take hold of him, but before they had completed their first step forward, Tavish vanished.

Panic engulfed Aidah—she screamed and bit down on the hand of one of the men holding her, kicked the other in the shin, and ran to Derg, screaming in her mind for him to get up, *get out of there.* Everyone in her vicinity ducked or cringed, many grabbing hold of their heads as if to shut out a great noise.

Brenton leapt to his feet, wrenched a saber from one of the men and then swung it at the other, felling him. From the corner of her eye, Aidah watched the man holding Arlene, go down. His nose bled from an unseen punch. A second man wrapped an arm around Arlene and held his sword to her throat. "Get back!" He cried, eyes searching for the invisible assailant.

Madhar turned around, lightning flaring above him in an echo of the rage on his face. "Tavish, show yourself and surrender, or I'll strike your mother down right now, I swear to you!"

"Keep order! No killing unless it is absolutely necessary!" The leader shouted, but things were moving beyond his control, as he strode towards Aidah to recapture her.

She reached Derg who at her mental shout had leapt up with a whine, ears flat against his skull. He snarled at the leader and leapt at his shoulder. He knocked the man down, but his teeth were foiled by a hidden coat of mail. Aidah ran past them to join Brenton as he brought down his second captor. They reached the door of the house, and Aidah felt the intense heat of the flames and cinders. Derg joined them, growling at men who had recovered from Aidah's mental shout and were encroaching in on them.

The leader struggled to rise, shouting orders to bring in reinforcements. Madhar scowled, looking at Darratn, then raised his face to the sky. Three booms of thunder sounded in quick succession. Towards the town they heard an immediate answering call, as men ran down the hill towards Darrant and his party.

Then utter chaos erupted. A fireball engulfed the area where Arlene and her captors stood. Men threw themselves to the ground to avoid spurts of flame shooting out, missing Tavish as he emerged from the inferno with one arm holding Arlene. She looked a little singed, but otherwise fine. They joined Aidah, Brenton and Derg in the doorway of the house. There they were trapped. The other men arrived and surrounded Darrant, Ethan, and the volunteers from the village. The flames were keeping everyone back from Aidah's group for the moment, but Tavish could not keep them burning forever.

"That wasn't exactly how I planned it," muttered Tavish, sweating profusely. His face was white with exertion, his legs trembling with the aftershock of his magical efforts. He'd be useless pretty soon. They had to reach safety right away.

"Darrant!" Arlene cried, holding onto to Tavish with one arm, the other outstretched to her husband. There was no way to get to Papa, and no way he would be able to escape to join them. He was surrounded by their enemies.

"We should go before they cut off the back. Tavish can protect us from the heat. You must leave him," Derg stated, brushing against Arlene's leg with his long tail.

The plan made sense, yet Aidah felt a wrenching pain in her heart at the thought. Leave her father to Rangwar's men? What would they do to him? And Grandpapa? And the others of the village—wasn't there any help for them? Where was the 'Great Protector's' protection?

"But my father, the healer..." Arlene murmured, echoing Aidah's thoughts.

Darrant must have seen them hesitate, or else Aidah was broadcasting her thoughts to her family. He called to them as he made a clumsy swing with his shovel, trying to take out a would-be captor, "Don't stand there, run! Get the children to Landaran! Don't worry about me, just go!"

Madhar approached Darrant when the others could not subdue him and reached out a hand to the shovel. A spark flew from his hand and Darrant yelped in pain, dropping the shovel. His arm fell to his side, paralyzed. The mage moved in to take hold of him as the others surrendered in fear.

Tavish grabbed Aidah's arm and turned her away, but she could hear some scuffling and what sounded like the smack of something connecting with skin as they subdued her father and his companions. She bit back a sob.

"Come on, now we go for it," he hissed, pointing down the main hallway of the house, still intact, towards the back door. The heat seemed to dissipate around him, and she knew he was shielding them.

She started to run forward through the cinders when she saw a figure blocking the doorway. She skidded to a halt, and pulled Tavish back. Brenton stopped and stared at Aidah, but Arlene gave a cry. "You!"

Rangwar was there, looking gray and weary and none too pleased. Aidah glanced at her mother. "You can see him?" Belatedly she realized her mother had not only seen him, but recognized him. "You *know* him?" What did that mean?

Arlene's eyes were wide and frightened. "I can see him, barely. It was thought when I was young I'd develop Talent, but it was only potential. I remember seeing him in a dream when I was very young. It only happened once."

Now they were trapped again, with a smoldering house about to collapse over them, the timbers creaking alarmingly above, steam rising from where the sleet was hitting the red embers. They could not stay here for more than a moment, or they would all die. Should they go forward, into Rangwar and gods knew what spell, or back to his men and their swords? Aidah looked to Brenton and Tavish for advice, a hope, anything.

It came instead from Arlene, as she charged forward into Rangwar.

"Go, children, run!" she cried and Aidah didn't know if it was because her mother had potential and could see spirits, or if Rangwar's earlier spell had so exhausted him, but when Arlene entered into the space the spirit was occupying, it seemed to interfere with his magic. A burst of magic, strength or life energy perhaps, threw Arlene back into the blackened frame of the door and the remnants of the kitchen pantry. Rangwar vanished—completely, it felt like, not just from sight. In a moment which seemed to stretch on and on, Aidah watched her mother fall through the pantry wall onto the earthen floor of the kitchen. For an instant it seemed the damage would stop there. Even as she thought that, hwoever, the rest of the pantry wall collapsed The back side of the house leaned in with a groan. Its last support snapped, then crashed down on top of Arlene, bringing with it a good section of the roof and the stone chimney.

"Mama!" Aidah and Tavish cried, even as Brenton pulled them back from the falling debris. Behind her, Aidah heard a cry of despair and disbelief from her father. As soon as the debris stopped falling Tavish ran forward, immune to the tongues of flame leaping up from the broken cinder. He pulled off what he could of the smoking wreckage to uncover Arlene's upper body. From there they saw that it was pointless to continue.

Her head lolled back at an impossible angle, her lifeless eyes staring out into oblivion as blood poured forth from a wound to her throat.

"No," Aidah whispered. Her heart pounded painfully in her chest as emptiness threatened to consume her. The pain was an avalanche, burying her, ready to sweep her down into an abyss where nobody could reach her. Beside her Brenton fell to his knees, and she *felt* him, and Tavish, and Derg, and the men outside. They could probably feel her too, for she was losing it, she was going to lose her mind right here and now. She pulled at her hair, shaking with the force of the emotions.

Then she noticed something. A shape emerged from her mother's body, drifting up and out, beautiful and incandescent, like her mother but far more true, not like the simple image she had seen of Rangwar only seconds before. That incredible thing, that essence of her mother, smiled and reached out to her. *I love you.* Aidah felt the emotion from it, in far more than what could be described in words.

Tears blurred her vision, but she could see enough to watch the essence drift upwards, becoming one with a shaft of light from the sun falling on the house…except there was no sun out today, Aidah realized.

The light vanished.

Time sprang back to its normal pace. Brenton regained his feet and shoved her forward as Derg strove to pull Tavish away from the lifeless body of Arlene. Aidah was choking on tears, yet she managed to grab her brother's hand and communicate both her pain and the urgency of the situation. "She did it for us to escape. Come on, we've got to go," she said. He nodded, swallowing hard, his face red with suppressed tears.

They ran out the collapsed section of the house into the snow as men ran around to intercept them. Flames erupted around them with a fury which mirrored the look on Tavish's face. The men fell back, fighting the flames which attached to their clothing. Aidah could hear their screams of pain as she and her group continued to run, leaping over the pasture fence into the deep snow of the fields.

"We'll never get to the woods through this stuff. Not in time," Brenton said with a grunt, trying to clear a patch for the twins and Lupas. Every step was an effort through the deep snow wet down by the unnatural thunderstorm.

"I can help, but I don't know how much longer. I feel kinda faint. Head hurts," Tavish gasped, stumbling to his knees. Aidah helped him to stand and he plunged forward, breathing hard. His face contorted with the pain she'd felt growing in him since the town fires by using his Talent far beyond what he'd ever tried before.

When a high drift blocked all progress, Brenton stopped and turned to Aidah. "Do you think you could repeat what you did on the mountain? Give Tavish strength? Not so much as last time, of course."

Aidah glanced behind her, just barely able to see the house through the storm and little black dots which must be the men, dividing up into two parties. They were still fresh, while her group was burdened with loss, with fear, and with the task of forging a path through sodden snow. An idea came to her. These men had to have come here through the same snow; the Storm Mage didn't have any power which could circumvent that. If they found that trail, they could use it.

"Derg, while I try this, could you run up ahead and scout? These men had to have made a path to get to the house. With their numbers, it should be a nice clear path," she said while helping Tavish to sit. He was pale and trembling, breathing hard and holding his fingertips to his temple, trying to massage away what appeared to be a massive headache. A low groan escaped him and he swayed. She knelt down to steady him.

"Excellent idea. I shall return shortly," Derg responded, and leapt up to the top of the drift, charging through it with endless canine energy and soon disappearing from view.

Brenton resumed digging the path for them with renewed fury,

"With all the tracks they must have made coming, we can easily hide ours. Then we can take to the woods. First, see if you can help Tavish. He needs your strength, Aidah."

Aidah nodded. She knew that better than he; she could feel the fever now taking hold of Tavish, combined with the terrible pain in his head, the other pain in his heart. She bit back a sob, knowing to acknowledge that pain would be to acknowledge her own, the emptiness. She couldn't cry now. If she started, she would never stop. They had to get away. For Mother, they had to.

With a hand on Tavish's shoulder—just in case physical contact was necessary—she closed her eyes, and wished. She didn't know how she had done it before, she didn't know if it would work now, but if the gods of goodness were listening, perhaps they would show her the way. She felt her strength like a tub of water within her; full, and Tavish's depleted strength; a void. To pour one into the other...

"Take my strength, take it," she whispered, wishing fiercely, wishing so hard her forehead ached. There wasn't much time.

Tavish grasped her hand, and it was like a floodgate opening in the spring thaw. Strength rushed out of her, and she had to scramble to keep all of it from leaving, trying not to put herself in the same situation that had occurred on Crooked Peak. She pulled away and drew back her aura tight against her, and it worked. She felt tired but not dangerously exhausted.

Tavish stood, still rubbing his forehead but with color returning to his cheeks and a light in his eyes. "Better. Head hurts, but I can go on now. So you need me to melt the snow?"

He put out his hand, and before them the snow began to melt, carving out a narrow corridor of muddy slush beneath their feet and icy walls supporting the snow to either side. They quickly went forward into the snow corridor, which soon became a tunnel in the high drift, blocking them from sight of their pursuers.

After several minutes of walking, passing out and into several more drifts, Brenton halted to check on their pursuit and on Tavish. There was no sign of either Rangwar's men or Derg. The storm, whatever the wishes of the Storm Mage, was sending a steady stream of sleet and snow. Tavish looked pale but unwavering.

"How long will you be able to keep doing this?" Brenton asked.

Tavish shrugged, moving forward a little to continue his work, "This is easy—I'm just rearranging the heat in the snow, melting here and freezing along the sides. I'll do it as long as it takes. Then I'm collapsing." He managed a sickly smile.

Aidah couldn't see the house, the woods, or anything else, but she felt something—the echo of the life forces nearby, perhaps.

The snow became deeper, and the corridor became a tunnel once more, going deeper and deeper, downhill. Aidah wondered if they would lose Derg as well as the pursuit. As she thought that, however, he appeared, racing through the tunnel, panting hard.

He spoke between gasps, "Steer towards the right—not too far—it hugs the tree line so once we've followed it a bit we can hide and rest."

They plowed forward, pushing melted slush to the sides to freeze to the ice created by Tavish's 'rearrangement of heat.' It took them several minutes more of tunneling to reach the trail. Derg, having caught his breath, related how he had evaded the men by burrowing and how on his return he had collapsed the mouth of the tunnel to hopefully confuse Rangwar's men.

Soon the snow became shallower and they reemerged just off the invaders' trail. Fresh prints in the snow showed the enemy had passed by recently. In the high drifts surrounding them, Aidah could see no one.

"It is fortunate they chose a storm as their main attack," Derg whispered, leading them down the wide trail. The sleet had turned to heavy snow, covering the tracks behind them and hampering visibility. Derg doubled back and forth to confuse his trail, while Brenton and the twins walked backwards at times, their footsteps merging with the foot prints of what must have been over three dozen men overtaking the small village.

They walked for what seemed like hours without hearing a sound other than the occasional rumble of thunder or the wind as snow continued to fall. They were wet, tired, and nervous, jerking at every hint of sound, looking through the dark gloom of the storm for signs of the pursuers. They met nothing, as the trail curved towards the trees, climbing up one of the foothills, eventually passing beneath the tall pine and fir trees. Derg ran up ahead again to scout, then returned in a rush.

"They're coming! They must have thought we'd move much faster than we did. There's a creek up ahead where the snow's been washed away. We should be able to escape down the embankment without leaving a trail. Come on," he urged, nosing their heels to get them moving. Aidah forced her tired legs to move faster.

They reached the ravine as sounds of the men ahead filtered through the trees. Tavish went first, melting any remnants of ice which might make the descent more dangerous. Aidah followed, then Brenton, while Derg kept watch on the trail. The ravine was steep but not deep enough to hide them from view.

When they'd reached the bottom where a trickle of water still flowed down the frozen creek, Derg called down to them, "They are very near—I can hear them talking. Go—I'll lead them away."

"But Derg!" Aidah called up in a fierce whisper, wondering how he would rejoin them.

"I can track your scent, angel. I'll be back." Derg disappeared from view as he ran off, in what direction Aidah couldn't discern from the sounds, muffled by the forest. She tried to keep up with Brenton and Tavish in the icy creek, but water began to soak into her skirts, dragging her down. Brenton noted her falter and picked her up piggy-back style to hurry her under cover. She glanced over her shoulder. Bandits, five ot them, up above the ravine. Aidah held her breath..

The men paused, probably noting their fresh prints on the trail. Aidah and Brenton held still, gripping each other hard. Aidah wastched as the men made a move towards the edge of the ravine, when Derg's bark rang out clear in the forest. With a shout, the bandits took off running. Aidah's pounding heart had a chance to calm.

"Now we can get away," Brenton urged them, setting down Aidah on feet which no longer had feeling. She stumbled, feeling the cold of her wet hem creeping up her legs, noting for the first time how cold her face was, her hands inside her soaked mittens. Exhaustion was setting in. They'd have to find shelter soon.

Brenton, supporting her with one arm, started them walking again. She forced one foot before the other, dragging her skirts through the snow, trying not to think about Derg, her father, anything. No matter how hard she tried to keep it from her mind, however, one image was always there in her mind's eye. Her mother, lying so cold, so lifeless. Aidah stumbled and fell.

Tavish was there instantly to help her up. "Come on, Sis, just a little further. Remember the cave overlooking the Jonstable's cabin? I figure we've got to be pretty close. Just up the hill a bit, then you can rest."

She nodded, stifling a yawn.

Time ceased to have meaning after a while, as they continued on, in a numb daze, but suddenly it grew dark. Before she was aware of a sunset, sheltered under the forest, night had fallen, and the temperature began to plummet.

"I see it—there, up ahead," Tavish gasped. Aidah could barely walk any longer; her feet and lower legs were a distant memory and cold had long since seeped through every last part of her body. She was so sleepy.

"I can't make it," she whispered, clutching onto Brenton so she wouldn't fall. The world went gray for a moment, seeming to fall away behind her, then she felt herself being lifted into strong arms.

"Come on, Aidah, stay with us. I'll carry you," Brenton said, his voice warm against the cold night. Aidah clung to him and cried, not sure why she was crying, only that in order to live she had to drop some of the intolerable weight in her chest.

"Come on Sis, come on," Tavish said over and over in a litany, his voice choked with tears. He reached over and grabbed her hand. Warmth flowed into her, easing the numbness. Together the three of them went up a steep hillside to a small cave almost invisible behind snow covered brush and rocks. It only went back about ten feet before becoming too small to crawl through, but it was enough. It was dry and out of the wind, lined with pine needles and brush of a former occupant's nest, probably a skunk or badger.

The three of them huddled together for warmth, not daring to light a fire lest it be seen from afar. Tavish tried to help as he could, but he was exhausted, too spent to control his Talent. It was enough, however. The moment she was warm enough not to worry about death by cold, Aidah closed her eyes and fell asleep. It was black as coal when she awoke to find a cold nose and a warm furry body next to her.

"What is it?" she whispered, feeling at Derg's long legs, still wet with either sweat or snow. He smelled, but it was a welcome smell, a smell of safety and home.

"We'll be safe here for a little. I led them off towards Crooked Peak and used game trails to return. By morning wolves will destroy any evidence of my passing. Rest now, child. I will protect you."

Derg nuzzled Aidah and she tried to relax, let herself drift off once more, but now the darkness was like a living thing around her, heavy and dense, silence a roar in her ears. Reality was trying to creep in on her, worse than any nightmare. Her father and grandfather, her town...Mother.

She bit back a sob, but the tears flowed anyway, stinging tears that brought no relief, only pain.

Derg tried to console her, softly licking her hand, his paw on her knee, but Aidah gently pushed him aside. This grief could not be shared with him, though he probably felt the loss as well. No, this rested solely on her—the pain, the damage...and the guilt. Would this have happened if she hadn't spoken to him? If she'd kept him out before she knew she had Talent? Learned how to make wards over her mind before she even knew what such a thing was?

No, this was Rangwar's fault, utterly and without question, and she hated him for it. If he ever showed up in her mind again...

The tears were flowing faster now, hot down her cheeks. It wouldn't help, nothing could ever undo the destruction to her life, not if she marched into Innis with an army and beheaded the vile man. A pathetic-sounding whimper escaped her and she clamped a hand over her mouth to avoid waking Tavish and Brenton lying on the other side of her.

And Papa, Grandpapa, Abel the Healer, everyone she knew in the village—what had become of them? Were they all dead now, or prisoners to be transported back to Innis?

She sat up shivering, both from the cold and from anxiety. Papa, how was he right now, if he was alive? That anger on his face had been so foreign. "Derg, did you see Papa or any of their prisoners while you were evading the men?" she asked in a whisper.

"I didn't see Darrant, but Rangwar's men were herding a group of women and children they'd captured from the farms near Hamstead. I think they planned on capturing the whole village, to leave no witnesses. They're probably being sent to Innis as slaves." Derg related, inching closer to stop her shivers.

"Slaves?" she repeated. To imagine chains encircling those strong wrists of her father was nearly impossible.

"Your father has hidden strength. Do not fear for him. He will survive, whatever the circumstances. I shouldn't be surprised if he even escaped."

A nice thought, but probably impossible. Her group had had two kinds of magic and they'd barely managed. Despair filled the darkness, closing in on her until it became difficult to breathe. How would they ever reach Landaran?

The shape next to her moved. "What are you two discussing?" Tavish sounded exhausted, but some things would always be the same—his curiosity, for one.

"Papa," she whispered, hoping they wouldn't wake Brenton as well. On the trail he'd looked so burdened, walking stooped with the responsibility of seeing them safely to Landaran.

"He'll escape. Or I'll come rescue him, once I'm trained a bit more. There's no way I'm letting Rangwar and his stinking Madhar keep Papa for long. I'll make them all pay." His voice shook.

Such anger, she thought, experiencing the heat in his blood, the dark intentions racing across his mind. She'd forgotten the feel of him for a little, lost in her own misery, but he was back in full force. Burning with his anger was grief as deep as her own, if not deeper, for he blamed himself for not being the one to attack Rangwar.

"It wasn't your fault, Tavish. You couldn't have done anything against Rangwar—that was only his spirit there. I don't know how she did it, but Mama saved us. I think maybe only she could have done it," Aidah said in her brother's ear, pulling him in for a hug. The fury faded to be swiftly replaced by aching loss, hers and his. It all seemed to merge in her.

She held onto Tavish's shoulder, lowered her head against his chest, and cried. His arms held her tightly, so tight they were almost suffocating, as he joined her, his voice hoarse as he said between sobs how he would protect her, how everything would be all right.

Though she nodded, in her heart she knew the terror had only begun.

7

Plundered

Tavish moved slowly through the holly bush, careful to hide any tracks of his boots and keeping below the snow laden branches to remain out of sight. Ahead he could see the Jonstable's pine cabin up against the cliff face of Mount Grinar. The Jonstables were hunters and tanners, and by the little curing shed, Tavish saw the carcasses of several deer, hanging out to bleed on the snow. Breakfast.

There was nobody home—he'd already checked that. Rangwar's men had swept by yesterday afternoon as Brenton, Aidah and himself had huddled in fear in the cave, sure that at any moment they would be found and dragged along to join the prisoners being herded to Innis. Derg had checked to see if Papa was there, but none of the men who had defended the village was among this group. It made Tavish shiver to wonder what had become of him.

For thirty-six hours they hadn't even stuck out the tip of their noses from their hiding spot, until Derg had reported no sign of Rangwar's men were within a two-mile radius. They had to move on, but not without food and some gear. That he meant to procure today from the Jonstable residence.

He crept up to the side of the curing shed, listening to the sound of snow softly falling from the boughs of trees in the warm sun, ready to flee at any unusual sound. As he approached the deer, he reached up a hand to unhook it, then saw the door to the house was wide open. A hand lay across the threshold.

Tavish gulped. Should he fetch Brenton to check, or should he grab the deer and run? The hand was an unnatural shade of white, and no heat; he didn't think it or its owner had any life left in them. Did it belong to a friend or foe? And what else was in the house? Any survivors? Perhaps he should go check it out.

He hugged the side of the shed and house where melting snow would obscure his footprints, and made his way to the door, watching the woods for signs of movement. At the door, he avoided stepping on the hand as he edged inside. What he saw made him jump outside again to bend over, retching.

Poor Mr. Jonstable. He'd probably tried to fight them when they'd come to take his family. But to leave him there like that— without his head—Tavish closed his eyes, but the image remained. He tried hard not to be sick.

Well, the man wouldn't be needing the blankets on the beds or the cloaks in his wardrobe. He'd gone on to better things, hopefully. Tavish sent a prayer to Meira in thanks for his aid to their mission. He stepped gingerly over the corpse, grimacing as his boots crunched on the frozen red puddle, and stole into the house.

Aidah paced the confines of the cave, walking stooped beneath the low ceiling, trying to comb through her bedraggled hair with her fingers. Brenton slept in one corner, having stayed up all night on watch against trouble. Poor Brenton. A welt left from one of the attackers' clubs had swelled up and turned purple on the side of his face, and he was in considerable pain. She could feel it even when he slept. She'd tried to take a little of the pain away or heal the bruise, but had only gotten a headache of her own in response. She couldn't wait to be trained.

As she paced, trying to ignore the empty gnawing of her stomach and the cold in her still slightly damp skirts, into the cave bounded Derg. He hurried to wake Brenton.

"We need to move. A party of Rangwar's men is headed this way. An hour perhaps, no more," he announced, breathing hard.

Brenton leapt to his feet and began to pull on his boots. Aidah was already dressed, so she grabbed a bit of dry brush and began to sweep out the cave and remove signs of their stay.

"Where's Tavish?" Brenton asked, tying laces on his boots.

"He went to the Jonstables to get supplies. It's been a while, but I don't sense danger from him, only—" Aidah grimaced, seeing the corpse in the doorway, the emotional impact it had hit Tavish with pummeling her gut. She swallowed hard. "Mr. Jonstable was murdered."

"You can sense all that," Brenton murmured in awe, staring at her. He blew out a nervous sigh. "We've got to warn him." He pulled the hood of his brown cloak over his head and put on his gloves, ramming them on in his haste.

"He's found food, blankets, clothing and fresh water. We should go help him pack," Aidah said, her vision clearer now of Tavish. He wasn't aware danger was coming, but he was being cautious. Brenton might not know it, but they were old hands at this sneaking around. She wondered though, how they were going to carry the goods he'd found. She and Tavish were hardly built for carrying heavy loads. If only they had managed to grab Muser when they were fleeing…if only a lot of things.

She finished cleaning and wrapped her cloak tight around her, pulling down her hood to protect against the cold. The day was perilously sunny, and temperatures would be dropping in the absence of snow. Outside the cave, Derg stood on a rocky outcrop, apparently calm, but his thoughts told a different story. Aidah tried to keep out his worries about everything from frostbite to starvation to cowering under the whip of an enemy mage. No effect. She still had little control over how to keep out unwanted thoughts and feelings.

Aidah and Brenton joined Derg on the rock, then the three of them descended the hillside into the forest, walking single file with Aidah leading and Derg last. The air was still, and painfully cold. Aidah was wondering why the air felt so empty, so…she concentrated harder, trying to sense something, gingerly reaching her senses beyond her group. The forest was dormant.

They were hibernating, she realized. The animals were asleep, and that what why everything felt so quiet. She could actually feel them. It was a strange sensation, even stranger than sensing people's thoughts. Once more she tried to block everything from her mind, concentrate on what she was doing.

They soon reached the cabin. Tavish stood against the side of the house, organizing a pile of stuff: wineskins, a deer carcass, leather vests and breeches, snow shoes, rope, carving knives and cooking wares, and blankets of soft wool, possibly even from Father's herd. Aidah rushed over to help him stuff food and other items into a couple of large travel packs, grabbing a bite of slightly stale bread to eat as she did so. Brenton stood over them, watching the woods, while Derg snuffed the wind.

"I hear the sound of hooves. Hurry," he said.

Though they struggled to fit everything inside the packs, there was too much; even when they left out all but a couple of blankets, bread, cookware and rope, they could barely close the packs, and Aidah found her burden of wineskin and pack impossible to lift. Tavish managed to shoulder the main pack, leaving the deer for Brenton, but Aidah doubted they could make a full day's walk with them.

Suddenly she heard the hooves as well. A single horse. Tavish heard it at the same time and staggered under his load to the side of the house to hide.

Brenton waved for Aidah to get moving, then ducked behind a fir tree. Aidah glanced at the packs and the stuff littering the yard, hesitating. She felt something familiar, something friendly. After Rangwar's false overtures, she wasn't certain how far to trust her senses, but she didn't sense any person's thoughts out there, just— and this was most odd—just sounds and smells. She wasn't alone in her hesitation. Derg sniffed the air curiously.

At the last second, Aidah threw herself down. Into view trotted not a mounted horse, but a mule. Old Muser! She sprang to her feet as it trotted right up to the cabin and stood before her, sides heaving with exertion. It looked into her eyes and she could swear it was waiting for instructions.

Brenton emerged from his hiding place and went to drape a rope across the mule's shoulder. It lowered its head, ready to receive a halter. Brenton looked askance at Aidah. "Were you wishing for this?"

Aidah ran a hand along Muser's damp coat, soothing the beast and silently thanking it for coming. "Well, sort of. I've been feeling bad about leaving him ever since we ran away. I wasn't sure if he'd escaped the fire."

Brenton found a halter and blanket, and set to putting them on Muser while Tavish ran to get a bucket of water. When he returned, Muser drank deeply, and the feeling of him was of warmth and contentment. Gently, Aidah began strapping their packs to his back.

Derg had continued his vigil in silence, sniffing the air occasionally. As they finished loading the mule, he padded over to inspect their handiwork. "Although I'm happy to see Muser made it out, we still need to hurry. I can't hear Rangwar's men yet, but they are coming. I don't know what they'll make of Muser's tracks, but its best we hurry on."

"Think you can make it, old fella?" Tavish asked Muser, scratching behind his ears.

The mule snorted. Aidah sensed his fatigue, but he wasn't exhausted yet. He should be able to walk with them, providing they not walk too fast. She took hold of his halter and nodded at Tavish. "He'll make it."

She began leading Muser in the direction of the trail, but Brenton grabbed her arm and shook his head. "It's too easy to find us on the main trail. We're going to make for the Gedar trail instead. Back up the hill with the cave—I know a way up the mountain. One of the hunting trails."

Derg's ears perked. "I can hear something! Hurry." Tavish reshouldered a much lighter pack and Aidah accepted a couple of extra wineskins to carry, then she turned Muser and began walking back up the hill towards the cave, following Brenton's lead. He led them to a break in the brush on the left, something which really couldn't be called a trail for anything but animals. In silence they climbed up the steep mountainside overlooking the cabin and the main trail.

They were climbing up an arm which would take them across the face of Mount Grinin, heading southeast, rather than due east like the main trail headed to meet the Southern Road for the Lowlands and Landaran. Rangwar's men had likely come from that direction and could be setting up an ambush for them. The Gedar Trail led south and then west, away from Landaran. It was a longer route, but if they could avoid trouble, it would be worth it. The only problem was that the Gedar Trail was on the southern edge of Mount Grinar in the valley before the next peak of Ranin. They'd have to cross the face of Mount Grinar to reach it, through dense forest and snow. Aidah sighed and set her mind for the long climb ahead.

They wound their way through the trees, moving from young bushy firs to older pine and spruce when they heard a commotion down in the valley at the cabin. The sound of doors slamming and men cursing rose up the hill as they scrambled to get out of sight.

"They've searched the house. It won't be hard to figure out

we've been there," Tavish whispered, eyeing the thin column of the chimney, all that they could now see of the house.

"We'll be easy to track through this fresh snow," Aidah added, her stomach turning over in knots.

Brenton crouched down, taking the pause in the march as an opportunity to check the mule's hooves and legs for rocks or burs. "We would have been just as easy to track on the main road. All we can do is keep moving. Unless you think you could use your powers, Aidah, to make them not see the tracks, perhaps, or to coerce them away."

"I don't know if that's a good idea. If she does it wrong she'll lead them right to us," Tavish argued.

"I think the mule's tracks already do that," Derg commented.

Brenton touched Aidah's arm. "Do you want to try? Or do you think it wouldn't work? If that's the case, we should hurry on."

Aidah shifted her weight against the burden of her pack, listening to the men as they chopped up something—she didn't want to think what—apparently ransacking the house. She saw their intentions: destroy the evidence, find the trail, acquire the Talents. They would not give up, no matter how hard the chase, and they were expert trackers. If she didn't find some way to throw them off with her power, she was as good as captured. She swallowed.

"I'll try," she said.

The three crouched down while Derg remained standing, gently nudging the mule away from chewing a rather noisy pinecone. Aidah closed her eyes and pictured the men below. That was easy—they were already focused on finding her, and that seemed to summon them to her mind without any effort. Then she tried wishing them away, wishing their senses to dull, their minds to grow sluggish. There wasn't any trail to find. There wasn't even a Life Talent to search for. It was cold, it was miserable, all they wanted was to go home...

Homesickness assailed her, real homesickness, not feigned. Her mother was irretrievably lost, her father missing, the house burned down. She *did* want, with all of her heart, to go home, to just forget about all of this, forever...

Tavish was shaking her. "Ok, Aidah, enough, please, that's enough. You're starting to affect us, I think. The men are leaving, anyhow."

She blinked away the moisture from her eyes, pushed aside the grief heavy in her chest, and stood to peer down at the cabin. Sure enough, the men were wandering back the way they had come, one man dropping a flaming torch into the snow from where he had been ready to set the house aflame. They said not a word to one another.

"What were we doing?" Brenton asked, rubbing his head. He stood and noted the men a moment, then mumbled to himself, blinking his eyes, seeming to come awake. He regarded Aidah. "Good job. Let's get moving."

Aidah led the mule up the hill into denser and denser forest, trying not to let her fear show as they hurried to put distance between themselves and the men below. With a vague sense of guilt, she wondered if the men would ever awake from her coercion. She only wished she could wake up herself, back in her bed to learn that none of this had ever happened.

They went as far as their legs would carry them that day, slept only enough to rest the mule, and continued on before dawn the next day. Under the cover of the forest, direction became meaningless, and they steered blindly based on the rising and falling of the land, hoping that with each dip into a valley they would find the little marker of the Gedar trail etched into the trees.

It was frightening to think that they may have missed the trail already, buried beneath several feet of snow. Aidah knew it had not been traveled on recently by any honorable folk, thanks to the recent storms. If they did see prints, what would they do? Follow them in the hopes it was a villager who'd managed to escape? Or avoid the tracks and find another way?

The one good thing Aidah could see in the new direction was that there hadn't been a whisper of any foe tracking them. They were alone but for the creatures of the forest.

Darkness descended over the woods, making the snow stand out in sharp contrast to the dark foliage and the glimmer of stars above. They took shelter under an old juniper whose limbs went clear to the ground, creating a soft bed under cover from snow and ice. The four crawled in under the heavy branches, careful not to disturb the snow on the tops of the branches which were helping to hide and insulate the little den. Aidah curled up with Derg against the trunk while Tavish kept Brenton awake for the watch, quietly whispering.

In no time at all, Aidah was asleep.

☼

Sometime later, Aidah woke. The shutters were open, letting in a view of a crisp winter morning through frost-streaked windows. Her bed was rumpled, the sheets twisted as if she'd been tossing in her sleep...

She blinked.

She was in her bedroom, Aidah realized, sitting up and throwing back the blankets. The room was cold and empty, so Tavish must already be up and starting the fire in the kitchen fireplace...but that fireplace had been destroyed, hadn't it? This whole house had been burned down to the ground by Rangwar's men. She leapt to her feet.

She was fully dressed, wearing her hiking boots, her woolen skirts and cloak; everything she had been wearing when she'd fled the house with Brenton and Tavish after Mother died...

It was a dream; it *had* to be a dream, and yet, just in case...

"Mama?" she called, hoping against hope that her call would be answered, that everything had just been a horrible nightmare. She could have fainted while out herding sheep with Brenton; that could explain her clothing. It could be possible that Mama would come through that door, even though she heard no noises in the rest of the house; it could be possible that Mama and Papa were simply outside...

Aidah knew it was a false hope. The crisp detail and the silence told her exactly what this was. That, and the fact her clothing was still wet from the snow, the smell of juniper in her hair. This was worse than a dream. *He* was coming.

She spun, searching the room for a weapon of some kind, preferably very long and very sharp. Aidah grabbed her knitting needle and tried to hide it up her sleeve. A chuckle behind her told her the effort to hide it was useless. Slowly, she turned around.

He was wearing a loose floor length robe of black silk, reclining against the wall on Tavish's bed, lazily observing her. His hair was damp as if recently washed, and he smelled of soap and rosemary. It was entirely the opposite of how she had expected him to appear, him knowing she was beyond his grasp. He had caused the death of her mother and would never be able to seduce her now. She glared, and brought her needle out to brandish at him.

He smirked, amused. "Do you think you can hurt me with that? Come, come, angel, think for a moment. This place doesn't even exist. It's all in your mind."

She looked at her hand, and the needle had disappeared. Looking down, she realized she was now dressed in her long flowing nightgown of white muslin. She concentrated hard to bring back her travel clothes, but without success.

Aidah kept her fear at bay, telling herself it was just manipulation. He was trying to make her feel vulnerable. It didn't matter what she wore for as he said, this was just in her mind. It was just a dream, even if it felt like she was awake. If she wished hard enough, maybe she would awaken. She closed her eyes to concentrate.

His hand brushed her arm, and she jumped. Eyeing him with as much contempt as she could muster, she scooted back. Her body might be asleep, but her mind was awake, and aware of her peril. So Rangwar could come when he pleased and keep her from waking. She'd take that as an invitation to attack.

"How dare you touch me! How dare you show up in my mind after what you did! 'I am only saving you from a horrible fate'—hah! You are the enemy, Rangwar, and now I know it. As soon as I'm trained, I am coming after you. You killed my mother!" She screamed, lunging at him to tear his eyes out, maim that perfect skin with a scratch or two.

In hindsight she would regret she hadn't lunged the other way, to leap out the window or door and escape.

He caught her with one hand, spun her around, and slammed her against the wall face first, arms trapped against the wooden planks, his elbow pressing hard between her shoulder blades. She grunted, the air knocked out of her, the rage suddenly replaced by terror. Pain shot up her arms and down her back. He let go and stepped back as she turned to face him.

The wood had scratched her wrist and she swore it was bleeding. A cold calmness swept over her, fear pounding in her heart. The pain was real. She could be hurt in this world between waking and dreaming. She might be killed here as well.

The sudden movement had mussed a few strands of his golden hair; he casually swept it back, his face calm, almost without expression. Aidah shivered, recalling the force with which he'd responded to her attack. It had been dealt with icy precision.

She made no move, watching him, waiting for punishment, a counter attack, something. A smile played at the corner of his lips, a smile not reflected in his eyes. He sauntered over to her bed and sat down. She remained standing.

Finally, he spoke. "I never intended to harm your mother, you know that. If you had surrendered, she would still be alive."

How dare he try to lay blame on her! "She wasn't going to allow me to surrender. Why should I? You're everything people say about you. You're manipulative and cold, a liar, a kidnapper, and a killer!" She broke off, suddenly remembering that her papa and grandpapa were in his possession. She didn't want to anger him. What sort of things could he do to them? She imagined plenty of things. Horrible things.

His eyes glinted. "Your father and the rest of the village are perfectly healthy, making their way towards Innis. I expect they'll probably be boarding the boats in about ten days."

Boats which would take them across the Krimean Sea, and out of reach. Even Korva never let her forces venture far out over the red waters of the cursed inland sea. Aidah didn't think her father had ever been in a boat before. What would become of him?

Rangwar watched her, reading her reactions, and leaned back to softly pat the space next to him. "Aidah, you are worried about the sort of life your father will have in Innis—after all, he is used to the mountains and pastures, not large cities and galley ships." His gaze bore into her. "Perhaps a trade could be made to allow him to remain in the Morgaine Range. Not in Hamstead, I'm afraid, but a similar village. If you would turn yourself in to a party of my men…"

"How do I know you would uphold your part of the 'trade'?" She asked, keeping her voice calm, nonaggressive. Her shoulder hurt from where he had slammed her into the wall. Though he seemed at ease, there was a growing tension in the air, and her instincts were warning her that something bad was about to take place. Was it merely her fears, or could it be his intentions she was sensing?

He stretched and stood, then advanced slowly on her, looming over her like a cat observing a mouse. "If you came to me, I would begin your training. Eventually you would be able to see your father or visit him out of body, even as I appeared at your house. I would have no way to deceive you concerning his treatment."

This was true. She felt it in her bones. "Then teach me this now. Let me see him right now."

He wagged a finger at her. "You ask me to put a roof on a house with no walls. First you must learn the basics. Then your power will increase steadily. I'm not one to brag, but I do consider myself one of the best teachers. Better than Korva; after all, I trained *her.*"

He chuckled and placed a hand on her shoulder. "I could make you powerful, ensure prosperity for your family, whatever you desire. However, I cannot wait forever for an answer. Will you come to me, yes or no?"

Her sense of danger peaked. Aidah glanced up at his face, and it was as calm as ever, placid, masked from any hint of what thoughts were stirring within. Where his hand was on her shoulder, however, there was a tension, a hardness of where his fingers pressed into her collarbone, clutching. She just wanted away from him, away from this terrible dream world. The mention of teaching Korva had reminded her—this man was close to three hundred years old. There was no guessing the power he had developed in that time.

"May I have a day or two to think on this? It's a big decision, you know," she asked in a small voice, wondering if she could find Korva before then, or at least somebody who could protect her mind. Surely there must be a way to keep him out.

He smiled, and again Aidah had the notion that he was reading her. "No, I don't think so. The further your uncle takes you, the more difficult it is for my men, and they can be quite testy after a long chase."

His hand left her shoulder to cup her cheek. "I don't see why you even need time to consider. I am offering you everything. Korva has not even visited you to make an offer. Doesn't that make you wonder? I would think if she found you important, she would have contacted you by now. Perhaps you will reach her only to be turned away."

"She's just busy. And she probably doesn't know yet—she told me I probably wouldn't develop any Talent, when I was seven. I'm sure if she knew she'd help," Aidah argued. She couldn't allow herself to think otherwise.

Rangwar shrugged, eyes hooded, his hair dangling down his shoulder, onto her face. "If you say. Regardless, she is not here to help you make your decision. Now what is your answer?" The hand cupping her chin tightened its grip to press into her throat. She gulped.

If she said yes, she could save her papa and grandpapa from a terrible fate, but she would also be betraying her country, her family, and most importantly her mother, who died to prevent this. To give herself over to Rangwar and his avid interest in her...she shuddered. No. She couldn't imagine staying with him, now that she knew who he was. She had to remind herself. He looked young only because he feasted on lives. Such a one would only cause her grief, whatever her decision. She didn't want anything to do with him, except maybe to bring about his death. Even if Papa suffered for it.

"I...can't," she whispered, closing her eyes, trembling, wondering what would happen next. He could beat her. He could torture her. Gods, she wished she knew how to wake up! She felt on the verge of tears, but swallowed them back.

"Of course you *can*," Rangwar said, venom and ire in his voice. Aidah whimpered, feeling that hand on her throat, but even as she felt it tighten, he released her. He remained near her, all too near. "What you mean is you *won't*. That sounds rather like a 'no'. Are you sure you want that to be your answer?" His lips were at the nape of her neck, hissing out the words, and Aidah pictured him with one fist upraised, ready to strike at her if she dared open her eyes. Never had she felt so terrified. Was it possible to die of terror?

She licked her lips, trying to think. Attack, or do nothing? What would keep her from harm? She couldn't use her powers against him; he could see whatever she did and defend himself with all his lifetimes of experience. It was a useless gesture to even try it. And he'd already demonstrated the futility of physical attack. What she most wanted to do was curl up, hide herself and pretend this wasn't happening. Unfortunately she was so scared she couldn't even tell her body to perform that simple act.

"Well, are you going to answer me?" He maneuvered behind her, grabbed her arms, and pulled her up against him. She gasped with shock and horror; he was aroused. She wanted to be brave, like her brother or uncle, but she couldn't help it. She started to cry.

He petted her hair. "Ah, now I see why you said 'can't'. You're a weak spineless thing who needs her decisions made for her." He all but hissed the words as he forced her towards the bed.

She looked into his eyes in a desperate plea, his intentions all too clear now. "You can't…" Her voice died.

The image of his face burned itself into her mind, into her memory, driven by stark terror, helplessness, frustration at her predicament. Tears slipped silently down her cheeks. The hard plane of his brow, cheek, and jaw, the stormy gray tinge which had stolen over his eyes, the flared nostrils. A look of lust, and determination. Most sickening was the familiarity of the setting—her bed, her room, her house. So cozy, with its little wooden plank walls, earthen floor, hand-quilted blankets and comforters, even her own needlecraft on the pillow covers. She was being pushed down onto her bed, pinned there, a feebly flapping little bird under the paw of a snow leopard. "Please!" She begged.

"That's right, say please," he murmured, on top of her now, robe slipping down his back to reveal more and more flesh. She turned her head to look at the wall, Tavish's bed, anything but him. She couldn't shut out his voice, "I am going to show you that we are more alike than you think. You are not what you think you are. I guarantee by the time I'm done you'll be begging me not to stop."

He proceeded to do just that, using his powers in ways she could never have imagined they could be used, to open up parts of her far worse than she could have guessed existed. Though she fought, screamed, tried to block him out or black out herself, the sensations began emerging from her body even without his help. There was no escape.

Time had no meaning except that it seemed endless; until finally it ended and he left her, lying sprawled in the bed, spent, moaning at the sensation of something wet flowing down her legs, seeping into the sheets underneath her. She glanced at the red stain on the sheets, ghastly against the white linen, and had to close her eyes against bile rising in her throat. A shiver of ecstasy ran through her.

A sob wracked her; dry, because there wasn't a tear left to shed. Her throat was parched and she felt hot and dizzy. She tried to rise but swooned, falling back against the pillow. A few more sobs escaped her, before she quenched them. She sat up.

Rangwar was gone, for now, and she was exhausted. When she fell asleep, she would fall asleep in truth—he had told her that, before he left—and she would wake up in the morning in her real body in the real world. Whether or not her real body would show the signs, she didn't know. It made no difference. He had succeeded.

She wanted him again.

8

Defeated

"Morning, Aidah! Time to get up," Tavish's voice woke Aidah from a sound slumber to aching limbs and a queasy feeling in her stomach. She swatted her hand in the direction of his voice to make it stop and blearily opened her eyes.

The snow had soaked into her back, making her bottom nearly numb with cold. Pine needles had somehow gotten under her blouse to scratch at her tender skin. She groaned, trying to stretch out her legs, and crawled out from beneath the fir tree towards the painful brightness of day. A sharp intake of breath from Tavish caused her to turn back. Where she had been lying, the snow was stained with blood.

"Uncle Brenton, come quick! Aidah's bleeding," Tavish called.

Heat suffused Aidah's cheeks, as she checked her skirts and realized where the blood was coming from. "Don't panic, Tavish, I think it's just my monthly flow," She hurried to explain. In all truth it could be that; by her reckoning nearly a month had passed since her last flow. There was a chance that it had no connection to the dream—that thing she most wanted to forget.

This was the real world. She wasn't in Rangwar's clutches yet.

She hurried to remove traces of herself, in case they were being followed, and went to the other side of the fir tree to attend to her needs. Sure enough, it looked like menstrual flow. She grimaced. How timely.

Once she had dealt with that, she joined her brother, uncle, and Derg in a little breakfast of salted venison and gruel. They eyed her with concern but asked no questions, leaving her to her breakfast in peace. Aidah welcomed the moment to figure out what she was going to do, if she should tell them or not.

Rangwar would probably watch her for the next few days, to see if she turned herself over to his men. By her actions, he would know her answer, and if she fled…she shuddered. She needed to find protection before he returned, or she needed to train herself to block him out, something. If she had to endure that—that horror one more time, she would crack. She'd been ready by the end to do anything, to promise herself to—

Suddenly breakfast was a cold lump in her stomach, ashes in her mouth. She put down her bowl and ran to a small copse of fir trees to be sick. The terrible quaking in her stomach was driven out, but cramps swiftly came to take its place. She ate a couple handfuls of clean snow to rinse out her mouth, struggling to hold back tears.

"Sis, you okay? What's the matter?" Tavish called from the other side of the screen of branches. Derg ignored their barrier of privacy to come trotting underneath, right up to her side. She flinched at his touch.

"Are you unwell, Aidah?" His deep brown eyes gazed into hers, searching.

"I'm—I'm—" She couldn't bring herself to say 'fine', because it wasn't true, and it was obvious to the Lupas that she was on the verge of falling apart. She struggled to compose herself, giving him any explanation she could think of, anything but the truth. "Actually, I'm not feeling too well right now. The running, and the stress—Mama's death—and now the woman's flow—" *That should be enough,* she thought, hiccupping back a sob and trying desperately to smile. She'd been through enough even without last night to drive most of the girls of the village to tears. Of course, she was tougher than them. Hopefully tough enough to pull this off until she decided what to do.

It wasn't anything vital she had lost last night. Physically she was probably still intact. It would be silly for her to let it affect her. She refused to cry, to let him be victorious over her emotions. She'd die before she gave Rangwar that satisfaction. Anger; that was what she needed to pull herself together. She imagined what she would to do him once she had her powers under control. After a few deep breaths, she was able to give Derg a real smile, though it was lined with iron.

At that moment Brenton came through the screen of fir,

followed closely by Tavish. Her stomach now settled somewhat and her emotions under control, she turned to smile at them as well.

"My stomach's upset. I don't really know why," she said to their questioning looks.

Brenton leaned over to check her brow for fever and gave her a brief looking over. She endured it, though she could not repress a shudder; Brenton's scrutiny was far too reminiscent of the attention last night.

"Well, nothing seems to be wrong with you. Could just be your Talent again. Can you walk?"

"I think so." She *had* to. There was no way she was going to hinder their progress if she could help it. She wanted as far away from here as possible, to get to Korva. She wished she could fly there, in fact.

To demonstrate that she was capable, Aidah led the way back to where Muser was tied up, and with grim determination, she made herself eat the remainder of her gruel, demanding that her stomach behave itself. She tightened the laces of her boots and adjusted her cloak for walking.

Brenton and Tavish eyed each other, shrugging, and began to shoulder their packs. Tavish made a point of taking more of Aidah's share, grumbling about females and all their excuses for getting out of work. Inside, he radiated worry. Derg shook his head and positioned himself close to her. She cleaned up the campsite and took her place at Muser's side to lead him. They began walking.

She concentrated on the cold, on her tired feet, the painfully bright sun reflected off of the snowdrifts—anything but last night and what it all meant. She was so tired, it was as if she hadn't had any sleep at all. The cramps and aches lodged in her side and refused to budge, no matter how she carried herself. Worse, she was still overly sensitized; she flinched if her waterskin brushed her unexpectedly, and almost backhanded Tavish when he casually touched her shoulder to check on her. It was awful—everything reminded her of his caresses, his oh-so-artful ministrations. She swallowed hard against another surge of nausea, shivering. The world felt vile.

She figured they had only gone a mile or two, when suddenly the peace of the mountainside was shattered by a quick succession of booms, sounding like explosions or thunder in the distance. Aidah froze; her heart pounding, expecting any moment for Rangwar or that Storm Mage of his to come waltzing out the trees. Brenton motioned for everyone to get down behind the mule, then waved Derg over and whispered something to him. The Lupas nodded and bounded off into the forest.

Tavish fidgeted and Brenton scanned the trees around them, keeping low to the ground. Aidah did nothing. Absolutely nothing—she hardly dared breathe, lest that alert whoever was out there. She was going to start crying, or screaming, or both, because she couldn't take this, she couldn't keep everything bottled up inside any longer, and that was probably just what Rangwar wanted. Her screams would tell his men exactly where they were.

Before she could break down, she closed her eyes and shut out the world. As a precaution, she checked her aura. It was so closely wrapped against her it was a wonder she didn't have a headache. Good. Now if only she could stay invisible. If only Korva would come.

Derg returned, winded. "We're alone on this mountainside, as much as I can tell. The sounds seemed to have come from the other side of the mountain, along the Gedar Trail, perhaps. It's difficult to tell with the echoes. I'm not sure if it was ahead of us or behind."

An hour later they were no closer to learning the truth. It seemed that if they had been spotted, there should have been some sign of pursuit by now. Perhaps it had been a communication of sorts, though for what purpose no one could say. Brenton said that he feared if it had come from ahead of them, that the Gedar Trail might have been discovered, and their last remaining escape path blocked. There was no way to know until they reached the markers. They moved on.

Aidah managed to make it to midday before she felt too ill to walk. They redistributed the packs, and bundled her on top of the mule to ride the rest of the day, miserable in heart and in body and wondering if she was being punished for some transgression by the gods.

Unfortunately, the inactivity made it impossible not to think about the slippery slope or how to walk without leaving an easy trail to follow. They were going down a fairly steep slope into the valley between Mount Grinar and Ranin. Hopefully by morning they would reach the Gedar Trail. Then they would know if Fortune smiled upon them.

As for Korva, any messengers she was sending would most likely have come up the Southern Trail, so it was unlikely they'd have help before they reached the Lowlands, but Aidah had to remind herself, Korva could probably do just about anything Rangwar could. If she knew of their plight, she should be able to contact them. *Please,* she prayed, hoping Korva would hear, *please help us.*

Aidah glanced at Brenton, plowing ahead through the high drifts of snow untouched by boot or hoof, walking bowed with the weight of his pack. Tavish was walking rather stooped as well, silent and determined. The only thoughts emanating from him were thoughts of a warm campfire and roasted pheasant on a spit. Even Derg had lost his bounce, walking just behind Muser to avoid having to bound through the drifts, tail low to the ground and ears back in contemplation. No one spoke a word.

Should she tell them? All signs of pursuit were behind them, and since she didn't really know where they were, she couldn't give away their location to Rangwar, even if he read her thoughts. It wasn't really their business, what had happened. It wasn't anyone's business but hers. And Korva's. When she saw Korva, she'd tell everything, she'd let that woman know all the pain she had just gone through, the humiliation and the confusion over what she was and what she was becoming, oh yes, she'd tell Korva all of it, and hold her accountable. She should have been warned—even if she only had a mild potential and might never develop Talent, she still should have been warned.

Brenton didn't need to know any of this. He was burdened enough with the care of them, and his thoughts were bleak. He planned to get them to Landaran, set them up for tutelage, and when he was sure of their safety. He would search for Father and the villagers. Aidah felt his yearning to free or avenge their deaths. If he knew what Rangwar was doing to his niece right under his protection, it would devastate him. She couldn't do that to him. And Tavish—well, he'd shoot flames if he knew, and run off to defend her honor. And Derg—he'd probably die of shame like he always said he'd do if he failed in his role as guardian. She didn't really know what he'd do, but it would be to harm himself, of that she was certain. He always kept things inside. Just like her.

The sun had fallen behind Grinar Peak when Brenton pushed through a particularly deep drift of icy snow to find trampled snow on the other side of the drift; snow with very fresh tracks. Derg ran forward to sniff at the crisscrossing tracks, and wrinkled his nose in distaste.

"Men from Innis. They went up the trail, and then back. We are most fortunate. They again overestimated our speed. I would not dally, however. They may return."

Brenton nodded, wiping at his brow. "What we'll do is backtrack to hopefully confuse the direction we're traveling, then up the trail a bit, then veer off the trail to sleep. I'm afraid I can only allow a few hours of rest. How are you doing, Aidah?"

Aidah hurried to dismount, then helped her brother return some of his load onto the mule. "I dozed a little while we were walking. I'll be fine."

The three of them worked on getting the mule repacked while Derg scouted. They followed their little makeshift trail back several hundred yards, making many tracks to be as confusing as possible. With Tavish's help, they then broke a new trail back to the Gedar Trail and disguised it to look like melting runoff. After following the Gedar Trail until the full setting of the sun, they then left the trail to climb up along the overhanging slopes and found a thick stand of spruce to camp within. Aidah sat on a matt of needles to watch Brenton and Tavish munch on some of the venison jerky. She herself ate nothing, but laid down to watch the two moons with their half light, half dark faces rising over the crest of the mountain peak, their pale glow bathing the snow in an eerie blue light, illuminating the exhausted faces of Brenton and Tavish. Derg rested beside her, soothing her with his warmth as he dozed off, ears twitching at any noises beyond the wind in the trees or the soft plop of snow falling from boughs.

It was probably safe to sleep tonight at least—the kind of magic Rangwar used to get inside her dreams had to be taxing, and Emperors surely had other business to attend to. She hoped he needed time to recover. Lots of time. Still, she couldn't shake the dread clutching at her stomach.

As the others drifted off, she tried to think of things before this, back to times spent with Papa, walking through snow and pointing out the tracks of elks and bears, or baking in the home with Mama, making gingerbread and honey cakes for the Winter Festival.

Around her, the sounds of the forest grew into a peaceful

melody, broken only by the occasional hoot of an owl or her own deep sighs.

☼

It was some time before dawn when Tavish awoke, disturbed by the sound of booted feet crunching through frozen snow and quiet muttering in a language he did not recognize. Across from him, Aidah was asleep huddled into a tight ball, and next to him Brenton was awake, crouched down peering through the brush. Derg was nowhere to be seen.

Brenton, upon noting that he was awake, held a finger to his lips and pointed through the brush towards the trail down in the valley. Very carefully Tavish crawled forward, trying not to make so much as a whisper of sound. Between branches of spruce and pine, he could see Madhar and his men coming down the trail from the southwest, heading back towards Hamstead. They moved swiftly but cautiously, checking along the sides of the trail for any disturbance of the snow, any possible traces of their quarry.

Tavish held his breath as they paused, hoping that Aidah wouldn't wake and make a sound, or that her Talent wouldn't manifest itself in any way until they were gone. She looked dead asleep. That was probably a good thing.

For long moments he watched the procession along the trail, until they were out of sight and out of hearing.

When all trace of them was gone, Derg ran out of the woods to crawl into their rest site. "They'll soon be upon our trail—even with the melting Tavish did yesterday, it may look suspicious. We'd better move on, right now."

Brenton leaned over to gently shake Aidah awake. She started away from his hand and yelped—a peculiar, high-pitched note of terror. Her eyes flew open and then recognition seemed to sink in; she flushed and scooted back a little, smiling timidly.

"Sorry, you scared me, uncle," she said by way of explanation.

Such odd behavior, Tavish thought, but well, she was becoming a woman, and who knew what things went on in their heads. Lucky for them that Madhar and his company were out of earshot.

Brenton explained what they had seen of their pursuers, and although she turned a shade paler, Aidah nodded and set to packing for the walk ahead. Tavish frowned as he brushed away their imprints with a sprig of spruce. She'd looked at Brenton yesterday like he was a monster or something, when he'd tried to check her health, and Tavish swore he saw Aidah flinching when he touched her. She was either taking this whole nightmare harder than she was showing, or something else was frightening her. Bad dreams, perhaps; gods knew he'd been having a couple of bad ones lately.

It was possible she might lose it, shatter with all the events that had recently occurred. Mama was dead, but he could live on—at least until she was avenged. He had a mission to keep him sane, but Aidah had never wanted any of this, and hate wasn't really in her heart. He didn't know how she dealt with the pain. He'd never really thought of her as weak, but she was no warrior either. It was hard to imagine her training to fight Rangwar.

Well, if he was successful, she wouldn't have to. He was going to string up ole Rangwar by his liver when he found him. After he was trained a bit more, of course.

Aidah stumbled as she went to Muser to pack a few things in the saddlebags, and Tavish hurried over to steady the mule, wondering if she was going to be fit for travel.

"I'm walking," she said in a low voice, glaring at him.

Well she didn't have to be so huffy about it; he was only trying to help. He waited until Brenton finished clearing up the campsite, then led Muser through the snow down the hillside towards the trail. He tried to ignore the fear in Aidah's eyes as she glanced back in the direction Madhar and his men had gone.

Gods, just get us to Landaran, he prayed.

☼

They walked until sunrise, stopped for a quick meal and to check if they were being followed by their pursuers, then set off again to march through the day into the afternoon. They followed a crisscrossing trail Madhar's men had made when they up and down the trail. The fresh tracks made the going easier, though Aidah worried that at any moment they'd find a straggler or guard left behind to watch the trail.

They made good time crossing between Grinar and Ranin peaks and down into a valley which wound itself around the next peak, Mount Neci, by whose odd-shaded dip at the top was thought to be a long extinct volcano.

In the late afternoon, when they were beginning to check for possible sites for a rest, the footprints they had been following suddenly stopped. A single file path veered off of the trail to a thin patch of forest on the hillside.

Aidah stopped behind Tavish and Muser, eyeing the narrow path with a shiver of fear. Rangwar's men were so close to catching her. They had passed by only yards away from her in the night—a night without any 'dreams', fortunately, but if she had awoken…she shuddered. And what had they seen here, that they had gone off the trail in what appeared to be a small group, single file?

"Should we follow it?" she asked Brenton.

He strode up to the path, then back, pacing. "Maybe I should go—but then you two would be alone—and if we continue on the main trail it could be a trap, or an ambush…" he inhaled for a breath and stopped his pacing, holding his forehead with one hand, head bent.

Derg stood up and nudged his leg. "Do you want me to go?"

Brenton stood a moment more, frowning and eyeing the mule and the group of them, then up at the open sky, then at the virgin snow of the trail before them, and shook his head. "No, I think we'd best stay together, pool our strengths. We'll do as they did; walk single file. I'll go first. Derg, you watch the rear."

They started walking, as the sun fell behind the mountains behind them, leaving them in the quickly cooling shadows. Brenton picked up a frozen branch lying buried just off the little path and began carefully removing needles from it, probably to use as a weapon in case of trouble.

The pathway went up the hillside behind the trees and allowed an excellent view of the trail below, now discernable only by the carved markers on the north sides of one of every dozen trees. There wasn't a sound other than the wind and the creaking of branches laden with snow. Aidah strained her eyes in the gloom to peer ahead, her nerves wound tight, ready to flee at the slightest hint of an attack. Tavish hung close to Brenton's side, also peering ahead.

"I can see something there down on the trail," Tavish whispered.

Brenton raised his hand for everyone to stop, and quietly crept ahead, keeping low. *Tavish is using his Talent to see in the dark*, Aidah realized, getting a flash of vision of what Tavish could see. So strange, she thought—he was seeing traces of heat from a fire. She sniffed the wind. Yes, she could smell it now, smoke from a fire only recently burned out. Yet they hadn't seen any smoke rising from the forest during the day...

"I can't see anything, Tavish. What do you see?" Brenton asked, returning.

Tavish squinted, standing tiptoe to peer over a stand of trees partially hiding the trail. "I see signs of several small fires, hours old. They're still giving off heat. Looks almost like a blast—an explosion or something. Can't see much else. Everything is the same temperature as the air and snow."

"Could be a trap," Derg said, with a low whine. He closed his eyes, sniffing. "Wait. I smell something. Humans, horses, food...." he sniffed a bit more, "...and blood."

"Could be allies!" Tavish exclaimed.

"Or the caravan that was supposed to come for me?" Aidah didn't know whether to be hopeful or afraid. If the humans were allies, were they alive or dead?

"Let me go check," Tavish urged, unslinging his pack and leaning it against a tree.

"No, it's too dangerous. I should go," Brenton muttered.

Tavish grunted. "You can't see what I see, and I'm trained enough to defend myself if there's trouble. You stay and watch Aidie. It'll only take a minute."

Brenton shut his mouth, but worry showed in his eyes as Tavish began to make his way down the hill through the snow to the trail.

Derg sniffed the air. "There's men nearby, not towards the trail but up on the hill. I'm going to go investigate." He tore off uphill into the trees.

Brenton gripped Aidah's arm. "Stay close to me, Aidah. Something doesn't feel right here."

Aidah tried to feel with her Talent to see if anything was amiss, but she felt absolutely nothing, save for the excitement Tavish was feeling on his little reconnaissance and the nervousness of Brenton and Derg. She concentrated on extending her aura to see if it came upon any other emotions or thoughts—such as readiness to attack. She felt nothing. Careful to draw her aura back in, she urged the mule forward a little from where it was munching on bark so that she could better view Tavish as he headed down the trail.

"Should we follow him on the path?" she asked in a whisper,

pointing to where their little path continued on into a patch of holly brush. "If there is an ambush, we could surprise them, or be close to help Tavish."

Before Brenton could respond, there came a cry from Tavish, now just out of sight in the shadows of the valley. "They attacked a caravan! Come down here and help me check for survivors," he called. Aidah grimaced; if they could hear him, so could any enemies lying in wait anywhere in this valley. Brenton gnashed his teeth and motioned for her to hurry.

They started forward, pulling along Muser to where the single file path ended, then urged the reluctant mule down the hillside to the main trail. Derg ran up to join them, reporting, "Nobody is hiding on this side of the trail that I can detect."

Brenton nodded, walking quickly and working to clear a path for Aidah and Muser. They went down a little fold in the land where trees blocked sight of the trail from the path above, and then suddenly there it was: an overturned caravan wagon with an arching roof, ornately carved and painted in the familiar bright reds and greens of the Gedar people. The roof had split wide open apparently from a blast that was too precise to have been natural. A lightning bolt had struck right through the woods, leaving a trail of destruction.

"Madhar did this," Tavish said with a growl, shoving away a wagon wheel that had been knocked off the wagon to one side. Bells attached to the spokes made an eerily cheerful ring in the silent evening. The rigging for the horses was blackened and torn, but apparently the horses had fled or been stolen for there was no sign of them anywhere. The humans had been less fortunate.

Bodies lay strewn everywhere, from inside the caravan to several feet away, hinting that some were probably brought down as they fled. Aidah hung back as Tavish and Brenton checked for life signs among the bodies, all of whom were dressed in the traditional garish costumes of the Gedar, people who typically roamed the land as fortune tellers and acrobats, staging shows and carrying messages. In the darkness, the bright colors of their blouses, tunics, skirts and breeches showed black against the snow.

At least the bold patterns disguised any stains of blood.

Aidah felt something of a shock from Tavish, as if she'd been doused with cold water, and hurried to the back of the caravan to where he was inspecting one of the bodies. Horror showed in his eyes.

She looked down at the corpse, shot through the chest with a blast which must have been lightning, dressed in a cloak of Gedar make. Beneath that cloak, however, she was wearing robes of the Doane. Sun Mage orange, it looked like. Aidah could just discern the face, more handsome than beautiful, with a square masculine jaw and rich black hair, graying at the temples. That face seemed familiar. Aidah struggled to remember.

"It's Nera," Tavish said.

The pain and suppressed anger in his voice startled her; for once he was shut off from her, his emotions solely on his face and not in her head. He gently closed the Sun Mage's eyes staring sightless into the sky, and took the medallion proclaiming her as a Protectorate Mage from around her neck to a secure pocket of his pack. His mouth was set in a hard grimace, his eyes downcast and clouded with grief. Brenton came over and gasped at the sight of the corpse. He tried to pull Aidah back from the sight, but she resisted, giving him a stern look. He dropped his arm to his side, a look of defeat on his face. His thoughts were loud in Aidah's mental ear, *Can't stop them from doing anything, can't even keep them in line. What a failure I'm turning out to be.*

Poor Brenton. She couldn't console him, however, for Tavish was acting strangely, a terrible smoldering fire now alighting in his eyes as he read a scroll which had been tucked away in Nera's pack.

He read it quickly, then crumpled it in his hand and threw it aside. With brisk purposeful strides he went to the side of the trail, looking out into the forest, fists clenched at his sides. He inhaled sharply, as if to speak, then slowly blew it out.

Without warning he was back in Aidah's head, and the pain was a blaze in his chest, as visions of memory flashed in his eyes.

She remembered Nera, but hadn't been close to the woman; the woman had bustled into their kitchen one morning during Tavish's confinement. She had taken Tavish by the hand, thrown his cloak and boots at him to don, then hauled him outside for immediate training. When they'd returned that nightfall, Tavish had been jovial and at ease, something he hadn't been since the abrupt appearance of his Talent some three months before.

Tavish's memories were far more immediate. She'd shown up in his life, confident and unafraid of what he could do. Strict, no-

nonsense—he'd wanted to grinde his teeth, had even tried to flame her as she taught him the basics of control. She'd swatted down his efforts as she would a fly, but hadn't scolded him, or gotten angry. That had earned his respect. She taught him how to use his temper to his advantage, and quickly a friendship had formed, as she patiently but firmly taught what he could and could not get away with. That joy he had felt the first time he successfully started—and extinguished—a fire, that he attributed wholly to Nera's efforts.

Now she was dead.

While he stood remembering and Aidah fought to block out the painful spurts of emotion and thought coming from him, Brenton strode over to pick up the crumpled message. He shook it out on his leg, and read it. He sighed.

"She was coming for you, Aidah. This is the message your father sent a month ago to Korva. I doubt it got all the way to Landaran. She probably intercepted it and rushed to come get you. What a tragedy." Now his grief poured over her as well, but this was more a sense of hopelessness and failure than true grief. Nevertheless, it was just as powerful, and Aidah staggered under the weight of both of them, her vision dimming.

She struggled to keep hold of her mind. "So Grandess doesn't know what's happened? There won't be any more help coming from Landaran for us?" Perhaps Rangwar was right. Perhaps Korva really didn't care what happened to her. Yet Nera had tried to come, and had been killed. *She* had cared.

Aidah hid her face, lost in the emotions around her and inside her. Was she going to cause death to everyone associated with her?

"Madhar's going to pay for this. And Rangwar! I'm going to flame the skin off of them and freeze their insides. Then I'll slowly kill them," Tavish uttered in a low voice, turning to face them. Aidah repressed a shudder. She had never heard true hatred in her brother's voice before. The death of Nera, combined with losing his mother, pushed him over the edge.

There were no words to answer him with. The only thought running through her head now *was what if he learns what else Rangwar's been guilty of? That he's defiled your twin sister right under your nose!* This time she could not repress the shudder or the wave of nausea that followed.

"Easy, Tavish. There's nothing you can do right now. Revenge will come later, but first you must get more teaching," Derg said, hugging close to Aidah as if he could sense her discomfort.

"Nera *was* my teacher!" Tavish screamed in fury. Derg whimpered and cowered back, while Brenton whirled, startled, to regard him.

His fury was an inferno, literally singeing Aidah's sensitivities, wounding her inside. She couldn't block it out, she couldn't do anything, and she was in real pain now, a physical pain in her head and all down her spine. She pleaded within her for him to do something, expend that anger, before her Talent decided to defend her against it.

As if on command, Tavish turned to a pine towering over the trail, so ancient that its lower third was bare of branches, its bark split with deep fissures of the many hard winters it had endured. It erupted into flame.

"Tavish, put it out now! Rangwar's men will see us!" Brenton cried, running forward.

Tavish ignored him, eyes narrowed, watching the tongues of flame as they leapt up and up the tree, throwing off dazzling sparks as the needles burned.

Aidah was torn; she should stop him before the men saw the light and came searching, yet this was diffusing his anger. Already he was hurting less, though the visions passing through his mind were not pleasant to witness. But if she fell into Rangwar's hands....

"That's enough, Tavish. Save it for the enemy," she said in a quiet voice.

He let the flames grow a minute longer, the light bathing him in a red glow, then just as suddenly, he extinguished them. He was thorough. Not even an ember glowed as he turned back to the caravan.

He blinked.

"There's someone watching us! Up there, on the hill!"

9

Allies and Enemies

Aidah and Brenton whirled to peer up the hill on the opposite side from the little path they had taken, but there was nothing either of them could see. In her head, however, Aidah could see what Tavish saw—a spot of bright red heat against the cold blues and greens of the forest, moving away rapidly

"He'll tell Madhar!" Tavish cried, and tore off up the hill to capture the onlooker.

He was still in a near-killing rage, Aidah thought, and for some strange reason, she didn't think the person fleeing was an enemy. She tossed aside her pack and ran after him, ignoring the frantic calls of Brenton and Derg.

Tavish's vision kept trying to invade her own, but she managed to keep it at bay as she followed him into the utter darkness until she was close behind. Then she let his vision replace hers. She tripped and stumbled a few times but was able to keep up as he swiftly overtook the fleeing form. Behind her, she could hear Brenton and Derg running far behind. Ahead, Tavish set another tree on fire to illuminate the forest.

In the light of the blazing tree—much smaller this time, thankfully—Aidah could see a young man, no more than sixteen or seventeen, dressed in garish Gedar clothing two sizes too small, leaping over a fallen log. His long skinny legs miscalculated the distance and he fell, long bony arms entangling themselves in the branches like a puppet whose strings had been cut.

Tavish was on top of him in an instant, waving high a hunting knife he'd taken from the Jonstables. From her link to her brother,

Aidah could see the youth gape in terror.

"Get back, demon! Let me and my people be!" the youth shouted, voice cracking. Aidah recalled the tales of Gedar superstition—that all mages had demon blood and were seldom to be trusted.

Tavish was furious. "What, don't like my fire? Tell me what you were doing spying on us, or you'll feel its heat, I'm warning you." He pulled the youth up, ignoring the fact he was half a head shorter, and kept the knife raised.

Aidah ran up to them to stop a tragedy before it occurred. "Tavish, put that thing away. We don't' even know if he's a foe or not. With your Talent, you hardly need it anyway."

Tavish glared at the youth, but sheathed the knife. "You understand that, I hope. I could flame you with a look. My sister there can do worse things; she's a Life Talent. She could reach right into your head to find out all your secrets, so you'd better start talking if you want her to stay out."

Aidah schooled her expression to appear neutral and fought not to roll her eyes.

With awe as well as fear in his eyes, the young man studied her, and she shifted uncomfortably. No one had ever looked at her with awe before. He was just on the verge of manhood. There came a sensation from him that felt like fabric stretched to the seam, or a rope pulled taut. *He's experiencing a growth surge,* she realized. *I can even sense things like that,* came the thought immediately after. Every day it seemed she could do more and more, even untrained.

She stepped forward and offered the young man a hand. Despite the fear in his eyes and the tattered appearance of his clothing, he had rather a nice face. The nose was too long and his adam's apple stood out, but these were things he'd probably eventually grow into.

Black hair hung past his ears growing out of what had probably been a close-cropped cut, and his eyes were wide set and dark brown; typical Gedar coloration with just a hint of a slant to the eyes and brows, also quite typical. Most prominent of all was his mouth—a wide, generous mouth made for smiling. At present it was pursed in anxiety.

He glanced at her hand, but did not shake it, balancing on the toes of his feet, like an acrobat. He spoke in a clear cultured voice towards Tavish, "Who are you to be ordering me around? I am Gair of the Malin Clan of the Gedar people. You have no right to accuse me of anything. Did you help in the attack?"

That brought Tavish up short; he stared up at Gair, uncertain of what to say. With a flash of movement, Gair snatched the hunting knife from his belt and held it aloft, out of reach, in a challenge.

Aidah stepped in before Tavish's temper flared yet again. "We're running away from the ones who attacked your caravan. They work for the Innis Empire."

Gair started to ask something, when Brenton and Derg arrived, out of breath. The sight of Derg startled Gair; he made a half bow and said something in a tongue Aidah didn't recognize. It sounded animal.

Derg replied in kind, then explained, "The Gedar have long been friends to the Lupas, long before Korva and the Doane. *Salos Marius.* Happy greetings, clansman."

"*Salos Marius son Lupas. Sono Gair tec'lana Malin.* I am sorry; I didn't see you down on the trail. These are your charges, or adoptees?" Gair asked, returning the knife to Tavish. Brenton quickly took the knife from Tavish to secure it in his own belt.

"Charges," Derg responded, walking in front of Tavish to nudge him back. Aidah remained where she was, watching Tavish's tree-torch slowly burn to a low glow. A bad feeling began to churn in her stomach.

When she returned her attention to Gair, he was staring at her, but upon her noticing, he quickly looked back to Derg. "Is what the boy says true? Is this one," he pointed at her, "a Life Talent? We were escorting Nera to find such a one."

Derg hesitated in answering, and Tavish leapt in, "How do we know he isn't working for Madhar? Isn't it suspicious that he alone survived the attack? Madhar could have spared his life for some small service—say, spying?"

Gair bristled, glaring at Tavish, but it was Derg who replied, "Gedar would never work for Innis. Too many of their people have been slaughtered in those lands. But you raise a good question. How did you survive, Gair of Malin?"

Gair stepped back, absently scratching a scab on his neck, his face clouding over. He gazed down on the trail, suddenly looking haggard, "I wasn't in camp. I was foraging ahead, gathering firewood and hopefully a rabbit or two. When the explosions started, it shook the earth. I lost my balance and hit the ground. I think I blacked out for a while; when I got up and ran for the caravan, it was all over. I doused the flames, but everyone was already dead." He looked at the ground, anger furrowing his forehead, though Aidah wasn't sure if it was directed at himself, or another. He muttered, "Nera was supposed to handle any magical attacks."

"Are you always that clumsy?" Tavish said with a snarl.

Gair shrugged, refusing to take the bait. "Last year I was shorter than you. I used to be really good at sneaking up on an enemy and fighting, but lately I've been a bit off in my skills. I was trying to prepare graves when I heard all of you."

Brenton gave Tavish a look, and strode up to Gair to offer his hand. "I'm sorry, I forgot to introduce us. I'm Brenton Dell; this is Tavish and Aidah Dernholt, and of course the Lupas is Derg—"

Derg nodded, "Of the Andari line, clan Durna."

Gair nodded, again staring at Aidah. "Dernholt, yes, that was the name. So what happened to send the four of you here?"

"We should be asking the questions, not him," Tavish muttered.

Brenton ignored him. "Now I know what those rumbles we heard yesterday morning were. The Storm Mage Madhar must have attacked your caravan. He also attacked Hamstead. It's probably burned to ashes now, and I fear there isn't a living person left."

Gair's eyes widened. "Dead?"

Brenton shook his head. "Just those who resisted capture. The rest are apparently headed for Innis, at least as far as we've been able to determine." He glanced at Derg, and Aidah could see new doubts in his face. His thoughts brushed her. If they were so thorough at the caravan and the Jonstables, who was to say the prisoners hadn't been killed someplace remote, and buried?

The discomfort in Aidah's stomach worsened, becoming a gnawing ache. "I'm sorry about the caravan. I'm afraid it was probably because of me," she offered, suddenly sensing yet another empty pang of loss—his. Still, the uneasiness remained. She patted Brenton's arm. "Don't you think we should get moving? I'm getting a bad feeling, standing here."

Instant alarm radiated from the whole group. Brenton advanced on Tavish, shaking a finger at him. "Tavish, you fool, douse that tree. We've probably attracted every search party in the Morgaine Range by now!" Tavish hastily doused the flames, including a small brush fire the sparks had set off near the base of the tree, and darkness enveloped them. Aidah could hear Brenton moving, and again used Tavish as her eyes to see him approach Gair. "Young man, I want to ask you a few more questions, but I think it would be best to do it on the move. Walk with us?"

Brenton returned to take Aidah by his free hand, and she in turn took Tavish's hand; he lead them back down the hill to where Muser was tied to a trail marker. Away from the shadows of the trees, they could see the trail ahead dimly lit by a rising half-moon. Aidah stuck close to Tavish and his night vision.

"One false move, one false look and I'll sear the skin off your flesh," Tavish whispered just loud enough for Gair to hear as they passed by him, leading the mule. Derg snorted, but Brenton continued, beckoning for Gair to follow.

Gair walked beside Brenton and Derg, slowly overtaking Aidah, Muser and Tavish. He seemed confident of his way, even in the dark.

"There is a break in the forest up the trail where we can leave the trail yet still move quickly. The area is rocky—it's a bit icy, but it should hide our passage. I've made camp on the other side among the trees," Gair said, lengthening his stride so that the others had to hurry to keep up.

"I don't trust him, not for a moment," Tavish whispered in Aidah's ear. "Let's both keep an eye on him tonight. If he's going to tell on us, it'll probably be tonight."

"I don't—" Aidah started to say, then held back. She didn't feel anything bad coming from him, but then her Talent wasn't particularly trustworthy. She hadn't detected Rangwar's evil, and if Tavish was right and Gair was spying on them to save his skin, she might not detect anything anyway. "Ok, I'll keep my senses open. All of them."

Tavish gave her a squeeze on the arm, keeping close to Brenton as they set off across the open hillside.

The first half-moon was high in the sky and the second had just risen by the time they reentered the woods, and true to his word, Gair had a tidy little campsite set up, complete with items scavenged from the caravan: a few packs laden with food and cookware, a beautifully decorated saddle which was slightly singed on one side, and a lute.

"You're a minstrel, Gair?" Brenton asked, looking over the spiraling designs inlaid into the wood of the instrument.

"No, my father was, or so I've been told. Always meant to take up the calling, but never got around to it. I don't even know why I rescued that old thing from the fire." Gair set to rolling out his sleeping pouch. Aidah helped Tavish to set out their blankets nearby, but not too close to Gair.

"I'm sure you must know lots of songs, though, traveling as you people always do," Brenton said, continuing to inspect one particular design on the base of the instrument. He pursed his lips, then set the lute back on a dry patch of pine needles.

Gair glanced at him, and shrugged. "Naturally. I know the tale of the Sundering of the Krimean Sea, where the Wild Folk came from, adventures of the Spice Lords of the Southern Sea, and many many more. Used to tell them for a silver or two in the off season, wherever we made camp."

Brenton nodded. "I might like to hear one sometime. For now I think it would be best to stay quiet and get some sleep. I'll stay on first watch, and if you can spare a few minutes, I'd like to hear how Nera came to be traveling with you. Would you happen to know if the message she carried ever got to Landaran?"

Gair shook his head. "She joined with us at the trailhead at Valleyforge and promised us good pay if we would journey with her to Hamstead. She has been known to my clan for many years; we didn't think there would be any trouble. Once again the gods show their hatred of *Murva*-blooded mages. We should have known better." With that, he flopped down onto his pallet, turning away.

Derg yawned, his sharp teeth gleaming in the moonlight. "Wake me at first moonset," he said to Brenton, and settled himself in the pine needle bed, next to the lute.

Aidah waited for Gair to close his eyes before crawling into her blankets, feeling somehow odd with this new traveler among them. Beside her, Tavish was softly snoring, but it was a lie. He was wide awake.

"Brenton will watch him. Best to sleep while we can," she whispered, moving her pack under her head to use as a pillow. The blankets did little to soften the feel of the rocky earth.

"Brenton's far too friendly with him. I'll sleep when I'm good and sure he's really asleep. Maybe," Tavish whispered back.

Aidah rolled her eyes and turned away. By the light of the moons, she could see the barren peak of Neci towering above them, blanketed in snow over bare rock, like a finger pointing skywards. One mountain almost down; only a half dozen or so to go to reach the lowlands. In their little camp, Brenton sat by the lute, head tilted back, gazing at the stars. Aidah could just make out the design that had fascinated Brenton. It seemed to sparkle in the moonlight; a crescent moon and three stars.

Looks like a heraldry emblem, she thought as she drifted off.

Tavish woke at an odd noise, something between a whisper and a groan. The second moon had set; only the dim stars cast their light on the forest now, half-hidden between wisps of clouds. He called upon his magesight to peer at where Gair had been sleeping.

The space was empty.

Instantly he was alert for trouble, rising up out of his blanket to search the camp for markings of heat. Brenton was asleep and Derg was nowhere to be seen. He cursed under his breath. How could they have left the Gedar thief out of their supervision?

He knew all about Gedar. They might play the part of musicians and tumblers but they were really just thieves, pickpocketing from the crowds they drew, ready for the opportunity to snatch from the unaware. He'd lost a good set of marbles to them once, and his favorite good luck charm.

As he turned to check the other side of the camp, another surprise sent his heart racing. Aidah had disappeared also.

"Aidah!" he called in a fierce whisper, running out to the edge of the wood where it met the rocky expanse they had crossed earlier. No sign of either of them, and no heat trail of footsteps leading away either. So the thief hadn't taken her that way. Perhaps to the north, through the woods. He crept back into the forest, ears straining, eyes scanning the cold landscape for the barest trace of heat. He caught a flash of red before it ducked behind some trees.

Oh, think you can hide from me, maggot, he thought, anger warming his insides against the frigid night. He'd bust that fool into a dozen pieces if the fellow had laid so much as a finger on Aidah. He'd flame him until he was white hot, like he'd done to a horseshoe for the blacksmith once. He'd—

He came upon them and stopped, uncertain. Aidah was backed up against a tree, holding herself and rocking back against the tree in a nervous sort of way, like a child of four made to stand before his elders. She seemed to have been crying; hot trails down her cheeks rapidly cooling in the night air could only be tears. Gair stood a few feet away, in front of her, one arm outstretched. He looked concerned.

An act, it had to be, Tavish reasoned; either that, or he was trying to cozy up to her, get her to like him. Well, he'd put a stop to that.

"Hey there! Whatever you did to upset her, you'd better stop right now and apologize. And stay back while you do that."

He ran up to his sister. "What did he do? Should I flame him right now?"

She struggled to compose herself, wiping at her cheek and moving away from the tree, and both of them, Tavish noted with puzzlement. Raising her head, she gave a weak smile and a false laugh. "Oh no, Tavish, don't be silly. I had a bad dream, that was all, and Gair here was just trying to reassure me. He didn't do anything, I swear."

Was she lying to him? She'd lied to others, often to protect him when they were 'spying' or 'borrowing' things, but she'd never before lied to him. He glared at Gair, trying to see any signs of ill intent, or find some clue to help explain his behavior. Had he threatened her? Hurt her? Or perhaps he was done touching her, and now she was trying to keep it a secret? He returned his gaze to Aidah, staring hard at her. For a brief moment, he wished he had her Talent.

She narrowed her eyes at him, some of her usual fire returning. "I said everything's *fine*, Tavish. Let's just go back to the camp and back to sleep."

Her voice faltered a little on that last word. Tavish stepped forward and took her arm, leaning in to whisper, but he nearly lost his balance when she abruptly pulled away. He growled. "Don't lie to me. I can tell when something's not right. Either he did something, or you had one heck of a bad dream. Either way, I'd like to know more."

Her eyes became shadowed as she seemed to consider her words. Tavish glanced over at Gair to check his face. Either he was completely befuddled, or he was an excellent actor. Given his heritage, that was certainly possible.

"It was a horrible dream. I dreamt again of how Mama—well, how she—you know, but it was even worse than the real event. You see, she was suffering terribly and Papa…" She broke off, turning away and holding herself.

Shame flooded Tavish, making his ears burn. Of course she would still be having nightmares; they both should be having them. His were a little different, however. In his dreams he rescued Mama and killed Rangwar.

He studied the two of them one more time, noting that while her words made sense, her body language was still rather odd, keeping herself away from both himself and Gair. Maybe she had in fact had a dream and come out here to walk it off, then Gair might have tried to side up to her…yeah, that was probably it. Even now he got a sense the Gedar boy was attracted to her, just by the way he was looking at her. He grimaced.

"Ok, I believe you, but you there, Gair Gedar or whatever your name is, next time my sister has a bad dream, you wake me up. Otherwise I might come to another conclusion about you and fry your hair off. Got it?"

Gair's face became stone like in its lack of emotion, and Tavish was sure his words had bounced right off. "I understand completely," Gair replied in a low voice. He turned his back on Tavish and walked back towards camp. Tavish snorted.

"Villain. You watch out for him, Aidah, I mean it. And if he does *anything* the least bit wrong, you tell me. I want to protect you, but you have to be straight with me."

Aidah placed her hands on her hips and looked down her nose at him. "Would you promise to hold your temper if something occurred and I told you?"

Fear clutched his heart. "Why, what happened?" he asked, reaching out for her hand.

She pulled it away and took a step back. "Nothing. I was upset and Gair was a perfect gentleman, asking me if I felt all right and if I wanted to talk about it—the bad dream—he said it was sometimes easier to tell a stranger. That can be true sometimes. You make it hard for me to talk to you. You always overreact."

Tavish opened his mouth to object, then reconsidered. He wasn't overreacting, but if he said that, she'd think he was. If he wanted her to be truthful with him, he'd have to play her game. "Ok, perhaps you're right. I do threaten, but you know its only words. I can keep my head when I need to, I swear. It's just that you're about all I've got left, you know? I'll try to do better."

Aidah pursed her lips, considering, then nodded. She came forward to give him a quick hug. "I'm sorry for frightening you. And if Gair does anything I don't approve of, you'll be the first to know. Believe me."

Well, that was better. She seemed over her fright, and back to her usual self. He sighed. "Okay. Come on, its freezing out here. Let's get back to our beds and I can create a little heat spell to warm them up."

Aidah shivered as if just noticing the temperature. "Last one back has to lead old Muser tomorrow!" She raced back and he was forced to follow, nimbly through the drifts of snow and dry patches of pine needles to avoid waking Brenton.

Aidah slid into her blanket so fast it sent a splash of snow onto his blankets. Tavish noticed that Derg had returned and was in quiet conference with Gair, apparently about two of them, Tavish figured by the way Derg gave him a withering look and a deep sigh.

For the next ten minutes he was forced to listen to Derg's lecture on safety with enemy close at hand, then he crawled into his blankets, rearranged the heat to envelope both himself and Aidah in a cocoon of warmth, and promptly thereafter, fell asleep.

☼

The following day they kept to the woods. Derg, from his nightly reconnaissance mission, reported that Rangwar's men were returning down the trail. They needed to keep moving and avoid the trail at least for a day or two to throw off pursuit. Brenton ordered Tavish to melt snow on the new path they were forging, hopefully to disguise it.

Aidah only hoped she hadn't ruined it for everyone. *He* had come again, last night, and she'd been so close to telling him everything. If he had the ability to read her thoughts, then he knew right where they were. Unlike the last time he had visited her, now she had a pretty good idea of where they were on the map. That was a bad thing. If there was some way she could communicate the need to stay 'lost', at least for her sense of direction, without telling anyone why, that would be the best way to evade Rangwar's mind tricks.

A shudder passed through her. It had been enjoyable this time, with Rangwar. Almost. She felt wanton, depraved, unfit for the kind of protection Tavish and the others kept lavishing on her. At least she was not a traitor yet—at least she didn't think so. Not for long, however. The next time she would either go straight to his arms, or she would go mad.

She jumped as Gair brushed past her to inspect a few scratch marks on the bark of a young pine. Brenton gave him a questioning look.

Gair patted the trunk of the tree, saying, "My people have on occasion been forced to leave the trail for a time..." he paused as Tavish sniggered. Brenton shot Tavish a look that could have peeled paint. Gair continued. "When that happens, we create a smaller trail with our own markings. If I could find a fresher trail marking, we could follow the trail to a winter campsite. I could convince them to accept your party as refugees. Perhaps they could even arrange an escort to Landaran."

Brenton glanced at Derg, eyebrows raised. "I like that idea. Might confuse our pursuers." He turned back to Gair. "Do you have any idea where a clan might be staying, near here?"

Gair frowned, shrugging. "My clan met with a larger clan, the Burris, about ten days ago. They could be down in Loweville by now, unless they decided to go north to the main trail."

Gair knelt down in the snow to draw a quick map. "To get to Landaran, you usually have to go on the Southern Road. That road passes through Thornton which is the doorway to the hill country, then down the Lamar River past Lothe, Colmsford, Bonnenville and finally the great city of Geraine. From there you follow the river of Glynnis on the Refugee Road to the coast and the city of Landaran." He drew a relatively straight line south from a pebble which represented Hamstead, with one sharp turn near the end.

"Right now you're heading west and south on the Gedar Trail. If you follow it all the way, it will take you exactly the opposite direction of Landaran, into the Lupas and Gedar lands. There is, however, a fork which runs south to meet up with a little mining town called Valleyforge, then you can follow the Radrich river—it's really more of a mountain stream—down to Bonnenville and back on to the Southern Road. That's a bit out of the way. The only other option, though, is to cut across to the other side of Mount Neci and

Scarath to rejoin the Southern Road before Thornton. Rough terrain."

Brenton nodded. "We'll just have to see what we run into. Since it seems that Rangwar's men used the Southern Road. I thought it best to use this one, but now they seem to be covering this as well. I was going to head for Valleyforge, but I'm concerned that Rangwar's put men into nearby towns to spy for us."

Derg growled. "I know of few places where Rangwar does not have spies. He has obviously found a way into the Doane without alerting the Guardians. He may even have spies in Landaran. The best we can do is get to the Lowlands and find other mages to protect us. I'd offer to take all of you to my homeland, but that is far in the west." A note of longing crept into Derg's voice; Aidah blinked in surprise. She doubted he'd ever even seen his people or his homeland. He'd been only a puppy when Korva gave him to the twins.

Gair brushed away the snow, destroying the image. "Very well. We'll swing back towards the Southern Road, across open land. Should take us only a few days if the weather holds."

"Then stop chatting and start marching," Tavish snapped, pressing a finger to his temple. He melted the spot where the map had been, and instantly Gair was on his feet, moving away, muttering something about devilry. He couldn't move fast, however, for his feet slid on wet needles and icy patches left in the wake of Tavish's magic. He almost tripped over a log and in recovery managed to entangle his hair in a prickly holly bush.

Aidah smothered a laugh, then frowned. When was the last time she had laughed? Before Mama's death, definitely, perhaps even before the discovery of her Talent. Following behind Brenton, Tavish, and the mule with Derg at her heels, she watched as Gair led the way up and down the steep side of the mountain, singing some song in a foreign tongue under his breath. In his hair dangled a solitary holly leaf from his tangle with the bush. Aidah smiled.

She'd told Tavish the truth last night. When she'd awoken fresh from the encounter with Rangwar, she'd been a little hysterical. Those queasy sensations had still been running through her body, the temptation to do something absolutely horrible; either to run out of the camp and deliver herself to Rangwar, or to take Tavish's knife and slice her wrists. She'd had to get away from everybody for a moment or two, and just cry. Let out the awfulness inside.

She guessed she'd been crying a little too loud. Gair came up and asked what was wrong; was there anything he could do to help? It was the way he said it that got inside where the pain and anguish roiled, and made it feel just the tiniest bit better. She didn't know a boy's voice could sound so tender.

He'd come forward, but then all the awfulness returned. Nothing of flesh and blood could touch her, because any touch reminded her of *him*. Gair must have sensed that, for rather than offer her an embrace, he kept his distance and offered her his handkerchief instead. Luckily she'd hidden it before Tavish had seen it.

And then what had Gair done? He'd told jokes; silly, crass jokes about old men and dancing girls, about wives and lumbermen. Not to mention lumbermen and lumbermen. She didn't know why, but it had helped, though she hadn't laughed. Not a single chuckle. At least she'd calmed down when Tavish found them.

As they passed a frozen stream, clambering over huge round boulders, Aidah allowed herself to be touched just long enough to be helped over a trickle of water down rocks frosted with ice. In the spring, this was probably a raging river. Though Tavish was quick to ensure that he was the one to help her, she caught a look of playful resignation from Gair, along with a conspiratory wink.

A warm breath of air ran through her heart. The memory of the dream faded as she followed Gair's lead down the mountain.

10

A Dark and Stormy Journey

It took three days hard marching to leave the peak of Grinin and cross the face of Mount Neci. Thanks to a continued presence on the trail by Rangwar's men, they were forced to keep to the woods, struggling through the snow as the weather turned sour again. Tavish felt pretty sure Madhar was controlling the skies, trying to flush them out.

He had to admit, he was thankful for Gair's presence, at least in his skill at trailblazing. They'd found a little Gedar path that snaked away from the main trail off to the east, skillfully hugging the land to be hidden from sight. Once again, it proved to Tavish that the true purpose of the Gedar caravans was to steal and make a quick getaway. At least Gair hadn't betrayed them to the enemy. There'd been opportunity enough for that. He might be a thief and a scoundrel, but he wasn't a traitor.

Gair had helped in other ways too. Aidah was sick with a bad cold. Gair knew a thing or two about treating her stuffy head with fir tree resin and soothing her cough with boiled holly leaves, but none of them could help with the fever. She took up all the space on Muser's back now, riding in the outlandish Gedar saddle covered with blankets and leaving the men to carry the packs.

Tavish walked ahead past Gair who was leading the mule, up to Brenton who forged the path through the snow in a blinding wind. He had to shout for his uncle to hear him past the wind and the scarf covering his face, "Has Derg spoken to you of finding shelter? This storm's going to be a long one, I can feel it!" Tavish had already been using his Talent to keep everyone reasonably warm, but with the wind increasing, even he could do little.

Brenton bent to speak to him, his eyes grave above his own scarf. "He went to see if that village Gair spoke of is reachable before the brunt of this storm hits." He glanced back at Gair and Aidah struggling to get the mule to keep moving as snow began to swirl about the animal's head, spooking it. Brenton turned back to Tavish. "I think we'll have to stop before we reach it. She needs shelter."

Brenton motioned for Tavish to continue packing down the snow for the mule to walk through, and went to check on Aidah. Though he could hear nothing of their conversation, Tavish could tell by the fear on Brenton's face that he didn't like what he found of her condition. Brenton said something to Gair, then returned.

"We've got to stop now; she's burning up. Use your sight, Tavish, and see if you can find any place a bit warmer than out here."

They were down in the valley before the next peak, Mount Scarath, through what in the spring was probably a meadow, so there wasn't much cover nearby. Perhaps up on the hillside they might find a cavern or hollow along the great falls which were purportedly ahead, though any such falls would be a tiny trickle right now. A stand of pine or a cliff side just wouldn't help much, but if they found a cave, they could have a fire, for the wind would scatter whatever smoke it made. He peered along the edge of the valley where the terrain was steep and sharp, as if a knife had cut into the land, searching.

A jutting rock pulled his gaze down to a dark area along the cliff that looked promising; a hollow of some sort. "I see something we might use. I don't think it's a cave, but that outcropping over there has boulders to shield us from the wind. We might be able to crawl under a space between them and light a fire."

Brenton nodded, and with a groan, returned to shoveling a trail. Tavish knew he'd have another headache tonight, but he assisted in his own way, leading the group to the rocky hollow. Thanks to him they got there in not more than an hour, and shortly after that he coaxed sodden logs to give up their moisture and burst forth in flame. Then he cradled his pounding head and lay back against a giant boulder while Aidah huddled beside him and Gair worked on melting some water to make a stew of their dried meat.

As wind howled above them over the tops of the boulders, sending snow whirling into tiny dervishes in the hollow, Tavish made another promise to make Madhar suffer.

☼

"You are making me very angry, Aidah," Rangwar's deep voice reverberated off the stone walls of an unknown chamber in an unknown fortress.

Aidah moaned, fighting against cold metal encircling her wrists and ankles, licking her swollen lips to taste the blood of an open cut. She felt fevered and dizzy, but still painfully aware of her circumstances. With a lance of pain to her stiff joints, she struggled to sit up on the hard wooden table.

"You aren't…" she swallowed with a dry throat "Aren't going to get me, no matter what you do. I'm far away now, and I'm lost. I can't even guess where I am."

He grabbed her chin to look deep into her eyes and she found herself fascinated by a small tic in his left cheek. Fear made her want to giggle for some reason. "I still see snow and mountains around you. You haven't left the Morgaine Range, and you're ill. Even if you survive to reach the nearest village, you won't escape me. I have agents who can find you anywhere."

Aidah said nothing, panting to regain her breath. This time he had hurt her. This time there had been no pleasure at all. She didn't know whether she should laugh or cry over that.

He watched her with a burning gaze, then suddenly his expression softened. He embraced her, speaking softly into her hair, "You must believe me when I say I want to help you. You can't imagine how precious you are to me, and I don't mean your power. I do most emphatically mean you, angel."

All of a sudden she could sense him; the shield of opaqueness was gone and she could feel his heart pulling at her. She could not deny his feelings because she could feel them. He was speaking the truth, at least in that in his mind he was certain he loved her. The notion haunted her.

She forced herself to speak, tired and fevered as she was, "If you care for me, let me go. If I saw by your actions that you meant everything, if you left me alone, perhaps I would come to you. There's a stubborn streak in my family. The harder you pull, the harder I push away."

Rangwar released her and smiled, and the shield snapped back into place. "Well spoken. See? You are learning from me already.

Very well, I will leave you alone for a while, let you recover from your illness and reach somewhere warm. Do not think I can let you go, however. Like Korva, I have waited a very long time for you. Sleep well, my sweet."

Aidah woke, shivering and sweaty, wrapped in several blankets by a crackling fire. Above her towered great rocks and the side of a cliff, and above that she could see clouds and blowing snow in a bleak morning light. Beside her hovered Tavish and Derg.

"Where's Brenton?" she whispered, her throat dry and raw. A coughing fit wracked her, giving her new spiking pains to a headache pounding in her skull. She swallowed the agony.

"Out hunting. Gair's helping him," Tavish said, pressing an icy cold hand to her cheek.

She glared at him."I know I have a fever. If it goes away, I'll tell you." Tavish snatched his hand away, looking hurt. Immediately she felt sorry—she didn't know why his touching her should annoy her, but it did, intensely. She reached out and put a hand on his elbow. "I'm sorry; I'm just cranky. I hate being sick. Think the two of them will be gone long?"

Aidah didn't know how long they'd been hiding in this hollow, waiting out the storm. A day, three days…it all ran together. She only remembered waking to sip hot liquids then dozing in fever dreams, then seeing Rangwar. Even in her fevered state, the time spent with him was all too clear. She bit back a moan, wondering if the bruises had been real or just the sensations of aches and pains in her illness.

Tavish shrugged and looked towards the dark line of trees on the hillside. "I haven't a clue. It's been a few hours, but they probably had to hike a bit to find any game. You've been asleep for a long time. I didn't want to disturb you. Feeling a little warmer now?"

It must have only been a day here, by that question. "A little, I guess," she answered.

"At least you're making sense now," Tavish said, sitting close to the fire to warm his hands.

Aidah stared at him. "What do you mean?"

Derg glanced over, looking at her down his long regal canine nose. "He is referring to some mutterings uttered while dreaming. You thought Rangwar had you, by the sound of it."

"Didn't make much sense—mostly your words were too

slurred to understand," Tavish assured her, trying to comfort her, Aidah supposed. It sounded like they had learned nothing about her secret visits from Rangwar. They wouldn't be so casual about it then.

"Oh yeah. I've been having a lot of bad dreams," she mumbled, trying not to let her fear show.

"That is not uncommon when fevered. The worst of it seems to have passed, for now. Can I offer you some porridge? It's warm, if not terribly appetizing," Derg asked, inclining his head towards one of the black pots they had taken from the Jonstables hanging on a makeshift stand over the fire.

Aidah nodded, sitting up. She felt lightheaded and hot, but at least she had her senses about her. On the trail, it had been terrible, thoughts and feelings from her past and from those around her intermingling and swimming around in her head until she lost all track of who and where she was.

She dug into a bowl of hot porridge, actually rather grateful at the blandness, when a feeling passed over her, like a summer breeze—hope, and excitement. That wasn't coming from her, she thought, then moments later two figures came into view coming down the mountainside towards their hollow. They took off their hats and waved, and Aidah smiled. Brenton and Gair tramped into camp, laughing and smiling.

"We've found the Gedar trail leading to a village, Minton. It's only about a day's march from here, up on the other side of Mount Scarath," Brenton announced, throwing down the carcass of a rabbit. Aidah suddenly lost her appetite.

"Hmm, that does not look like a deer," Derg said, sniffing and licking his chops, "But it will do."

Gair sighed, looking sheepish. "Sorry, it isn't much, but at least it will give us a morsel or two to eat. Didn't see a single deer."

"We'll eat well once we reach Minton. It's a tiny place, just an old mining town barely surviving, but it should have an inn." Brenton pulled off his boots to dry by the little fire and sat down.

"Or it's possible we'll find some of my people staying there. Minton's a good place for us because it is so small. Plus, they have gold to trade." Gair looked almost cheerful, red spots of color showing on his dusky cheeks.

And to steal. Tavish's thoughts were so loud in Aidah's ear, she thought he'd actually said it aloud. She glared at him, and he gave her a bemused look.

"When do we start?" he asked aloud, impressing Aidah with his success at holding back his prejudice.

"Tomorrow morning, if the weather eases up. It will still be snowing tonight, but I am hoping this storm will move on. Rangwar's Storm Mage can't possibly know where we are now," Brenton said.

That was true, at least for the moment. Hopefully they could stop briefly in Minton and then move on, out of her range of knowledge before the next dream came. She didn't really know where Minton was, but she could be sure Rangwar did, or could find out. Once again she wondered when Grandess Korva was going to come to her. Surely she had the same power Rangwar possessed to enter dreams or come out of body. Was she really so ignorant of what went on in the land she was supposed to be protecting?

"Well, let's get this hare cooking before the fire burns out," Tavish said with a chuckle, taking the hare before Derg could be tempted to pull a leg off of it, hair and all.

Aidah laid down to sleep again, unable to convince her stomach to eat something whose head had been bashed in.

She dreamt instead of hot mutton stew and a warm downy bed.

☼

By morning, six inches of new snow had been dumped on the mountain, but the sun rose in a clear sky, reflecting its brilliance off the snow covered landscape. The trail Brenton and Gair had forged the day before was still mostly intact, except along a cliff where a small snow slide had try to bury it. Aidah rode Muser, watching for any signs of man or beast. Her head was clearer today, but her cough had grown worse, wracking her body until it hurt to breathe.

They traveled across the valley and up the northern shoulder of Scarath, if Aidah's recollection from maps was correct. If it was Scarath, then the mountain should grow gradually rounder and they should finally reach the main Southern Road that they'd wanted to use in the first place, the most direct route to Landaran. They found the marking of a small trail, one of the offshoots perhaps, and followed it across a deep valley choked with snow up to a rocky pass climbing higher and higher, slowly circling the mountain as they marched throughout the day and into the evening, heading ever eastward. This couldn't be right, Aidah thought. It must be another mountain. Or they were on the trail to some town or settlement. She wasn't sure whether to be relieved or disappointed.

As night fell, her suspicions proved correct. They spotted the lights of a small town high up in the arms of the mountain. A mining settlement.

Aidah could have wept; she was exhausted. The fever was coming up strong again to make the lights swim and dance before her eyes. She wanted nothing more than to march up to one of the cottages up there and beg for shelter, but Gair had other thoughts.

"Wait here a moment. I'm going to check the miner's trailhead and see if any Gedar have camped nearby—that's usually where we conduct business when in town." He dropped his pack at Muser's feet. It was hard to make him out in the near darkness, even in his gaudy clothing. Aidah swayed, clutching at the mule's short mane.

"I'll accompany you. I do hope it is not far. Aidah can't go on much longer," Derg offered, still full of vigor, despite the day's march.

Tavish sighed and sat down. Brenton expelled a nervous breath, then nodded. "Please hurry. I want to get Aidah inside tonight if at all possible."

Aidah dozed off while waiting, limbs heavy with fatigue, and was woken by a gentle shake when the first moon had risen, casting its waxing glow upon the forest in a clear starry sky. It was rapidly growing colder.

"Can you ride just a little more, sweetie?" Brenton asked in a whisper. Behind him stood Gair and Derg, looking tired but triumphant. Tavish stood to the other side of them, holding Muser's lead.

She couldn't feel her feet, and her face was nearly frozen, a fact exacerbated by the fact her nose was running and her cheeks felt like they were on fire. "Get me to a warm bed," she croaked, sitting up on the mule.

They hurried up the trail Gair and Derg had made in searching for the Gedar encampment, passing through a patch of trees, climbing steadily, then suddenly the trees ended at a wide stone trail worn down with frequent use. In a flat little cove of the mountain were parked eight Gedar wagons, brightly lit with hanging lanterns. The sound of an old woman singing, of horses shifting and snorting friendly greetings, and the smell of mutton stew traveled fast upon the clear night air to warm Aidah and her party.

Gair led them up to a large bearded man in a red vest with gold tassels and blue trousers. He grinned, showing several gold capped teeth, and bowed to Brenton and Tavish.

Gair introduced him, "This is Montrose of the clan Burris, head of the Burris family here. He specializes in the crafting of tinware and is also an accomplished dentist." Gair took Montrose's hand and placed it in Brenton's.

"Montrose, this is Brenton of the Dell Family, and as I understand it he is the uncle of these two *murva*, Tavish and Aidah, Dernholt family. They have recently fled Hamstead."

Montrose nodded, beard wagging. Aidah glanced at his hand as he released Brenton's—it was gnarled and thick with calluses, yet adorned with rings of silver and gold. The look he gave Aidah and Tavish was friendly, but cautious. Aidah had heard the word *murva* before, when Tavish started showing his Talent. The rough equivalent in her tongue was 'witch', but it generally had a derogatory meaning.

Tavish had not missed the word. He stared at Gair with dislike, arms crossed over his chest. When Montrose came to shake his hand, however, he smiled and politely shook hands, before stepping back again. Aidah held out her gloved hand to shake as well, but Montrose instead brought it to his lips and kissed it, giving her a friendly wink. She blushed.

Montrose released her hand with a little smile. "If you're headed towards Landaran, dear, you're going to have to get used to that type of greeting. You'll find things mighty different in the Lowlands. I reckon men will be falling all over you." He grinned, again flashing his golden teeth, and led her and the others to the largest wagon, which was nearly covered by rows of hanging pots and pans and other tinware, jangling in the breeze. A plump old woman in a bright orange apron appeared at the door and waved them to follow her inside, into a spacious cabin where from the curved walls were hung four shelves which served as beds or benches; two of them were ready with blankets and pillows.

"Poor little things! You must be frozen," the woman said, snatching sodden cloaks right off Tavish and Aidah's backs and wrapping them with blankets, then moving forward to assist Brenton and Gair. "Call me Eomma, and if yer wanting anything, I'm a holler away. Don't have much to feed you right now, but—"

"We have food. We appreciate the shelter, but there's no need to take your beds—" Brenton assured her, but she carried on as if he hadn't said a word.

"—I think there's a bit of stew left and boiled cabbage and I'll get straight away to fixing ya some. Here—sit on the beds there, take off your shoes, and let's get the little sick one here—" she wrapped a meaty arm around Aidah "—straight into bed."

Montrose looked on, beaming. "That's my good wife, Eomma. She'll see to all your needs. I've got to watch tonight over the fire, but we'll spend tomorrow on the help young Gair requested. You just sleep secure until then. We're accepting you as friends of Gedar."

A young boy came up to Aidah with a steaming bowl of stew, and she gulped it down gratefully, not caring if it burned her tongue as it traveled down, to warm her insides. She wanted to stay awake and talk to these strange people, but exhaustion and her cold took hold of her, and she found herself being tucked into bed.

Drowsily she heard Brenton talking to Eomma as he slurped his stew, but she was too tired to care about the words. The last thing she heard before sleep overtook her was the sound of a young man singing and playing a lute, and the soft jingle of bells mixed with the clatter of many tin pots swaying in the wind.

It took Aidah nearly a week to recover from her illness. During that time, Tavish tried to keep himself out of trouble and his eyes and ears wide open, waiting for the inevitable attempt on his personal items from the little pickpockets around the Gedar camp. Their thievery was no secret to the Gedar—the little Gedar children went daily into the village, and by nightfall they had returned with new trinkets: a brass belt buckle, a gold thimble, a ring. It made his hair stand on end thinking how innocent they looked, and yet so conniving.

"How do they escape the villagers' wrath?" He asked Derg as they sat mending their gear, torn by numerous brushes with rocks and thorny brush. Derg held the fabric straight with his paws while Tavish sewed.

"Gedar children tend to be quick and deft, so they are rarely discovered. When they do get caught, they manage to look cute enough to escape most trouble," Derg responded, tilting his head as he looked to Tavish so that one ear drooped a little, "Rather the same tactics you and Aidah typically employed on your excursions?"

Tavish flushed. There must be an argument for that, but he couldn't think of any right now. "It's still surprising, considering they spend the entire winter here." He broke off the conversation as on the trail of group of miners haggled with Montrose over the sale of one of his trinkets—a hand sewing machine, brought by the Gedar out of the Lowlands.

Derg spoke in his ear, "You see, the Gedar bring items from the Lowlands to sell at well below the merchant guild prices, including the items not normally exported for sale. They also act as message carriers and traveling craftsmen. The village reaps its benefits."

From his pouch, the miner produced a large blue-gold beetle, with a brightly glowing spot on the crest of its thorax . *A Miner Beetle,* Tavish thought, breathless. How had a simple mining town gotten a hold of one of those? They were magical constructs, left over from the ancient mages of Innis.

A chill touched his heart, as the miner, a grizzled old man with a swarthy complexion, glanced at him. Could he be an agent of Innis?

Montrose made the trade of the sewing machine for the beetle, carefully storing the creature in a wooden box with some quartz to chew on. Miner beetles had been created to prefer gold and diamond above all other minerals to feed upon, but they could subsist upon plain quartz. It made them cheap to maintain and loyal to work while searching for veins of ore.

"Pretty good deal," Tavish whispered to Derg.

Derg yawned and laid down at his feet. "You mean for the Gedar? I would say so, but then I have heard they breed quite a few of that beetle here."

"They hardly know their value, then," Tavish said, wondering about the small town. "When will Brenton be back?" Just as Gair had promised, Minton was nestled against Mount Scarath, and they were once again within reach of normal trails to the Lowlands.

"Hard to say. If he is successful in finding a message carrier and all the supplies we require, it could be after sunset. More likely, he won't be able to find half of what he seeks and will return sooner."

Tavish fidgeted. "The more time he spends in town, the more likely he'll be noticed by one of Rangwar's spies. Aidah said she felt the presence of enemies in the town."

Derg snorted, shifting his weight a little. "She was dreaming."

Tavish looked hard at Derg, waiting for the Lupas to settle a bit before saying in a low voice, "She's Life Talented. Who knows how that affects her dreams?"

Derg gave a low whine, lowering his head. "I must concede that fact. We should take it as a warning, but it is not a certainty. Brenton will try to blend in, I assure you."

In a village of eight hundred, he'd still stick out like a blue sheep. Down the sparsely forested slope of the mountain, Tavish could see little red roofs of the village, sticking out above the trees like little red spears. A clear trail ran from the village up the mountain past the Gedar camp to the mines, with a steady flow of traffic as men dug out precious silver and gold by the cartload.

He hoped that somewhere down there was also a Protectorate employed message carrier, or maybe even a visiting mage. If they didn't find help in the village, it was possible Brenton might follow Gair's advice and ask Montrose to take them to Landaran. Then he would have to spend weeks with these people, and Gair would have an excuse to get closer to Aidah.

Tavish had seen little of Gair around the camp, though he had caught him twice looking at Aidah while she was asleep. The other Gedar looked at her with sad eyes, calling her 'poor *laruna*', which Derg had roughly translated as 'orphan'. There was a lot of gossip going around, complaints about how Gair had brought *murva* into the camp, and that he was a carrier of bad luck. Tavish almost felt sorry for him. Almost.

Down on the trail, the sound of hooves broke off his musings. Tavish stood on the log he'd been sitting on, and caught a glimpse of Brenton and Gair on a Gedar draft horse, riding back to camp at a fast trot, bells on the horse's harness chiming in steady rhythm. Giving Derg a look, Tavish hopped off the log, and the two of them ran over to the trail, where they were soon joined by Montrose and Eomma.

Brenton craned his neck, looking for something, leaning forward on the horse's back, kicking it to urge it even faster. When he saw Tavish, he waved for him, coming right up to stop in front of him. He was out of breath. He dismounted, and took Tavish by the shoulder. "We've got to pack and move on. Rangwar's men are in town."

11

The Southern Trail

"Should I wake Aidah to hear this?" Tavish asked, wondering how quickly they could get her up and moving. She was past her near brush with pneumonia, but she was still recovering; he wished they had just a few more days for her to gain strength.

Brenton held him back. "No, don't wake her just yet. I don't want to stress her. Her Talent could draw the mage to us."

Ooh, he'd forgotten that. "How many did you see? Was Madhar among them?" If he was, Tavish might have to take a little detour out of town to flame the miserable mage.

Brenton must have known what he was thinking. "No, he most definitely was *not*." He gave Tavish a stern look.

"You wouldn't tell me if he were, would you," Tavish said in a low voice, eyes flashing.

Brenton smiled. "With your temper? No, I wouldn't. But in this case, I am telling the truth. There were three men, masquerading as miners. I heard them talking in a dialect no one this side of the Krimean Sea would use. I have a feeling they've been in town a while—the locals seemed to trust them."

Montrose growled. "You mean I may have been doing business with *Intaka*?!" He turned to the side and spat at the ground, showing exactly what he thought of the notion, while Tavish dug through his knowledge of Gedar to try and remember the word's meaning. *Taka* was a vulgar expression for dog droppings, he believed.

Brenton shrugged. "I only happened to stumble across them when we made a wrong turn from the livery. Unfortunately, I didn't get to hear much. They stopped talking as soon as they saw me. It's possible they know my description. We have to hurry." He started towards the wagon where Aidah was resting.

Gair ran to catch up with him. "But what about my idea?"

Brenton cut him off. "I can't ask them to leave. Winter hasn't even reached its peak yet, and they've got their business to manage here. I don't expect you to come either, Gair. Your help to us already has been invaluable."

Well, there was good and bad then in Brenton's decision to head off without the Gedar, Tavish thought. Bad, for they'd again be subject to the elements and enemies. On the trail between the mining town and the valley cities could harbor bandits as well as Rangwar's men. On the other hand, Gair would be gone, and he wouldn't have to live with the Gedar and their questionable ways.

Montrose frowned, glancing from Gair to Brenton, a shrewd look in his eye. "What is this about?"

Gair spoke up before Brenton could say a word, "When we came to this camp, we were hoping to travel with a Gedar tribe to Landaran, for the safety and shelter of numbers."

Brenton broke in, "It sounded like a good idea while struggling through a blizzard, but now I see it is impossible for us to displace your entire caravan—"

Gair glanced at him and went on, "The fact is, it was originally my clan's task to take Sun Mage Nera to pick up the Life Talent, then accompany her back to Landaran. There was, of course, a fee involved."

Tavish's jaw dropped. Gair hadn't mentioned that before! "You mean you just wanted to help us for *money*?!" All his suspicions about the Gedar confirmed, he thought heatedly.

Gair groaned and rolled his eyes. "No, we were happy to do it, but we have to make a living. We knew we wouldn't be able to camp for the winter like the Burris clan here, so the mages offered us compensation." His tone and the way he glared at Tavish made it clear he thought poorly of Tavish's ideas. Tavish stifled a retort. Brenton was watching.

"Compensation? Gair, Brenton, would you mind accompanying me? I think we should discuss this matter with all the clansmen," Montrose said, taking Brenton by the arm in a way that broached no argument. Tavish glowered; he had been pointedly left out of the invitation. He watched them gather up the men of each wagon and disappear into the eldest's wagon. Derg ran to join them, wriggling his way in between legs. He must have been allowed, for he did not re-emerge. Tavish sighed and kicked a rock.

Thinking black thoughts towards the Lupas, who could get away with pretty much anything, Tavish stomped up to Montrose's wagon and banged on the door. Eomma flung open the door with a finger to lips, "You're going to wake the little—oh—you're her brother, right? Come on in, master—ahh—"

"Tavish," he supplied, trying not to snarl. These people were so slick, and yet could be so dense at the same time. "I want to see Aidah." He tried to see around the woman's body into the wagon, but her girth prevented that. Either that or the loud colors of her skirt.

She bustled back as he climbed the stairs, "Oh, of course, of course. She's doing so much better—should be able to get out and move around a bit tomorrow. By and by, have you seen Montrose?" She blocked his path to Aidah's bunk, smiling sweetly. Tavish wished he could tell if her sincerity was real or feigned.

"He just called a bunch of clansmen and went into one of their wagons. The red and gold one." Tavish pointed his thumb in the general direction, still steamed that they had excluded him.

"Thanks. I'll leave you two some privacy." She stood aside to let him pass, then bustled out the door. Tavish counted to ten a couple times, then went to wake Aidah with a little pat to the arm. She must have been sleeping lightly, for she came awake at once. Or perhaps she'd only been faking.

Aidah looked better, the color coming back into her cheek and some of the old life back in her eyes. She looked to where the woman had left, rising up onto her elbows. "What's going on? I could feel your anger outside the wagon."

Tavish gaped at her. "You felt that?" He felt suddenly ashamed at himself. And a little spooked.

Her eyes, so clear and blue a second ago, suddenly clouded over. She'd just blurted out something she didn't want him to know, Tavish realized. What else could she detect from him? She brushed a hand over her eyes, and Tavish could see that she was still recovering from the illness; her hand trembled. "Oh, uh, yeah—I still get snatches of emotion…especially when they're intense," she explained, blushing.

He guessed he did have rather intense emotions at times. It was not something he'd ever really been conscious of, but now, he'd try to remember to keep his temper down, for Aidah's sake. "We're leaving. Brenton and Gair saw some spies from Rangwar. They're discussing with Montrose right now whether the Gedar will come with us or not." He didn't mention that Gair was fighting for the Gedar to accompany them. The guy was still busy trying to charm Aidah, and he could swear she liked it.

"Spies?" Aidah had suddenly grown pale, and a wave of something cold passed over Tavish, making his heart pound—fear, he realized, coming from her. He found himself clutching at his chest. "When are we leaving?" The urgency in her voice was unmistakable and Tavish was reminded of Brenton's words to him. He hoped he had not just made a terrible error in telling her.

"Now don't get scared. We're taking care of things, Sis. I don't know exactly when we're leaving, but it'll be soon. They won't be able to get you here, anyway. It's just three old miners by the sound of it. Just keep eating and sleeping, and get your strength back." He searched the narrow wagon for the food shelf, and upon finding it pulled out a sack of dried fruit and honeyed grains. He shoved a handful at Aidah.

"I'm not sick any more, Tavish. Stop babying me."

This was good. She had some of the old spunk back. "I know. But you still look a bit pale."

She took the handful and began eating, talking through a mouthful, "And what about Gair? If the Gedar decide not to come, will he still come with us to Landaran, or stay here?"

He *knew* she'd ask. "Stay here, I'd imagine. They're his people, after all." His tone sounded pretty good, he thought. No emotion, light-hearted, as if he didn't care either way. Damn that Gair.

Aidah wasn't so good at hiding her disappointment. "Oh, I guess you're right."

He was about to ask her if she felt anything—either of the Gedar debating whether to stay or go, or of the Innis spies, when a bell began ringing on one of the wagons. He opened the shutters of the small window and saw women and children running over to the elder's wagon, in sort of a clan gathering. "Something's happening. Wait here. I'll go check," he told Aidah.

"Wait—I'm coming too," she said, but he was already running

out the door, following a group of young boys over to a rapidly growing crowd around the elder's wagon. Montrose and Brenton stood with heads bowed together, talking. There had to be over fifty people in the clan, all gathered close together. It was an impressive and colorful sight. Tavish squeezed between a boy wearing a vest trimmed with tiny bells and a woman wearing a cloak which looked like an entire fabric shop.

The owner of the wagon, a wizened old man with a braided beard, rang his copper bell one last time with a pull of a rope, then stepped aside as Montrose raised his hands to the crowd. A hand tugged at Tavish's sleeve and he found that Aidah had ignored his request and followed, looking pale as the snow, swaying as she stood.

He gave her his arm to hold her steady. At her side appeared Gair, from where, Tavish had no idea, lending his arm to support Aidah from the other side. How heroic.

"Gair of clan Malin has presented our clan with a task of great reward," Montrose began, and Tavis was forced to turn his attention away from the pesky thief. Montrose was speaking in the proper tongue of the Doane Republic rather than the strange Gedar tongue, probably as a courtesy to Brenton, Tavish and his sister. Montrose continued, "The heads of our families have discussed this, and we agree it is worthwhile to pursue this task, but we felt it necessary to get the full clan approval, as there is danger involved." *What a dunce*, Tavish thought with a scoff. He couldn't even believe they were considering it.

Montrose paused, watching the reactions of his people. "Gair's clan held the task of accompanying a rare and powerful sorcerer, a Life Talent, from her home in the mountains to the Protector in Landaran." He took a deep breath, staring at Aidah with worry. "We all know the demons which may be stirred by a sorcerer's abilities. It is dangerous to associate with them in normal circumstances, but especially this one. She is being hunted by the Empire of Innis."

A rumble of fear and disapproval ran through the crowd, and Aidah shrank against Tavish, eyes large as she looked around. Tavish couldn't miss how some of the Gedar threw her dark looks. Tavish didn't know if news of their power had spread. They hadn't been bothered by any of the Gedar, and now that he thought about it, that seemed strange. Montrose must have kept their Talents a secret.

Montrose nodded, his beard wagging at the mutterings of his

clan members, and spoke again. "Yes, it is a grave matter, absolutely. And I must be truthful. Some of you have heard Gair's tale of clan Malin. They were ambushed by a Fire *murva*, whose name I understand is Madhar. This *murva* may strike at us if we harbor the Life Talent. But we would have a Fire *murva* of our own, to protect us. If we transport these sorcerers to Landaran, the payment is a hundred gold pieces. Per family."

"A fortune!" Murmured the woman of many fabrics next to Tavish.

"But *murva?*" The woman next to her muttered, shaking her head. Tavish swallowed; she was staring at him. Despite Montrose's discretion in not naming his own ability, it was pretty obvious who the '*murva*' with the Fire Talent had to be. He considered backing Aidah and himself out of the crowd in case things got ugly.

Too late. The boy with the bells and several of his friends turned to Tavish and began whispering, "*Murva*, bloody *murva* been staying here under our noses!"

A man with yarn braided in his beard yanked back the boy, hissing something into his ear. The boy glowered, but waved back his friends to leave Tavish standing there with one fist raised, unsure what to do next. Around him he could hear heated discussions in the Gedar tongue between man and wife, and between fathers and sons. The prospect of gold seemed to nudge them away from their usual superstitions about magic, but it was anyone's guess if that would hold. Probably that was why Korva had offered so much.

A few of the Gedar shouted questions at Montrose, which he answered in Proper, "Yes, Trevan, she is just a child, and no, Mora, she is not trained, but the fire,uh,'Talent' is trained." A little at least, Tavish thought. Montrose was trying to use the polite term as he caught sight of Tavish, but nothing could mask the uneasiness in his voice. Having a firestarter stay for a few days was one thing. Trusting a young half-trained one to defend his clan against a mature expert one was something else entirely. Sometimes Tavish didn't need Aidah's Talent to know what people thought about him. It had been the same in Hamstead.

Montrose answered more questions about what had happened to the other clan's caravan, making a point of not mentioning Nera, though whether it was because he thought poorly of her protection or because he wanted to encourage his clan to go for the gold, Tavish couldn't say. In the end, they decided they could live with a couple of Talents for a while; long enough to get them to Landaran. Tavish sighed. His feeling were as mixed as those around him who would be his escorts for the next few weeks.

Beside him, Aidah shivered. "I hope we don't lead this clan to its doom."

Aidah rode upon Muser's slowly swaying back, smelling the welcome scent of fresh grass on the hillsides. Behind her towered the great Morgaine Range; ahead of her was the hill country, scattered with farm holdings and herds of sheep and goat. Here the snow only lingered in small patches on the ground, melting in the sunny afternoon.

Beside her, Montrose's wagon squeaked and jangled along, pulled by two draft horses named Ring and Clang, for the bells on their harnesses which mixed with the jingle of pots and pans on the wagon to create a whole sort of orchestra. Tavish sat on an unhitched horse, a young stallion named Buck who was as good as his name, giving an irritated kick and a buck every couple of miles, testing Tavish's control. Buck was too young to pull wagons and normally ridden by one of the Gedar boys, but Montrose had decided their designated protector needed a steed and had made it a gift to Tavish so that he would have freedom of mobility if Madhar attacked.

Brenton sat beside Montrose at the front of the wagon, struggling to study a map of the lowlands written on old oiled parchment, in a way that wouldn't disrupt Montrose's handling of the reins. Derg sat on the footboard between Brenton and Montrose, looking rather uncomfortable with the rocking motion of the wagon.

Aidah felt the horror and the pain of the last few weeks fading away in the crisp morning air, breathing deep lungfuls that were finally clear once more, exulting in the energy that slowly returning. The flight through the mountain, the burning of Hamstead—even the terrible dreams of Rangwar—all seemed to be fading away, lost in the bright sun and milder temperatures of the hill country. She could see spots of civilization dotting the landscape between dark green swaths of forest and farm and grassland. Landaran was growing closer, day by day.

The Gedar camp at Minton had been a blur for her, between fever and coughing and taking down copious amounts of Eomma's 'special brew.' Obviously it had worked. She felt fine now, and strangely enough, her Talent seemed to have gone into remission; other than a continued presence of Tavish in her mind, she sensed little else of other people and creatures. Perhaps she was blocking her own power. She had reason enough to do that, after all of Rangwar's pressure for her to surrender herself.

She hadn't had any 'visitations' from him since the night before they reached Minton, and two weeks had passed since then. It was too much to hope that he thought her dead. He had to be up to something.

Gair trotted up beside her on a donkey, leading along a couple of sheep a herder had traded for some tinware just yesterday. Behind him rolled the seven other wagons of the other Gedar families in the caravan, creating a snaking line up the hillside. Aidah stifled a laugh at Gair's riding; it wasn't necessarily that he was a bad rider, but he was much too tall for the donkey. His feet nearly brushed the ground and his knees stuck out at odd angles. Gair caught her muffled giggle; he grinned, which only made him look more ridiculous, the wind touseling his dark hair.

Aidah tried to imagine what it must be like for him. "That has to be uncomfortable."

Gair shrugged, reaching down to scratch at one of his ankles which kept catching against bits of brush. "It's no worse than riding in one of those wagons. You're looking much better. I think Eomma was smart to make you ride." He looked her over, and there was a warmth in his eyes that made her blush.

Eomma had insisted that the fastest way to recover from an illness was to spend a little energy, get a little fresh air and exercise. Aidah couldn't complain; it was cramped in the wagon, and the bumpy ride was hardly good for her stomach. She didn't know how the Gedar could live this way, traveling most of the year.

"I guess so," she answered, leaning over Muser to pet his neck fondly and stretch her muscles. Around them, the brush lands were full of the sound of birds, and every now and again the wagons would startle a rabbit out of hiding, the animal bounding across the hillside. Up ahead she could see a swath of forest. "How long before we reach the lowlands, do you think?"

Gair squinted into the distance, holding a hand over his eyes. "Couple more days, I'd say. We should reach the first real city in a week. From there, the going will be easy—probably an escort of a couple mages, and roads guarded by soldiers of the Realm. We'll have you in Landaran inside three weeks, I should say." He almost sounded wistful.

Aidah didn't know what to say. It had made a huge difference, joining up with the caravan. Yes, they were forced to use main trails, but with numbers to hide among, even that had become an advantage, getting her to the Lowlands much faster than Brenton could have managed alone. With burly men who could pound out a dent in a pot in two minutes flat and children who could juggle knives, she felt safer. Then too there was a sense of belonging to something, even if conversations had a tendency to stop short when she approached Gedar other than Eomma or Montrose. It felt like a shield around them, blocking out her fears, the terrible dreams. She only hoped she could reach Grandess before Rangwar tried to contact her again.

They began passing fir and spruce trees, heading towards the little swath of forest cutting across the hillside, its edges trimmed back by lumbermen so that it looked like a saber or scythe, hard-edged against the faded yellow landscape. As they passed under the canopy of pine and fir mixed with ash and elm, Aidah started to get a prickly sensation down her back. The woods were thick and dense here; it had probably been the heart of a much greater forest, slowly chipped away by man. The undergrowth was young and dense between the towering pine trees creeping up on the road. Despite the heavy snow in the mountains, it looked like it had remained dry here, with scarcely a patch of snow even in the cool shadows of the trees.

Tavish rode up beside her, the clomp of Buck's hooves eerily loud in the hushed forest. The sun was all but blotted out by the trees, dappled spots on the thick carpet of pine needles. He glanced up ahead at the trail which seemed to disappear into the dark depths of the forest. "Maybe it's just me, but this seems like a perfect place for an ambush. Are you sensing anything, Aidah?"

His words sent a wave of cold through her, and suddenly she couldn't tell if the fear she felt was her own or his. She looked at the trail, trying to separate, trying to decide if her nerves were instinct or only a morbid imagination. "I'm not sure." She wasn't sure if she wanted to know if disaster was about to strike.

"Close your eyes, and concentrate. Better some slight warning than none at all," Gair whispered, gripping at the donkey's bristly mane, eyeing the dark forest closing in around them. Behind them the second wagon was just crossing into the shade of the forest.

Aidah closed her eyes, sending out her aura just in case she needed to attack with it as she had at the house. She sensed briefly a rabbit's pain as it was struck down by something. Next she felt Tavish's fear, and got a tiny thought from Montrose, "*And then with the money, I could—*" She lost that thought before she could learn what he meant to do. She reached farther, but there was nothing. As far as she could discern, the forest was empty of threats, other than natural ones. "No, I guess not," she confessed to Tavish and Gair Their steeds, followed alongside Montrose's cart as the pathway rounded a corner, heading downhill.

She tried to feel for the rabbit again, but there was nothing, just the quiet of the trees. She began to ask Tavish whether the three of them should go back and check on the other wagons, when movement in the corner of her eye stopped her.

The last wagon had entered the forest, the caravan snaking its way down the narrow trail. A shadowed figure walked out from the woods onto the trail just ahead of Montrose's wagon, broad shoulders wrapped in a purple and black cloak, face hidden by a low hood.

The Gedar halted their wagons, murmuring nervously in their native tongue, and looked to Montrose. Tavish reined in his horse, scowling. He held out an arm out to tell Aidah to halt as well. Gair stopped beside her, fingering the wrist sheath where he kept his knife, watching the figure carefully. The figure just stood there, silently.

Tavish brought his horse slowly forward. "Who are you? What do you want from us?"

As Tavish drew nearer, Aidah got a sense of impending danger—not a thought or an emotion, just an inexplicable sense that she must not let Tavish get too close to the stranger. "Tavish, watch out," she called, not even sure of what he should be watching out for.

"Now," the figure whispered in an all-too-familiar voice, and removed the hood to reveal a ghostly pale image of Rangwar, the black of his cloak in fact the shadows of the forest, tricking the eye into making him look solid. Aidah's heart stuttered in terror, all the memories of the dreams crashing in on her.

To the right of Montrose's wagon emerged Madhar, grinning like a mad man. Everywhere around them, Madhar's ruffians revealed themselves, stepping out from behind trees, standing up from hiding behind bushes, swords in hand, ready to strike. Madhar held aloft a long metal rod with a copper ball at one end, pointing it like a weapon towards Tavish. Aidah was sure that it had something to do with lightning, as the skies above had been clear when they'd entered the forest.

Now she knew why she hadn't felt anything. Rangwar was blocking her. He strode towards Tavish, and Aidah remembered that neither she nor Brenton had warned Tavish of what Rangwar was capable of even out of body, as he again seemed to be. "Tavish, don't let him touch you!"

"Don't worry, I won't," Tavish growled, backing the horse up as Rangwar drew closer. Tavish raised his arm, and flame erupted around Rangwar's figure, but he passed through, unaffected. The fire only served to startle Buck, who gave a squeal and raised up on his hind legs, forelimbs kicking at the air. Tavish gave a cry, holding on for dear life.

Rangwar walked up with one arm raised, unafraid of the slashing hooves, and touched one foreleg as it flew past his head, clouding his image for a brief second. The horse screamed. It fell backwards, and Tavish only barely managed to dismount and roll away as it collapsed, shuddering. It gave a long sigh, eyes rolling, and then was still.

"You killed it!" Tavish was aghast, horrified that anyone could commit such a callous act.

Tavish didn't have time to react further; Rangwar drifted forward, reaching out to touch him. Tavish stumbled back, just managing to keep out of reach. With grace learned by countless escapes over rooftops, Tavish leapt and went into a tuck and roll to end up next to Gair and Aidah as Rangwar continued to come forward. "Stop or I'll flame this whole forest!" Tavish shouted, his voice quavering, eyes wide with fear.

"You would kill your friends as well as your enemies. Surrender! We do not wish to hurt any of you," Madhar called from his position standing on a fallen log off the right side of the trail. The man who had been commanding the force in Hamstead did not seem to be present; Aidah assumed he must have been in charge of leading back the prisoners, hopefully including her father and grandpa.

Tavish snarled. "Fine. Just you, then."

In her mind, Aidah heard Rangwar's voice for her alone. *"Come to me, angel. I will spare all of them—your brother, uncle, all the Gedar, if you come to me right now. This is your last chance."*

She didn't allow herself time to consider the option. "No!" She screamed, sending out that cry through her aura as well as her voice, hoping it would do the same thing it had at the house when she'd warned Derg. At the same instant, Tavish struck at Madhar with a column of fire, and Madhar threw a small fork of lightning from his rod at Tavish. The two of them staggered back, clothes smoking, but the attacks had cancelled each other out, broken their concentration. Around them, half the ruffians struggled, clutching at their heads from Aidah's mental scream, but the other half remained standing, holding weapons crossbows aimed at the Gedar. Tavish sagged against Muser, holding onto him, and looked up at Aidah.

"Do that again and we might be able to escape," he whispered, rubbing his head. So her attack had affected him too.

Brenton too was looking pained, but he stood up and climbed down from the wagon, heading towards the twins slowly, a hand raised as if he could hold off one of Madhar's bolts. "Madhar, if you let the Gedar people go, the twins and I will come with you, but you must let them withdraw first." He paused, as one of the ruffians took aim at him. Tavish muttered something under his breath.

"No, you can't," Aidah cried, watching Rangwar smiling so pleasantly, as if this were just a simple chat among friends. He was fading in and out of view, however, showing the trail behind him, and she remembered that it seemed to take him a lot of concentration and energy to remain out of body. If she could distract him somehow, and if Tavish could deal with Madhar...

That left only the twenty or so armed men under Madhar for Brenton to deal with.

She leaned over to Gair. "Gair, if Tavish and I take care of the mages, will your people fight the men?" Rangwar could probably overhear her, could perhaps even sense her thoughts, but she had to take the chance. Tavish against Madhar, herself against Rangwar— was she crazy?

Maybe if she could avoid thinking about it, she could fool him.

She concentrated hard, and only belatedly noticed that Derg

had left the wagon as well, and was suddenly moving swiftly past her, heading straight for Rangwar. Images of her mother slamming through Rangwar, distracting him, falling into the burning debris of the house flashed in her mind. "Derg, no!"

He moved so fast, even Rangwar never saw him until he was leaping in midair, passing through the ghostly image of the Emporer. Rangwar staggered and disappeared, and Aidah felt as if a heavy curtain had been lifted. Derg crashed into the soft carpet of pine needles and was still. Aidah tried with difficulty to disperse her aura where it touched friend and concentrate it where it touched foe and sent a silent psychic scream out, pouring all her desperation, all her fear into it. All their enemies, even Madhar clutched at their heads, swaying, and a few of his men passed out, dropping their weapons as Montrose called for the Gedar to defend the wagons.

Tavish screwed up his face, and threw a massive fireball at Madhar. The flames engulfed the wizard, setting his robes ablaze, spreading to the thick underbrush in a rush of hot air, quickly growing in size and ferocity. Aidah gasped. It was far beyond anything Tavish had done before. Ruffians cried out, trying to escape the growing fire; the horses pulling the wagons screamed, throwing their heads as their drivers tried to control them. Madhar fell down, screaming as the flames consumed his robes, a rising inferno. Tavish watched in horror, seemingly frozen, as the flames climbed higher and higher, beyond the point where they even needed his help.

"Run!" Montrose ordered as in desperation Madhar's men began firing their crossbows. With a crack of the whip, Montrose drove forward the horses, and the rest of the caravan began following, intent on escaping the forest before the trail became impassable.

Tavish stumbled and fell, his face pale, and Aidah could feel the drain the large scale use of his Talent had cost him. She pulled him onto Muser's back and urged the mule forward to check on Derg, lying motionless on the side of the trail, as Montrose's wagon caught up. Dismounting, she ran to Derg's side. He was breathing, but unconscious. With Gair's help, they picked up Derg and carried him over to the wagon, handing the Lupas over to Brenton who resumed his place beside Montrose. "Hurry," he urged Aidah, but she needed no urging.

The fireball had turned into a forest fire now, spreading quickly, as ruffians were forced out of hiding and onto the only cleared area, the trail. Gedar men and boys attacked them there, throwing little cunning daggers that no armor seemed proof against. Aidah mounted Muser again, with Tavish holding onto her from behind, and quickly they began riding forward, trusting that the wagons would follow. She could feel Tavish's pang of loss as he glanced back at the still form of Buck—already in their short time together, they had begun to form a bond. The last of the ruffians fled the few directions where fire did not block their path, and shakily Tavish concentrated, trying to quell the flames so that the Gedar people could pass. By the time the last wagon had passed where Madhar had fallen, the flames had died down for the most part, sparing the trees but leaving a carpet of ash and embers in a wide circle, at the center of which was a blackened spot that had been the mage.

They all drove the horses quickly, saying nothing, awaiting any moment the return of Rangwar, or the few of Madhar's men that might have escaped. All was quiet again, except for the crackle and pop of cinders.

As the afternoon wore on, the group finally emerged from the forest, into sunlit grasslands gently sloping downwards. In the distance they could just see the first of the Lowland settlements and farmland. Tavish had recovered enough to sit up, but the headache still radiated off of him, combining with Aidah's to make her lightheaded and dizzy. When he spoke, his voice was just the softest of whispers. "I killed him, didn't I."

12

Thornton

Tavish was silent the rest of the day, even when the caravan rolled into the town of Thornton the following morning. Thornton's population was about three thousand, larger than any town either Tavish or Aidah had ever seen. Aidah let Tavish to ride Muser so she could sit at the front of Montrose's wagon, drinking in the sights of a bustling agricultural center. The streets were crowded with men and women, donkeys, boys leading sheep off to pasture, an occasional goat, chickens scurrying about, and even a militia guard riding a horse in glistening studded leather armor.

The guard smiled at Aidah, and she blushed and looked away. The men looked different here; instead of the ruddy complexions and brown hair common to the mountain folk, they had pale skin and a variety of hair colors—like Tavish and her, who had always taken after their mother. It drove home more than anything the fact her ancestors had left these lands to marry hillfolk. Fleeing their kind? Aidah had to wonder.

Most amazing to Aidah, however, was the technology available here, even on the outskirts of the Lowlands. She saw a woman working a giant loom for her weaving instead of the tiny hand looms she had learned on. Surrounding the town was a high stone wall, with a large wooden gate, presumably for protection. Some of the buildings were four stories tall, unheard of in Hamstead, leaning against their neighbors near the heart of town. She even saw a merchant trying to peddle something called a harpsichord, a harp laid on its side played by pressing ivory levers.

Yet Tavish seemed blind to the wondrous sights. He rode

stoically beside Gair, head bowed, his sandy hair falling into his face to cover his pale skin. She should go down and comfort him, let him know he'd had to do it. He'd saved all of them. The feeling she got from him, however, warned Aidah that he wanted to be left alone.

Gair was respecting that wish as well, perhaps unconsciously, by staying back a bit and keeping his sheep out of Tavish's way. Every so often he glanced up to look at Aidah; when she caught him looking one time, he grinned and tipped his hat at her. She rolled her eyes at him; he was still riding the tiny donkey and drawing laughs from the children of the town. None of it seemed to bother him.

Once they reached the center market square, the Gedar halted to peddle their wares, and the women came out to sing and dance, attracting a small crowd and the clink of welcome coin into shawls laid at their feet. Montrose's wife and the older women gathered some of the coin and made their way to local merchant stalls, purchasing bread and meat. There would be plenty of food for all in the caravan tonight. Aidah sat with Brenton, observing it all.

She spotted Tavish seated alone, beyond the Gedar wagons, on the steps of the town temple. He watched the dancers with a sullen look on his face. Gair was performing acrobatics not far off, though he fell more often than not, to the delight of his onlookers. His antics were earning him his own collection of coins.

"An interesting people, aren't they?" Brendan commented, chewing on a piece of bread. The jingle of bells on the dancers' feet kept time as the musicians played a lively tune on pan pipes and lute. Aidah found herself tapping her foot along.

"Yeah, they are. Though I get the feeling Tavish doesn't agree," she said. Brenton glanced over at Tavish, sighing.

"He's having a rough time. Rough age for it, too." Brenton looked Aidah up and down, a worried look in his eye. "You're looking better, at least. All of your strength back now?"

She stretched, easing out the kinks from having ridden for most of the day. "I feel much better, thanks."

Brenton nodded, staring at her. "And how has your Talent been lately?"

Aidah actually smiled. "Hasn't bothered me much lately." She almost told him about her deepening link to Tavish, but what insights could he offer? She'd tell Korva once they reached Landaran. She still wasn't sure if the link was strong because they were siblings, or because Tavish was just so open with his feelings.

"Yes, I remember you having nightmares when you were sick. You thought there were spies all around us. Tavish said you were telling them to leave you alone." Brenton frowned at her. "I do hope those were only dreams."

Aidah tried to hide the sudden wash of fear over her. That was right—Tavish had overheard her talking in her sleep during one of Rangwar's visits. She didn't think he knew what Brenton knew, that Rangwar had actually visited her before the attack on Hamstead, so perhaps he had thought it was only a fever dream. Brenton would figure it out if she wasn't careful. He must not. He already had too much on his shoulders. Besides, it was all in the past.

"Oh yes; I was having really odd dreams—even dreamt I was locked in this incredibly high tower, filled with spiders," she exclaimed, making spider motions with her hands up her arms.

Brenton laughed uncertainly. "Then you don't think it was a warning from your Talent, or perhaps Rangwar—"

A commotion in the square over by Tavish broke off their conversation. Three local boys, around Tavish's age, stood to either side of him, and as Aidah watched, they began shoving him around, harassing him. Aidah listened closer, climbing down off the wagon so that she could hear better, coming closer. One of the boys accused Tavish of stealing a pocket watch, a gold pocket watch. The tallest and supposedly eldest of the three youths, he was just starting to grow facial hair, a fine line along his jawline and upper lip, the color of honey. He had somewhat curly hair, reddish blond, tucked under a fine cap of dyed wool, with a pheasant feather for adornment. His fair skin was lightly freckled.

Tavish, though he was the shortest of the group, looked ready to take them all on, fists clenched, an angry glare in his eyes. "I tell you, I didn't take it!" He tried to take a step back, but the third lad was behind him now, blocking his way. Tavish rounded on him. "I'm not even Gedar. I'm from the mountains. See my clothes?" He pinched the dull brown of his tunic, a color that no Gedar would ever choose to wear, displaying the rough woolen fabric, lined with fur. The boys looked at each other and laughed. Their clothes were almost as bright as Gedar, though not so garishly patterned, with soft russet red tunics, green leggings and dark blue cloaks held by silver pins. The tall boy wore a fine green woolen cloak and a fur trimmed doublet with pewter buttons. Aidah's heart sank. He looked like he might be the son of a steward. Definitely not a simple herder.

"So you're a dumb hillboy. You're still a thief! Give it back to me, or I'll make you pay in full for it," the tall one ordered, giving Tavish a hard shove. Tavish fell back on his rump, and Aidah knew if she didn't stop things right away, there would be flames soon. They were burning full force already in Tavish's eyes.

Brenton was ahead of her, striding up to them. "Boys, what seems to be the problem? Why don't you all stand back, and we can discuss this?" Easy for him to say; it was obvious in his stance and by his broad chest that he had at least some weapons experience, even if it was only a tiny village's militia. Two of the boys stepped back, uncertainty in their faces, but the tall leader remained undaunted, arms crossed, glaring at Brenton as Brenton helped Tavish to his feet.

Behind her, another presence tickled at Aidah's awareness, and she turned around to find Gair had left his circle of young admirers to come see what was happening. Aidah felt a flutter in her stomach. The look on Gair's face was serious, and concerned, not his usual jovial smirk. "What seems to be the problem, gentlemen?" he asked.

The tall one gave Gair a nod, possibly of recognition. "Gedar. We were strolling past, and this runt bumped into us. Next thing we knew, my pocket watch was gone. It was my father's, and it's valuable. Tell the runt to return it, or I'll press charges."

His words sounded funny to Aidah, as if he had marbles in his mouth. It had to be the Lowland accent, she decided. Gair's voice took on a similar quality when he responded, "Well Tavish here is my friend, and if he says he didn't take it, then there must be another explanation for what happened to it. He'll allow a body search to make you feel better, won't you, Tavish?" He gave Tavish a hard look, smiling pleasantly.

Tavish fumed, but he raised his arms obediently to be searched, silently challenging the tall boy to take advantage of his position. The tall boy grinned mischievously, but he was gentle as he patted at Tavish's cloak, tunic, vest and trousers. Aidah tried to think if he was carrying anything he shouldn't be. Probably a hunting knife—but that was common for mountain folk.

Aidah hoped that the Lowlanders wouldn't take offence.

The boy finished his search and scowled. "He must have hidden it."

"Why you pompous, stuck up…" Tavish lunged at him, but Gair and Brenton held him back. Aidah cringed, feeling his fury inside her, just waiting for the sparks to appear on that lovely green cloak which might soon burst into flame. She could almost smell the smoke, so intense was Tavish's desire.

Instead, however he choked back his anger and stopped struggling. His eyes threw daggers, but he only spoke in a quiet voice, "I don't know what trash you're trying to pull, but I'm innocent. Now leave me alone."

The tall one grinned. "You're a Firestarter, aren't you?" All malice had suddenly left his face, and Aidah suddenly had the feeling that it had all been a joke. Or perhaps a test? But that didn't make any sense, she thought. She was getting conflicting impressions from him. She almost wanted to like him, and yet he had been so rude to her brother…she shook her head, baffled.

Tavish was not so inclined to be friendly. "Who are you? Why do you ask?" Beside him, Brenton tensed, and very clearly Aidah got the picture of Madhar and his men. Ah, he feared this was another of Rangwar's spies, she realized. She didn't think so, though she couldn't say why.

"My name is Kendrick Thorne. My family owns an estate just north of town. May I ask your name?" Aidah noted his well-manicured hands, his polished boots. Was this a noble? She'd heard tales of the rich families who traced back to their heritage to noble families of Innis, from before the Great Flight. She'd never met such a person before.

"Tavish Dernholt." Tavish half mumbled the words, standing with arms crossed firmly over his chest.

"Of Hamstead?" Kendrick asked.

A shock went through Aidah—not just her own, but Brenton's and Tavish's as well. Tavish reached into his pouch where he kept his hunting knife and Brenton grabbed Kendrick's arm, fear filling his face. "Who are you with? How could you know that?" His fear was a black choking thing, making Aidah struggle for breath as it surrounded her. She made a frantic gesture at him, trying to warn him that her Talent was acting up again, that she couldn't think how to control it while he panicking like that.

Kendrick, however, only smirked, and pulled out the supposedly missing gold pocket watch. "Obviously you don't keep genealogical charts in Hamstead. Doesn't matter, though. If the short one's Tavish, then the girl—" he pointed at Aidah before she could duck behind Brenton, "—must be the twin sister? The one with the Life potential?"

Tavish drew his knife. "Did Madhar send you?"

Brenton reached for his own knife. "Or Rangwar?"

Kendrick paled, raising his hands in supplication. "That's good. You know who your enemies are." He sighed, glancing over at his friends. "But you obviously don't know who your family is. I'm your cousin, well, 6th cousin, to be exact. There was a pretty straight line down from Korva until it came to her great-grandchildren. She had seven total. You two came from Davina, the eldest great-grandchild, and I came from Gothmir, who was Davina's younger cousin. Long story short; we're both part of Korva's family tree. You might have heard of my great-grandfather, Gabriel Holt—he's one of the last surviving Spirit Mages other than Korva."

Brenton had lowered his knife, and motioned for Tavish to put his away as well. "Gabriel's your great-grandfather?"

Kendrick grinned. "Yes, sir. Fought with Beven Dell in the Hunt for Mahala in 1071."

Brenton laughed, shaking with relief, and the fear dissipated like so much smoke, allowing Aidah to breathe freely again. "Okay, now I know who you are. Your grandfather is a Sun Mage, is he not?"

Kendrick nodded, relieved as well. "Jardan Thorne. He's instructing me in the craft." He poked Tavish. "That's why I asked if you were a Firestarter. We'll be in the same class. Maybe you'll even get my grandfather as Master!" He held out his hand for Tavish to shake, but Tavish held back, eyeing him with a frown.

"How do I know you're who you say you are? And what about your accusation that I was a thief, not to mention 'dumb hillboy?' You sure have a strange way of introducing yourself!" He put his knife away but crossed his arms, looking sullen.

Now that the danger was past, Gair and the other Gedar who had gathered to watch the commotion backed away to continue selling their wares and performances. The two boys with Kendrick turned to watch them, looking bored. Aidah looked closely at Kendrick, searching for a family resemblance. The eyes were similar, she noted, large and wide set with a grayish cast to them which probably changed with mood, as hers did. Now that he wasn't angry, or pretending to be angry, she saw he had a handsome face, with lips perhaps a little fuller than most men. That too was similar, though Kendrick's jaw line was more angular, lined with the fuzz of probably his first attempt at growing a beard. With his fine clothes and gold watch, he probably *was* nobility. Korva had been the daughter of an Emperor, after all.

Kendrick rocked back on his heels, looking sheepish. "I knew you were a Firestarter from a mile away—you have the look," he smiled, "And the smell. You ever notice how the smoke clings to us? Impossible to wash out. Anyways, I saw the company you were in and figured out who you must be. There's been a lot of talk in Landaran about whether you were going to come for your training. I thought I'd test you, see if you're ready. Having a temper's fine, but if you act with haste, they'll never let you become a Sun Mage."

Brenton broke in, relief in his face, "Is Korva looking for us? Did they receive word of our coming?"

Kendrick flipped the watch over his knuckles, from one hand to the other. Aidah was struck with another similarity—Kendrick and Tavish were both agile. And show-offs. "Yes. Didn't know which trail you'd be on, but we posted mages at the three most likely." He put the watch away. "By the way, where's Nera? She was supposed to be with you."

Brenton averted his eyes, and Aidah felt a flash of horror. He didn't know! That probably meant that nobody here knew. Not about Nera, not about Hamstead, none of it. Tavish looked to Aidah, trying to judge from her what attitude he should take with their cousin. She felt his doubt. "I think we can trust him," she murmured, trying to feel deep into Kendrick's thoughts or emotions. Instead, she got a barrage of voices from all the people in the town square, and a headache. She groaned, holding her head and wishing all the other minds away. Eventually they quieted down.

"She has the Talent, hasn't she?" Kendrick said in a near whisper. He looked concerned.

"Aidah? Are you all right?" Brenton asked, bending down to look at her.

Through the pounding pain, she gave a slow nod, smiling weakly. "It's acting up again."

Kendrick leaned closer as well, which was a bit disconcerting for Aidah. "What exactly are you experiencing?" He looked into her eyes as if trying to see inside of her.

She blushed and backed away. "I get thoughts and emotions from those around me every now and then. I got the entire square just now, but it passed. Except for the headache."

Kendrick reached into his vest pocket and pulled out a packet of herbs. He handed it to her with a bow. "One pinch in hot water, sip slowly and inhale deeply. It'll help with the headaches, though it won't dull your Talent at all. We'll get you to my great granddaddy, Gabriel. He'll teach you how to shield yourself."

Finally some training! It was good enough news to make Aidah smile despite the pain. Tavish regarded her, then Kendrick, nodding to himself. "You seem all right, though I think your taste in jokes stinks. I guess I'll trust you though, for now."

Kendrick grinned and bowed again. "Most gracious of you. But if you think that's bad, wait until you get to the academy. They test us all the time, knowing we have to deal with all kinds of people. You won't believe some of the stuff they spring. They stuck me in a situation with a woman I thought was in her childbearing pains!"

Even Tavish had to smile a little at that. With a deep sigh, he offered his hand. Kendrick took it and gave it a hearty shake.

"So where's Nera?"

Aidah opened her mouth to speak, then looked to Brenton. Tavish bowed his head, looking away, his gray eyes unable to hide the pain of loss. As the pause lengthened into an uncomfortable silence, Brenton leaned forward to answer. "She was killed in an ambush. We've been fleeing Rangwar's men since they attacked Hamstead. The whole town was attacked. They took anyone who survived, presumably back to Innis."

Kendrick staggered back, the blood draining from his face. Any doubts that Aidah might have had about his loyalties were swiftly quenched. "She's *dead?!* Do you know who killed her? How she died?" He looked ready to faint, so Aidah gestured for Brenton and Tavish to help him to sit on the curb of the street. Tavish looked shaken; apparently he was not the only one Nera's death had touched. More important, Aidah thought, was the fact news of her death had not reached the Lowlands. That meant Korva might not be aware of her predicament.

Kendrick took deep breaths, staring up at them while Brenton tried to explain what had happened, from Madhar's attack on

Hamstead, the loss of friends and family, and the remains of the caravan they had found on the trail. Aidah glanced over at the square as Brenton mentioned Gair's help, looking for him. He was on the other side, entertaining some older folk with what looked like a lively tale. As she searched for him, he glanced over and their eyes met. She turned away, embarrassed.

Kendrick shuddered as Brenton finished his tale, and bowed his head, strawberry blond curls falling into his face. Aidah bit her lip; she saw tears clinging unshed to his lashes. He sighed, and raised his eyes again to look at Aidah and Tavish. "I had no idea. Believe me, I wouldn't have been fooling around with you about the pocketwatch if I'd known what your group had been through. I can't believe it. She was one of the best..."

Tavish fidgeted, lips pursed in thought, strands of his hair falling into his face. He reached out a hand, then drew it back, unsure how to deal with this new distant cousin of theirs. Finally he patted Kendrick on the back. "Yeah, she was. Madhar must've surprised her. That's the only explanation."

Brenton leaned over to speak to Kendrick, keeping his voice low, "I understand if you want some time alone right now, but can we talk to you later, perhaps tonight? The Gedar tribe is accompanying us to Landaran, but we could use extra protection if either you or your master can come. There have been repeated attempts by Rangwar and his agents to capture Tavish and Aidah."

Kendrick rose to his feet, blinking away tears and nodding. "Yes of course—it's the reason I came to see you when I heard the Gedar were in town. I have to talk to my grandfather, tell him what you told me. We'll come back by this evening. Is there anything you need while you're in town? I can give you some money. My father's the Earl of Thornton."

He pulled out a silk coin purse, and Aidah found herself gaping. She'd never seen a gold coin before, much less the handful he was offering. Tavish looked to Brenton for a cue, licking his lips. Aidah was getting all sorts of images from him, from swords to a new cloak to pastries. She had an idea or two of her own, most particularly a visit to the local bathhouse.

But Brenton pushed Kendrick's hand aside. "I can't ask for you to spend your gold on us. I'm sure once we reach Landaran our needs will be taken care of—"

"But the journey—we need weapons," Tavish whispered.

"Absolutely. You passed the test. I'll leave it to you. Any trouble from the locals, just say you're Kendrick's cousins," Kendrick insisted, pressing a few coins into Tavish's eager grasp.

Before Brenton could disapprove, Tavish was grabbing Aidah by the hand to pull her towards the shops. Her headache was all but forgotten in her excitement, but as he pulled her away, she looked back over her shoulder to wave at Kendrick. "Thank you so much. We'll see you later!"

Kendrick smiled, but she felt him fighting back tears. Nera's death had hurt him perhaps even deeper than Tavish. He stepped away, nodding at her. "I'll be by later, wherever the Gedar set up their wagons. Have fun—I'll wager it's your first time in the Lowlands?"

Aidah nodded, smiling.

"Have fun—there's lots to see!" With a swirl of green, he pivoted and began walking, waving at his friends to join him. In the hustle and bustle of town traffic, he soon disappeared. Aidah ran off to follow Tavish and explore the town.

☼

That evening, after a heavenly soak in a hot bath and a change of clothing into a new woolen dress of pale lavender—her favorite color—Aidah sat on the step of Montrose's wagon, playing cards with Brenton, Gair, and Montrose. Tavish was busy in the wagon sharpening his newly purchased short sword.

Gair put down a ten of cups, studying her out of the corner of his eye. "You look very nice. Lowland fashion suits you."

Aidah grinned, flushing with pleasure. She'd worn her hair down, freshly washed and combed, shining blond, and she looked like a proper woman, rather than a pile of mismatched clothing stolen from the Jonstables. The local fashion favored a low neckline to reveal her shift up to its ruffles on her neck, but it was a simple enough dress, lined along the hem and sleeves with rabbit fur about bought second hand. Brenton muttered to himself as he put down his card, watching her.

Aidah matched Brenton's four of staves with a four of cups, struggling to concentrate on the game. Above them the stars were beginning to appear out of the violet sunset, and from town she could see light from the houses, and in the tops of the watchtowers.

They had camped in a field under furrow by one of the town wells outside the walls.

A farmer and his three sons were chatting with some of the Gedar, and among them, Aidah recognized one of the boys who had been with Kendrick. Kendrick himself had not shown up yet.

It was strange finding a family member—even a distant one— so far from home. In the mountains none of this had really touched her, that they'd be traveling so far away into the heart of the realm. Each town and city would only grow larger until they reached Landaran. She felt small all of a sudden, and yet here was a connection. Family. She imagined Korva and her descendants strung out across the countryside, little sparkles of Talent here and there, all connected in some inexplicable way to the Protector herself, like a great spider in the center of her web.

She couldn't wait to meet more family members.

As she thought that, Kendrick appeared at the edge of the campsite dressed in a funeral red jacket over a white tunic, red hosen, and black leather boots. Beside him stood a man of perhaps fifty or so with long amber hair streaked with silver, a short neatly trimmed beard, and a broad forehead with heavy brows and deep set blue eyes which gave him a hawkish look. He was definitely not of Korva's line. By his badge of flame and his orange robes, she knew he must be Jardan Thorne the Sun Mage.

Brenton noticed the newcomers about the same time as Aidah and rose to go greet them. Aidah stood up, uncertain of proper etiquette. From their wagon, Aidah felt Tavish's attention shifting focus. He descended the steps slowly, exiting the wagon and staring at Kendrick and his master with a mixture of awe and fear. His fear was vague—Aidah wasn't getting any specific images from him, just a sense of nervousness. Perhaps a fear of inadequacy? That wasn't Tavish; if anything, he was too sure of himself most of the time. Aidah frowned.

Tavish had also purchased new clothes in town, including an olive green cloak and tan tunic and trousers, and new boots. The old pair were worn through from their trek across the mountains. He strode up beside her, and before Aidah could ask him what he thought about their related Fire Talents, Brenton was leading Kendrick and Jardan back towards the twins. The Gedar stepped respectfully out of their way, giving them a wide berth, whispering among themselves. Montrose and his wife came forward to shake hands with the two, offering up stools around a small makeshift table where meals were served or games were played. Jardan declined the seat offered to him and Kendrick sat instead on the step of the wagon, flashing a smile at Tavish and Aidah. Around his neck he was wearing a talisman of some kind of stone in three interlocking circles—the emblem of Doane Republic, Aidah realized with a start.

Kendrick leaned in as Montrose and Jardan spoke, whispering to Aidah, "Now you two look like Lowlanders. Much better." He reached over to take Aidah's hand and brought it up to his lips for a quick kiss. Tavish rolled his eyes.

"Now why didn't I think of that?" Gair asked with a chuckle and a sigh.

Tavish glared at him. "Don't you dare."

Their little conversation was broken up as Jardan strode over and also bestowed a kiss on Aidah's hand, with a great deal more grace and dignity than Kendrick had managed, then the old man shook hands with Tavish. "I've heard good things about you, young man. I assume you have been practicing your Talent at every opportunity?"

"Yes, sir," Tavish immediately responded, standing almost at attention. "I even learned a new spell. Invisibility. Used it to escape Madhar when he—" his shoulders slumped. "—burned down our home."

Aidah sensed him struggling to remain composed; he was thinking not only of that terrible event, but the one from yesterday. He'd killed with fire, not just one man, but possibly as many as twenty. With a nod and a heartfelt smile at her brother, she came over to take his hand in support. "He's saved us over and over, Master Jardan. You'd be amazed at the stuff he's pushed himself to accomplish. Just ask my uncle."

Brenton took the cue, "And I'd be happy to tell you about it at length. The children are holding up, but it's been hard for them." He didn't even have a clue how difficult, Aidah couldn't help thinking, trying to keep up a brave smile. Korva would understand. If anyone could, she would.

Jardan's voice was soft, serene. "I understand. It's remarkable you made it this far on your own. We had no idea that Rangwar could get agents into the Realm so easily. He must have found a way past the Guardians." He frowned, thinking, and Aidah felt a shiver of fear. What did that mean? Was their enemy becoming more powerful, then?

"We have to warn Korva," Kendrick said. His jaw was set in a firm line that Aidah knew only too well, both from her brother and herself. Kendrick probably had the same stubborn streak that ran in her family.

Jardan nodded. "We'll get you to Landaran as soon as possible, to meet with her. My wife is at court. I can deliver a message to her via carrier pigeon to get to Korva."

That in itself was a huge relief, to know that word of their coming, what they were facing, would reach her Grandess. Aidah nodded, looking between Jardan and Kendrick, at the differences in their features.

She wondered at Kendrick's wide-set eyes, that heart-shaped face, so different from his grandfather's straight jaw. "Might I ask which of you is related to Korva? And how?"

Jardan blew out a soft breath, eyebrows raised. "That could be a course in itself, Aidah, but I'll try to make it simple. My wife is of Korva's line, Brenna, 6th generation. Korva currently has eight generations of descendents. Seven individuals of her line are alive right now and Talented. It comes down from her daughter, Elidi the Sun Mage. Elidi had two children who married. Your line fromes from the elder, Gendar, who wanted to live in the mountains, away from the sea. My wife came from the younger sibling's line, from Terene's, who remained in the Lowlands. My own family, the Thornes, also trace our line to Innis as well, and fought with Korva in the Great Rebellion. We were granted an Earldom in the Doane for our assistance.

"You're an Earl?" Tavish blurted out, eyes wide. He clapped a hand over his mouth, too late it seemed by his mortified flush. "Sorry, sir—I didn't mean to interrupt."

Jardan smiled. "Not at all. I actually passed my Earldom down to my son—he manages the town far better. I imagine it must be strange for you, living all your life up in the mountains. I have been there a time or two, though not to your village. But just think! Your great-five-times-over grandmother could have had any title she wished. Instead, she married a peasant."

Tavish and Aidah looked at each other. So that meant they

could have been nobles? The notion was laughable. Tavish looked back to Jardan, at the crest of the Realm on his robes. "Should we be bowing to you?"

Jardan's smile grew wider, laugh lines crinkling around his blue eyes. "Not at all. Regardless of your upbringing, it is you and Aidah who are the heirs to Korva's legacy. Which brings me to you, dear lady." He leaned over to take both of Aidah's to gaze into her eyes.

She sensed his Talent, and not just through the intensity of his blue eyes. Kendrick was right. There was a smell, like wood smoke, but beyond that she realized he had something of an aura, like a fine sheen of mist clinging to his skin. Orange, like his robes.

He turned her head gently, from side to side, taking in all of her. A shiver passed through her and she suddenly wanted to pull away. The image of Rangwar blazed bright in her mind, though this man's study of her felt entirely different. It was just men—any men—touching her. She feared she would never be normal again. He seemed to notice her discomfort.

"May I be permitted to speak with you alone? Please, don't worry." This he addressed to Brenton and Tavish. "I mean no harm, and we'll talk within sight if you like, but there is a private matter we must discuss."

Aidah felt a cold stab of fear in her breast. Was he with Rangwar, perhaps even Rangwar in disguise? Or could he possible know what had been happening to her in the dreams? He couldn't possibly know. He was Fire, not Life. It was probably something silly, like Abel the Healer's test to make sure she was really what she claimed to be.

Tavish nodded immediately; apparently the Sun Mage robes were all the proof he needed of Jardan's identity, but Brenton paused, no doubt wondering what this distant relative possibly had to say to her. He shrugged and turned to her. "Aidah?"

"We'll just go to the edge of camp. You can still see us there," Aidah suggested, lifting the hem of her skirt to navigate her way past Gair and Montrose, who had been watching the entire conversation in quiet awe.

"I understand your caution. Believe me, I wouldn't let her out of my sight for a moment. She's the first female Life Talent in Korva's line we've had in over a hundred years. But this should only take a minute," Jardan said, then crossed to Aidah's side to offer her his arm, gently leading her away.

Aidah tried to calm her pounding heart, knowing her trembling would give her away to the Sun Mage, but she couldn't help it. As always when she was afraid, her Talent became sharper, stronger, and she began getting images and thoughts from various members of the Gedar tribe. She suddenly saw an image of herself—from which person she couldn't determine—wrapped in a halo of light, more beautiful than she could possibly look right now despite the new dress. Head bowed, she looked so uncertain, perhaps on the verge of tears...she shook her head, shaking off the other person's thoughts. Aidah raised her head and tried to look confident. Who had that been? Someone by the table, surely, by the vantage point. Kendrick, perhaps. Or maybe her brother?

They moved out of earshot—even Derg's, though he was probably enjoying himself too much to overhear, lying on some Gedar mother's lap enjoying an ear scratching. Beside her, Jardan stood still, looking thoughtful. He crossed his arms over his broad chest, rocking back on his heels, rather like old Abel used to do when confronted with a difficult problem. Aidah waited, shaking either because of the cold, or her fear.

Jardan cleared his throat. "How old do I look, Miss Dernholt?"

What an odd question! It was leading somewhere but Aidah didn't know where. "Fifty...fifty-five, perhaps?" He was just beginning to develop wrinkles around his eyes and across his broad forehead. The mixture of gray and gold in his hair and beard also hinted that while older, he was by no means ancient.

"Sixty-eight, in fact. I can thank my dear mother for the youthful looks and the spring in my step. Bless her heart, she was a Life Talent like you. Korva's not the only line of mages in the Realm, though our lines are few and our numbers are steadily decreasing. It is from her that I know a little about Life Talents."

He paused, gathering his thoughts, then looked her in the eye. "Now tell me truly. Are you hiding something? I noticed you lurch away from personal contact. You keep your gaze lowered. And you may not be aware of it, but you're sending out waves of anxiety, even as we speak."

Was she? Aidah checked for her aura, and saw with horror that it was far extended again, out of her control. She struggled to draw it in. "I don't know what you mean. I've been through a lot lately, and

I've grown a bit...suspicious...of strangers." She wanted to hug herself, but she forced her arms to stay down at her sides, tried to force herself to look relaxed, unafraid.

He frowned. "That's not it, and you know it. I received a healthy dose of Life potential from my mother, though not the Talent. I can sense a few things. You're afraid of men. And touching. And above all, you don't want your brother and your uncle to know. Am I right so far?"

How could he know? They had barely met, and she doubted if Kendrick had noticed. But perhaps he had. "Did Kendrick say something to make you think this? I'm just shy. Get to know me, and you'll see what I'm really like." She pushed her chest out, tried to look taller, braver.

He reached out to touch her cheek. It was a fatherly gesture, but she flinched at the touch. She didn't mean to; it was involuntary. Jardan nodded, as if confirming something.

"Rangwar has contacted you in your dreams," he said.

13

A Choice of Paths

Aidah pulled away sharply, but she didn't know what to do. She wanted to run away, but that was ridiculous. Where would she run? He could walk back over to Brenton and tell him of his suspicions. And then where would she be? Better to talk to him now, try to settle his mind as she had Brenton's. Only she feared he would not be as easy to convince. He was a mage and had known Spirit Mages.

Biting her lip, she nodded.

Jarden nodded as well, looking solemn. "I'm sorry, child." He was silent a moment, weighing his words, while Aidah wondered what exactly he was sorry for. What did he think Rangwar had done, visiting her? Frightened her, surely. Perhaps that was what he thought. But when he asked his next question, she knew she was wrong. "How many times? How many times has he touched you?"

Aidah stared open-mouthed at him, horrified. "I—" she stuttered, for what could she say to that? The truth, she decided. At this point there was no use in lying. "Three. Maybe four times," she answered quietly, glancing back towards her uncle to see if he was still watching. He was. "He hasn't come in a few weeks, though," she added, a note of hope in her voice. Perhaps she'd unconsciously learned to shut him out.

The expression on Jardan's face was a mixture of sympathy and distress. "I'm so sorry. It wasn't your fault, you realize." He sighed. "And you're not the first he's done that to. The Gods willing, I hope you'll be the last to endure it." He placed a hand on her arm, just a simple gesture of comfort, moving slowly so that mentally she had time to prepare for it, accept it. But what did that mean, that she wasn't the first?

"Who?" Aidah asked, miserably. Rangwar was almost three hundred years old, she reminded herself. How many in that long life, had he molested? Tortured? "What did they do?"

Jardan stared off into the fields, and for the first time, he looked his age. "My mother was not of Korva's line. But she was a Spirit Mage, and those you must know are a rarity. The Emperor has long made it his policy to subvert or kill as many of our Talented as he can—he's always been most interested in his own, in Korva's line. But he takes delight in corrupting or harassing any mage born here. Because of our proximity to Landaran and our aid to Korva, he took it upon himself to drive my mother mad. She was strong, for many years. She warned me, because I had the potential to become a Life Talent and my children would also carry the potential." Jardan looked back to Aidah. "But yes. He used to visit her in dreams too, when she was young like you, when her Talent first appeared. I know it must be awful to have to endure that. But it will stop. Just know that." He grimaced.

"It has stopped," Aidah insisted, because she needed things to stay that way, and because they were safer lands now, among more mages, almost under Korva's protection. She had endured it. And it was over.

"Of course," Jardan said, nodding, but Aidah sensed he was not convinced, and that worried her. It would stop—he had told her that. It would stop when she learned how to shield herself, whenever they met up with a Spirit Mage who could teach her. She only had to hold out a little longer. Tears threatened at the corners of her eyes. She couldn't fall apart, not now, not like this.

Jardan bent over to look her in the eye. "I know you can't talk about this right now, because the others are watching. But if you need to let some of it out, if you need to scream or cry or just talk…it's a long road to Landaran. I will remain with your party until you are safe with Korva. You can tell me, and it will not go further. Do you understand?"

Aidah took a deep breath, releasing it slowly. She looked back towards Brenton and Tavish, who were both watching with anxious expressions, obviously wondering what was going on. She nodded slowly. "I understand."

"Good." Jardan smiled, straightening. "I see a lot of Korva in you. Her strength." He offered her his arm again. "Let's return to the others. It's late, and I have much to discuss with your uncle and Montrose. We need to decide which route to take, and who will come. The Gedar may or may not want to accompany us all the way to Landaran."

And if they left, that meant Gair too would probably leave, Aidah thought. She'd grown so used to his antics, it was hard imagining how it would be to travel without him.

They returned to the table where Montrose and Gair were recounting the tale of their travels to Kendrick. They had reached the part where they had been ambushed by Madhar and Rangwar's men and how Tavish had set the forest on fire. Tavish was sitting back a bit, squirming as they described things, as if he'd like to be invisible. That made Aidah realize he hadn't tried to do any practical jokes, any mischief since they'd left Hamstead. He seemed almost a different person now, quiet and withdrawn. It didn't suit him.

She sat down beside him. "They're going to be talking about how we're getting to the city," she said in a low voice as Jardan sat down to listen to the tale.

Brenton scooted close and leaned in towards Aidah. "So? What did he want? Is everything all right?"

Aidah tried to stay composed. What could she say? "His mother was a Spirit Mage," she said, thinking furiously. "He knew a few things about the, uh, problems a new Talent can have. Things that are…uh, private." Which was all true, she decided. Just not the full truth.

"Ew, sounds like something I don't want to know about," Tavish whispered, looking happy to have a distraction from the tale. But Aidah could see Jardan was watching them even as he listened. She had a feeling he missed little that was going on.

Brenton looked embarrassed. "Oh. All right," he said, and let the matter drop. At least Aidah knew how to deflect their questions. It never would have worked with her mother. She felt a keen prick of pain at the thought.

She looked at Tavish, wondering if he would answer her earlier question to him. "Want to wander the camp a bit? Learn to juggle? I bet we could be good at that," she suggested, remembering all those stolen tarts and pies in Hamstead, the rooftop walks. She wanted to leave the adult business to the adults tonight. Have some fun.

Tavish shrugged. "I'd rather stay here. I want to know about the plan, where we're headed." He looked so serious. It cut at her heart.

"Don't go off by yourself," Brenton cautioned Aidah, and returned his attention as Montrose concluded the tale. Aidah sighed. She didn't want to know their plan, their path. She'd already learned that knowing too much could be dangerous for her.

Gair glanced over, looking from Aidah to Brenton. "I could go with her, if she wants to walk around a bit. We'll stay in the camp." He grinned. "I could even show you juggling."

It said something that Tavish didn't even glare. Instead he seemed engrossed in his own thoughts.

Jardan spoke up. "Was that the first time your Talent has killed someone, Tavish?" Aidah felt her jaw drop open—how could she have forgotten? Small wonder Tavish didn't want to play!

Tavish's head snapped up, and he glared at Jardan. "Who cares? They were bad. They killed our mother." His tone was defensive, ready for a fight.

"Tavish!" She hissed, nudging him with her foot. Her little gesture only earned her a full out wave of emotion from him of self-blame, despair, pain and grief. She doubled over with the force of it, clutching at her heart.

"It's all right, Aidah," Jardan said in a calm voice, as Aidah struggled to separate her emotions from her brother's. Tavish looked somewhat horrified, realizing that something was wrong with her. Jardan continued. "It should still hurt you, Tavish, even if they were bad, as you say. It should never be easy to kill another person."

"Aidah," Tavish said, ignoring Jardan. Aidah knew that, because at the moment she was him; she was watching herself struggle with her Talent through his eyes, she was feeling his fear, his concern, and she was hearing his frantic thoughts. The separation wasn't working; instead she was being drawn further and further into him. She could even feel his Talent. It felt like she could reach his hand out and make him use it. Control him...

"Don't touch her," She—he—heard Jardan's sharp voice, and stopped the hand that had been reaching out to touch herself. She—Tavish—looked in confusion to Jardan. "It wouldn't be a good idea right now," Jardan continued. "Everyone, keep a little distance." Aidah watched Jardan look at her from Tavish's eyes. "Aidah? Where is your aura?"

Probably all over the place, she thought, but she couldn't bring herself to care at the moment. The realization dawned upon her. *She had moved Tavish's hand.*

"What's happening?" Brenton asked, and just like that, she was in him, feeling his worry, and it seemed it would be even easier, him being without any Talent, to cloud his mind, to make him do whatever she wanted. Deeper down, she felt a powerful sense of despair, but that wasn't from Brenton. Aidah wasn't sure where that was coming from. Herself?

"Her powers are surging," Jardan explained. "Give her a moment. It should hopefully pass."

Why can't I touch her? That thought came clearly from Brenton, though Aidah was pretty sure he wasn't voicing it out loud. She blinked, and then it was like seeing out of two sets of eyes: her own, and Brenton's. She could see her aura, and they were all within it, just as Jardan suspected. She couldn't seem to draw it in tighter, however. She felt a buzzing in her veins, something new she hadn't felt before. There was such an urge right now to touch one of them, to control them. It would be so easy, especially with Brenton. She knew him. He was family. And he cared deeply about her.

Jardan looked at her. "Are you back in control, Aidah?" She could sense him, but it seemed like the instant she did, there was something pushing her back out. His own Talent, perhaps. Or that Life Potential he'd mentioned.

"I need to...take a walk," she said uncertainly, and it felt like her voice was coming from far away.

Jardan nodded, and picked a spoon off the table. "One thing first," he said, and suddenly smacked her on the arm with the spoon.

"Ouch!" she yelped, but suddenly she was back in her own body, and the buzzing had stopped. She blinked and looked at him in confusion.

He nodded and said to the others, "That won't always work, you must understand, particularly if she's upset. But sometimes a physical sensation can pull them back when they're 'floating,' as they say. When they're new to this, you can tell by the facial expressions." He smiled at her.

Aidah flushed in embarrassment. As if she didn't have enough to deal with! "What would have happened if they'd touched me?" She had a feeling she didn't want to know. But she needed to learn.

Jardan frowned. "One of several possible things, and few of them good. Draining or giving life force, creating illness or health, charming, possession…the list goes on. Where your brother would have been predicable when his Talent flared up—literally—yours tends to be more unpredictable until trained."

Possession. Was that what she'd been trying to do? Why would she want to do that? "Oh," Aidah said, because really, what could she say to that? Perhaps the healer had been right. She might be better off hiding in the wagon until they reached Landaran.

"I'll still take her on that walk, if that's all right," Gair offered in a quiet voice as they all stared uncomfortably at her, making her once again wish she had Tavish's power to be invisible. Tavish looked shaken. Aidah wondered if he had felt her, poking around inside his head.

Jardan looked at Aidah. "Are you all right now?"

In the deeper sense of things, Aidah would have to say no, but her power seemed to be under control once more. "I think so," she answered quietly, feeling the gaze of Montrose and Kendrick on her. In particular she worried about Montrose. He was Gedar, and more superstitious about magic. What must he be thinking now?

Happily her Talent remained silent on the matter, as Jardan continued, "Then I think that might be a good idea." He smiled at her, in that calm, encouraging way of his. She wasted no more time but stood up, fumbling out a thank you as she hurried to follow Gair. Let them all discuss her in her absence. She just wanted to forget about things for a while.

"Too serious around here," Gair said in a mocking tone, making Aidah smile despite herself as they walked towards the firelight where the Gedar were singing, playing instruments, and dancing. She saw a fair number of townspeople among the crowd, mostly men, watching the dancing and playing cards with the Gedar. Even at night it seemed that the Gedar were making money. Gair pulled her over to a group of children practicing at various things, including dancing and card tricks. And juggling.

"I need to borrow this," Gair told one young girl who had dropped a bright red wooden ball, bending to pick it up. He looked around for another and managed to find a yellow ball of similar size, but the other balls were being used, so he shrugged and took off his cap, then began to juggle the three objects with an ease that Aidah found fascinating. It had to be quite awkward, she thought, with the different shaped objects. The children clapped, delighted by his show.

Aidah watched, trying to follow Gair's hands with her eyes, but it was difficult. "So can you show me how to do that?" She asked. If nothing else, it would be a welcome distraction.

Gair caught his woolen cap with a flourish and took a bow, a ball in each hand. "I'd be happy to," he replied, setting the balls down. Aidah raised an eyebrow at him as he took a handkerchief out of his pocket. "It's easier to start with these," he explained, handing her the handkerchief and then digging around in his pockets for another one. She hoped they were clean.

He shook out another one, then started tossing them up into the air, plucking them back as they floated down and sending them back up in a kind of dance that looked magical. Aidah stared, struck by the gracefulness of it.

Gair chuckled. "You should have seen my tumbling skills before I grew taller. I used to be so much better at this." He snatched both handkerchiefs and offered her one. "We'll start with something simple and work up," he said as she took the bit of fabric. Where he had made it seem weightless and airy, now it seemed leaden and ordinary in her hand.

She attempted to toss it up and catch it, but it had none of the grace that it had with Gair. "There's some trick to this," Aidah mumbled, trying it again.

"Of course there is," Gair said, coming around to stand behind her. The movement distracted her, making her almost miss catching the handkerchief. "The trick is to make your hands almost unseen, by moving them quickly. He touched her arm from behind, pressing in a little closer. "Allow me?" He asked, his hand closing over hers, guiding her movements.

Aidah expected to feel that all too familiar dread at his touch, the shameful fear. But there was nothing diabolical or predatory about his actions; if anything, she felt safe with his arms around her, comforted. He was only Gair, after all. Silly and awkward and young. "All right," she answered softly, feeling herself blushing.

His touch on her was gentle but firm, showing her how to flick her wrists up when she tossed the handkerchief, quick little movements as Gair had said that were almost too quick for the eye to follow. The handkerchief fluttered down a little more gracefully than before, and Aidah found herself grinning as she started to do it all on her own, Gair taking a step back to observe. "Like that?" she asked.

He nodded. "You're getting it." She practiced it with one cloth for a while, then he handed her a second kerchief, once again guiding her on how to alternate them from hand to hand. She laughed when she overreached for one, losing her balance and sending them both falling over each other's feet. It was the most normal she'd felt in weeks.

By the time she had graduated to three handkerchiefs (with the help of another boy who lent them his kerchief), it was late, and Aidah fought not to yawn. She caught sight of Tavish standing at the edge of the crowd with Kendrick, their heads bent towards each other as they talked, watching her. She wondered how the planning had gone. After a very sloppy toss, she sighed and handed the kerchiefs back their respective owners. "I'm beat," she announced to Gair, and walked over to her brother and cousin. Tavish took a step back as she came near. Apparently Jardan's warning had taken root in him. Yet another person afraid of what she could do—and her twin brother, at that. She sighed.

"The Gedar still want to come," Tavish said, which wasn't really a surprise to Aidah. Despite their initial misgivings, they had come to accept her. And she in turn felt comfortable here. She nodded, and Tavish yawned. "And I'm heading to bed."

"We'll be heading home for the night as well," Kendrick said, as they began walking towards Montrose's wagon. "But Jardan and I will be back in the morning. We'll be accompanying you all to Landaran." He was smiling, no trace of fear or hesitation as he guided them through the other wagons and campfires. Then again, he was a trainee, Aidah reminded herself. Perhaps he had seen other Life Talent trainees and their accidents. He glanced at her. "The juggling was looking good. Was it fun?"

Aidah smiled. For at least an hour or two, she had felt perfectly natural. Normal. "It was," she replied, nodding at Kendrick. "Was there much discussion before the Gedar made their decision?"

Kendrick shrugged. "They're committed to helping out—and they'll be well rewarded for it. We'll all head out in the morning. Shouldn't be too tough a road from here. Korva will probably send a Spirit Mage to help you with your power until we reach Landaran."

Aidah let out a breath of relief. That would indeed be a great help.

With that, Kendrick gave a little bow and headed back towards his grandfather. Tavish and Aidah headed towards Montrose's wagon. Gair followed close behind, escorting them until they had reached the steps. Tavish headed inside, but Aidah paused, turning to face Gair.

"See you tomorrow," Gair said, looking shy and ungainly. He dug his toe into the dirt, looking down.

Aidah found herself blushing and looking down as well. She could still remember his arms around her, helping her with the juggling. But she didn't want to remember it as anything more than a friendly gesture. The desires were too new. Too frightening. "I guess so," she agreed, taking the first step up. The question burned in her. What would he do once they reached Landaran? Would he remain with Montrose's clan? It wouldn't be long now, and she might never see him again after that. It was best that they not get too close. "See you," she finished, and headed into the wagon.

Despite how tired she was, it was quite a while before she fell asleep.

☼

Arms around her, from behind. Hot breath on her shoulder, warmth of flesh against flesh, the feel of a firm chest, tight grip, securing her. Entrapping her.

And then a sharp pain of penetration, and suddenly Aidah realized this was not some simple dream of being held in someone's arms, but *him*, Rangwar, come again to her in her head. "No," she whispered, struggling, but she was hopelessly outmatched. "No!" She cried out, scratching at the strong arms, but she might as well be scratching marble—any scratch she managed to inflect, he immediately healed. She screamed as he bit her shoulder, shuddering at the sound of his laughter as he languidly raped her.

"And you thought I would go away so easily. Foolish girl," Rangwar chided her.

"We're almost there," she hissed at him, feeling hot tears sliding down her cheeks at the burning shame of being violated once again. She wanted him out! She willed him gone. But even as she sensed her powers trying to reach out to attack him, he batted them away, as simply as batting away a pathetic fly.

"No, you're not quite there. I may yet be able to retrieve you.

And if I don't, well then, I suppose you'll just have to say farewell to your father and grandfather." Rangwar's hips stilled a moment as he played with her hair. "Hm. Perhaps I can do some damage to your little entourage as well. Kill your little Gedar friends—filthy things. I can't believe you let one of them touch you."

Aidah gritted her teeth, determined not to show weakness, even though all she wanted to do right now was curl up and cry. "You're a monster," she said, thankful that she hadn't sat in on the meeting, that she didn't know the plan. He couldn't take from her that which she didn't know.

For several moments there was no talking, as he rutted against her, until he was spent and satisfied. Aidah didn't feel much pleasure, for which she was grateful. She hated this. She hated him. Afterwards, he petted her hair, one arm still holding her, though she longed to pull away from him. "I sense that wasn't as fulfilling for you this time. A shame. I'll make it up to you, next time." He kissed her cheek. She flinched. "You may not know your direct path, my morsel, but you're traveling with a caravan of wagons. Truthfully, there are only a few different options they can take. And while Jardan—ah yes, and I do remember his mother, sweet thing—might be able to protect you from most things, he can't protect you from everything." His kissed her again, this time on the lips. She resisted the urge to press her lips together or bite back—both of which she knew he would take as an opportunity to punish her further. It was better to have as little reaction as possible. Sometimes.

What did he mean, 'not everything?' What could he be planning? It could be a ploy to make her worry, Aidah reasoned. But then again, maybe not. As for her father...her heart clenched. "How do I know you haven't killed him already?"

"I'm afraid you don't," Rangwar told her matter-of-factly. "Not unless you want to come with me astrally to see for yourself." And trust him to get her spirit back into her body? Aidah didn't think so.

Rangwar chuckled and she frowned, wishing, hoping that he was done with her for the moment. He pet the side of her face. "Poor Aidah. Even if you do make it to Korva, you will not be rid of me. Accept it. You will be mine. Or I will torment you until you go mad. I let Jardan's mother go. She grew too old, and I tired of her. But it was not for any defense of hers. You will never keep me out. And if you do not submit, I will destroy you."

Aidah wanted to shut her ears, drive him out; she wanted not to believe him. But she remembered that solemn look on Jardan's face, the way he had said the wording. *It will stop someday.* She had the sinking suspicion that he had known that Rangwar would torment her again. And if what Rangwar said was true…if there was no way to block him ou…

"No," she whispered, feeling perilously close to the edge already. She couldn't bear this night after night, month after month. She couldn't even imagine it continuing longer. Years. "No!" She screamed, pushing at him with everything she had, with muscle, with mind, with spirit, anything.

Rangwar chuckled. "Yes," he said, quite amused by her ineffective attacks. And then just like that, he released her.

☼

Aidah felt hands on her, holding her down. It seemed like the world was shaking, until she realized it was her that was being shaken. Someone—her uncle—was calling her name in a frantic tone. She opened her eyes and saw that she was in the bunk bed in Montrose's wagon, being shaken by Brenton while Montrose and Tavish looked on worriedly. She sat up, alarmed. Had they known what kind of dream she'd been having? "I'm awake!" she told them, brushing off Brenton's hands. "What's happening?" Was it possible that the camp was being attacked, as Hamstead had been?

"You were dreaming," Tavish answered, looking scared. He hung back, and Aidah noticed he was trembling.

"You were screaming," Brenton said in a soft voice, his hand still on her shoulder as if afraid to let go. "You kept saying no, and then something about already killed, and 'monster'," he continued and Aidah thought frantically, wondering exactly what all she had said, while Rangwar had been with her. Could they tell what had been happening to her? Apparently her reaching out with her Gift had done one thing. She didn't know if that was a good thing or not.

"It was…a very bad dream," Aidah said, quietly hoping that the excuse would work again. She wasn't sick this time, nor fevered. By the looks on their faces, they weren't buying it.

"Aidah…" Brenton said with a sigh, shaking his head, the worry coming off of him in waves. "Was it—you know? The Emperor?" He almost whispered the last word, as if Rangwar would hear and immediately appear. For all that they understood about the

178

powers of the Spirit, perhaps he could.

She said nothing, but he read the answer in her eyes, in her silence. "I'm so sorry, Aidah," Brenton said, holding his arms out in an invitation to be held, if she wanted. Maybe it was because the visit was too fresh in her mind, or maybe it was the stress of having journeyed through so much without guidance. Aidah hiccupped, and a sob escaped before she could hold it back. She dove for the safety of her uncle's arms as the tears overtook her, crying hard as he held her tight, letting it out, the grief for her parents, her grandfather. Herself.

Aidah felt a hand on her head, gently pushing her hair back— her brother's hand, she knew, just from the feel of it, the energy. She could feel his heart, inside and out, how much he loved her, how angry he was that this was happening to her, and that he couldn't do anything to help her. It was dangerous for him to be near her, when she was like this, when she was barely in control.

"Tavish," she said, quietly wiping at her tears so that she could look at him. "I need you to go outside for a moment." She immediately felt his hurt, as she knew she would. At least the anger stopped, and that was good. She couldn't handle anger in her head at the moment, even if it wasn't directed at her.

The hand on her head lifted, and Aidah could sense as her brother moved away, out of the wagon, until feel of him was soft and dull. She breathed a sigh of relief even as she felt guilty for sending him away. They were so close, and she knew he only wanted to protect her.

Brenton cleared his throat. "He's gone." He pulled back a little, enough for Aidah to see his face. He looked like he was at war with himself, between being afraid for her and being afraid of her. "Now, talk to me, Aidah. What happened? Can I help you in any way?"

Her walls were crumbling; Aidah felt raw and exposed. "Torture," she said, because that was the best word for it. She still couldn't bring herself to tell Brenton the details. They were too ugly, and too shameful. She didn't think she needed to tell him the details anyway. He probably could guess. "He said his men have Papa and Grandfather. He said that he would kill them, unless I come to him."

"They're still alive? Did you see them?" The hope in Brenton's voice told Aidah that he had long since written them off as dead. She shrugged unhappily.

"He said that he could show me, but I didn't want to try it," she replied, wondering if she should have. It would have been nice to at least see them, and know the truth.

Brenton looked alarmed. "Right—don't let him. Don't agree to anything or take up any offers from him." He swallowed, running a hand through his hair. "You realize even if they're still alive, that he's never going to release them. They would be too useful to control both you and your brother."

Aidah nodded glumly. She knew that in her heart, even if she didn't want to think about it. A man who could do such things to a girl...she shuddered to think how prisoners were treated in that realm. "I'm not going to surrender to him, ever. But I don't know..." she looked away, feeling miserable, heartsick. "I don't know how much I can take." Already, thoughts of death seemed less frightening and more appealing.

A moment of silence stretched between them, before Brenton laid a hand on her shoulder. "We're going to get you to safety, soon. Korva will protect you. I know it must be hard, but we need you to last just a little bit longer." A look of pain crossed his face, a show of weakness that Aidah couldn't ever remember seeing in him before. "I've done my best to try to protect you, and Tavish. I'm sorry that I haven't done better."

A stab of guilt struck at Aidah. This, she told herself, was why she must not talk to others about the horrors that she was going through. This was why, perhaps, Jardan had offered himself as someone she could go to. Breaking down was not something she could afford to do, for her uncle's sake. She gave Brenton a fierce embrace. "You've done great. We're here, not in the Innis Empire. You can't protect us from everything."

Brenton nodded. "I know. But I wish I could." He stood up. "Are you okay for now? Do you think you could sleep, or do you want to sit up front with me? We're going to try to get moving with the first light."

Aidah had no idea what time it was, but it must still be late, for it was dark. "I don't think I could sleep right now. Can I sit with you up front? And perhaps with Derg too?" It didn't matter that neither Brenton nor Derg could truly protect her from Rangwar, but at least she could feel safe, snuggled between the two of them. As she had clung to Derg's soft fur when she was young after scraping a knee, she could do the same now, at least for a little.

"I'm sure Derg would be honored," Brenton said with a smile, and led Aidah out of the wagon.

14

The Road to Landaran

The caravan was on the move again, thank the gods, Tavish thought, as he tried to get used to yet another horse. This time he rode a more seasoned mare named Leya, one of the horses from Jardan's stable. Tavish had been a little hesitant to take another steed, especially given the fate of his first one, but both Jardan and Kendrick agreed that for any kind of fight, he needed to have his own horse. When he'd related what had happened to Buck, Jardan had nodded solemnly. "You will lose many horses over a lifetime of service to the Doane Republic. Know that their spirits reside with the love of Meira for their devotion and assistance. Leya will be a good companion; she will not shy away from loud noises or explosions."

Hopefully that meant that she wouldn't buck him off, Tavish thought, trying to imagine how one fought from astride a horse. Clearly he had a lot to learn.

That was one of the objectives today, as the Gedar caravan slowly wheeled along the main trail towards Lathe, a small village which supposedly was the last town still in the Morgaine foothills, before the larger town of Colmsford at the proper beginning of the Lowlands.

The debate yesterday had hinged on two paths south. One veered to the southwest, following the Lamar river down to the city of Geraine, then turning east down the Glynnis River and reaching Landaran at the mouth of the Krimean Sea. This was a major road. The alternate trail veered towards the east from Colmsford, across the open plains to meet with the much smaller Turis river, then cutting south across the Guardian Foothills to Landaran. This route was shorter, but less populated and nearer to the Krimean Sea. If Rangwar had found a way past the Guardian statues lining the coast of the sea, he could very well have men hidden in the small towns there. Maybe even a small army.

In the end, they decided to stay with the main route down the Lamar River, even if that added a few extra days to the journey. Either way, as far as Tavish saw it, he was going to try and use the travel time to take advantage of the fact that he had a full Sun Mage traveling with them; someone who could continue his training in case Rangwar tried to pull anything else.

Jardan rode beside Montrose's wagon, where it would be the easiest for him to protect Aidah in the case of an attack. Aidah sat wrapped in a blanket between Brenton and Montrose, but she had fallen asleep sometime in the early morning, missing the packing up of the caravan or the sights of the lightly forested hillsides as the wagon creaked along on the wide dirt road, lightly dusted with snow. After Aidah's screaming in the middle of the night, Tavish could hardly blame her for sleeping now.

Since Jardan was staying near Aidah, it was only natural for Tavish and Kendrick to ride alongside him, with Kendrick just slightly in the rear. Tavish had to admit that while he still thought Kendrick's taste (and timing) in pranks stunk, he'd regained a lot of Tavish's respect by his reaction to the death of Nera Holt. Now they were chatting as if they were brothers, regaling each other with stories of the mishaps from when their Talents had first appeared.

"And that's how I set Garl's hair on fire," Tavish finished, basking in the glow of attention from Kendrick and Jardan.

Jardan laughed. "At least you didn't set fire to your Nanna's, erm, 'derriere.' But setting fire to the town bully definitely counts a close second." His gray eyes twinkled, matching the hazy brightness of the day.

Kendrick snorted. "I still think flame-broiling Mama's prune pudding at Winterfest was the funniest."

"You did that intentionally," Jardan remarked dryly.

"Why would you flame dessert?" Tavish wanted to know.

Jardan and Kendrick exchanged glances, and Kendrick grimaced. "You haven't tasted my mama's prune pudding."

Tavish couldn't help but laugh. It felt good, the weight of things lifting for a moment. Last night he hadn't slept well either, dreaming of the faces of the men he had set fire to in the wood, the smell of their burning flesh. He needed talk about lighter things, but of course they couldn't do that all day. "So what am I learning about today?"

Jardan rubbed the pommel of his saddle, looking thoughtful. "Let me review a few things with you first. I assume that your previous instructor taught you about the basic nature of your gift, yes?"

Tavis appreciated that Jardan's hadn't named Nera. "My Talent means I can see and control things called 'light waves' and 'heat waves'—mostly heat waves, at the moment," Tavish answered. He still didn't exactly understand what it all meant, but he did know that the light waves were a lot harder to control. That was why the invisibility spell had been such an achievement.

"Very good," Jardan said, pausing as a few young Gedar on donkeys raced past them, apparently bored with the slow pace of the wagons. "You'll learn more about those lines that you can see with your third eye when you take classes in Landaran. You'll also learn reading, science, and mathematics, if you haven't already."

"I have to read?" Tavish was horrified. He'd learned his letters in Hamstead, but it could hardly be called a strength for him.

"You're going to have a ton of reading," Kendrick chimed in, giving a dramatic groan. "We're not only the protectors of the realm; in many places we're the closest thing to law enforcement, and they expect us to know just about everything in case they need to mediate something, or if they need someone upstanding to testify at a local court." It was obvious that it was something he didn't relish doing, and Tavish couldn't blame him.

"There's a lot to being a mage, isn't there," Tavish said, feeling more and more overwhelmed at the prospect. He'd always envisioned himself fighting wars, perhaps saving a village from a forest fire or defeating a monster. One thing he had not ever imagined was making decisions or judgments. He was going to be powerful. The notion was more than a little frightening.

"You'll have plenty of time to learn," Jardan assured him. "You'll be apprenticed to a Master Sun Mage until you're twenty. You'll assist them in the duties, gradually learning the art as well as the station." He smiled at his grandson. "It's not always the case that they pair up relatives. But in my case it worked best to be able to attend to my holdings and the local area's needs while training Kendrick." He stretched in the saddle, popping a few joints. "We're allowed a maximum of two apprentices. So it would be possible for you to be assigned to me as well."

Tavish smiled, but he wasn't sure if the idea appealed to him or not—on the one hand, he would enjoy learning and practicing with Kendrick, and Jardan seemed like a decent fellow. The only problem was that if Jardan stayed here at his estate much of the year, then Tavish wouldn't be near Aidah, to watch over her.

"In any case," Jardan continued, "That will be decided by Korva or Grant Gail, Head of the Sun Mage House." At Tavish's bemused look, he chuckled. "The numbers of mages are few. Storm Mages are the most common; we currently have over a hundred of them roaming throughout the Doane Reuplic. There are currently somewhere around forty Sun Mages at this time. About half of them live either in Landaran or Geraine." Tavish glanced at Aidah who had woken up some time during their conversation. Jardan continued. "There are only seven with the Life Talent currently living in the Doane."

So few... Tavish could see the consternation in his sister's eyes to be such a rarity. He knew she hated to be singled out; she preferred to stay in the background, unseen. He doubted that would be an option for her any more.

Aidah sat up a little straighter, and Jardan reigned in his horse to ride just beside the wagon so that she could join in the conversation, despite the constant jangling of the bells and pots on the wagon. "Will I be trained directly by Korva?" she asked, her tired voice just barely loud enough to hear over the clatter.

Jardan nodded. "She'll want to keep you close, and I don't think she's had an apprentice since Gabriel, who is nearly 90 now. It's high time she took another."

Yet again, Tavish thanked the gods that his Talent was Light, not Life. He couldn't imagine having The Protector as his teacher! "So wait a minute. If firestarters can see light waves, what do Spirit Mages see?"

"They see life energies—spirit, and the astral plane," Jardan replied, glancing over at Tavish. "You would have to ask your sister as far as what it looks like to her. The Life Talent, in addition, works very differently than the Light Talent—there are other 'senses' that they have that don't really correspond to the usual that either Storm or Sun Mages possess. Their gift is more nebulous, harder to define."

"Is it harder to control that Tavish's?" Aidah asked, the look on her face telling Tavish that she probably already knew the answer. She sighed as Jardan nodded.

"My mother said the Life Talent is not only the rarest, but the most confusing and frustrating to control." He gave Aidah a sad smile. "But it is also considered the most powerful. They say the god Ughar was once a man, who unlocked the secrets of the brain and produced the first Life Talents. He later unlocked the key to immortality—without need for feeding on life energy." He looked down. "They say Rangwar is trying to do the same."

Tavish stared at Jardan in horror. "Is that even a possibility?" Just one more reason why he needed to train so he could go and kill the man!

Jardan shrugged. "I don't know. We know the Ancient Ones could do things like create new creatures; there are written works describing their experiments, and the Life Talent was a part of that. But I don't know if I'd go as far to say that men can become gods. Much knowledge has been lost since those times."

It was probably better not to dwell on such things, Tavish thought, shifting uncomfortably in his saddle. A stray butterfly lighted on his horse's mane only be shaken away by the animal as they passed under the shadow of cottonwood trees. "I'm sure even the most powerful Spirit Mage burns in a fire," he said under his breath.

Kendrick muttered something under his breath and Jardan frowned as he replied. "Not necessarily. You've only seen the Emperor in his astral form so far, from what I gather. Believe me when I tell you he is far more powerful in person. Without your own Spirit Mage to shield you, you would not even be able to formulate the thought of attacking him."

To Tavish, the topic had become old very fast. "So I'll surprise him," he insisted. He fidgeted in the saddle, noting that the steady pace of his horse was beginning to chafe areas he never knew could be chafed. Even though they were leaving the mountains and the highlands, the air was still bitterly cold. "So teach me something. Assume I have Sis or some Spirit Mage helping me. What can I do then?"

Jardan chuckled, looking between Aidah who was avidly listening, and Tavish. "All right. Then assuming that Aidah is actually shielding her side—while possibly trying to subvert or close the minds of the enemy—you could perform an area attack to hamper the enemy mage's attention. A favorite of mine includes melting the ground beneath them. It's less showy than a fireball, but it is particularly effective against large numbers or against enemy mages who might otherwise deflect a personal attack."

That gave Tavish a thing or two to think about. In the forest, he had done something of an area attack, hitting multiple targets. But melting the ground? That was impressive. Would he really be able to do that?

A crazy thought occurred to Tavish. "Is that how the Krimean Sea was formed? Did Sun Mages melt the ground too much?"

Jardan chuckled, shaking his head, but there was a nervousness to his laugh that rubbed at Tavish's senses. He had a feeling there was more truth to his guess than the mage wanted to admit. Jardan looked at the road before them, sighing. "We don't know the full truth, to be honest. We have tales about the Ancients, that they had skills and devices of unimaginable power. They could cure any disease, it is said. They travelled to the heavens and back. They could kill an entire city with an object no larger than a travel sack. And as I mentioned before, some of them claimed to have achieved immortality. But they were still human, with human faults. Including such things as greed, envy, pride, and anger."

Tavish leaned in closer, his attention fixed as Jardan told the tale. "We don't know what provoked them, the Ancients. Perhaps it was territory. Perhaps it was the love of a woman. What we know, however, is that there was a great war, greater than any that have happened since. With all their power, all their knowledge, they fought each other in the city of Inniswold. The mountains rose up; earthquakes tore the land apart, and the sea came crashing in. Thus the Krimean Sea was formed. It is said that beneath the Krimean Sea, hundreds, perhaps thousands of feet below the water's surface, one can still find Inniswold. It is also said that the waters are red, for this reason, because of the blood spilt, and the red dust of the mountains that were demolished."

"Wouldn't have wanted to be around in those times," Kendrick said with a nervous laugh. He came up close and poked Tavish in the side with his scabbard. "We know those tales are true. We know, because every once in a while, strange artifacts wash up on the shore. The scholars have tried to figure out what they are, but nobody knows."

"Wow," Tavish said, shivering. A thought came to him. "So…we're what's left? Since they discovered the Talents and all?" How many people had died?

Jardan nodded. "The Ancients had spread wide, which is why there are still the Talented in many lands, including our own. I believe, however, that we have become more rare over time. But that is only my theory. It is possible we were always a rarity." He shrugged. "In any case, a great deal of knowledge was lost. Spirit Mages were said to have created several breeds of magical creatures, including the Gerenuk, wyrrets, rocs, and Lupas. We don't know how to do that anymore."

"Well that's too bad," Tavish said, grinning over at Aidah. "That would have been neat if you'd been able to create something. Maybe a flying horse!" She laughed, which made him feel good. She looked a ton better than she had in recent days. Then another thought came to him. "Wait—so the Doane touches the Krimean Sea, but I thought the Doane Republic started with Korva the Protector. How is that possible?"

Jardan looked grim. "The remnants of the Ancients regrouped, and formed new cities, and a new empire: the Innis Empire. The Doane here was nothing but a tiny land of Gedar, Lupas, and common families in sheepherding, farming or mining. Until Rangwar. Korva led a rebellion against him, and fled the lands, crossing the Krimean Sea. Two thousand refugees came with her. Those were the seeds of what the Republic is today."

Two thousand, Tavish thought—and now there were cities ten times that in population. How the realm had changed in just over two hundred years. Of course it was possible there had been more refugees that had arrived since then, as well as the integration with the local peoples. Including his relatives in the Morgaine Range. "So what made Korva start a rebellion?" Tavish caught a look from Aidah, one of caution and fear. Did she have an idea?

Jardan opened his mouth to answer, but then he paused. He squinted, looking towards the south, and Tavish noticed something—a little group of black specks in the air. Birds, perhaps?

But if they were, he realized they must be uncommonly large, for they were swiftly growing bigger, travelling towards the caravan. Jardan grimaced. "Aidah, get into the wagon. Now."

Aidah was looking at the sky as well, and then with a whimper, she was scrambling to get back into the wagon, as Montrose scooted his large frame over, trying to cover the doorway behind him, looking scared but determined. Tavish blew a breath in relief; whatever the flying creatures were, they would have a difficult time of getting Aidah out of the wooden house on wheels; the windows were small, and with Montrose protecting the door leading to the front of the wagon where it was tethered to the horses, that left only the small door at the back of the wagon for him and the others to defend. "What are those things?" he asked, trying to get a feel for what to use, what to expect. One thing he didn't want to do was set the wagons on fire.

"Vespyres," Jardan snarled, brandishing his sword. "I'd wager that Rangwar sent them; they're impervious to fire and heat. Magical constructs—they are typically found living in or near volcanoes in the south. Use cold and steel to attack them."

Steel? Tavish pulled out his short sword, thinking it was probably worse than useless, and wondering how he'd be able to use any *cold* magic, seeing as he hadn't really learned that trick yet. Kendrick's face was set in a grimace as he pulled out a thin-edged rapier; he waved Tavish to come join him at the rear of the wagon, leaving Jardan near the front.

"Also watch out for their blood—it's molten!" Jardan shouted back at them, and then he pulled on the draft horse's reins, slowing the wagon to a halt. Tavish wondered if it would be better to make a run for it, but where would they run to? The next town was days away. He keps his eyes on the sky, able to make out more and more features now, as the shapes started to descend. There were six of them. They appeared somewhat humanoid in the body, with large batlike wings, dipping and soaring with the wind. Their heads reminded Tavish of raptors, or vultures. Their feet were claws like those of a great hawk, outstretched, ready to grab, or rend.

The Gedar gave a shout, halting their horses, pulling out swords, axes, and even pitchforks to use as weapons, but the vespyres ignored them entirely, diving straight for Montrose's wagon. Two of them landed on the roof, and Tavish saw that they actually had little hands like bats as well, at the crook of their wings, which they used to hold onto the wagon as they hung upside down, trying to enter through the small windows. From inside the wagon, he heard Aidah shriek.

"Jardan!" Tavish screamed, seeing now that being on horseback was useless; the creatures moved like mad things, scrambling over the wagon and trying to find a way in. He rode up to the back of the wagon and leaped off of his horse, just barely managing to grab hold along the side, clinging to that with one hand as he swung his short sword with the other, aiming for one of the vespyres' feet. The metal of the sword clanged uselessly off the wagon as the creature leapt onto the roof, heading for the other window.

Jardan brought his horse around, his sword glinting oddly in the sunlight—with ice, Tavish realized. He stabbed at the wing of one of the vespyres, and Tavish saw the wound hiss and steam. As blood dribbled out and touched the ground, a small flame appeared in the grass beside the drops.

"Tavish, if you can't perform cold magic, keep an eye for fires to put out. Their skin is hot and their blood even hotter." Tavish hurried to put out the flames with his Talent.

Kendrick, meanwhile, was sending off little ice darts from his hands, his face showing the amount of effort it was taking him to do the exact opposite of a Sun Mage's nature, to pull heat rather than gather it. He managed to strike one in the chest and it crashed into a bush, but two others succeeded in joining their brethren on the wagon. Tavish found himself face to face with one of the hellish creatures.

He squeaked in surprise, thrusting out with his short sword, but the creature was quicker, darting to one side. A searing pain struck his hand as the vespyre raked its claws into Tavish's skin. Tavish was barely able to hold on, switching the sword to his left hand to hold onto the wagon with his right and thankful that he was nearly ambidextrous. He thrust with the sword again, but the creature took flight, flapping its wings just enough to dive towards Montrose and the horses, screeching with its claws extended. Montrose fell back from the creature, looking panicked, but Jardan was there, stabbing forward with his frozen sword. He ran the creature through and Montrose yelped as a drop of fiery blood landed on his trousers, setting the fabric smoking. Tavish again quickly worked to disperse the heat. The vespyre fell to the ground in a steaming heap.

Two down, and four more to go. Tavish thought furiously to figure out how to take out the others. The vespyre who had managed to crawl into the wagon emerged from one of the windows, arms wrapped tight around Aidah who was desperately trying to struggle free. She grimaced in pain, her eyes desperately seeking Tavish's. "Help!"

Jardan was too far away to use his cold steel. Tavish scrambled onto the top of the wagon, intent on stopping the creature from flying off with his sister at any cost. He wasn't sure whether to use his short sword or not. What if he accidentally hit Aidah? Tavish settled for grabbing hold of the creature's legs, wincing as he felt the heat. Its skin felt like stone burning from within.

The vespyre squawked in Tavish's face, its beady black eyes showing more intelligence than Tavish expected. Its hands were busy holding onto Aidah, dragging her further and further out of the window, its wings folded tight against its body. It gripped the rim of the window with clawed feet, and snapped at Tavish with its sharp beak.

Tavish dodged to the side.

He charged forward, but unfortunately, there was still the other vespyres on the roof behind him; One vespyre grabbed at the leather of Tavish's vest with its talons, lifting him off the ground with powerful thrusts its wings.

It was more instinct than anything else. Tavish knew that heat would be useless, but he remembered how he had bent light for the invisibility spell. With a sudden surge, he threw as much bent light as possible at the creature. Light flashed and blinded it, half blinding Tavish as well; he blinked to clear his eyes. The creature let him go, and he swung hard with his sword, feeling it connect with flesh, sinking in. They landed back on the roof of the wagon and Tavish grabbed onto the side to keep from falling off.

He heard a whoop of joy from somewhere—Kendrick, maybe—but Tavish didn't have time to celebrate. The other vespyre still had Aidah, and he wasn't about to allow it to carry her off. He let Kendrick put out the fires started by the spill of vespyre blood, and jumped to grab onto Aidah's ankles, as the vespyre lifted her from the roof. Tavish felt himself lifted up into the air as the vespyre struggled to fly. But the two of them were too heavy for the creature.

Despite powerful strokes of its wings, they all landed in a heap on the ground, the impact knocking the breath out of Tavish, rocks on the road scraping his shoulder.

Tavish no longer had his short sword—he'd left it stuck in the other vespyre in order to grab onto Aidah. As he tried to pull the infernal beast off his sister, the remaining two vespyres landed nearby, clawing at him, trying to get a hold of his arms. Tavish wasn't sure if it was to keep him from fighting back or to carry the both of them off. He didn't want to find out.

The vespyres, however, had apparently forgotten about the two other mages. Before they could secure the twins, Jardan and Kendrick attacked, one stabbing with his icy sword, the other with his ice darts. Before Tavish had even regained his breath, it was over. He felt flames on his clothing and instinctively doused them, as Jardan shoved the dead vespyres off of him. Taking stock of things, Tavish found that his sister and he were scratched and singed, but otherwise fine. Aidah sobbed and hugged him hard, crying against his shoulder.

He held on tight to her, uncomfortably close to tears himself. That had been just a little too close. If one of the other creatures had managed to properly grab him...

They both would have been on their way to Rangwar.

"I've got you," Tavish said over and over, letting Jardan and Kendrick take care of the bodies, not wanting to let go, even for a moment. He wasn't going to lose his sister. He wasn't going to let Rangwar take anyone else.

Sooner or later, he'd find a way to kill the Emperor.

15

Tales and Ghosts

The rest of the day, Aidah rode behind Tavish, unwilling to be apart from him and no longer trusting the safety of Montrose's wagon. That was fine with Tavish. Despite the little scare the night before and the whole possession thing, he trusted his sister, and it felt better to have her near him. If that was her doing or just his nature, he wasn't certain. Nor did he care.

After the attack of the vespyre, they rode in silence for several miles. As the day began to wane, Jardan led Tavish and Kendrick in exercises to pull heat from things, trying to make them as cool as possible, just in case there was another similar attack. Tavish was able to produce a little frost on an apple at one point, but that was about it. Still, it was progress.

They reached the hamlet of Lothe just after sunset. Lothe was much more like Hamstead in size and character, though in the hilly forested land here, it was timber and woodworking that seemed to take precedence over mining and sheep herding. The Gedar set up camp just outside town, and once again, the locals came to watch the Gedar perform and buy wares. As children of the Gedar found a patch of ground to perform their acrobatics and juggling, Kendrick pulled Tavish aside, a mischievous grin on his face.

Tavish raised his eyebrows in question at Kendrick. He could see Aidah over with Gair, trying her hand at the juggling scarves thing again. Though she looked ungainly, it looked like she was having fun. Kendrick leaned over to speak softly in his ear, "Have you ever tried throwing miniature fireballs? You can play catch with them, if you're with another Firestarter." He chuckled. "Even juggle with them. I've done it before; it's a real crowd pleaser."

"They don't get scared?" Tavish had to admit it sounded like fun. Also, it was practice. Anything he could do at this point to increase his skills, any training, he would grab at.

"Actually, it's one of the tricks we use to help people get over their fear of fire Talents, because you know typically they hear the stories about us as children burning down the village and whatnot." Kendrick took a few steps back. "Come on—I'll show you. It's no harder than holding a flame—well maybe just a little, but not that much." He reached out his hand, and flame erupted, hovering just an inch above his flesh, in a tight little ball.

Tavish squinted, looking at it, trying to figure it out. Generally he just gathered the heat together enough to start the fire, or increased it to build the flames higher, because fire had to consume something. But the way that Kendrick was doing it was a little different. He was continually intensifying the heat, and it was almost *sucking* air into the midst of it, to fuel it.

It was actually the way he'd flamed the enemies in the forest, but in a much smaller, more controlled form.

Before Tavish could dwell long on that, however, Kendrick was tossing the ball of flame towards him. "Catch!"

"Hey!" Tavish cried, worried that he'd have to dispel it the instant it caught on his clothing. But he managed to catch it in his hand. Fire couldn't touch him; it was as if he had some kind of barrier always in place, protecting him. Thus it rested just above the skin of his palm, as he stared at it in wonder.

"Perfect! Now this is the tricky part. I'm going to release control of it, and you'll have to keep it going. That's how it works— we just take turns fueling and controlling it. That way it doesn't make either of us too tired." Kendrick kept his hand outstretched, concentrating on the orb of flame. Tavish noticed that they were gathering a small audience, of locals and Gedar alike.

Tavish wrapped his senses around the fire, trying to mimic what he was seeing with his own Talent. He felt the control slip, as Kendrick drew his own influence away. The flame flickered, dangerously close to snuffing out, but Tavish managed to push harder, bringing it back to life. It wasn't as easy as starting fires, but Kendrick was right. It was within his ability.

Wrinkling his brow in concentration, he tossed it back, trying to keep the ball from disintegrating or flashing out of control. And then Kendrick's hold was on it, both physical and magical, and Tavish was able to let go. Tavish grinned. He was sweating with the effort, but he was also having fun.

He readied himself as Kendrick made the next toss.

Aidah tried her hand at juggling for a while, but it became apparent that even the youngest Gedar children were better than her, at least at the moment. She needed more practice, but it was disconcerting to practice in front of an audience. So after a bit she stopped and turned to watch some of the others, including Gair who not only was juggling, but had found a smooth log to balance on as well, rolling it as he tossed colored balls into the air. Either he was growing used to his new height, or he simply loved performing, for he wasn't making any errors that she could see, as graceful as a cat. Or a monkey, she thought, smiling and trying to hold back a giggle.

After watching him for a few minutes, she began to hear murmurs from the crowd, something about fire mages, and a game of catch? Aidah turned, and she saw a flash of orange in the midst of a crowd that had gathered to watch. Curious, she walked over, and soon saw the source. Apparently her brother was back up to his antics—only this time, with Kendrick as a partner. The two of them were sweating, exerting themselves, but they were also laughing, as they tossed what looked like pure fire back and forth. The spectators cheered, and a few onlookers tossed coins at the boys' feet.

It was good to see Tavish laughing and being himself again, even though there was a faint twinge of regret that it wasn't her that he was having fun with. Still, Kendrick seemed like a decent fellow. It was also nice to know they had family, and youths around their age in this land that was growing more and more unfamiliar with each coming day.

Aidah struggled to find a decent vantage point to watch, silently cursing her lack of stature, when someone pulled at her sleeve. She turned and found a young girl in peasant skirts staring up at her, and a concerned looking mother holding a crying baby. The baby couldn't be more than a few months old, but its skin looked waxen and pale. The mother looked at her with a mixture of awe and need. "You are the Spirit Mage, are you not?"

Even though the woman looked harmless, Aidah couldn't help

the twinge of fear that went through her. She looked around, but neither Jardan nor Brenton were near. Rubbing the back of her neck, she shrugged. "I'm Talented in Spirit. But I'm not a mage yet." Even that much information was dangerous to divulge. But the woman looked desperate.

The woman bobbed a curtsy, her tattered skirts brushing against Aidah's new dress. "One of the Gedar told me you might help. We haven't had a Spirit Mage in the village for a long time. We live too far from Landaran." She tilted her hold on the baby, so that Aidah could see it. It looked unwell, with grayish skin and a runny nose. "My baby is dying—consumption. Can you heal him?"

Aidah opened her mouth, horrified at the thought. Fortunately, at that moment, Jardan appeared at her side, casually taking her elbow in a move both to reassure her and to protect her. The woman blanched at the sight of his orange mage robes but curtsied to him as well. "My baby is sick."

"I'm truly sorry to hear that, madam," Jardan said in a soft voice, leading Aidah and the woman away from the crowd where they could talk. "But Aidah is completely untrained in her Talent. She cannot heal your infant."

The woman looked adamant. "She says she has the Spirit Talent," she insisted, holding her baby tighter. "She can heal."

"I don't know how," Aidah said. Could she heal him? Was it even possible, if she tried? Those types of powers had never even occurred to her before, nor the ramifications, for small villages like this one.

The woman looked ready to cry. "Then my baby will die. Please—could not she at least try? It might help a little." She looked imploringly at Jardan, and then at Aidah, and Aidah couldn't help but feel an ache in her heart. There had been deaths of infants in Hamstead, when she was younger. How difficult was it to try? She looked at Jardan as well, hoping he could tell her something, help in some way.

He sighed, looking at her. "Aidah…" he started to say, then shook his head, looking at the woman again. "You don't understand the risks. Not only could she fail to help your baby, she could kill him. Or you. Or mutate that simple influenza into something that could attack your entire village. It's too risky."

Aidah sucked in a breath, feeling suddenly dizzy. "How is any of that even possible?"

She could see Jardan was debating with himself to even answer. "Spirit Mages can see the disease, inside the body. They can see everything alive, in fact, and affect or even alter them. Such as stopping a heart, or damaging an organ." He stared hard at Aidah, his face grave. "Because you can affect things, it also means there is a good possibility that you can also contract the disease—you'd be opening yourself up to it. That's not a risk we can take right now."

The woman looked devastated, and Aidah found herself trembling with the strength of her emotions, her frustration. It wasn't that she didn't believe Jardan—his words were reminiscent of the healer's when her Talent had first shown a glimmer of existence. But to just let a baby die... It just seemed so incredibly unfair. She looked pleadingly at Jardan. "I have to try. I'll be very careful. Maybe I can't do anything. But I have to try. I can't just walk away." She hoped he had some insights, given his mother, but she knew he might very well not know anything about how to do this. So before he could protest, she closed her eyes, focusing on that third eye, the one Rangwar had taught her, looking at her own aura, and then at the auras around her, Jardan, the woman, the baby.

She could see a problem in the baby right away.

It wasn't his aura, precisely—that was a pale blue, held very tight against the skin of the child. But there was something else there, a darkness of some kind, a *wrongness*. It was so closely connected with the aura it was almost a part of it, marbled in and throughout, but somehow Aidah knew that was a lie, and the key to healing the child. That taint had to be removed. She frowned, considering it. "I can see it," she said in a low voice. The mother gasped.

"I imagine that you can," Jardan said in a low voice, staying cautiously near Aidah but not touching her in any way. "But that does not mean you can help."

Aidah knew instinctively that he was right. If she touched her aura to the child's she had a feeling that darkness could spread to her, and that would be bad. And how else was she supposed to control it, but by touching it? It wasn't as if there was a mind there that she could control. She tried experimenting a little with her aura, wishing for some kind of otherworldy 'hand'—something that perhaps was a part of her and yet not, protected in some way so that it wouldn't be able to merge into her actual aura. She had a feeling that was the key, but it was difficult, trying to control her energies with any kind of precision. She could tell the blackness to die...but that would probably also kill the baby.

It was so frustrating! She wanted to make the taint go away, but without exposing herself, and without knowing how to protect herself...there was no way. When Aidah opened her eyes, her vision swam with her misery. "I'm sorry. I can't help you." A large tear spilled down her cheek. It felt like her heart was trying to tear itself out of her chest.

Immediately, Jardan's arm encircled her, a barrier against the desperation and the sorrow on the mother's face, a protection from the few who had stopped to gather around. Thankfully it seemed most of the villagers were still entranced by the firestarters. Aidah turned her face, burying it against the Sun Mage's shoulder so that she wouldn't have to look at her failure.

"Thank you for trying," the woman said, and Aidah knew she was trying to sound brave, but it was a useless gesture, because Aidah could feel her emotions. They were raw and without hope.

Jardan nodded at the woman. "As you can see, we are very sorry. My best advice would be to keep your infant warm, give her boiled willow bark tea to drink, for the fever...and pray."

The woman's words were softer this time, barely audible to Aidah above the crowd. "Yes, Sun Mage. Thank you for your time." Aidah felt Jardan gently guiding her, leading her away from the people to head back towards Montrose's wagon. Once she was certain that the woman was gone and could not see, Aidah let herself cry. She clung to Jardan's robes, ashamed to let him see her this way, so weak, and so ignorant. How was she supposed to become this great mage when she couldn't even deal with one woman's simple request to heal a sick child?

"It's all right, Aidah. You'll encounter things like this sometimes, situations where as much as you want to help, you can't. We aren't gods. We can't stop all death from happening. Not even once we are fully trained." He petted her hair, speaking low and soft, as they halted near the entrance of the wagon. "It was too much to ask of you. You do realize that, right?"

Aidah nodded, scrubbing at her eyes with her sleeve. She paused when Jardan touched her wrist, offering her a handkerchief. That was right—she was going to be considered close to royalty now, wasn't she? She supposed she would have to learn that part as well, using a handkerchief instead of her sleeve. Sighing, she took the handkerchief and did her best to dry her tears. "I know—I do. But…it was just a baby. If I'd known just a little more, if…" If Grandess had come to fetch her, rather than force her to travel without any kind of trainer, she would have felt better. More prepared. But she knew they were trying to get someone to her, as quickly as possible. It just wouldn't be soon enough for this town. And somehow, that just seemed all so unfair. "I'm not doing well. With all this power." And the responsibility.

The sounds of the crowd were not that far off, just on the edge of town between the Gedar camp and the first houses, but even so, it seemed quiet in the camp, with only a few Gedar men working away at their wares, little hammers tinking away at metal. Jardan nodded, rubbing at Aidah's shoulder. It felt reassuring, just the way it was supposed to, for which she was grateful. "It's never easy, for any of us. It takes a long time to get used to your abilities, and what you can do with them, and even more, when you should do it. But for you, I imagine it is even harder—knowing that you are kin to the Protector. You have to deal with all the expectations we have of you."

Aidah nodded. "I don't—I didn't want any of it. I didn't even really want to be Talented, except for the fact it would mean I could go to Landaran with Tavish. But this…" She closed her eyes, feeling unsteady for a moment. "I did not wish for this."

Jardan took her hand, gripping it firmly. "In these times, I doubt that any person would. But as they say, the gods and the stars write our destinies. We must deal with what we are given. I assure you, Aidah, that there will be many great people there to help you and to guide you. Myself included. You must have faith that you are strong enough." He sighed. "And forgive yourself for the things you cannot control."

Aidah took a deep breath, and let it out slowly, anchoring herself to the firm feel of his hand. Jardan was right, of course. She couldn't change what she was, so what use was there in bemoaning that? And she certainly had help; even as Jardan had been speaking to her, she noticed her uncle and Derg had emerged from the crowd, watching them worriedly. She held her hand out to her old companion, part pet and part protector, and Derg strode up, head held high, tail long and relaxed. She hugged him hard, pressing her cheek to his soft fur.

"What happened?" Brenton followed Derg over, but right now, Aidah couldn't face him, because she had failed him too, as she had her parents, and Grandpa. She released her hold of Derg but kept a hand on him, and looked into his dark brown eyes.

"Will you come sit with me a while?" she asked the Lupas.

Derg looked at her calmly, confidently. Both emotions were helping to keep her grounded. "I would be glad to, my friend," he replied.

Aidah led Derg into the wagon, settling herself on the little fold-out bed with Derg beside her, keeping a hand on him the entire time. Outside, she could hear Jardan explaining to Brenton what had happened. Let them talk about it, she thought. Let them do the worrying. She laid down next to Derg and wrapped both arms around him, trying to remember times now lost, of home and safety. Simpler times.

She caught a glimpse of Derg's ears, turned back, focused on listening to the conversation even though the rest of him was focused on her. Derg noticed, and nuzzled her. "Sleep, child. We'll keep you safe."

So she slept.

The next day, Aidah was given the option to stay in the wagon, or ride behind Jardan on his horse. With the attack by the vespyre still fresh in her mind, she opted for the latter. Tavish spent the morning complaining that he was sore and that he wasn't convinced that travel by horseback was the best way to travel, but when he found out Aidah would be on horse as well, he shut his mouth. He rode close by, and Aidah was able to listen as Jardan continued his lessons on controlling heat and cold.

It was a cold day, colder than the previous, and even though they were still winding their way out of the hills into warmer country, there was an icy wind that blew without relent, forcing everyone to sit hunched forward, their cloaks wrapped tight around them in a vain effort to keep the fingers of cold from reaching in. The Gedar travelled slower, the women walking huddled together, the children staying inside the wagons. It wasn't snowing yet, but Aidah had a feeling that up in the mountains, back in Harrow, it probably would be. The Gedar stopped for a short lunch of cold meats and bread before resuming. They passed none on the road other than a solitary trapper carrying rabbit furs for sale.

Aidah had hoped there would be another town by nightfall, but this time, there was not. She was at least heartened by the fact that there hadn't been an attack of any kind—nor any dreams. Jardan told her that it would take Rangwar at least a day or two to recover after each one, and that attacks took planning. The Emperor might not even yet know the fate of the vespyres.

The evening was much quieter this time, without anyone to entertain or sell things to. The Gedar gathered around a large fire as the evening meal was cooked—including a few rabbits purchased from the trapper. There was singing, but it was more subdued. There was also storytelling.

Gair had promised to tell them a tale, and so he did, standing in the light of the campfire with the two crescent moons above and his father's lute in his hand. He played two chords—the only chords he knew, he had told Aidah earlier. And he sang.

It was the tale of Calder and Dain, which Aidah had never heard in its entirety. Twin brothers born of the sun god, Ughar, a proud and violent ruler in the times before the stars. Dain was fair-hearted and good, always looking out for his somewhat misshapen brother, but Calder was cold and mean, and had a vicious temper. He killed a tree spirit, angering the wildfolk, who came to Ughar and demanded that Calder be punished. Ughar was furious. It was his gift, and also his curse, that when he was angry, flames engulfed him, for he was the father of fire, and fire dwelt within him. Dain came forward, to spare his brother's life, saying that it was his smaller form that made Calder bitter, but Ughar would not listen. With both hands, he struck his sons' cheeks, slapping them both once. They both cried out, as their father's fire burned them, Calder on his left cheek, Dain on his right. Then they fled, afraid to face Ughar's wrath again, lest they be killed.

Gair finished his song. "And to this day, Ughar chases them, though whether to punish or to apologize, we cannot know. The sun follows the moons, each with their half burned face, around Jael, their Mother Earth. On most nights the moon brothers travel together, but now and then they quarrel, and smaller Calder races past Dain, separating, only to reunite two months later. Thus the moons have their paths across the night time sky." He took a bow, and several of the Gedar applauded, together with Brenton, Jardan, and Aidah. Gair smiled at Aidah, but she didn't smile back, this time. There was just too much going on in her head to accept his little flirtations today.

Once the storytelling was done, Aidah hung close to Jardan for the short walk back to the wagon. She had decided the best place for her to be while journeying was near Jardan. He more than anyone seemed able to not only protect her, but recognized when her Talent was acting up, and knew best how to deal with it. While her sense of safety in sleeping near Derg and her brother was more of an emotional, instinctive urge, rationally she knew that her best chances were if Jardan were near to intervene.

It was very dark, the stars gleaming above with only a little help from the two moons in their last phase before they hid their faces, so Aidah had to take care where she stepped. They had almost reached the wagon when on the side of the road she caught sight of something pale and glowing, like a miner beetle, but much paler. She glanced worriedly at Jardan. "Do you see that?"

Jardan leaned over a little to gaze in the direction she was pointing. "I'm not sure. What do you see?"

Aidah wasn't sure she wanted to go any closer, but she took a couple steps towards the side of the road. The glow seemed to take form somewhat, and she realized it was a little boy, sitting next to one of the mileage posts. "There! Do you see it now?"

The little boy turned and looked at Aidah, and she felt a shiver go through her, noting his near transparency. Jardan put a hand on her shoulder, cautiously. "Yes, I do, although if you asked most people, they wouldn't see it. It's a ghost, Aidah."

Aidah felt her heart go cold. "But he's just a boy!" She wanted to go nearer, but was it safe? The boy smiled, waving shyly. She gave a hesitant wave back. "Can I speak with him?"

"Yes, you may. Death comes to all ages, all locations. But understand, not all dead become ghosts. He must have died on this road. Because he's young, he's still here, possibly waiting for his family to join him before he moves on." Jardan kept a hand on her shoulder, but led her closer, staying close by her side. "It's probably best you keep a little distance. I don't know all the ways that your Talent can interact with spirits."

Aidah took that advice to heart, staying back, but she wanted to speak with the boy. "What is your name?" she asked him, wondering why he looked different than the spirit of her mother, when she'd seen her ascending. That must be what Jardan meant by 'moving on.' She could still remember the great sense of love and peace. Wherever her mother's soul had gone, it must have been a good place.

"Tomas," the boy said, in a voice that seemed to come from far away. He did not appear to be upset nor surprised by her speaking with him, but merely curious. In fact, he looked for all the world as if he were merely waiting for something, a rider perhaps, to come sweep him away. "Are you here to take me to my mama?"

Aidah glanced at Jardan, who seemed to be just standing there. He looked back at her. "Is he speaking? I can see him. But only you can hear him."

Well that made sense, she supposed. "He wants to know if I'm taking him to his mother." Aidah frowned, concerned. "Am I able to do that?"

Jardan smiled a little. "Someday you will. But you'll have to tell him that for now, he'll need to wait for his parents to come get him. And that it might be a long wait."

Not another person to let down, Aidah thought, her heart sinking. She opened her mouth to tell Tomas, but it seemed he could hear the living just fine. He gave a little shrug. "I reckoned it would be a wait. But you two are the first who could see me at all. At least I can talk to you. It gets very lonely out here." He tilted his head, looking at the Gedar wagons. "I'm glad you decided to camp here. I liked hearing the singing and the tales."

It was better than hearing him cry, but Aidah still couldn't help but feel again the sense of helplessness. That a small child should be stuck here between worlds, simple watching and waiting…it wasn't right. Even though she knew Jardan was right, she still wanted to help. "We're glad you enjoyed it." The question gnawed at her. She wasn't sure if it was wise, but she really wanted to know. "May I ask what happened to you? How did you…die?"

Just as she feared, the little boy sobered, looking down at his hands. "It was an accident. I was riding on the wagon, sitting between Ma and Pa, and my older brother Clavis. He was minding the sheep. We was bringing them to market at Colmsford. And then something spooked the sheep, and they started running, and that spooked our horse, and he started running, and then the wheel broke. I fell off the wagon and hit my head. The wagon hit me too, I think." Tomas grimaced, looking up at Aidah.

What could she possibly say to a story like that? "That must have been awful," she replied, trying not to feel creeped out about the fact she was talked to the deceased about the manner in which they died. Aidah could sense Jardan's presence still near and wondered what he must think of the one-sided conversation. But she couldn't take time to explain right now, because the boy continued speaking.

"It hurt," Tomas said, squirming a little and making a face. "But then it didn't. And then, nobody could see me, but I could see myself, stuck under the wagon. I didn't look so good." He tilted his head, peering at Aidah. "But I look all right now, don't I?"

"Yes. You do," Aidah hurried to reassure him. It was something that she was spending a few minutes talking to the spirit, temporarily easing his loneliness. Wasn't it? At least this helped her to feel like she was helping in some way. "I'm glad you enjoyed the singing."

Tomas nodded, kicking his heels against the post, rocking back and forth a little. "I wish I could come with you, but I can't seem to leave this spot. It's probably best, though. My Ma and Pa will know where to find me. I'm waiting for them." He shrugged, looking so young, and yet so old at the same with what life—and death—had served him. Aidah felt a painful constriction around her heart.

"That's probably best," she said, and finally looked at Jardan. "He fell off the wagon while traveling with his family. He says he enjoyed the singing and dancing and wanted to come with us, but can't." She didn't even know what question to ask him, so she left it at that, feeling oddly at peace even though once again, she was helpless to do anything.

Jardan nodded at her, smiling. "You're doing fine, just by talking with him. Did he say he was lonely?" Aidah nodded. And when she looked back, it appeared to her that Thomas had faded somewhat, becoming more of a nebulous mist, hovering. Jardan took her gently by the arm. "I think he's good for now. Most spirits cannot leave the place where they died, but from what I've read, there's a timelessness to death. It takes concentration for them to interact with the living—even Spirit Mages. Time for you to get some sleep. We should reach Colmsford tomorrow."

Aidah waved a hand towards the spirit, just in case Tomas was still paying attention. "It was nice meeting you!" She was indeed tired. Quietly, she followed Jardan's lead, and when they reached Montrose's wagon, she bade him good night and went to her pullout bed, finding Derg already curled up asleep at the foot of it. It took a little to find a position that would not disturb the Lupas. It had been a very confusing day, but also an enlightening one. More and more, she was starting to understand just how much she would be able to do, how she would actually be able to help people with her Talent. The possibilities sparkled in stark contrast to the horror of the future that Rangwar wanted for her.

16

Rumors From the East

Aidah dreamt that night, but it wasn't any visitation from Rangwar. Instead it was just a normal dream, one where she was surrounded by children who were all asking her questions. There was a gypsy woman dancing, and her brother was eating fire, like a circus act. When she woke up, she actually felt refreshed.

The Gedar made quick work of packing up the camp, eating breakfast on the go so that they could get the wagons underway. Aidah tried not to listen, but she couldn't help but hear that they were due to arrive at a larger town today, Colmsford. There was excitement and relief among the Gedar. Apparently this would mark their entrance into more habited lands, and they would start to see more traffic on the road. Opportunities to sell and make money.

In fact, as they neared the town, Aidah began to see what the Gedar were talking about. Colmsford was twice the size of Thornton, at about six thousand inhabitants. To Aidah's eyes, it was huge, with farmland sprawling for miles dotted with little farmhouses and wheat silos, pastures of sheep, and even smitheries where lumber and ore from the hills and mountains were processed. The town lay beside a rushing white river that streamed down from the mountains, providing both fresh water and a way to transport goods.

Aidah was riding beside Jardan when they passed by one smithery on the side of the river, with a great wheel where diverted water made it turn steadily. Black smoke streamed from a chimney with an acrid smell that made her grimace. "What is that?" she asked.

"Smelting house," Jardan replied, and Aidah could see that Tavish was gawking as well, leaning over in his saddle. "The water

206

rushing down from the mountains provides power for the waterwheel to work the bellows for the melted ore, refining it. They burn charcoal and wood dust from the lumber yard to produce the fires to melt the iron. Our land is blessed by the things which come from the mountains where you grew up."

"Is that to make swords?" Tavish asked. Aidah rolled her eyes at him; leave it to him to think first of weaponry.

Jardan chuckled, shrugging. "Some of it. But also to make tools, nails—many other things. You'll see quite a lot of technology that is new for you in Landaran. And they say the Doane is a rustic hovel in comparison to the Innis Empire. Landaran is the closest that we come to the old technologies that were lost."

The town appeared to have once been a village that grew quickly. There were no walls or armaments, although they did pass by a manor estate of the local lord, surrounded by an orchard of nut trees. The Gedar set camp next to a riverside market square which Aidah understood was not even the main town market square, although it looked more than large enough to her eyes. Once the wagons were anchored and the horses were watered and fed, Tavish and Kendrick went off with Gair and a few other Gedar boys to explore town, but Jardan recommended that Aidah stay with the wagons, for her own safety as well as to avoid any problems with her Talent. While normally she would have felt confined and disappointed not to see the sights, this time she agreed with him. There would be plenty to see in Landaran. For now, she just wanted to feel safe.

Even from the confines of the wagon, she saw a great deal she had never seen before. Town lawmen wore swords and carried flintlock pistols—the latter she had heard about from Brenton, but she'd never actually seen one before. He said pistols were rare, found only in the countryside, and useless against Sun Mages who could make them misfire.

She spotted women wearing dresses dyed in colors so vibrant that at first Aidah thought they had been sewn from flower petals, with fine delicate patterns stitched in needlepoint. There were actually other Lupas in the town as well, and she could see Derg conversing with them, the others standing with such a similar pose, ears focused forward, tails held proudly high, so that it became difficult to tell Derg from the others.

With all these wonders, Aidah didn't really have time to feel lonely or upset about her confinement. But as she watched, she began to notice other things as well, things that she probably wouldn't have noticed if she had been out there, running around People regarded the Gedar with friendly eyes, but here and there, she saw looks that were not so friendly. Suspicious, even. And then she remembered Minton, and the spies that Rangwar had planted in the village, searching for her. Could such spies be here as well? As Rangwar had told her, there were only a few ways to reach Landaran. He could have foreseen that they would pass through here. Did they know of her? Would such spies even know which wagon was her refuge?

Aidah found herself looking at each person more closely, trying to determine if they were merely an innocent citizen or a dangerous enemy. Her Talent reached out—she couldn't stop it—and she began to gather snatches of emotion and thought. Most of it was innocent. Thoughts of purchasing bread, happiness about a new baby, boredom, thoughts of bed and sleep. However, here and there Aidah began to pick up other things, snatches of rumors, rumblings that Landaran was preparing for war.

War?

It was the first time she'd heard of the possibility in her life time. Of course Brenton had talked of war all the time, regaling her with tales of her great-grandfather and the battles he had fought in defense of the Realm. But that war had taken place eighty years ago. And yet, it made sense. Rangwar wanted her. Could he be gathering up his forces, preparing to attack the Doane again? He had tried twice before. It was certainly possible to try it a third time.

When Montrose stepped into the wagon, she tugged on his sleeve to ask him about it.

"I have heard these rumors you speak of," he began, pulling out some bread and cheese from his pack and handing her a chunk of each to eat for their noon repast. He sat down on the cot across from hers, where Tavish had been sleeping each night. "There have been times before where rumors passed through towns like this one, but it is different this time. There hasn't been official word yet, but I think there soon will be. The lords are inquiring as to how many men are old enough to fight. This makes me think that those men will soon be called upon."

"It's because of me, isn't it," Aidah said quietly. It was impossible not to feel guilty. Her mother had already paid the price for her resisting Rangwar's call, for not turning herself over to him. How many more would die?

Montrose looked at her solemnly, then shook his head, the curls of his great beard brushing against his knuckles. "No. It is because the cursed Emperor is greedy. He has always been. He took lands from our people many years ago, and he still is taking land, whenever he can, and wherever. You are but a convenient excuse. Do not blame yourself."

That helped, although Aidah wondered about Montrose's people, the Gedar, and what their ties to the Innis Empire were. "But he does want me."

"Your powers increase his powers. And he wants a wife. Why he wants one of his own line, I don't know. It is said that the Emperor is insane, and I think they are right. But truly, the Emperor is like a sick bloated toad. He wants to eat and eat until there is nothing left to eat. And so it is good, and it is right that we must fight such a man." He petted her hair. "We, the Gedar, love your Protector, because the Doane lets us be as we are, lets us wander the lands and make trade. Not all people have this freedom. It is worth protecting." He bit into his bread.

Aidah ate her bread as well, mulling things over. She had grown to care for the head of the Burris clan; Montrose was like a beloved uncle to her now, and she appreciated his insights. So he thought war would come. "Do you think we'll reach Landaran in time, before things grow worse?"

He was silent for a moment. "I hope so, little lady. I really hope so."

☼

They left Colmsford early the next morning. Tavish had found a few new trinkets in town including a slingshot made with a strange elastic material from the south, smaller and more compact than the long leather strap Aidah had seen him play with as a child. He also had purchased something for her—a dagger, which actually fit inside her dress in a way that onlookers wouldn't be able to tell she was carrying it. For her protection, he said.

The next major town was supposedly about four days away, Bonnenville, and it would be an even larger town than Colmsford had been. But now they would also find small clusters of habitation along the way, for they were now following the one of the forks of the great river Lamar, which they would follow until they reached the fork at Geraine, the second largest city after Landaran and the capital of the Doane.

Some time before that, they all hoped to at least hear from Landaran, or even better, be joined by a Spirit Mage to start training Aidah.

They made good time during the first day out from Colmsford, though the weather did not seem to want to cooperate. About midday, a light snow began to fall. It was not enough to slow their progress, mostly melting on the packed dirt of the road. They passed several farmers on their way to Colmsford for market, as well as a messenger on his way to Landaran on a sleek black horse. He barely stopped to acknowledge them as he galloped past. After the past few days of riding behind Tavish, Aidah wondered how the man's legs could stand the pain of trying to sit anything faster than a walk. Eventually she supposed she would get used to it.

The snow fell heavier as evening approached, and Aidah abandoned Tavish's horse for the warmth of the wagon. They halted early as it became too dark to navigate, and this time there was no bonfire, and no dancing. Tavish came into the wagon and they ate a cold meal of jerky and dried apples. Aidah wondered about the messenger that had been hurrying earlier. What if it was word from Landaran? What if they were looking for her? "How long do you think it will take for Grandess to send a Spirit Mage to meet us? And how long until we reach Landaran?" At this point, Aidah didn't think it would matter what she knew. The river was too easy a landmark. She knew the names of the cities. For her own peace of mind, she wanted to know how long before she could find true safety.

"From here, it will be about ten days for us to reach Landaran with the wagons. That of course is assuming the weather holds up." Brenton blew out a nervous breath. "However, if Korva sends out a single horseman, and they ride top speed, they should be able to reach us in under a week. And actually it would be sooner, since we sent out message by carrier pigeon back in Thornton. Maybe just a few more days before we have some additional help."

A few more days. Aidah nodded, feeling her knotted insides easing somewhat. "Then I can start to learn things," she affirmed.

"I hope so," Brenton murmured.

The wagon creaked in the wind as Aidah closed her eyes to sleep.

☼

There was a dream, one of houses burning—Hamstead perhaps, or possibly Thornton. Or Colmsford. Aidah was vaguely aware of people running, of herself trying to fight the flames. For a moment, she even thought she was Tavish, and that she had her brother's powers.

And then suddenly the flames and the town were gone and it was just her standing there, herself again. Rangwar was there.

He looked winded, tired even, but pleased with himself, and he was in full battle gear, molded chestplate and leather studs, very different from other visitations. Aidah's mind was sharp and focused again, but there was no bed, no dungeon, not even a real setting. They seemed to be standing in a fog, just herself and him. He looked at her with irritation. She braced herself for another fight, another defeat.

"No time for pleasure or pain tonight, my dear," Rangwar said, wiping sweat from his brow. He didn't attempt to come closer, and for that, Aidah was grateful. However, she wondered, what was he up to, if not to torment her?

"We're nearing Landaran," Aidah told him, though she doubted her bluff would work.

He laughed, harshly, and she knew he was not deceived. "I know precisely where you are, my sweet, and I know that you will not reach Landaran. My troops are closing in and will soon surround the city." He smirked. "Oh, and tell Gabriel, when you see him, my compliments to his choice in steeds. The stallion was a tasty treat to my energy." Rangwar laughed again, more heartily this time, with confidence. He finally took a step closer, though he did not attempt any physical contact with her. Still, Aidah could feel his strength, his energy. It terrified her.

"Sadly, I won't have time for a bit to see you, other than a quick little drop in like this. But have no illusions, Aidah. You shall be with me soon." He reached out and cupped her cheek in his broad palm.

Then he was gone.

Aidah slipped back into other dreams.

It was barely dawn when Aidah awoke. The sky was clear, and it was almost painfully cold, the air sharp in her lungs as she stepped out of the wagon with her blanket still wrapped around her shoulders. There was a thick cover of snowfall on the ground, but even at this early hour, many of the Gedar were awake and moving about the camp. Apparently, so were her brother and uncle, for as she sat down on the steps to the wagon, she spotted them, sparring on a cleared part of the road, circling each other as Jardan and Kendrick looked on.

Aidah wasn't sure how she felt about Rangwar's latest visit. On the one hand, she was relieved it had been short, and he hadn't touched her. On the other, it didn't matter how long he had stayed; he had still come by, and every time she saw him, every time she heard his voice, it was like a great black hand covering her, suffocating her. All she wanted to do was crawl into a hole and hide forever. What had his words meant? She wasn't sure, but they filled her with foreboding.

"Steady with your feet there, Brenton!" Kendrick called out, and Aidah shifted her focus to watch Brenton and Tavish parry with wooden swords, happy to take her mind off darker things. Tavish was doing well with his speed and agility, not surprisingly. But what Brenton lacked in those areas, he made up for in size and strength. She cried out in surprise as he struck hard at Tavish's side and connected, feeling a touch of pain herself.

They stopped, noticing her. Kendrick stepped forward and stood beside Tavish, and Aidah could hear him clearly even though they were several feet away, telling Tavish, "You always want to watch your opponent's shoulder—their hand has to follow that shoulder, so if they're about to strike, you'll see the trunk of the body move before their hand starts moving. That's how you can get out of the way in time." It made sense to Aidah, but it also told her that she was connecting with Tavish again. She checked her aura. It actually was fairly close in, so she wasn't sensing him through that. Another question she would have to ask Grandess.

Aidah walked over, deciding that it was better to not rely on her Talent to carry the conversation. For once, her heart was undivided on her decision to speak about her dreams. "Rangwar visited me last night," she told them.

Abruptly all conversation ceased, and all pairs of eyes were intent on her. Aidah flushed. "It was a very short visit—he was sending me a message, to give to someone named 'Gabriel'. He says we won't make it to Landaran. His troops are surrounding the city." As it had last night the fear gripped her, making it difficult to breathe. "Is that possible?" She looked at Jardan.

He looked grim, but not surprised. "It is...but it's not likely. It would take him time to gather his forces and cross the Krimean Sea. It's more likely that he's taunting you. But why he would want you to relay the message to Gabriel..." He shook his head, his brows furrowed, gray eyes clouded. "I don't like it. The real message here, as I see it, is that he knows Gabriel is trying to reach us, and he expects it to happen. On the one side, that's good news. But I have a feeling there's something he's not telling. And that's what worries me."

Brenton's brows were furrowed with worry. "Should we separate from the Gedar? So that we can reach the city before he closes in?"

Jardan shook his head, stroking his beard as his gaze turned inward. "We must wait for Gabriel Holt to reach us first. He's the second highest Spirit Mage in the land, and we need both his protection as well as his guidance. Once he's here..." Jardan shrugged. "Then we'll see what the best course is." He let out a breath. "For now, I think you and Tavish should continue on with your lessons." He gave a nod, and motioned for Aidah to stand beside him as Tavish and Brenton took up their positions in the road again.

☼

Later, as they were riding, Aidah rode beside Tavish to talk about the things he had been learning lately, including the sparring. The wagons slogged their way through snow that was starting to melt, and the horses plodded alongside, as their riders strove to avoid icy patches. The sky was gray but didn't seem ready to release more snow on them just yet.

"So I've been working more on the invisibility thing," he told her, reaching out his hand which was holding the rein. Aidah watched as his hand became invisible as he'd done in front of their house in the desperate attempt to save her. She was about to ask him if he was only practicing or learning something new, when as she watched, the reins began disappearing as well, slowly melting away. She blinked.

"You can make what you're touching invisible too?" Aidah asked.

Tavish nodded, grinning. "Imagine the pies we could have stolen back in Hamstead if I'd known then!"

Aidah chuckled. Trust Tavish to first think of nefarious ways to use his powers. Although, she supposed if townsfolk had seen a pie floating its way down the main avenue, that probably would have raised a fuss. "Do you like learning under Jardan?" She asked, as he brought his hand and the reins back into view.

"Jardan's great," Tavish said with enthusiasm, touching next the saddle and making it disappear. "And Kendrick's great too—who would have thought we'd actually have family, you know, to hang out with? He teaches me almost as much as his grandfather. I really hope I get to stay with them as an apprentice." His face, which had been filled with joy, suddenly fell. "But I guess that means you and I wouldn't see as much of each other. Since you'll have to stay in the city, and all that."

Right now that was the least of her concerns. "We would have to separate at some point anyways," Aidah said, trying to console him. It was foolish to think they could live their entire lives along the same path, in each other's company. But she knew Tavish seemed to have a particularly strong need to stay close to her. "And you'll be able to come visit me often, I'm sure." At least she hoped he would. It still wasn't clear what their roles would be, once they were full mages. Kendrick had spoken of traveling the Doane and helping in different locations, but that was mostly for Storm and Sun mages. From the sound of the last village and the sick baby, Aidah had a feeling that Spirit mages didn't travel as often.

"Yeah," Tavish said in a low voice, but he didn't sound convinced. Beside them, the wagon slowly creaked along, and Aidah could hear Montrose and Brenton arguing about something. She wondered if Montrose had told him of the conversation they had shared in Colmsford, in the wagon. Just ahead of Tavish's horse, Jardean and Kendrick were riding side by side, not speaking. It was a rather cheerless day, Aidah reflected, looking up at the hazy skies. To her left beyond the road, Aidah could see rolling hills, for as far as the eye could see. To her right was the winding river, ducking in and out of sight behind stands of large trees which had lost their leaves for the winter. She listened to the muffled clomp of horse hooves on the muddy road, just letting her thoughts wander for a moment.

And then she began to hear a noise that clashed with the slow pace of the caravan. The sound of galloping hooves, far away ahead of them. Aidah glanced at her brother first, and then her uncle. Someone seemed like they were in a rush.

Brenton motioned to Tavish to bring their horse closer, while Kendrick fell in beside their horse, acting as a shield. Aidah watched as Jardan gave his steed a light kick, urging it into a trot to overtake the slower wagons. He headed to the front of the caravan, presumably to get a closer look at what was approaching. She felt a flutter of fear. What if it wasn't the Spirit Mage?

She needed to see what was happening. She knew exactly how as well; closing her eyes, she used the third eye trick to find out where her aura was, and began extending it forward, until she sensed Jardan. Rangwar was correct about one thing. It was easier to sense those with Talents, particularly those with potential Spirit Talent. She knew she couldn't read his mind; she remember the sense of being pushed out before. But there was a perfectly ordinary Gedar man riding in a wagon next to Jardan, leading the caravan. It was easy to slip inside and use his eyes to look at the road ahead.

Back in her real body, however, Aidah could still sense things, hear things. She heard her brother ask, "Are you doing something?" She forced herself to nod, which was strange because it felt so far away. The Gedar was still watching the road, the sound of galloping hooves growing closer. She thought she could see it then, a faint speck in the distance.

"I'm watching what's happening up where Jardan is," she heard herself say from her own body. She couldn't risk opening her eyes to see Tavish's reaction, but hoped he wouldn't tell Brenton. This time it wasn't a random flaring of her power. She was controlling it.

"Oh, that's intense!" Tavish whispered back, and by his tone, he was in full cooperation with her. She smiled. The speck was growing steadily larger, a man on a horse, but she couldn't see any details yet.

A question came to her. "Do you know what this relative of ours, Gabriel, is supposed to look like? Is he old or young?" Rangwar looked young but was incredibly old, she reminded herself. Korva looked older even though she was Rangwar's daughter. Gabriel was younger than Korva, but by how much? She knew he was older than

Grandpa.

"Um, I think he's supposed to look really old. Kendrick mentioned something about it that first day we met. Do you think they'd let an old Spirit Mage ride out alone to meet us?" Tavish abruptly broke off his questioning, and Aidah wondered if Brenton had noticed that her eyes were closed, that there was something strange going on. She didn't break off the contact, however. Let him think it was beyond her control.

The horse was brown, and moving very fast, as she saw from the eyes of the man in the front wagon. The rider was wearing leather, no pack that she could see, and he didn't appear to be old. Aidah's heart sank. She couldn't imagine that Gabriel would be riding at such a fast clip, and in such good physical condition. This looked to be a messenger of some kind again, perhaps coming from Landaran. But to where?

She pulled back from the man and drew in her aura, feeling it contract around her as she opened her eyes. Brenton was looking over at her curiously, but said nothing. She flushed, feeling guilty about deceiving him and leaned in close to whisper to her brother. "It's not him."

Her confirmation came soon enough. She heard the rider slow the horse down to a trot, the sound carrying down the road, and then the faint sound of voices talking. Aidah was considering extending her eyes and ears again to overhear what was being said when she heard the horse give a whinny, and the rider spurred it forward. Very quickly, the rider drew near Montrose's wagon, and then he was past them, continuing towards Colmsford. Jardan rode back towards them looking grim. He brought his horse in close, on the other side of Montrose's wagon, as Brenton stood up to exchange words with him. Tavish made sure to pull his horse in close as well, leaning over so that he could hear better.

"It's a messenger bound for Colmsford," Jardan reported, as the caravan, which had stopped, began to get moving again, the creak of wheels and clop of hooves competing with Jardan's smooth voice. "He states that war is coming and they're asking the towns to send able-bodied men to defend Landaran." He glanced at Aidah. "It's as you feared. Invasion may be imminent."

For a moment, Aidah couldn't have replied if she'd wanted to. It was all too real, the dream and then the news today. She was glad

216

that she was leaning against Tavish, holding onto him. If she had been standing, she probably would have slumped to the ground. Her heart was pounding too fast. The world seemed to be closing in on her.

"It's all right," Tavish said by her ear, turning slightly in the saddle as if sensing her distress. Or perhaps she was projecting it; anything was possible at the moment. She nodded mutely, reminding herself that it hadn't started yet. But war! They were going to send people to fight.

To die.

"When?" she finally asked, though she doubted that Jardan had an answer.

He shook his head. "I doubt even the commanders know exactly. But obviously it is coming soon, for him to be hurrying so. Days, weeks." He sighed, but then added, "The messenger did say that he passed by a mage dressed in purple on the way here, who was also riding. That should be Gabriel, and it was only yesterday. So that's encouraging. We may see him either today or tomorrow, depending on the pace that he's riding."

Again, that followed what Rangwar had said in the dream. That wasn't particularly encouraging to Aidah. If Rangwar knew so much, could follow not only her movements but other Spirit mages as well, what chance did she have? What chance did they all have? She shivered, holding tighter to Tavish, wishing the Talent would somehow leave her, make her normal again. She didn't care how much Korva needed her. She just wanted to be left alone.

There didn't seem to be much to say after that. The Gedar caravan continued forward, and Aidah heard murmurings around her as word spread of the messenger, and the message he was carrying. Aidah could almost feel it, a darkness coming from the east. How far was it from here to the Krimean Sea? And what of the Guardians, who had always been supposed to protect the land?

She urged Tavish to ride closer to Jardan, hungry for more knowledge, more insights. He had been quiet for most of the day. It was unsettling. "Jardan? Can you tell Tavish and me about the Guardians? Aren't they supposed to help defend the Doane from attacks across the sea?"

Tavish perked up at that as well, scowling. "Yeah, weren't they supposed to stop people from Innis entering our land at all? Like the men who attacked our village?"

Jardan glanced back towards Brenton before answering. "Yes, they were supposed to. And they have protected us, for many years. But their power is not limitless. The Guardians are stone statues which line our beaches and mountains to the east. Each statue holds the soul of a past warrior, who gave up their body and their afterlife to keep vigilance and report to the Protector. What you have to understand, however, is that even though the spell that bound them to stone increased their senses, they were once human. They are not infallible." He sighed. "Even so, their power has been weakening, over the last twenty years or so. Korva is old, and she is feeling her age." He rubbed at his temple. "I think the spells are beginning to break down."

Even though Aidah had only heard about the Guardians in passing talk prior to today, she knew this was big. And frightening. "What will that mean for us?" she asked, because if the Protector could no longer protect, why were they all risking their lives to head right into the heart of danger?

Brenton leaned forward as well, trying to listen in. "Surely they have at least some standing troops stationed in Landaran for the defense of the city. They've been attacked before."

"They have," Jardan confirmed, and that eased Aidah's mind somewhat. So at least Landaran was used to being in a constant state of readiness. But then why send such an urgent message as far out as this? She listened as Jardan continued, "And as soon as you are there, as soon as Korva begins to train you, you will be able to start helping her. Your strength will add to hers. The Guardians should be able to assist us more, as they did in the past." He sat up a little straighter. "My father's family has a link to one of the Guardians, who was one of our ancestors. It is said they not only see all within their stretch of territory, but can create a barrier no enemy can pass, if they are at full strength."

So once again, the sooner she reached Landaran, the better. Aidah didn't want to speak up; she didn't want to again acknowledge that Rangwar was contacting her, could contact her any time he pleased. But she felt it was important that they understood. "He's going to try and get there before me. The Emperor, that is." Fear was a fist clenched tight around her heart.

Jardan glanced over at Brenton and Montrose, and Aidah didn't even need her Talent to sense their unease, their fear. "We'll figure something out," Jardan said softly. She wasn't sure she believed him. And if they couldn't think of a way to get her to safety, then what? Would she then have to stay on the run indefinitely? She remembered Derg offering to take her to his kind, the Lupas, to hide with them. Suddenly it didn't seem quite such an outlandish idea. Otherwise, at this point, her best hope was that other Spirit Mages had means to get her to Landaran safely.

☼

The rest of the day was uneventful. By nightfall, snow began to fall again, and they set up camp just off the side of the road. Again, there was no singing or dancing. Word of war had darkened the mood of the entire camp, and though there was a campfire, activity around the fire was limited to quiet conversations and eating.

Aidah dreaded sleep, afraid that another visitation would occur even though Rangwar had told her that he wouldn't have time for her for a while. Jardan instructed Brenton and Tavish in more sword technique. Aidah was prepared to spend her evening watching them, but Gair approached her, looking hesitant. She gave him an apologetic look. "No juggling tonight, I think," she told him.

He shook his head. "Actually, when I saw that your brother and uncle were learning swordplay, I thought there might be something else somebody should be teaching you." He flicked his wrist, and suddenly a dagger appeared in his hand. "It wouldn't hurt for you to learn a trick like this, for example."

Aidah blinked, taken back by his concern. The fact that he was thinking of her safety warmed her. Sadly, it also reminded her that time with him was running out; whatever happened, she knew she could not stay with the Gedar forever. "Yes. Can you teach that to me?" It was a simple trick, of course, and there was the fact she barely knew how to wield a dagger. But it was something.

He sat down beside her and showed her his simple leather wrist sheath, taking it off to show her how she could make one as well from scraps of leather. He then proceeded to show her how it worked, how to flick the wrist muscles just so in order to pull on the cord and release the dagger into her hand. She practiced, and while she wasn't nearly as fast as he was, she at least felt it was something she could do, given enough practice.

Since merely holding a knife was useless without actually

knowing how to use one, Gair next taught her a few precise moves both to defend and attack. He kept it simple, making sure she had a move right before showing her the next one. By the time she had learned three or four moves and countermoves, it was late, and she was exhausted. She felt a great deal better, however. Brenton and Tavish and even Jardan often treated her like she was fine china, likely to break if they even mentioned anything too terrible. Gair, on the other hand, treated her with the confidence that she wouldn't lose control of her Talent around him, and would be able to handle whatever he was showing her, or telling her. It was refreshing.

When it came time for him to leave for the wagon where he'd been sleeping, Aidah was almost tempted to give him a kiss. Almost—but it was still too reminiscent of Rangwar, of the perversions he had made of that simple act. She touched his hand instead, smiling at him. "Thank you for helping me. It really means a lot." She hoped he understood. She liked him, and she wouldn't forget him, no matter where their paths might go.

Gair actually blushed a little. "It's no sweat, really." He seemed about to say more, then just grinned, rubbing the back of his neck. "See you tomorrow night for more lessons?" She laughed and nodded. "Excellent!" He exclaimed, then hurried off back to the family who had unofficially adopted him.

No dreams, for which Aidah was profoundly grateful. The next day dawned clear and bright, but it was obvious that storms would continue to beleaguer their evenings by the clouds that could be seen drifting from the northeast over the snow covered mountains.

Once again, after they had been riding for a few hours, as Jardan was instructing Tavish and Kendrick on the finer points of invisibility and deception, Aidah heard the shout from the front of the caravan train that there was a lone traveler on the road ahead. This time, however, the traveler was on foot.

They thought little of it, until the wagons drew near and they were able to see the purple robes of a Spirit Mage.

The instant that Jardan heard the news, a look of grave concern crossed his face. Without another word, he spurred his horse forward, galloping until he neared the figure, then dismounting. Kendrick swore, holding back his horse as it bucked, eager to follow. "Wait until he verifies who it is," he told Tavish and Aidah. "It might be an imposter."

They waited, for several tense moments. Then Jardan waved to them. Kendrick breathed a sigh of relief. "It's him! Come on—let's find out what happened. He should have been on horseback!" He too urged his horse forward, but kept to a fast trot. Tavish muttered under his breath something about unpredictable beasts and gave a little kick. Their horse jumped a little, then trotted after Kendrick's horse, weaving through the wagons and ponies and horses up to the front and then further up the road. Jardan had dismounted and was offering water to an old man with short white hair and royal purple robes. The man looked weary and upset.

Aidah and Tavish dismounted as well. Aidah wanted to hold back, but the moment Jardan saw her, he hurried over to take her hand, leading her up to the man. His robes were covered in mud, but his face was regal, and his eyes were the familiar blue gray of her mother's. Aidah swallowed as the man put down the waterskin and extended a hand.

"Hello, Aidah. I'm Gabriel Holt, Dean of the College of Spirit Magic."

17

The Spirit Mage

Aidah reached out her hand, but did not take Gabriel's hand right away. Part of the reason was fear. How did she know for certain that he was who he claimed to be, and not some imposter sent by Rangwar? Then too there was the feeling of standing at the edge of a cliff, knowing that the next step would send her plunging into depths unknown. And he was male. Could she trust a male teacher again?

He saw her hesitation, and put his hand down, smiling tiredly. "It really is me. I can see by your aura that you've already had at least one lesson. And yes, I know who taught you that lesson." His eyes showed the seriousness, the gravity of things. Aidah flushed, feeling exposed and vulnerable, but he carried on, "You will see, however, that you have nothing to fear from me. My shields are down. You may know what you wish." And with that, he reached out and took her hand.

Instantly, she could sense him—really *sense* him. Just as he'd said, he had lowered any shields, not only letting her see inside, but inviting to see, to know. She saw his thoughts, memories, emotions, and most importantly, his aura. It was pale blue, and nothing at all like Rangwar's. He was not her enemy. More, she saw that he was hurting all over from walking all day, parched and cold. She felt the horror he had experienced at finding his horse dead yesterday morning.

It really was Gabriel! Rangwar had visited him, just as he had told her in her own dream. Aidah pulled her mind back, but when she sensed Gabriel's disappointment, she hurried to explain, "Rangwar told me to say hello to you, and that he 'complimented your choice in steeds'. He said something about the energy being tasty?" It all came together then, the meaning. Aidah felt the blood drain from her face. "Oh! He killed your horse and *drank* its energy?" It seemed too terrible to contemplate. And yet, hadn't he also killed Tavish's horse?

"I hate when he does that!" Tavish exclaimed, watching her with a puzzled expression. Of course, he couldn't sense all the things she was sensing. And he didn't truly understand about Rangwar. Tavish turned to Gabriel. "Is that why you were walking?"

Belatedly, Aidah let go of Gabriel's hand. Her awareness of him faded, but she still sensed him a little, which probably meant he was still leaving himself open to her. She wondered about that—was it to gain her trust? Or some other reason? Gabriel nodded to Tavish, reaching for a flask of water from Jardan. "Yes. I received a dream message from the Emperor—his usual foot stamping and sabre rattling, going on about attacking Landaran. The next morning, I awoke to find that apparently he had visited astrally and killed my horse." He smiled wanly. "I hate when he does that as well. Usually I can protect the animals, if I'm awake. But the riding has been a little hard on my old bones."

Aidah smiled back, warmed a little by the humor. He seemed to have an easy-going manner to him. She had feared that her tutor would be hard and cold. After all, wasn't Korva?

Tavish shuddered, fidgeting. "Yeah, we found out he could do some pretty bad things out of his body—that's what you mean, right? So let me ask you. What would happen if you went there the same way? Could you kill one of his horses or something?" He was testing the Spirit Mage, Aidah realized, in his own way making sure that she was safe with him.

Gabriel nodded to Tavish, acknowledging him. "Traveling astrally is dangerous, unless like the Emperor, you are extremely powerful. There are ways to disrupt the astral form, to send them back to their bodies, or even in some cases break the link connecting spirit to body. While I might be able to kill a few of his horses—or men—in the end, he would likely kill me as well." He chuckled sadly. "Believe me, I wish it were that easy to rid ourselves of him!"

Tavish made a face. "All right. It was a thought, anyway." He looked at Jardan, unsure what to do next.

Jardan took the lead smoothly and efficiently. "Let's get you over to the wagons so that you can rest your feet, Master Spirit Mage. I think perhaps it would be best for you to ride inside with Aidah so that the two of you can become acquainted. We'll continue on towards Landaran. After you've rested, we can discuss what next, what our strategy should be."

Gabriel nodded, looking weary. "I agree. There's much to be discussed. But at the moment, all I can think of is sitting for a bit. He handed Kendrick the saddlebag he had been carrying which presumably held his food and other belongings. Jardan offered the mage his horse, but Gabriel shook his head. Jardan nodded and offered him an arm to lean on. In that fashion, they walked back towards the Gedar wagons with Kendrick following on horseback, leading Jardan's horse. Aidah and Tavish both climbed back onto Leya the mare's back and rode her to Montrose's wagon. Then Aidah dismounted and climbed into the wagon. It wasn't her favorite way to travel, but she was eager to have some of her questions answered. She had a trainer now, an actual trainer. Even if Gabriel couldn't stop the dreams, it was still something to know that she would have someone who understood things, understood what if felt like to have her abilities.

It wasn't long before she heard Jardan's voice outside the wagon, telling Gabriel of the attack by the vespyre, and then the two of them were climbing into the small wagon. She sat on her foldout bed with her knees against her chest, to take up as little room as possible. Jardan only stuck his head in and nodded at her, but Gabriel climbed in and sat down in Tavish's bed across from her.

"It will be all right," Jardan assured her. Then he left her with the second most senior Spirit Mage of the Doane.

Aidah looked down at her feet, unsure of what to say. If what Jardan had told her about his mother was true, then other Spirit Mages, the women at least, had probably also been visited, tormented by Rangwar. Why had no one stopped him before this? Aidah thought if there was even the smallest chance a child would be born with this Talent, the Spirit Mages should take them under their protection when young, trained them early, rather than leave things to chance. She was angry at Gabriel, she realized. She had never met the man, yet she was angry just the same.

For Gabriel's part, he looked weary and grateful to be sitting. He took another drink from his waterskin, groaning as he sat back against a cushion. Aidah jumped a little as the wagon began to move again, rolling slowly towards their destination.

At last, Gabriel fixed his gaze upon her. "You want to know why we were so late. Why you have been suffering so."

Aidah glared at him, her chest hurting. "My mother is dead. Did you know that?"

He winced a little, though whether it was because of her words or the rock of the wagon and his old bones, Aidah didn't know. "I didn't know that. I am sorry for your loss."

At the moment, she wanted nothing to do with his condolences. "And why didn't you know? Why weren't we warned about this, that something could happen, that people might come for me? Why wasn't I warned about the Emperor? Why did you all let this happen?" Aidah was crying now, and she didn't much care. Let Gabriel think what he wished of her. Let any of them think as they would. She was scared, she was tired, and she was hurting, in places they couldn't see and couldn't possibly understand.

If Gabriel had come closer at that point, if he had tried to reach out to touch her, console her in any way, Aidah was sure she would have struck him. Perhaps she was small, perhaps she was young, but it wouldn't have mattered. She would have hit him with all her might, trying to inflict damage. In her heart, she knew he wasn't really to blame. Perhaps it was simply that he was a safer target than the one she truly wished to strike at.

He adjusted the pillow behind his back before answering. "Korva told me that she went to witness your birth, astrally of course since she cannot physically leave the city. She felt a strong likelihood of Talent in your brother, but did not think you would develop anything more than the potential that your mother had. She made a terrible mistake, and she knows it. You should have grown up safe in Landaran, and been trained from the first day you showed signs of your Talent." Gabriel rubbed his hands together, looking pained but keeping his gaze on Aidah steady as he leaned forward. "But nothing she did, nothing she could have said, would truly have prepared you for him. The Emperor is the oldest, and most powerful Spirit Mage alive today. Our greatest failing is that we have not been able to find a way to keep him out of the young Spirit Talents' dreams."

Aidah bit her lip, looking down. She didn't want to cry in front of a man she'd barely met, and yet all the emotions seemed to be welling up inside her, and she was powerless to control them. She clenched her hands into fists, digging into the palms with her sharp fingernails, as a hot tear escaped. "This is the worst Talent anyone could possibly be cursed with. I don't want anything to do with it."

Gabriel tilted his head, his wizened face thoughtful, as if pondering whether to speak or not. After several seconds of silence, he finally did speak. "You may change your mind, once you have saved someone's life. Once you fully understand your Talent."

Aidah shrugged, not wanting to admit that he might be right, because she was still angry, and she was still hurting. She had waited too long, and lost too much already. "Then teach me. How could I have saved the sick infant in Lothe?" She looked defiantly at him, her eyes burning, but resisted the urge to wipe her tears. Let him see her pain. Let him also read her emotions or her thoughts, because she really couldn't care anymore.

Gabriel took a deep breath, letting it out slowly. "Let us start with a few basics. You already know of your 'Anja', your third eye, and perceiving auras. Let's start there, and then let's go deeper and look at all the points of energy in the body. In understanding these energies, it is possible to restore health from illness."

Aidah nodded, because for all her anger, for all her pain, she knew she needed this, had been needing training from the very first day strange things had started to occur. She closed her eyes, forcing herself to relax, taking slow, deep breaths. The wagon shook a little as it passed over bumps in the road, the steady plop of the horse's hooves a calming sound to her ears. "Are you going to just tell me what to do?"

She felt rather than heard Gabriel shifting, moving closer. Aidah had to quell the urge to move away. She still couldn't quite trust him yet. "Actually, it would be quicker if you would allow me inside to show you." He paused, waiting for an answer from her.

She didn't want to. It was bad enough that one Spirit Mage had been in her mind. She didn't really want to invite another one. However, Aidah knew at once there was a difference. Gabriel was asking. While at first he'd asked, later Rangwar had simply barged in. She frowned, opening her eyes again, looking at him. She sensed that he was still being open, readable, but it wasn't really helping. "Promise to ask me every time? And if I say no?"

Gabriel's gaze on her was steady, as was his aura, confirming his words. "Then I will not enter. And we will do things the hard way, by my instructing you and you trying until you get it right."

Aidah nodded, reassured. "All right. This time, you are allowed." She steeled herself for the feel of him inside her head, unsure what exactly to expect. Would it be like Rangwar in her dreams?

At first it was barely noticeable. It was definitely not like the dreams, because she was still awake, in the real world. But Aidah did start to feel an *otherness* inside her. She could feel age, a weariness, aches and pains in her joints that were not hers. With her third eye, she saw that Gabriel's aura was now wrapped around hers, permeating it. A little thrill of fear went through her, but just as soon as that happened, it was as if ghostly arms were around her, calming her. Inside her head, she heard Gabriel. *It's all right. I'm not going to hurt you.*

She breathed in, and let out her breath slowly. "I'm all right," she said. She said it out loud because she needed to hear herself, needed something to ground her in the world she had always known.

Close your eyes, Gabriel told her, and she did, letting him take control. It was if he were taking her 'hand' so to speak, directing her attention down deeper. He showed her how to regulate her breathing, her heart rate, and even her temperature. Then he showed her the energy points of which he had spoken of earlier. Seven points, from the crown of her head to the base of her tailbone, each controlling different parts of her.

The crown point will be one of your most powerful tools—it is from here that you can separate yourself from the rest of your energy points and travel through the spirit plane, the Astral. But you must not try it alone, until you are older and understand all the risks. Gabriel drew her away gently from that shining point of power. Aidah knew there was more, so much more. Oh how she wanted to understand it all! It felt right, like a missing piece of a puzzle that had been tormenting her for ages. She also understood, however, that it would take her time and practice to fully gather all the knowledge of her Talent.

She attempted to use her own voice inside her head, as he was. *And what would I have used to heal the sick baby?*

Gabriel's hands—his real hands—gripped hers. *Not yet, child. Before you would be able to heal another, you would have to know how to anchor yourself and shield against the illness. The first step to that is called Grounding.*

This is also what you must understand to control all those times when your Talent flares up unexpectedly, when you find your awareness floating without your conscious control.

Excitement filled her. Shielding! *Yes, please teach me,* Aidah told Gabriel, and he did, showing her how to sink her energy deep into the earth, connecting herself in a way that clearly outlined what was her and not her. Once it was clear what was not her, she was able to keep outside influence and energies out, which was essentially the same as shielding. She could do that even if she was not centered within her own body, extending her consciousness to another person, as she had when borrowing the Gedar's eyes and ears.

With your permission, I want you to practice something which we do frequently as Spirit Mages, Gabriel told her, as she practiced for a moment, grounding then reaching out of the wagon, seeing out of Montrose's eyes for a moment. The sky was gray and there was a cold breeze again from the east. Tavish was riding with Kendrick as usual, but she couldn't see either Jardan or her uncle. She pulled back before answering.

What is that? It must be something important, she reasoned, if he was waiting until he had her full attention to ask her. Not once yet through their mental training session had she sensed any 'wrongness' from him. It was day and night from the one training session she had received from Rangwar.

One of the simplest ways to heal another is to share energy with them. This is also useful between mages of all three Talents. When we overtax ourselves, we can be vulnerable. A Spirit Mage may draw upon their own inner strength and transfer it to another. This helps the body deal with stress, illness, wounds, and simple exhaustion. Aidah sensed something shifting within Gabriel, almost like a ripple in the current between them. Again, Gabriel was moving in and out of her it seemed like, adjusting something here, tweaking her attention there. Thinking his thoughts, she Looked at him, and she sensed his energy was low, that he was weak.

As they were sharing thoughts, she knew just what he needed. It sparked a memory for her. *This is how my Talent first showed up,* she said, and then it was suddenly all there, in her head, how to transfer energy without giving away too much, without taking in any of his aches and pains, his weariness. It flowed effortlessly from her and he sighed audibly as he accepted. He only took a little, and then showed her how to stop the flow.

They sat silently for a moment afterwards. It was a breakthrough, Aidah thought. She had controlled energy flow. "That's how I could have saved that baby" she said, understanding. Her chest hurt, but it wasn't the pain and anger she had felt moments earlier. She felt calmer now. Centered. She looked up at Gabriel, and he looked better than he had before, less exhausted. "Thank you," Aidah said in a soft voice.

They fell silent after that, and Aidah watched as Gabriel laid back and closed his eyes to sleep. Strangely enough, the little lesson had taxed her as well. The gentle rocking of the wagon slowly wove its spell over her as well. She slept.

18

Time Running Out

Tavish couldn't help his frequent glances at Montrose's wagon.

The caravan was moving along steadily, just as it had day after day, the steady plop of horse hooves the main sound along with the jangle of pots and pans and bells. Tavish couldn't hear much else above that, but he knew the Gedar were whispering among themselves, discussing the newest visitor joining their trek to Landaran. That old man hadn't looked like much to Tavish, not compared to the quiet strength of Jardan or Kendrick's fiery youth. But now they were all putting their faith in Gabriel, that Gabriel would be able to help Aidah—help train her, and help protect her.

Tavish glanced over at the wagon again, wondering what they were talking about in there, if Aidah was having her first training, and if she would be less moody afterwards, more like her old self. Not that he had been, of course. But he had a mission, and nothing could come in the way of that. They weren't children any longer.

"You're going to wear a hole in the side if you keep looking over there," Kendrick said in a half-teasing tone, bringing his horse in closer.

Tavish blew out a breath in frustration. "I just want to know what's going on. What we're going to do now."

Kendrick shrugged, and Tavish envied him, the confidence he always seemed to possess. "I expect we'll keep going as we have. You could use some more work with the blade as well, cousin."

That was an understatement. Tavish wondered if he'd ever be as good as Kendrick, and Jardan too, even if Jardan wasn't in his prime of youth any longer. He nodded. "I'm pretty useless with a sword." He was better standing off to the side and throwing fireballs if they were attacked again, which he fully expected they would be. He worried nightly about it, about a shadow in the dark sneaking into camp and stabbing Aidah. It gave him nightmares.

"I think my grandfather is right. We should concentrate on what you're used to first, the knife and dagger. Once you've developed some skill there, then we can focus on other weapons. I mean, it's not like you were raised to be a soldier. It's going to take time and a lot of practice."

But Tavish didn't have time. The closer they drew to Landaran, the more he was certain of that. Rangwar was coming, and now he was bringing an army with him. And his encounter with the vespyres had taught him that while short swords and daggers might be fine for a human assassin trying to kill them in the night, it wasn't going to work in a battle. He needed to perfect his sword skills as well.

As the cold wind from the north blew and the skies threatened snow again, Tavish returned to the latest tricks he was trying to perfect. Jardan had taught him how to make things colder. He had taught himself the invisibility trick. Kendrick had taught him how to hold and toss fire.

It was time to start combining things.

Tavish brought out what he'd bought for himself in Colmsford, a medium weight saber. The good thing about this blade was that it wasn't as heavy as a long sword, which Tavish knew he could barely wield. But the reach was longer than his short sword. Or a dagger. He held it out in front of himself, concentrating on the first trick. The blade began to cool down, until frost started to form along the edges. Good. He was getting better at that part.

Then he started making it invisible.

Light waves fought against his intentions, making the blade at first half invisible but warm, then cold but visible. Spots danced in front of his eyes as Tavish concentrated harder and harder, and a sharp pain lanced through his head. For an instant, only an instant, he had it, then everything fell back to normal, his hand and dagger visible, the metal warming up. A trickle of something dripped onto his lip; he tasted blood. Embarrassed, Tavish swiped at his bloody nose. A full blown migraine was starting to develop.

So perhaps he'd have to take things a little slower.

Tavish did his best to conceal the pain the rest of the day, but by nightfall he was in agony, and unable to perform even the simplest drills for Jardan.

"You've been taxing yourself too much, pushing your Talent," Jardan admonished him, as he heated up some water on the campfire for his famous headache tea. Tavish nodded weakly, cursing himself. Here he wanted to prepare himself, become a fighter, and what had he done? He'd sabotaged his own training, that was what.

At least Aidah looked more like her old self. Once they had parked the wagons, she had emerged with Gabriel with an actual smile on her face, speaking animatedly with the old man as they joined everyone at the campfire. Jardan rose and gave the Spirit Mage a proper greeting, grasping both the man's arms in a sort of embrace and offering him a place to sit. Montrose and his wife had left the 'murva' alone to be with the other Gedar, so it was just Brenton, Aidah, himself, Jardan, Kendrick and now Gabriel. Tavish had an idea that they would be discussing strategy again.

"So what exactly happened to you?" Jardan asked between sips of mutton stew. The weather was remaining calm but cold, clouds blocking out the stars above. It was so quiet out here in the hills and plains, Tavish thought. No howling of wolves, no cry of hawks. He had seen several rabbits and a fox or two, but little else that day.

Gabriel sighed, shaking his head. "I was foolish. Korva gave me the order to get to Aidah as quickly as possible. So I rode my gelding hard, six hours a day, as hard as an old man like me can manage. I was making good progress, and so once I passed Bonnenville, I stopped on the road for the night, even though there had been merchants who had offered to let me make camp with them. I was so tired, I forgot to put up the mental protections for myself and my steed that I usually do. That was a huge mistake."

"Protections?" Aidah asked, but Gabriel shook his head at her.

He continued. "The Emperor visited me to tell me that he was bringing an army, and that the city of Landaran would be attacked within a fortnight. He also threatened that as long as I was on this path to support Korva, he would be throwing 'obstacles' in my way." Gabriel grimaced. "When I woke up the next morning, my horse was dead. I was forced to walk, and that is how you found me earlier today. I'm only thankful that your company was only days, not weeks away. I've been walking for the past two days."

Tavish shook his head to himself, realizing for the first time what could have happened. There had been snow in the last few days. Gabriel was old, even if he was a powerful Spirit Mage. At some point, however, he could have succumbed to the elements and died. And where would they all be now, if that had happened?

"More obstacles?" Jardan asked, looking nervous. "We were attacked by a handful of vespyre a few days back. And now you tell me that there's going to be an army between us and Korva by the time we draw close. What other obstacles could he be talking about? And why tell us?"

Gabriel shrugged, as he reached for tea. Tavish wondered if he had a headache as well—he must have been using something, all this time, to keep himself warm when he was traveling. And who knew what kind of training Aidah and him had done today? "I don't know. We must be cautious, but we must move with all speed." Gabriel cradled the mug in his hands. "I've been warring with myself. Part of me thinks it would be best to take one of your fastest horses tomorrow morning and ride with Aidah to hopefully make it before the attack."

Brenton looked up at that, his brows drawing together in alarm. "Do you think that is wise? What if he kills that horse as well? You could be stranded..." He looked to Jardan for help.

Jardan nodded, sitting forward on his stool. "It would be a perfect trap—strand the two of you, and then stage an ambush. I'm not sure I like the thought of that."

One thing was sure. Tavish was certain he didn't like the idea of Aidah just riding off on her own, Spirit Mage with her or not. He wouldn't be there to protect her. And who had saved her the last time—not to mention the two times before that? Tavish stared hard at his sister. "If you're going, so am I." His tone said there would not be argument, not from the Protector herself.

She looked surprised. "But you can't ride hard like that—you're still learning!" Truth be told, they both were. Tavish had the sore thighs to prove it.

"I'll learn," Tavish insisted. He wanted to say more, but when Gabriel raised a hand, he reluctantly held his tongue. He couldn't help but give the old man a glare.

"The objective would be to outrun the army, and yes, Brenton, you are correct—it is possible the Emperor would find a way to strip us of another horse. But the closer we draw to the city, the more help will be available, both in the towns and on the road. We would still be faster than this caravan, even if we had to go through several animals. I fear that if we all remain together, we may not be able to reach Landaran at all. Either way has its risks." Gabriel, who had been sitting on one of the Gedar's little wooden stools, stood up and began pacing. Tavish had to admit that for however old he was, he still moved with a fair amount of grace and speed. He supposed the Life Talent probably helped a lot with that.

"And what if Rangwar set assassins upon the road or in the towns to confront you? I'm sorry, Gabriel, but you and I both know that our track record for keeping young Talents out of the Emperor's grasp haven't been great. Particularly for Spirit Talents." Jardan remained sitting, and perhaps because of this, he seemed to be the more confident of the two. Tavish couldn't help but nod in agreement. Fire Talents were renowned for their achievements in battle. What did Spirit Talents know of assailants in the dark?

Gabriel turned to look at him. "I understand your concern. Believe me, I've been thinking about this for some time, weighing the options. Unfortunately, it all comes down to one thing. Time. The longer we take to get all of us back within the safety of Landaran's walls, the more likely it becomes for the Emperor to succeed in his plans. He will continue to make attempts until either he succeeds or it becomes an impossible task. My duty is to bring Aidah to Korva, and make it impossible for Rangwar to capture her."

Tavish shivered at the coldness of Gabriel's tone. He had thought that Jardan was battle-hardened, but now he was starting to wonder. There was a presence to the Spirit Mage that he couldn't define. He didn't look imposing, but he *felt* powerful, if such a thing was possible. Tavish looked worriedly at Aidah. Surely they couldn't leave without him!

When he looked over at his sister, Tavish saw that she too looked distressed. Her gaze, however, kept returning over to the fire where the Gedar were gathered. Tavish leaned in a little closer, trying to trace the line of sight. Gair, he suddenly realized. She was glancing back over at Gair.

He wasn't sure that sat well with him.

"You make a convincing argument," Jardan said, rubbing his brow. "We had this debate before, but we had decided that having the safety of numbers within the company of the Gedar was better."

"That was before we heard this talk of war!" Kendrick spoke up, then at a look from his grandfather, fell silent again. Tavish understood him. Neither he nor Tavish wanted to be left here if all the action was going to be taking place elsewhere. And what would the Gedar do, if they split up? He doubted they would want to try to enter a city under siege, no matter how great the reward.

Brenton shook his head, hugging himself. "Do we really have to get her to Korva? What if she stayed with you, Gabriel, until the siege was past? I don't like this. I don't like it at all."

Gabriel shook his head. "Korva needs her because her own strength is failing. The weaker our Protector becomes, the weaker the Guardians and our borders. The easier that Rangwar can invade all of the Doane and sweep us all into his fold. At that point, no place would be safe for your niece. I can train her, but only Korva can bestow upon her the magics she designed as Protector."

Aidah stood up, her hands clenched into fists. "Do I get to have a say in this?" She looked uncertainly first at Gabriel, then at Jardan. Brenton looked conflicted. Jardan and Gabriel both turned to look at Aidah. There was something in her expression that seemed different to Tavish. Adult, almost. She squared her shoulders and looked them both in the eye.

"Absolutely," Gabriel said. "Please, speak your mind."

Tavish wondered if Gabriel realized what kind of a rant that might produce from his sister, but Aidah was already speaking. "None of you understand what it's been like for me. You don't understand having to live every day…knowing that every night when you fall asleep, you could wake to a nightmare." She looked on the verge of tears, but her voice was steady. Powerful, even. "I want to get to my Grandess as fast as I can. Just get me there."

Brenton looked despondent. "We're trying, Aidie. We're all trying to get you there. We just don't want to make the wrong decision. Sending you the fast way only to have you be captured doesn't help you, or anyone else."

Aidah sighed, crossing her arms and looking at the fire. "I know. But look what has already happened to us. I agree with Mr. Holt. My best chance of reaching Grandess is riding there as fast as I can." She rubbed her arms as if cold, but Tavish doubted that could be so, with them all sitting close to the fire. Perhaps it was a different kind of cold. "I want her protection."

Jardan and Gabriel looked at each other, and Tavish could see some kind of unspoken agreement pass between them. Jardan gave a nod. "I think that settles it, then. But understand me, Gabriel. I will be accompanying you, along with both my apprentices. You know that you could use our protection, and we each have our own horse. You can ride with Aidah—once we find you a new horse."

That would mean they would have to wait until they reached Bonnenville, Tavish realized. But then again, that was only a day's journey away. Another thought occurred to him, now that he knew he would be able to join them. "What about Brenton? Derg?" He found his gaze drifting over to his uncle, and saw the question in Brenton's face as well.

Gabriel's tone was firm. "There is no way they can accompany us. They are untrained in warfare and UnTalented. They would be a liability, I'm afraid."

Brenton opened his mouth to speak, looking shocked and angry. But Jardan held up a hand to him. "I have to agree with Mage Holt about this. We need fast riders who can fight if need be. Tavish is still learning his horsemanship skills, true. But his fire-wielding capabilities are more than adequate. I have every confidence he could defend himself or protect others; he has done so in the past, with even less training. But we can't be protecting someone without Talent that the Emperor could use as a distraction, or worse, a hostage. Even if you were fully proficient with the sword, I would hesitate to include you in this matter."

"But I'm their uncle. I got them away from Hamstead. I got them over the mountains," Brenton replied, and there was a note of pleading in his voice. "I just want to see that they arrive safely. I owe it to my sister." Tavish had to look away as he heard his uncle's words, heard the slight crack in Brenton's voice. It hadn't occurred to him how hard that must have been for his uncle, facing all the dangers as they had. For himself, Tavish had just taken things day by day. Let his elders worry about the big picture. But Brenton had a point. He'd succeeded when there had been almost no hope. Tavish saw Derg, quietly laying by the fire near Aidah, but the Lupas didn't speak up. A sharp pain lodged in Tavish's throat. Would he see them again if they separated? He honestly didn't know.

Gabriel Holt stood up, and walked over to put a hand on

Brenton's shoulder, smiling sadly at him. "And we thank you for your hard work, and your sacrifices. You must know that Korva will see to it that you have anything you need, whether you make the rest of the journey and come to Landaran once it is safe, or if you should decide to return home. You are a hero, and will be celebrated as such. But this task, right now, is not yours. For their safety, I ask that you hand over guardianship. We will keep them safe. Whatever the cost."

Tavish wondered if the Spirit Mage was using some of his skills, for at once, Brenton's shoulders relaxed, and he smiled a little, though there was still worry in his eyes. "I know," Brenton said, glancing over at Tavish, and at Aidah. "I just wanted to see them meet the Protector." He looked sheepish. "I wanted to meet her too."

"And you shall," Gabriel asserted. "In good time." He returned to his stool. "If the Gedar do not continue towards Landaran, I'm sure that there will be many others who will. You've seen the messengers. The towns will be sending troops. I'm sure you—and Derg—could join up with one of those companies. Mark me; the road that direction will still be dangerous for you. But I think you'll be less of a target if you are not with us."

Silence fell over the group, as they all contemplated Gabriel's words. The man made sense, Tavish had to admit. He didn't have to like it. Piece by piece, it felt like he was losing his family, his connections to home and the past. Would he even see his uncle and Derg again?

Derg finally spoke up, raising his head although he remained lying down. "We knew this day would come. I am satisfied that I have fulfilled my honor in carrying out the Protector's request. I have watched over my charges and seen to it that they were delivered to others to train and watch over them." He nodded to Brenton. "Your honor should be satisfied as well, Brenton. You led them out of the mountains. They each have a mentor and trainer now. Rest easy, and let the pups leave the den."

Brenton chuckled a little at that, but it wasn't a happy sound. He nodded, still looking a little torn. Tavish couldn't blame him. In his place, he doubted he would have handled things well. "I know. I wasn't supposed to be the parent letting their children go." He looked at Tavish and Aidah and gave a sad smile. "But I reckon that Derg is right. We would have had to say our goodbyes at some point."

"Hopefully only for a short time," Jardan interjected. "If you continue on towards Landaran, I'm hopeful that all of you could meet up again, even if only for a short time between their studies."

That was of course assuming they all managed to reach the city alive, Tavish thought with a shiver. But then again, he supposed they all had to hang onto what hope there was. "We'll be fine," he told his uncle, if only to help assure himself. They would make it. They had to.

"Then is it settled," Gabriel said. A feeling of peace came over the group. Tavish wasn't sure if it was real, or a fabrication from the Spirit Mage. "Once we reach Bonnenville, we will part ways and make a hard push for Landaran. If things go well, we will reach Landaran in four or five days. That should put us ahead of an invasion."

Unless Rangwar had other tricks up his sleeve, Tavish thought.

19

Goodbyes

It actually took the Gedar caravan another day and a half to make its way to Bonnenville. As the wagons rolled along, Aidah continued her studies with Gabriel, practicing shielding and centering, over and over. They spoke only through their minds, another exercise in control for Aidah, because all too often instead of simply hearing Gabriel's thoughts, she heard Montrose or Brenton. Or even what passed for the horse's thoughts.

She didn't like the snatches of Brenton's thoughts that came through. He was second-guessing himself, still wondering if he should allow Gabriel and Jardan to ride off with his sister's children. There was a lot of self-blame there, and worry. It made her feel uncomfortable. It shouldn't be so easy to intrude on another's privacy, but it was. She almost couldn't keep him out, so strong were his thoughts.

Aidah had caught glimpses of Tavish's as well, but his were much more comfortable, excited, even. He was off riding towards the front of the caravan with Jardan and Kendrick again, undoubtedly learning another new trick or two. Aidah smiled. Her brother seemed much happier these days, having the two fire Talents with him. He needed other people around.

That had never been true for herself. While Aidah needed and valued Gabriel's lessons, she was perfectly content to sit alone with her thoughts. One thought in particular continued to plague her, as they drew nearer to the city, passing a small village or two where the bleating of sheep penetrated the wooden sides of the wagon. One thought distracted her, as she practiced her centering. Gair Malin.

Like Brenton, there was no possible way he would be able to accompany her on the hard push to Landaran. Today they would reach Bonnenville, and she would have to say goodbye, perhaps forever. It weighed heavily on her heart.

She hoped she would be given the chance to say goodbye. On the one hand, having the chance might make her feel better, being able to see Gair again, speak with him. But on the other hand, perhaps it would be easier if her mentor simply whisked her away. If Gair never came to Landaran, if she never saw him again, what would a goodbye matter?

"I think we are drawing close," Gabriel said, pulling Aidah out of her thoughts. He stood up carefully in the slowly rocking wagon, making his way towards the front to pull open the shutters. Montrose and Brenton were there, seated on the little bench as Montrose guided the draft horse with his whip and reins. Beyond them, the view was mostly blocked by the other wagons, but in the distance, Aidah thought she could see something.

"Is that Bonnenville?" she asked. She felt more than saw Gabriel nod; already between them there was an unspoken communication, a link of some kind. Gabriel had explained that it commonly occurred between Spirit Talents because of the nature of their abilities, and that she shouldn't be concerned by it. It wasn't thought-sharing, precisely; it went deeper than that. Feelings was the best word she could find to describe it.

"You can see the mayor's palace from here. There, to the right," Gabriel said in a low voice, pointing.

Bonnenville seemed to fill the horizon, Aidah thought, taking in the view. Yes, she could see the palace, rising towers of stone with turrets and a steepled roof. It was an actual castle, just like in wildfolk tales. The castle had high walls, but those were not the only walls; in fact, the entire city was walled and fortified. Towers rose in regular lengths along the stone walls and she could just make out the movement of guards on top of them. Beyond the wall, dozens—nay, *hundreds* of shingled roofs of buildings of all shapes and sizes, including a few tall buildings of stone which must be temples.

Aidah looked at Gabriel. "They have more than one patron god?" At Hamstead of course, they had only had one, devoted to Meira the Good, Giver to mankind.

"Bonnenville has four temples," Gabriel explained. "Jael,

Aghar, Leta, and Elidi," pointing out the buildings for the sun god, earth goddess, rain goddess, and goddess of the harvest. It made sense, Aidah supposed. In the rolling plains here, they probably concentrated on farming and sheep herding. "They also have smaller shrines for the lesser deities including Iduna and Meira." Iduna was the goddess of love. Aidah wondered if there were also shrines for some of the darker ones like Ulmer, God of War.

"What do they do in Bonnenville?" It seemed wrong that she knew so little of a large city like this. Other than Landaran, however, her tiny village had not maintained contact with many of the lowland cities. She had known they existed, but that was about it. If Korva had her way, she would soon be responsible for protecting all these lands.

"A great deal of things," Gabriel answered, returning to the little bench to sit. "They're well known for their clothing production, including both wool and linen. As you can see from the periphery wall, they are also known for their stone working. The people of Bonnenville are a sturdy folk. The winters here are still quite harsh, and the summer can be brutal as well. The lands around here are better for grazing than farming, other than flax."

Aidah nodded, not really listening to him. She had caught sight of Gair riding his little donkey again, near one of the other wagons. Her heart seemed to lodge in her throat.

"You're thinking of people you're going to miss, aren't you," Gabriel said softly, startling her out of her thoughts. She turned around guiltily to look at him.

"Am I that obvious? Or am I sending again?" They'd spoken earlier about how with his fully developed Talent, Gabriel would be the first to know if she was 'leaking' either thoughts or emotions. She generally had a better idea of when she was doing it, but this, today...she couldn't seem to hold things inside.

"Just emotions—that and you seemed to be focused on something other than the city. It's all right. I know this must be difficult for you. You've been traveling with these people for quite some time, a very stressful time for you, in fact. And your uncle. I'm sure you are concerned about what will become of him." Gabriel's voice was gentle, as opposed to the sternness it had held last night when they'd reached this decision. Aidah supposed that he wasn't used to dealing with children. After all, Jardan had said that he hadn't taken on an apprentice in a long time. She doubted, however, that he truly understood what she was going through.

Looking out window with the wagon's rocking motion made her feel ill, so Aidah closed the shutters. They would be in Bonnenville soon enough. "I just want a chance to say goodbye to everyone who has helped me." Montrose, for certain. And then perhaps she could steal a private moment with Gair.

"I'll make sure you have that chance," Gabriel assured her. "Know also that this is only the beginning for you, Aidah. You're going to meet many, many people, many new friends. We are a long-lived group even without stealing extra years. So please, do not be sad." Aidah had a feeling she knew what Gabriel was trying to tell her, that while she might have a liking for a young Gedar right now, there would be other young men, others who would be interested in her. She didn't care. At the moment, she only wanted to keep the ones she already had.

The caravan was stopped twice on the way into the city, first as they left the main road to take the trail leading towards the perimeter wall and gatehouse by guards who were stationed at the road. They were keeping watch over a company of men departing the city— recruits for the army, Aidah learned, as she and Gabriel took a look out the wagon's windows. The second time was at the gatehouse, with a burly man asking what their business in town would be. It seemed the locals had grown wary of strangers, including Gedar. This second time, Gabriel was forced to exit the wagon to speak to the guards, explaining who they were. Things went much smoother from that point, and they even received an escort to the marketplace where the Gedar could camp and sell their wares.

It was time to say goodbye.

Aidah ignored the look from her uncle, leaving her brother to keep him busy for a moment as she hurried to find Gair among the Gedar youths setting up their acts to perform for the townspeople. She didn't have to look hard; he was waiting for her, and the instant he saw her, he gave a nod, taking her arm and guiding her behind one of the wagons where they could have at least a little privacy.

Once there, however, she had no idea what to say. Aidah looked down at her hands, aware even as she did so that Gair was avoiding her gaze as well. The two of them stood close, and she could almost feel Gair's longing, matching her own. She finally reached out and grasped his hand. He squeezed it hard.

One question she had to ask. "Will I see you again?"

Gair looked up, startled. "Of course. If I have anything to say about it, that is. Do you think they'll let you see me?"

That thought hadn't even occurred to her, but she could see that it had worried Gair. It made sense, she supposed. The Gedar, while allied of the people of the Doane, were still something of an underclass. Slightly undesirable. It struck her anew—she was going to be like nobility, like royalty, even. They would probably keep her sequestered away. "If they don't, I'll sneak out. They'd better not try to pick and choose my friends."

Out of the corner of her eye, she caught Gair smiling. "Good. I'm worried that they'll try to change you. Make you into some kind of ice princess. They say the Protector is cold. That she doesn't smile much. I want to see you smile." He looked up, and Aidah finally allowed herself to look directly at him as well. "Maybe I could get a job as a court jester!"

Aidah laughed. "I'd like that. Even if it was just your clan, coming to the city to perform once in a while..." That reminded her. She needed to thank Montrose and his wife for all they had done, allowing them to sleep and travel in their wagon, helping her during her sickness. She also had to say goodbye to her uncle and Derg. She bit her lip, needing to go, but wanting to stay.

Gair saw her look and understood immediately. "You need to say goodbye to your uncle." He smiled. "And don't worry. The mages will get you to the city. And when it is safe enough, I will find my way there. I promise." He reached into his pocket, fumbling around for something, and brought out a coin, one that Aidah hadn't seen before. He handed it to her, and she flipped it over in her palm, gazing at it. On one side there was stamped an image of a little wagon, just like Montrose's. On the other, there was a man playing a lute. She looked at him curiously.

"Is this what I think it is?" She had heard rumors of coins the Gedar people stamped for themselves, but she had never seen one. It was said that it was a way they identified one another, that they only traded the coins among themselves.

Gair nodded. "If you need help, you can show that to someone in a Gedar clan, any clan, and they will know that you are a friend."

He blushed a little. "I figured it was also something to help you think of me. When you are worried or just plain down…look at it, and think of juggling." He grinned.

Aidah couldn't help but laugh a little at that, imagining him and his crazy antics. It also brought to mind his teaching her, arms around her. She blushed a little herself, and pocketed the coin. "Thank you. I hope to see you soon." That was as much as she could say. With a final glance at him, a brief meeting of gazes, Aidah turned and hurried back to the wagon where Tavish was busy packing up things in small satchels that he and Aidah could easily carry while riding. He looked up at her approach, and immediately his eyes moved to where Gair was also emerging from behind the wagon, narrowing in speculation. But Tavish said nothing, for which Aidah was grateful.

Her uncle stood to one side, looking frustrated and pensive. Derg mirrored his mood, pacing in front of Brenton, long tail lashing back and forth in agitation. Brenton looked at her, and there was a wounded look in his eyes. She heard his thoughts; he was cursing the fact that he wasn't Talented, that he didn't have the training or skills needed to accompany them the rest of the way. She ran up and hugged him hard.

His grip on her was vice-like, and he only reluctantly let her go. Aidah could see him struggling to find words. "You and your brother…" He swallowed.

"We'll take care," Aidah promised him.

Brenton nodded uncomfortably. "I would really hate to have to explain to your mother in Murd's hallways that I let her down and the two of you perished. So just…do whatever you need to do. Listen to your teachers and stay safe."

"Yes, Uncle. Thank you, for everything," Aidah said, putting emphasis into her words. This was not supposed to have been Brenton's task, keeping her and Tavish safe, delivering them to Landaran. She suspected she knew where he would go next. "Will we see you? Before—you know—" Aidah looked to the east, to the storm clouds there.

"Before I go to try and rescue Grandpa, you mean?" There was steel in Brenton's voice. Aidah had a feeling he would die trying to rescue Grandpa Ethan and her father, if needed. She shivered.

"Yes." The thoughts weren't new to her. Gods, but it seemed

like Tavish dreamt of revenge scenarios every day.

Brenton smiled. "Of course I will. I want to see the two of you, in your new stations, safely inside the city. But then, yes, I plan to head east. The longer your father and Grandpa are there, the more I worry about them." Neither of them spoke of their greatest fear, that the two were already dead.

"You take care as well, then," Aidah said, hugging him again. "Love you, Uncle." And she meant that. One by one, it seemed like she was losing family members. At least she still had Tavish.

She hugged Derg next, who wrapped his long tail around her in his own sort of embrace. "I'll miss you," she told the Lupas. He has always made her feel safe.

"I'll miss you as well," Derg said, sounding almost whining in his sadness. "I'll stay with Brenton, and see to it that he doesn't get himself into too much trouble." He placed a paw on her hand. "If you ever need help, don't forget that you can always go to the Lupas, and tell them my name and clan. They'll help you." He rubbed his furry face against her—his way of kissing, Aidah supposed.

Finally, Aidah moved to say farewell to Montrose and Eomma. She thanked them for their hospitality, knowing that she and Tavish had probably displaced them from their beds. Eomma waved a hand and stated that they'd long before stopped using the little cots in the wagon and taken to sleeping outdoors; their old bones preferred more room than the little wagon provided. Eomma gave her a Gedar vest of brightly embroidered red and yellow, complete with little tin charms sewn in along the neckline.

Montrose clapped her on the back. "Don't you worry, little dear. We'll make a stop in Landaran, as soon as the roads are safe and the threat of war is a bit less imminent. Have to get our reward, you know!" He winked. "I'd also love to see how you and your brother are getting along."

"I'll be sure to tell Korva how much you all helped us. I don't think we could have made it this far otherwise," Aidah said.

Montrose grinned, his gold tooth gleaming. "Yes, tell them! A bit of fame could help us out, and I'm not ashamed to show off for the rich Landaran folk. Should be a prosperous year!"

They both laughed, and Aidah shook his hand and bade him farewell. She found Tavish hugging and rubbing Derg's belly, two packs sitting on the ground beside him. As she walked up, he sighed and hugged Derg one last time, then grabbed his pack and stood up, motioning for her to take the second pack. He didn't look particularly sad to be moving on. Aidah supposed he had been ready for this for some time—probably ever since Nera had come to Hamstead to train him in his Sun Talent two years ago. He loved adventure.

She wished for a quiet life

20

Bonnenville

Aidah and Tavish made fast work of packing up and leaving the Gedar caravan once Jardan and Gabriel returned from the castle. Afternoon had crept into evening, so they decided to stay the night in the castle, which Aidah learned belonged to Duke Harcourt, a cousin to Jardan by way of marriage. Gabriel, in his official role as Spirit Mage Holt, hailed them a coach, and stated that it was likely the Duke would want to meet Aidah. A faint sense of unease assailed her; it seemed it was already starting, the fame that came with the rarity of her Talent. There seemed to be something more to it as well, something about her place in Korva's family, but it was beyond her comprehension. At the moment, all Aidah really wanted to do was sleep so that she could ride early in the morning and finally reach her destination.

Aidah had never ridden in a coach before. It was much more comfortable than Montrose's wagon, with velvet-lined seats and shocks to absorb most of the jarring from the cobblestone roads. Out the window, she could see all manner of shops as they passed through the Merchant's District, all bustling with activity as shoppers made their rounds. The clothing was brightly colored, and there were styles reminiscent of the Gedar—scarves worn over skirts on some women, and embroidered vests on the men. There didn't seem to be a lot of nobles in this town, but Aidah did spot one or two. The men wore velvet doublets and cloaks, while the women wore gowns of some material she was not familiar with. It looked very soft.

Once again her attire, which had seemed so new and wonderful back in Thornton, now seemed drab and quaint in comparison. She supposed, though, that it would continue like this, richer and richer, until they reached Landaran.

The coach turned off from the merchant district onto a straight wide road heading directly towards the inner ramparts and the castle. From her vantage point, Aidah couldn't see much, but she could see guards at points along the road, standing straight in bright red and blue livery, their spears held tightly in their right hands. They passed through a stone archway with a portcullis, the entrance to the inner courtyard. The wheels of the coach clattered against the stones of the road, making Aidah's teeth hurt. Beside her, Tavish was engrossed in the sights as well, his head hanging out the window in his efforts to see everything at once.

During the entire trip, Gabriel and Jardan had been engrossed in quiet conversation with each other, sharing news, not that Aidah had paid much attention. As the coach rolled up to the front steps of the castle, however, they swiftly ended their talk, looking as if they were preparing for something. Would there be trouble? Aidah wondered. Kendrick, who had been half napping during the ride, came awake and stretched. "Nice not to have to ride for a bit," he commented, as the coach came to a halt.

Two footmen, also in blue and red with a rampant white horse on their livery, hurried forward and opened the doors of the coach. Gabriel and Jardan exited first, and then Kendrick. Aidah looked at Tavish, and she could see her own nervousness mirrored on his face. They'd never been anywhere fancy. How were they supposed to behave?

"Come on," Kendrick said, and the moment was broken; Tavish grinned, as irrepressible as ever, and climbed out of the coach, leaving Aidah to climb out last. She imagined that Gabriel had already sent word of their coming and more specifically, who she was. Flushing, she kept her eyes lowered as the footmen assisted her, then went to stand by Gabriel's side, as his apprentice.

Aidah raised her eyes at the sound of footfalls, quickly approaching them. A bald man in a full-skirted blue jacket and parti-colored hosen hurried up to them, wiping at his brow with a handkerchief. He looked comical in his haste, and Aidah couldn't help but stifle a chuckle. He bowed to all five of them with a flourish of his handkerchief. "Welcome, Sirs and Lady Mages. The Duke is at his repast, but bids that you join him. He understands that you have been traveling for some time, yes?"

"Indeed," Gabriel said, immediately taking the lead, which made sense to Aidah. He was the most senior, both in his position and in age. He carried himself with confidence, and Aidah had the sudden realization that he was used to this, comfortable with it. Jardan too, looked to be in his element.

"Our apologies to the Duke for our appearances in that regard; we haven't had time to freshen up," Jardan said. Even he was dressed only in dusty travel clothes, though they were of a finer cloth. It actually made Aidah feel a little better—at least they all shared the fact they were dusty from the road.

"Nonsense, nonsense—we know the reason of your haste. The Duke of Bonnenville is grateful for the opportunity to host such company. My name is Dunby, and I'll be at your service for anything that you require." With a wave of his kerchief, Dunby motioned for them all to follow. He walked at a more leisurely pace, but there was still quickness to his movements that reminded Aidah of a little brown hare, or a deer perhaps. She glanced sidelong at Tavish to see what he made of the odd fellow.

He glanced at her and pointed to his head, indicating that he too thought Dunby was a little touched.

They followed Dunby into the castle, and the fellow rattled off some of the history of the place, mostly for Tavish and Aidah's benefit, Aidah was sure. Apparently the castle predated the Doane Republic, and had been a small fiefdom in the days of the old Innis Empire before Korva and the other refugees fled the tyranny. The Duke's lineage ran back to that original line, though he'd intermarried with the descendants of the refugees. There had been a Storm Mage or two in the line, but not much else.

Dunby allowed them to wash their hands and faces before bringing them into the main dining hall. At the far end of the hall, sitting on a long table heaped with food, sat the Duke, his wife, their two sons, and a few other guests, including one fellow who wore the black and gold uniform of the Doane—a soldier of some kind, Aidah guessed. Dunby led the group over to stand in front of the Duke, a middle-aged man with a receding hairline and a round face. He looked regal enough in a brocaded doublet and a bright blue cloak, but for some reason Aidah could imagine him as being more comfortable in plainer clothes, perhaps surrounded by books. He had a scholarly look to him. Gabriel and Jardan both gave slight bows, and Kendrick gave a low bow, giving Aidah and Tavish looks to follow his actions. Aidah did so, feeling awkward and remembering at the last second that she was probably supposed to curtsy instead.

Dunby held his arm out towards the duke. "The esteemed Duke Harlan Radcliff of Bonnenville, his Lady Gwenna, and his sons Alric and Frederick. Sir, may I present to you Spirit Mage Holt, Sun Mage Thorne, his apprentice, Kendrick, and the newest Talents, Tavish and Aidah Dernholt." Aidah blinked as Dunby rattled off the names without hesitation.

Duke Radcliff nodded at their group, and Aidah could feel the man's eyes on her, assessing her. It made her feel distinctly uncomfortable, but it wasn't like the looks Rangwar had given her. It was something different—more like how the town bullies had used to look at Tavish, as if trying to decide if they could best him or not. She stared back, then realized it was probably rude to stare; relunctantly, she lowered her eyes.

"Interesting. Thank you, Dunby," the Duke said in a smooth cultured voice. Aidah heard the scrape of a chair and glanced up again to find the Duke standing up and indicating the empty chairs at his table. "Please, won't you all join us? I understand you have been on the road for some time." He chuckled, looking at Jardan. "I imagine the cuisine has been basic at best. My cooks are known for their roasted wild pheasant."

"It would be a delight, Your Grace," Jardan replied. He placed a hand on Tavish and Aidah's shoulders, leading them around to sit nearest the Duke, taking his own seat just down from them. Kendrick and Gabriel quietly took their seats at the far end of the table, and Aidah realized she had no idea who was considered the highest rank here, or how that all worked. More than ever, she felt like a 'dumb hillfolk' as Kendrick sometimes teasingly called them.

Aidah sat down gingerly, almost afraid to touch the fine embroidered cushions on the high-backed wooden chair. She'd never been in such a lavish place before, and she feared that the dust of the road which clung to her would mark everything she touched. A servant hurried forward to lay a plate in front of her, heaped high with steaming pheasant, roasted carrots and buttery rolls. Her stomach growled loudly. She blushed to the roots, feeling everyone's eyes on her. "Excuse me," she said in a small voice.

The fellow in the uniform surprised her by laughing, a deep hearty laugh that reminded her of Montrose. "It seems you're right, Your Grace. I'll bet they haven't had a decent meal in ages." He offered Aidah a thick hand hardened with calluses. "Captain Caleb Murdock, at your service, Miss Dernholt." Before she could even respond, he was taking her hand and giving it a firm shake.

He too looked her over, and again Aidah flushed, feeling uncomfortable. She'd known that she would be scrutinized like this once they reached Landaran—she'd gathered that from the rarity of her Talent and how the Talented had responded to her so far. But she hadn't realized it would begin now, before they even reached Landaran.

Beside her, Tavish leaned in a little closer, and she could feel him measuring the captain right back, letting the man know that nobody was going to ogle his sister while he was near. The Duke broke off further ponderings.

"So I understand the two of you are twins, is that correct? And by all means, please eat. I'm curious about the circumstances of your arrival, but I can be patient." Duke Radcliff had almost finished his plate, and as Aidah began digging into her roasted pheasant, a servant took the Duke's plate away and replaced it with a dish of custard and raspberries. The meat almost melted in her mouth. She'd never had anything so good before.

"Twins, yes," Jardan answered for them, before he took his own first bite. "Oh my—that is excellent. My compliments to your chef."

"I'll be sure to tell him," Duke Radcliff said, with a smile. He looked at Aidah again. "And which one of you—dear me, I hope this isn't rude. But which was born first?"

Now that was an odd question. Aidah looked to Tavish, hoping he would answer. He was having a bit of trouble spearing a baby carrot with his fork, but looked up when she didn't answer. "I was. They said I was really loud." He managed to impale the carrot and stuck it into his mouth.

"Hmm," the duke said, and Aidah wondered what he meant by that. Radcliff looked to Jardan. "He's the fire Talent, yes?"

"Correct," Jardan said, after another bite. "Aidah is the Spirit Talent. She already knows she's to be groomed to be the next Protector."

"Right, right, of course," Duke Radcliff said, popping a berry into his mouth, but Aidah had a feeling that now his curiosity was shifting more towards Tavish than herself, which didn't make sense. Sun Mages weren't common, but there were certainly more of them than Spirit Mages.

Tavish, of course, did not seem concerned at all. He was halfway through his meal, eating like he hadn't eaten in weeks. Aidah turned her attention to her food as well, as the Duke and Jardan began making small talk about local issues, including the crops and the strange weather lately. Apparently Jardan's son, the Earl, and Duke Radcliff were friends. That made sense, she supposed—it wasn't that far to Thornton from here, so they probably shared a lot of the same concerns with their townships.

Gabriel surprised her by asking the captain a question. "How many troops are you sending to Landaran? Have they left yet?"

"About a thousand foot soldiers and two hundred archers, fifty cavalry. They'll be leaving in the morning, actually," Captain Murdock replied, taking a sip of brandy. He'd finished his custard, and was sitting back now, relaxing.

Gabriel nodded, taking his time to chew and swallow a bite. "Is that the first regiment you've sent? What did the news say as far as an expected timetable?"

Captain Murdock set down his glass. "I see where you're going with this. We received word from Landaran of a likely attack in the next two weeks. We sent our mages first, along with a small party of scouts to try and pester the enemy should they arrive earlier than expected. The word is that there are blind spots along the line of Guardians and Korva is anticipating an initial strike soon—perhaps in about a week to two weeks, so the call was urgent." He glanced at Aidah. "I think we all know why. I don't think there's been this kind of tension since your son—" he abruptly broke off at the dark look that crossed Gabriel's face, glancing at Aidah again. "Sorry," he finished taking his brandy glass again and looking down at it. "I spoke of things I shouldn't."

Aidah blinked and stared at Gabriel. It seemed there were more secrets being kept from her. He ignored her look but nodded to the captain. "Indeed, Captain. There has not been a new Spirit Talent in the family for many years. Thus the urgency of our mission," he said.

She was growing full, but it was difficult to concentrate on food with the talk that was going on. Beside her, Aidah could feel Tavish fidgeting; he'd finished his plate. "Would it be better if we travelled with the troops? I mean, that's safe, isn't it?" Tavish asked, pushing one of his carrots around.

Gabriel shook his head. "They're mostly on foot, so they're going to take longer to get there—perhaps as long as the Gedar would have taken. The troops which are being sent to Landaran will most likely be used in a ground battle outside the city. Landaran has its own forces, which should be sufficient to fortify the city, but Rangwar's troops could create a barricade and seal off the city from resources, like food and munitions. Our intention is to reach Landaran before any such barricade can occur."

So the only troops *outside* the city once they reached it might be Rangwar's troops. Aidah shivered. She was full, and the weight of everything started to come down on her again, making her droop in her seat.

Jardan took note. "The young ones are tired, and we have a long day of riding tomorrow. With your leave, Your Grace, I think we'd like to retire for the evening." It dawned on Aidah that while they'd been talking, everyone had finished their plates, with the exception of Gabriel.

Gabriel nodded at Jardan. "I'll join you all shortly. I'd like to catch up on a few things with the Duke first. My last time through here was a bit rushed." He sat back and offered his glass as a servant brought forth the brandy bottle.

No custard for the guests, Aidah supposed, but then again, they hadn't really come with a lot of notice. She stifled a yawn. Jardan was right. She was exhausted. "Thank you for dinner," she said, trying to be polite, and then remembered she was supposed to be using titles. "Uh—Your Grace." She blushed.

He chuckled. "You are most welcome, my dear. I do hope that when things are settled, we'll be able to see a bit more of the two of you," he held his palm out, indicating both her and her brother. "When Court's in season in the summer, perhaps." He scooted back his chair and rose, and instantly everyone at the table stood up. Aidah and Tavish hurried to follow suite.

There was a chorus of "good night" from around the table, and Aidah remembered this time to curtsy as she followed the butler and Jardan out of the room, leaving behind Gabriel. As she passed through the doorway, she heard them sitting down again, chatting about things like the upkeep of Bonnenville's defenses and how the trade was this year. She was glad to leave that all to the adults.

Dunby led them up a stone staircase and down corridors decorated with hanging tapestries to a couple small rooms at the end of the hall, guest bedrooms, Aidah supposed. Each room had two beds, a chest of drawers, and a wash basin. Servants had warmed the beds for them, and set their bags against the outer wall. Aidah felt grateful for the bed warmers; it was cold in the castle, not at all like the thatch cottage where she had grown up. She and Tavish were to share a room; Jardan and Kendrick would share the second. Apparently Gabriel was an esteemed guest and merited a guest chamber of his own.

Aidah hurried to dress for bed, used the room's chamber pot, and washed her face and hands at the basin. The Gedar hadn't been a big change for her in terms of how people lived, but everything felt strange here, almost too clean. She sat on the feather mattress awkwardly, trying to decide if she liked the feel of the soft mattress over firm straw and hard wood. Across from her, Tavish glanced up from where he was trying to decide what to do with a scrub brush beside the basin. "Do they expect us to clean the floors here?"

"I think that's to scrub the dirt from your fingernails," Aidah replied, but she wasn't positive about that.

"Oh," Tavish said, setting it back down. He rinsed off his face and wiped it with a towel. "This is going to take some getting used to. Do you suppose they're going to make us wear their fancy clothes? In Landaran, I mean."

"Definitely," Aidah answered. She couldn't imagine that they'd let them wear the rustic homespun clothes they'd always worn. By the way that the Duke had been treating them this evening, it was like they were royalty or something. She hadn't paid much attention to the Duke's wife, but as she recalled, the woman had looked rather stiff in some kind of bodice. It looked uncomfortable, and Aidah wasn't looking forward to trying something like it. "I suppose eventually we'll get used to it." She sounded doubtful.

"Yeah," Tavish agreed, yawning. "Well, to bed then. I don't know what time Mage Holt means to wake us, but I'll bet you it'll be before dawn." He crawled into the bed. "I feel like I'm sleeping inside a goose."

Aidah laughed. "That sounds awful!" But the humor did help to allay the strangeness of everything. She pulled the coverlet over herself, then leaned over to blow out the candles. The room plunged into near complete darkness. Even though she was warm in the bed, Aidah shivered.

"Good night, Sis," Tavish said in a small voice. He sounded a little frightened himself. For some reason, it actually helped Aidah to know that. As her eyes adjusted to the sliver of moonlight coming through the narrow glass window, she realized she could at least make out the objects in the room. She sighed.

"Good night." Sleep felt far away. As she tried to relax and drift off, Aidah listened to the sounds of the castle. Down in the courtyard she heard the clip clop of a horse, probably a night patrolman. She heard the soft sound of Tavish's breath as he dropped off to sleep. Moments passed, where she couldn't hear much of anything at all. Then she heard just the barest sound of footfalls out in the corridor.

Aidah heard a tiny creak as the door opened. In the dark, she saw a cloaked figure standing—Gabriel perhaps, checking on them?

But when the figure raised one arm, and when Aidah saw moonlight glinting off the steel dagger, she knew it wasn't her mentor.

21

A Knife in the Dark

At the sight of the dagger, Aidah sent out a wave of pure fear, similar to what she had done at the house when cornered by Rangwar. She hoped it would alert Jardan and Gabriel, but she could feel as it struck something intangible, a shield of some kind, and bounced back at her. It hurt, as the wave collided with her, and Aidah suddenly gained some notion of what it had felt like to others to be hit by such a wave. Dimly, she heard Tavish cry out in pain.

Light flared in the room, a bright flame in her brother's hand as he leapt to his feet, facing their assailant. Aidah was never so grateful to be siblings with a Firestarter. By the light of the small flame, Aidah could see their foe, but what she saw confused her. At first, she thought it Gabriel, but as she looked closer, she saw that the man was younger by a good many years. He held a long steel dagger and was dressed from head to toe in black, his long hair held in a pony tail, gray at the temples. He looked at her and sneered.

"Now come along like a good girl. Or I'll kill your brother."

Just like that, Aidah watched as her brother's eyes rolled up and he collapsed, his flame going out. The room plunged back into darkness, but before Aidah could think to scream, the door opened and fresh light poured in, illuminating the room from a candelabrum held by none other than the real Gabriel. Aidah sobbed in relief, hoping, praying that her brother was all right, that whoever this man was hadn't killed him already.

At the sight of the stranger, Gabriel paled, and his eyes grew steely and hard. "Alaric," he said in a low voice. Aidah held still, wondering how the two knew each other. She wanted to go to her brother to check on him, but it seemed like a bad idea to draw attention to herself at the moment. The man, Alaric, turned to face Gabriel, brandishing his weapon.

"Hello, Father." He sneered, and Aidah gasped. Mage Holt had a son?

Alaric's pause gave Aidah the chance to check on Tavish, but as soon as Aidah moved, Alaric dashed towards her. She didn't know if he meant to kill her with that knife or only threaten her with it, but she had no intentions of finding out. Ducking low, she kicked out with her foot at the man's knee, intent on breaking it if she had to. She felt her heel connect, heard the crack, but then suddenly all the strength seemed to leave her; she crumpled to the floor, unable to even find the energy to stand, let alone fight. Alaric grunted, then flexed his knee with a pop. If Aidah had held any doubts before, she didn't now. Alaric, like his father, had to be a Spirit Mage.

"Back away, Father, or I swear I will kill them both," Alaric said, moving closer to crouch down beside Aidah, working an arm around her to pull her unsteadily to her feet. She feebly tried to push him of, but it was like a toddler trying to break a parent's grasp. She simply had no strength. She gulped as she felt the cold metal of the blade at her throat.

Gabriel's mouth set in a hard line, but Aidah saw no fear in his eyes. It helped steady her a little. "You aren't going to kill her. I know that Rangwar wants her alive. So unless you have recently broken off from him and decided to start your own little empire, you're bluffing. The Emperor would hardly go to the trouble of organizing a full blown invasion for a dead girl."

Behind Gabriel, Aidah saw the shadow of movement—Jardan, most likely. Against her skin, the metal seemed to be growing warmer.

Alaric noticed the additional help as well. "Call him off." Aidah could hear the frustration in his voice. This obviously wasn't going as planned for the enemy mage.

"No," Gabriel said. "I have two Sun Mages under my shields. You are but one, without support, it seems. Give yourself up. Come work for a government that actually cares about its people."

There was a shift in the room; Aidah could feel it. She didn't dare try to move against Alaric, but she also couldn't see how he could possibly escape now, and he knew it as well. She heard him growl softly under his breath. His muscles were tense, his heart beat elevated.

Alaric spit at the floor, snarling. "Not today, dear Father. We'll have her soon enough anyway."

In a blur of movement, he released Aidah. She hardly had time to turn her head, then he was climbing up on the night table and diving through the room's narrow window, breaking the glass in a loud shatter as he passed through. Gabriel ran to her side and immediately strength flowed back into her, making her heart race. She stared at the broken window in horror. The room was high in the castle, over cobblestone. "Is he—" She couldn't bring herself to say it. Even if he was working for Rangwar, it seemed a terrible thought that he should be dead.

Gabriel shook his head. "Alaric is a Spirit Mage. A fall like that might hurt him, but he would be able to heal most of the damage quickly. He'll mostly likely pull the rest from an unsuspecting guard. I'll have to alert the Duke. I doubt Alaric will give up so easily." He bent down and touched Tavish's forehead, frowning. With a gasp, Tavish awoke, looking startled.

"What—?" Tavish asked, looking wildly about. "Was I dreaming?" He looked over at Aidah, then at the broken window.

"I'm afraid you weren't," Gabriel said, after looking him over. "You were accosted by an enemy mage. He's gone now. You and your sister are safe."

Tavish started to ask about the window, but Aidah touched his shoulder, shaking her head. "I'll explain later." She wasn't sure she could believe it herself, that a man could fall from a height like that, onto a stone floor, and not be dead. She feared that Gabriel was correct, however.

Jardan entered the small chamber as well, heading for the broken window. He bent over, careful not to touch the broken glass and peered out into the courtyard, then sighed. "I don't see him." He beat his fist against his thigh in frustration. "Just when we thought we could feel safe for a moment. How long do you suppose he hid out here, waiting for us?"

Gabriel shrugged, looking perturbed. "It's difficult to say. He likely altered the palace staff's perceptions of him, and made them think he belonged here. We'll take what precautions we can, but I doubt he'll trouble these walls further. It is more likely he'll take refuge among one of the companies of troops heading to Landaran, so that he may lend his strength in terrible ways behind the scenes. There are many pieces at play in this game." He stood up. "I'll be back shortly." He strode out of the room, as Jardan began picking up pieces of glass.

Tavish and Aidah watched Jardan curiously, as he meticulously searched for pieces. "Do you need help?" Aidah watched, just to be able to do something, and not have to think about enemy mages running loose nearby.

"Find as many pieces as you can—the larger, the better. Don't bother with the tiny ones," Jardan said in a low voice, a look of concentration on his face. He held up a larger piece of glass and held it next to the window frame. It glowed orange for a few seconds, and then he drew his hand away, leaving the piece fused to the frame, effectively back in place "It isn't a perfect fix," he told Aidah and Tavish, as they held up pieces for him to add, "But it should keep the cold night air out." He set another piece of glass up, and Aidah realized that the orange glow was the glass itself, being heated up until it melded to the piece beside it.

"That's handy," Tavish remarked. Aidah knew what he was thinking—it would have been useful when they'd broken things in the past.

Aidah tried to keep her nerves at bay, as they continued to help Jardan with the window repair. Smart of him to keep them busy while they waited for Gabriel to return. Fear pricked at the edges of her consciousness, making her palms clammy. She thought it was her own emotion, but she couldn't be certain of that. At the moment, she didn't feel grounded, and she still needed Gabriel's help to find that center of balance.

By the time they were done, there were only a few holes left in the window, and those Jardan filled with wax from the candle, in order to keep out the cold. He sighed, looking at the two of them. Before he could speak, however, Gabriel returned.

He took a few seconds to look them over before speaking. "I've notified the Duke and the Guard, so there shouldn't be any other issues this evening. I think it best that we all try to get some sleep." Something in his face told Aidah that he wasn't including himself in that statement. Her suspicions were confirmed when Gabriel gave a nod to Jardan. "I'll keep watch over them. I've already had one of the guardsmen volunteer up his energy. It should get me through the next twenty-four hours at least."

Jardan looked relieved. "I was going to volunteer. But we both know I can't protect them from Alaric." He stepped closer to Tavish, inspecting him. "Do you need to examine him? He doesn't seem worse for wear…" He glanced back at Gabriel. "But you and I both know the kinds of things Spirit magic is capable of."

Tavish paled. "What does that mean?"

Gabriel drew closer, reaching out to touch Tavish on the forehead. He closed his eyes briefly, while Tavish's eyes never left Aidah's, silently questioning her. She shrugged in response; she had an idea of what Gabriel doing, possibly checking the energies or the living energies within Tavish much like she had with the baby, but there was much she didn't know yet. One thing she felt certain of, was that if there was a problem, Gabriel would find it.

Gabriel opened his eyes. "He's clean. Alaric merely knocked him unconscious."

Aidah sat down on the bed, feeling suddenly very tired. "I don't think he realized we were still awake. Or perhaps that we'd be in the same room." Whatever way it had gone wrong for the enemy mage, she was grateful.

Jardan stood up, brushing the last vestiges of glass dust from his robes. "To sleep then for both of you. Morning will come too quickly." He smiled reassuringly, then headed out of the room.

Morning did come too quickly.

It was still dark outside when Gabriel shook Aidah to rouse her, and with the cold chill of the room, all she wanted to do was crawl back inside the blankets to sleep more. She didn't, but set to pulling on her travel leggings and boots, trying to pull on things as quickly as possible so that she wouldn't have to be cold long. According to Tavish, riding fast could be strenuous, so hopefully that would get her blood moving.

Tavish dressed quickly as well, and as they repacked their bags and headed out of the room, Jardan strode up and handed them both a cold pastry with sausage inside. "Eat as we walk. They're readying horses, and we'll be mounting as soon as we reach the stables."

Aidah bit into her pastry; it was cold but the sausage was well spiced, and it eased the hunger pains. The castle was quiet for the most part, the dining room empty, table cleared, and for most of the walk there was only the glow of their candlesticks to light the way. It seemed the Duke would not be seeing them off. Once they had reached the ground floor, however, Dunby appeared with a small satchel, which he handed to Gabriel. "The gods' speed with all of you, and may all this talk of war blow over. I do wish that some rogue would just put a knife in that old Emperor's heart. Save us all a lot of trouble." He smiled at Aidah and she couldn't help but smile back. He seemed a nice fellow, and this seemed like a decent enough place. Perhaps she would be able to come back someday and actually get to visit. Her life seemed like just one giant blur at the moment.

The sky was only starting to lighten in the east when they reached the stables across the courtyard. Here activity was buzzing, with stable boys running around checking the tightness of saddles and strapping on packs. Guards also strode through the area, preparing for an early morning patrol, it seemed. Four bay horses stood ready to ride, stamping their feet in the cold morning air, steam drifting from their flared nostrils. Holding the reins of one of them was Captain Murdock. He acknowledged Gabriel with a nod as they approached.

"These four should serve you well. I understand you're keeping the little lady close, correct?" Murdock asked, as Jardan inspected their packs and made last minute adjustments. With a wave of his hand, Jardan motioned for Tavish and Kendrick to mount up. They did so, without fuss or words. It was probably the first time Aidah had ever seen her brother behave so well.

"She'll be riding with me," Gabriel confirmed. He touched Aidah gently on the shoulder. "You up first—the Captain will assist. I know you haven't ridden much before."

"Definitely best, if she's not experienced. And I expect harder to grab and carry off," Murdock said, bending over and interlocking his fingers to give Aidah help up. Feeling awkward, she placed her booted foot in his handhold and felt her stomach lurch as he lifted her up. She managed to get her leg over without too much trouble and sat on the large horse feeling small and higher up from the ground than she preferred.

Murdock stepped back as Gabriel came forward, offering him no assistance despite the fact Gabriel was probably old enough to be the man's grandfather. Murdock continued to speak even as Gabriel hauled himself up into the saddle. "I'm sending word ahead via carrier pigeon so that they'll know your new method of travel. Shall I also send word to Geraine?"

Aidah could only see Gabriel's back from her position behind him. "Go ahead, but let them know we probably won't be staying in the city. After last night, I think it best if we stay to smaller places. Places that won't be expected."

"Best of speed, then." Murdock saluted, then headed back over to where the cavalry were preparing to depart with the footmen. Jardan mounted last, then with a nod to Gabriel, the four of them rode out into the streets. It was barely light enough to see, but Aidah did spot groups of farmers heading out towards the fields, ready for another day's work.

"Keep an eye out. There may still be enemy agents in any groups we come across," Gabriel said in a low voice, just loud enough for Tavish and Kendrick to hear. "I'll keep my sense open for Alaric, but there are others that could be utilized, including peasants." The shadows seemed deeper as Aidah looked around. guardsmen waved them on out as they passed the city gates.

As the sun peeked out over the eastern horizon, they reached the main road headed towards Geraine. They wouldn't make that city until tomorrow, but as Gabriel stated, it wouldn't matter because it was too risky to stay in a large city other than Landaran,. The road still followed the Lamar River, heading almost due south to where the Lamar would join in with the Glynnis River. It was at that meeting point where the city of Geraine. lay. From there they would head due east to Landaran. If things went well, they would reach Landaran in three days.

Gabriel kept them at an even pace, a loping 'canter' as he called it, which would supposedly eat up the miles without tiring the animals too quickly. It took a little bit before Aidah could accustom herself to the rhythm; at first she tried to fight it, but Gabriel showed her how to relax into the horse's movements, just let her stomach roll with the gait. She spent several moments counting it to herself, like a waltz, one two three, one two three. It was nothing like walking, or even trotting.

Light suffused the land, and once Aidah was able to divert her attention from riding to their surroundings, she realized that the road was quite busy. She didn't know if it was typical traffic or not, but as they passed by a company of armed horsemen, she suspected a lot of this activity was related to the oncoming invasion. What made her curious was that a great deal of traffic wasn't headed in the same direction as them, but rather back towards where they had come from. She tapped Gabriel's arm. "Are there normally so many travellers headed for Bonnenville?"

Aidah suddenly sensed unease from the man. He wasn't shielding that from her, she realized, and wondered why, until he spoke. "No. What you see right now are townspeople and villagers fleeing for the safety of Bonnenville's walls if a full invasion should occur. And don't fear to read my emotions. I want you sensitive to others right now. You can use your abilities to detect spies and possible assassins. If you feel nothing from a person, let me know. That may be the sign of a shielding."

"I'll keep that in mind," Aidah replied, feeling anything but reassured. People preparing for war—was it really coming to that? But it seemed that it was; even as she looked ahead, she saw armed soldiers dressed in chainmail with fierce-looking crossbows trudging down the road. The men hardly looked up as Aidah's company passed them, the horse's hooves stirring up clumps of mud on the road. She quelled the urge to shout an apology as she saw one soldier spattered, but he hardly blinked. She wondered what town or part of the Doane he was from, how far he had come. He had a hard face and sullen eyes.

They barely stopped to eat but rode hard all day changing horses once at a message post, until Aidah's legs were aching and her face was chapped and burned by the cold eastern wind. They passed two more companies of soldiers, and each time it was the same news. Everyone knew that fighting would begin soon. It was merely a matter of when.

By late afternoon, the pain of siting astride and riding became so bad, Aidah could barely move. She watched the landscape fly past in a sort of numb haze, clinging to Gabriel until her fingers cramped up. At the moment she wasn't sure which was worse—the dreams that she'd been blishfully free from for the past few nights, or the reality she was living now, riding hard into what might be only bloodshed and horror. What if the city was already surrounded? What would they do then?

Gabriel noted her discomfort. He tugged on the reins, slowing his horse to a walk, and at once Jardan, Kendrick and Tavish were doing the same. The sun was low in the west, and with the dark clouds in the east, it was likely they would only have another hour to ride before nightfall.

"What are you doing?" Aidah asked in concern. If they were stopping because he was tired, that she could understand, but she didn't think exhaustion had struck him yet. As for herself, she didn't care if she hurt. She wanted to be safe, first and foremost.

"We ride for as long as we can," Gabriel explained, patting her hand at his waist. She instantly felt warmth and energy flowing into her.

"But you—you need it!" Aidah protested, as Jardan brought his horse closer, watching them. The aches lessened considerably, however, and she was able to sit a little taller in the saddle. The throbbing in her head eased and faded away.

"Don't argue, child," Gabriel scolded, but he hardly sounded displeased. Aidah watched as Jardan gave a nod, and there was an unspoken communication between the two master mages. "We need to ride until dark," Gabriel told him, then he gave the horse a swift kick, spurring it into motion. Aidah nearly lost her balance, but fortunately between the saddle and Gabriel's back, there wasn't anywhere to go. She clutched at Gabriel's robes as the horse broke into a gallop, and had to learn all over how to sit to fit the new faster rhythm.

22

City Under Siege

It was a visitation, and yet not.

Aidah stood on the snow-dusted road. A pale moon shone up above, and a breeze rustled through the tall grass of the plains, the only sound on the deserted road. She could see the tent where she had been sleeping, where she might in fact still be sleeping. She remembered when she had drifted off that Gabriel had set wards around the two tents and promised her that Rangwar would not be able to make one of his nightly encounters. She could even hear the old man's heavy breathing and see slight movement from the tent where her brother and Kendrick were fast asleep. Jardan was supposed to be on watch, but she didn't see him anywhere.

At the sound of a chuckle, Aidah whirled. She saw Rangwar, but he didn't seem entirely solid—just a wisp, in fact, floating beside her. Aidah felt heartened. Perhaps Gabriel's wards were working after all.

He spent no time at all gloating or coaxing, which was another surprise. "Look east, Aidah. Look at the city of Landaran."

She looked. It seemed they were much closer to the city than she remembered being when they had decided to stop for the night. Distantly she could see long straight walls with high towers on a hill by the wide river, with pendants flying from each pointed tower. A great dark mass swarmed outside the gates; Rangwar's army. Above the city the sky glowed orange against black smoke; the sight reminded her of the smelting plants they had passed on the way to Colmsford.

Landaran was burning, Aidah realized.

"You're lying to me," she said against the fear clutching at her heart. She shouldn't be able to see Landaran yet, not from here. That meant it was probably an illusion of some kind, some vision that Rangwar wanted to have her see, and despair.

"I could be," Rangwar said, nodding. He didn't look amused, however. "I am sure you will see the truth for yourself soon enough. Landaran is surrounded. You can run and hide, but you will not evade me forever." His cold blue eyes pierced her, and Aidah shivered.

She started to make a retort, to tell him to rot in Murd's Halls, but as Aidah opened her mouth, he faded away. The next instant she found herself back in her sleeping roll inside the tent. Gabriel snored beside her.

A dream, she told herself, and only a quick one at that. He hadn't even touched her. Perhaps Gabriel's wards weren't perfect, but it was better than any protection she had received thus far. Aidah rubbed at her arms to dispel the chills, listening to the wind rustling outside. She heard the crunch of gravel under a booted foot—Jardan, walking around.

Waking Gabriel seemed like a bad idea. He had looked worn out after the life energy had run out, and Aidah had to remind herself that he hadn't slept in almost forty-eight hours. Going back to sleep, however, would not be easy. What if Rangwar returned? She was tired, but she needed to double check things and see if he had been speaking the truth.

Carefully, Aidah eased out of her sleeping roll and crawled out of the tent. It was bitter cold outside, and she shivered, seeing her breath wafting on the breeze. Still, this cold was nothing compared to the deep of winter back in the mountains. Jardan stood near the fire, the glow illuminating the lines of care in his face. He glanced over as she approached, and raised an eyebrow. "Nightmare?"

Aidah nodded. "Not as bad as they usually are, though. But he did come. He said the city is burning." She looked to the southeast where supposedly the city lay, but all she could see was the long grass bending in the wind. The sky was clear, for once. She breathed a sigh of relief; she could see no signs of smoke or fire in the distance. "We can't see Landaran from here, can we?"

Jardan shook his head, watching her intently. "No. And I doubt the city is burning. He's only trying to frighten you."

That brought a sigh of relief. "I thought as much. But you know...I just had to be sure." Aidah stood closer to the fire and rubbed her arms. "Just when would we be able to see it? You know—in case he returns and tries to trick me again." It was almost comical the way she both longed and dreaded seeing the city.

"You won't be able to see the walls until we're past Freemont, which is past Geraine. If there is fire, however, we'll be able to see evidence of that in the skies tomorrow morning." Jardan tossed a small log onto the fire, and Aidah watched as the sparks flew up into the starry sky. She startled a little as he patted her shoulder. "I'm sure they're all fine. We'll get there in time."

Aidah nodded, but she wasn't convinced. While Rangwar might exaggerate, she hadn't caught him outright lying to her as of yet. It seemed more his style to stretch truths and manipulate her with twisted information.

After a few minutes of warming herself by the fire and listening to the sounds of night, the horror of the dream began to dim. Aidah felt her lids grow heavy, the exhaustion from the day's ride settling over her once more. "I'm heading back to sleep," she told Jardan, and made her way back to the tent. Gabriel hadn't stirred. She crawled into her bedroll and closed her eyes once more.

It seemed hardly minutes before she was standing near the field on the road again. Aidah whirled, fear clutching at her heart, wondering where Rangwar was hiding this time. She expected him to be standing right behind her, glorious in his youth, in his armor for battle as he'd been before. This time, however, he was nowhere to be found.

Instead, there was a very old woman standing several paces away, staring at her.

Aidah gasped. It couldn't be, could it? And yet how many old female Spirit Mages could possibly know of her? She turned to face the woman but didn't speak, uncertain of what she should say. It could still be a trick from Rangwar, Aidah reminded herself. Gabriel had a son who was evil. Surely there were other evil Spirit Mages?

She swallowed in a dry throat as the woman took a few steps toward her. "G-Grandess?" Did she dare believe it was really her?

The woman gave a slow nod. She looked tired. Rather, she looked exhausted. Drained. Like the Emperor, she was only partially solid, and Aidah could see right through her. She didn't know if that was Gabriel's attentions again, or Korva's apparent weakness. "Aidah," Korva said, and somehow managed to convey a lifetime of regret into a single word.

"How do I know you're real?" Aidah demanded, and suddenly all that rage, all that hurt she had felt when Gabriel had arrived was back in full force, nearly choking her. Rangwar had told her that Korva hadn't visited via dream before because she didn't think Aidah important enough. Aidah wondered if there was some truth to that.

A flash of anger passed over Korva's face. She strode forward and suddenly took Aidah's hand. Aidah gasped as images surged through her of corridors and towers and underground tunnels. Knowledge seemed to pour into her about ways into the city of Landaran. Secret ways. Korva dropped her hand, and the images stopped. Aidah staggered, trying to digest what had just happened. One thing was certain. This was definitely Korva.

"I don't have time for your anger," Korva said brusquely, standing still as Aidah fought to regain her balance. She wanted to ask Korva why the sudden invasion of her mind, but the woman was already answering her. "I've given you the layout of the city walls, towers, and passageways to help you gain entrance in case Gabriel is killed. The northwest tower may be your best option."

Aidah started to ask why, but the answer was already in her head. The entrance was underwater, in the Glynnis River. That certainly seemed like a place nobody would look to find her. "Is the city burning?" she asked instead.

"Have Gabriel teach you how to hold your breath," Korva said, and shook her head. "Not burning, no. But the first ships from Innis have landed on the beach. The Guardians have grown weak. They cannot hold back the invasion. By the time you reach Landaran, enemy troops will stand between you and the city."

A chill went through Aidah. Just as she had suspected, Rangwar's warning was not far from the truth. "What do we do?" she asked, but Korva wasn't paying attention. The woman was glancing around, as Rangwar had done before, apparently seeing Aidah's real surroundings outside the dream.

"Gabriel and Jardan have solid plans—follow their direction," Korva said at length, turning back to Aidah. "Continue to learn what you can during your ride, particularly shielding and mental attacks. We'll do what we can to clear your path." She shivered, or perhaps the air around her shimmered, and she faded somewhat. "I came tonight at great risk—it isn't safe on the ethereal planes while he is afoot. Just remember. Northwest tower." She faded entirely, and Aidah was left again with the soft night breezes and the stars.

That faded away too, as Aidah slipped into dreams. The next morning, however, Korva's words were clear in her head, and the knowledge of underground passageways in the city was present as well. It felt odd to know things she shouldn't know. She rolled over and shook Gabriel awake; outside she could hear Tavish and Kendrick already up, both groaning about their sore muscles. After whatever Gabriel had done yesterday, Aidah's legs felt surprisingly all right. She wondered if she would pay for it later.

Gabriel rubbed his eyes and looked at her, then sat up, instantly alert. "Time to make the last push for it," he said, popping a joint or two. Aidah blushed, busying herself with the repacking of her bag, stuffing her blanket into it. She had slept fully clothed, but she still couldn't quite bring herself to feel comfortable sharing a tent with a male who was not her brother. She knew the reason—only another Spirit Mage could provide full defense against Rangwar, and being nearby helped. Still, she couldn't help the unpleasant reminders of the innocence she had already lost.

The dreams were still fresh in her mind. The urge to spill everything to him tugged at her, but she made herself wait until he was rolling up his bedroll as well, moving slowly but with confidence. She looked down at her hands, which were shaking. "Korva visited me last night."

Instantly he was alert, staring at her with astonishment. "Did she? What did she have to say?" By his reaction, Aidah realized it must not be a typical occurrence, the Protector visiting people's dreams. Korva had said it was dangerous. Why? Aidah wondered.

"She gave me knowledge about the city and secret ways inside. Through my head," Aidah replied, hoping he would understand.

His brows drew together, and she knew that he did. "She sent you the knowledge—to your mind, yes?"

She nodded. "She said it was just in case you and I were separated, or..." She didn't want to say the alternative, that he could be killed. She didn't even want to imagine the possibility of being alone, of having to figure out things on her own.

"Or if I was killed," Gabriel finished for her. He looked

serious. "An excellent idea. She knows even more of the secret passageways than I do. Did she say anything else? I imagine it was a short conversation."

"It was," Aidah said, and realized Gabriel hadn't visited her dreams ever, even though he'd had to have an idea where she was when he was riding out to meet her. It must be as dangerous as Korva had warned. "She said to tell you the Northwest tower. And she said you needed to teach me to hold my breath." That one had stuck out in her mind. She didn't really know how to swim, it was true. But how hard could it be to hold one's breath?

Gabriel's white brows drew together in concern. "She means for us to use the underwater entrance."

An image flashed in Aidah's mind, of the entrance, a metal trap door on the bottom of a little square room jutting out from the circular tower, only beneath the water where no one would even know of the chamber's existence. She shrugged, not liking the idea one bit. Still, she had to admit it was crafty. "I don't suppose many know of that. Do they?"

"No. Only a handful of those alive, in fact. Korva designed the city walls in her youth, when she and her kindred fled Innis." With both their bedrolls neatly tied up, Gabriel opened the flap of the tent. "We'll wait and see what sight presents us at the city gate. We still have two days travel. A lot can happen in that time."

That was precisely what Aidah was afraid of.

There was little talk around the campfire as everyone prepared for a second day of riding. Tavish heard only a snatch or two, but he gathered that Rangwar had made another appearance, and not just him, but Korva as well. The day dawned bright and sunny, but Tavish felt a cloud over all of them, knowing that they were in a race now, and that they might not make it in time. As they mounted up, Jardan waved him to ride closer.

"You've heard that there may be fighting at the city when we arrive?" Jardan was all seriousness today, and Tavish realized there was something different about his dress—he was wearing a leather chest piece over his robes.

"I heard," Tavish said cautiously. He didn't think it was possible for them to leave him behind at this point. Was it?

Jardan nodded, as they began at easy trot, letting the horses warm up. Ahead of them Kendrick was staying close to Gabriel and Aidah, leading them down the road and acting as their protection for the moment. Jardan smiled with approval. "I know we can't really train you in use of the sword or knife, riding hard like this. But I do want to discuss some tactics with you that you can use if we encounter enemies. You've already proven that you can fight and kill an enemy mage. But realize that you probably surprised your foe. They won't underestimate you again."

Tavish felt an itch between his shoulder blades, the kind of itch that meant he wasn't going to like what Jardan was going to talk about. He still wasn't sure how he felt about killing those men. He'd kind of enjoyed killing Madhar. Was that bad? But he wasn't looking forward to having to kill again. "You think we'll see combat?" Ironic how he'd waited for this for the past two years, fighting with his powers, and now that it came to it, the idea made him sick to his stomach.

Jardan's steel gray eyes scanned the road ahead of them, hard and unreadable. "I think it is likely at this point, yes. The most important thing you'll need to do is listen to my orders, and obey them. Without question. Or hesitation." He stared at Tavish.

"Yes, sir." Tavish gulped. He was starting to feel light-headed.

Jardan went on. "While on the road in the Doane you'll find single mages or a mage with an apprentice. On a battlefield, it is entirely different. Companies will have footmen, archers, cavalry, and all three types of mages. We will be at a disadvantage without a Storm Mage."

"Why is that?" Tavish had always thought the Storm Mages were the weakest. Of course, it had only taken one Storm Mage to completely destroy his home and village.

"Because their gift is too different from ours. You can't stop a lightning strike with heat or cold. And if they have a Sun Mage working with them, then your invisibility or light tricks won't be able to protect you."

That made sense. "But Spirit Mages are rare. They can't possibly have enough for every Storm Mage," Tavish said, as they quickened their horses' pace to a light canter. Ahead of them he spotted the farm houses and fields. They had to be getting closer to another city or town.

"You're right. I doubt we'll see more than two of Rangwar's

precious Life Talents here in the Doane. But they'll try to coordinate things, just the same. We learn to work together, sometimes with ten or twenty Storm Mages, four or five Sun, and a single Spirit Mage as company leader." Jardan clicked his tongue, encouraging his horse to go a little faster. He glanced over at Tavish. "By the way, we'll be stopping by the stables in Geraine to change horses."

That made sense, Tavish supposed. They could hardly keep pushing the horses at this pace. "So how do they use all those Storm mages?" he asked to keep Jardan talking. Anything to keep his mind from envisioning how it would be, when they actually had to fight.

"It takes more than one Storm Mage to create weather—both sides utilize them to stir up the atmosphere before a battle, so that the Storm Mages can use bolts of lightning at will. In fact, the term 'Storm' is a misnomer—Storm Mages need help from Sun mages to create a storm, if they want to do it with any speed, that is. We heat the air; they pull the moisture. I've never understood exactly how they do it, but they can move things to a certain degree. Something about impacting their magnetic fields."

Tavish struggled to understand it all. "So let's say Aidah and I were going against a Storm Mage—like we did. He can zap us, but I can blind him or flame him, and Aidah could take his strength or possess him. But if he had a Sun Mage with him, then it starts to become more even because he can counter pretty much everything I can do, right?"

"Essentially, yes," Jardan said, and then motioned for Tavish to be quiet a moment. They rode up abreast of Mage Holt and Aidah, and Jardan leaned over to get their attention. "The River stables, correct?" At Gabriel's nod, Jardan dropped back again, and Tavish kept pace with him. After a moment, Jardan spoke. "When each side has the same kinds of magic available, it basically becomes a battle of wits. You try to outsmart each other and act quickly."

That didn't sound great, but then again, Tavish figured it would be the same between two fighters wielding swords. Of course, he had to ask the other burning question. "So are we going to find a Storm Mage to travel with us?" Was there one they could trust? It seemed strange to think of someone else joining their small group now.

Jardan shook his head. "They're all going to be needed for the war effort. It shouldn't be an issue, though. If there are enemy troops at the city, there should at least be some of our fighting forces as well, and that will include Storm Mages—they excel at warfare. They should be able to protect us. We want to slip by unnoticed if possible, so the fewer we are in number, the better."

Tavish let out a breath, feeling the butterflies in his stomach again. "So we're going to want things that are quiet and sneaky. Like no big explosions. Right?"

That earned him a dry smirk. Jardan smoothed back his beard. "That would be advisable, yes. If we run into mages, my hope is that Gabriel will be able to take care of them before you or I or Kendrick need even think about it. But I felt it was important that you have an understanding about how we work as teams."

That made sense. Tavish wanted to ask more, but as he looked ahead on the road, he saw they were approaching the outlying areas of a larger city, much as they had outside of Bonnenville. This time, however, Tavish saw no city walls. Instead, on the north side of the road there seemed to rise taller and taller buildings in the distance, and a haze of smoke and steam, from what kind of buildings, he couldn't say. The city seemed to stretch on and on into the distance. He gulped. "That's Geraine?"

"That's Geraine," Jardan confirmed. "It's actually larger in size than Landaran, because it doesn't face as great a threat of invasion, being deeper into the Doane. As you can see, it has long outgrown its original walls." He pointed and Tavish could see that the city stretched far to the west, beyond what he could see. He'd never imagined a place with so many people.

"We're not going in there, are we?" They could waste hours, days, in such a tangle of roads and buildings!

Gabriel answered this time. "No. We'll take only the time necessary to obtain fresh horses and continue riding. In light of last night's visitors, I'm hoping we can reach Landaran by tomorrow night."

It seemed too soon, and yet too far away.

☼

Their stop on the outskirts of Geraine seemed unbearably long to Aidah. First of all, the road was packed, and all Aidah could think of was that there might be a possible assassin among any one of the people passing by. It felt like there was a big target right in the middle of her back. Second, it was noisy, not just to her ears, but to her senses. One thing nobody had ever warned her about before was how it would feel like to be surrounded by so many minds, so many emotions. Her head spun, making her queasy.

The stables were huge, with several buildings, some housing horses for local militia, others for visiting nobles, and still others for 'official Doane business.' They stood outside this last building, waiting as boys hurried to transfer their packs from their tired animals to fresh horses stamping in the cold, their coats clean and shining. On the road, Aidah could hear the steady drone of men and horses walking, heading towards Landaran. The preparations for war were in full swing.

Three times, Aidah swore she saw something out of the corner of her eye—Alaric, lurking among the armored troops. But each time she looked closer, it wasn't him. Still, something dark and cold brushed her senses, though she wasn't sure if it was real or just her imagination. She told Gabriel about it, but he felt nothing. It was probably just her nerves.

A little over an hour, all told, and then finally they were told that their new steeds were ready. Several messages had arrived during that time for both Mage Holt and Mage Thorne, one supposedly from the Prince Mayor. Aidah wasn't sure which term exactly was his title; she was still trying to untangle the mixture of Old Empire royal titles and the newer democratic stations that the Doane had created after the forming of the Republic. Either way, it was the man in charge of the largest city in the Doane, and that meant the news must be important.

Gabriel read over the notes as they waited. Another servant approached their party with pork sandwiches, which Tavish and Kendrick immediately set to eating. Aidah, for her part, could barely nibble at hers. She stood near the Spirit Mage, both because it felt safer there, as well as to hear the news. When he was finished reading, Gabriel sighed.

"Apparently my son came through town last night," he said, staring at the parchment rather than at Aidah. "And apparently Alaric 'persuaded' twenty soldiers to commit treason and go with him to Landaran." Aidah gasped.

"How?" she asked, but she had a feeling she already knew the answer. He'd told her that Spirit mages could overcome the minds of unTalented, could distort their perceptions. How much more could they do? Could they cause men to mindlessly obey? Or worse, to love and change loyalties?

Gabriel shook his head, crumpling the paper and throwing it to the ground. "It doesn't matter. What does matter is that he now can wreak havoc even as he approaches the city. We can't dally further. Take some food for the road. We ride as soon as our mounts are ready."

She did so, promising herself that she would eat later. Their new horses were sleek, built for racing. Despite this breeding, however, they stood calmly as Aidah and the others mounted. It was only as Gabriel set heel to the dark brown flank that their horse charged forward, braying loudly. People instantly moved out of their way, which was good; in seconds they were riding at a full gallop.

At first Aidah kept her eyes open, trying to sense if there was anything dangerous in their path, a rogue archer aiming for them, perhaps. But the rough movements of the horse and the crazy path they took to avoid pedestrians made her ill, so she ended up closing her eyes, holding on tightly. Her heart hammered in her chest. Surely they would run someone over!

"I rode this way to reach you," Gabriel said, or perhaps thought in her head—Aidah wasn't sure because the wind was whistling past them. His tone conveyed his confidence, that they wouldn't have any horrible accidents. She relaxed a little bit, but it was impossible to truly relax with the jarring movements of their steed. She assumed that Tavish, Kendrick and Jardan were behind them, but she dared not turn her head to look. A day and a half left to go.

The zigging and zagging movements stopped, and finally Aidah opened her eyes again, to find that they had ridden past the thickest part of town by the road. Ahead of them the road turned, heading east.

The sky was darkening again, threatening more snow. It was noon, or just shortly after, yet it seemed that evening was approaching. The sense of foreboding threatened to overwhelm Aidah, and she had to take slow, deep breaths to keep herself calm. As fast as they were moving, it didn't seem fast enough.

They passed by several mills and factories, as well as a few buildings that stank of fish—fisheries, Aidah assumed. She had never seen buildings so large before outside of the castle in Bonnenville. These buildings were nothing like that. Most were made of wood, but here and there stood buildings that were actually made of metal. She couldn't help but stare as they passed by. "Isn't that dangerous if there are lightning storms?"

Gabriel spared a glance for the buildings before answering. As before he answered directly to Aidah's mind; she supposed with the thundering sound of the horses' hooves, it was better than having to shout. "They each have rods attached to the rooftops. The rods draw the lightning down the sides of the buildings into the ground. I don't understand exactly how it works, but the Storm Mages say it protects them. So far, it's worked."

The mills and strange metal buildings gave way to farms where huge herds of cattle and pigs grazed; beyond the animal enclosures on Aidah's right side, she could see the river—it must the Glynnis, she reasoned. Bridges crossed at regular intervals, and ships making their way up and down, some stopped at docks to the farmhouses, others at the mills. Most of them were low barges that fit right under the stone bridges.

If they hadn't been in such a rush, Aidah would have wanted to take a closer look. This was so far beyond anything she could ever have imagined. She'd known there were technologies near the capital that were unheard of back in her home village. But the actual sight of such things boggled her.

Finally they passed the last of the big buildings, though there were still farms scattered here and there, mostly on the left side of the road. Rich farmland stretched north of the road instead of the hills that they had avoided for so long. Here in the fertile valley of the Glynnis, even with the onset of winter, Aidah could see crops growing, like winter squash and turnips. Her stomach growled.

It was difficult with the constant rocking of the horse, but Aidah managed to unwrap her sandwich and ate as they rode ever eastwards. She didn't feel any evil presence now. It must have simply been the press of so many minds, weighing down on her. Once she was done, Gabriel handed her the carafe to drink from. They slowed to a trot for a bit, to rest the horses. That allowed them to finally speak without shouting.

"It's time to teach you about holding your breath," Gabriel said, surprising Aidah. She'd forgotten all about Korva's message and the lessons she had recommended.

She couldn't help but squirm in the saddle. "Yes, Mage Holt." She wasn't sure what exactly to call him. 'Gabriel' seemed far too familiar. Sir, perhaps? She mentally slapped herself. She knew she was delaying things, because she didn't want to learn, didn't want to contemplate diving under the flowing river, especially now that she could see how deep and wide it was. She sighed. "I don't know how to swim." The lakes near Hamstead were like ice, even in summer. It would have been folly to jump in. And why would one want to, anyway?

She couldn't see Gabriel's face but she didn't need to; his silence was reaction enough. "Oh dear," he said after a long pause. Aidah felt the back of her neck heating up. Did all Lowlanders know swimming, then?

He cleared his throat and tried again. Behind them, Aidah could hear Jardan speaking with Tavish and Kendrick again, probably instructing them. Hopefully in some kind of magic that would get them all safely past enemy eyes. "There are two main aspects to swimming. The first is breath. The second is how to propel yourself through the water."

"And how can you teach me that, without actually taking me into the water?" It wasn't as if they had time to stop and try along the shore. The sun was already heading for the horizon behind them.

"The same way that Korva taught you about the city entrances—directly into your mind," Gabriel answered serenely, even though the notion of having someone tool around inside her head still gave Aidah the chills. He continued, "However for that, it would be best that we're sitting and not riding horseback. So I'll leave that tonight. For now, we can practice some breathing exercises. Take a few quick breaths in and out, then expel all the air out of your lungs and take in a deep breath. Hold it for as long as you can."

She tried doing that, and immediately ended up coughing. The dust stirred by their travel didn't help matters. He had her practice as they moved into an easy canter, and after a few times, she was able to at least hold her breath for a bit. It felt strange, trying not to breathe and trying to ride at the same time.

"Just keep practicing that as we ride," Gabriel said when she mentioned her concerns. "If you start to feel light-headed, then stop. You've taken the first step to swimming and diving. The other parts will be learning how to move your body, and then using your Talent to slow your body functions. With that, you'll use less air and be able to swim deeper."

"I'm scared," Aidah found herself saying. She didn't know why it just suddenly came out like that, why the swimming lesson of all things should be what was pushing her over the edge. But there it was. She didn't want to risk her life diving into a freezing cold river while being attacked by gods knew how many enemy troops. She wanted to be safe in a bed somewhere, far away.

Gabriel reached back and grasped her hand. "It's all right. You're allowed to be frightened. I—we—aren't going to let anything happen to you. Have faith in that."

But she didn't. Hadn't her parents tried to protect her? And her uncle? And even though Korva had finally spoken with her, finally given her at least some kind of help, it seemed so weak in comparison to the promises Rangwar made. Aidah squeezed Gabriel's hand, both because she couldn't think of what to say to him, and second, because just the fact he was trying to reassure her actually did make her feel a little better. It was nerves, she told herself. After all, they were headed into battle.

They fell silent, and Gabriel kicked his horse into a steady canter, as they rode into the afternoon, inexorably towards Landaran. They continued to pass by small farms and ranches as well as the occasional inn or guard post; the road was well travelled. Often they had to ride past troops or farmers and villagers about their daily business. As the sun began to set, they caught sight of the last town before Landaran, more of a dock station and way station, really. Gabriel told her that they'd be exchanging their tired mounts first thing in the morning, and by late afternoon they should reach Landaran

Before they reached the town, Gabriel and Jardan reined up their horses to decide whether to actually stay in town or make camp as they had the night before. The arguments were the same as they had been for Geraine. Staying in town was safer on one hand because there would be guards and troops staying there as well. And it would be more dangerous for the exact same reason. More people meant more chances that a silent assassin or a mind-possessed servant could try to take Aidah and Tavish.

As the older men debated, Aidah took a moment to stretch her legs. She dismounted and walked around gingerly, wincing at the pull of sore muscles in her thighs and buttocks. Tavish handed his reins to Kendrick and dismounted as well, coming to join her. He blew out a frustrated breath. "I wish they'd figure it out already. I'm ready to just fall asleep on the ground right here." They stood on the outskirts of yet another farm, this one with rows and rows of short fruit trees, bare for the winter. Aidah's stomach growled. Why couldn't they have faced all of this in the summer when there would have been fresh fruit?

She didn't have much in the way of a reply for her brother, so Aidah merely shrugged, letting her gaze wander eastwards, towards the pointed rooftops of the village only miles away. She couldn't see anything beyond that, but as she watched, a tiny plume of smoke rose in the distance. She frowned and tugged at her brother's sleeve. "What is that?" She pointed at the plume, just visible over the rooftops of Freemont.

Tavish squinted hard, looking at it. "That's smoke. It must be far away. I'm not seeing any heat from it." He glanced at Aidah. "You think it's from Landaran?"

Aidah felt her heart go still. "I don't know. Do you?"

He stared at the little plume, which was slowly growing larger. "Yeah. I think it is." He leaned over and tugged at Kendrick's sleeve, then pointed over at the dark spot, even as a second plume began to rise up beside it. "Could that be from the city?"

As Kendrick's face grew pale, Aidah had her answer even before he spoke. "I think it is." Kendrick stared at it for a moment then took a deep breath.

"Landaran is under attack."

23

Going Dark

At Kendrick's words, Jardan and Gabriel stopped their discussion and stared at him. Kendrick pointed east, towards Freemont and Landaran. Gabriel's eyes narrowed, and he stood for a moment observing, concentrating. Jardan seemed to be concentrating hard as well. Aidah looked to Tavish and Kendrick in confusion. Tavish held a finger to his lips before she could open her mouth.

"There's little heat to the smoke—it's not a great fire, whatever it is," Jardan said at length. Gabriel closed his eyes a moment, and then nodded.

"They're probably burning some of the outlying farms." Gabriel opened his eyes and regarded Aidah and her brother. "It's begun. This seals it, then. We'll change horses again in Freemont and take some energy, all of us. If we're lucky, we can make it to the city outskirts before dawn's light. There's no time to waste now."

Fear struck Aidah, making the edges of her vision go dark. Her heart pounded inside her rib cage and it felt like the world was tilting, spinning. She thought she might faint, but then Gabriel was there, taking hold of both her shoulders. Calming thoughts enveloped her; the spinning stopped as Gabriel's presence steadied her. She felt the earth beneath her, felt her connection to the energies there. Slowly, she took a deep breath and let it out, feeling grounded once more.

"Better?" Gabriel asked in a soft voice. She nodded. He gave her a pat on the arm, then turned to Tavish and Kendrick. "Mount up. We're going to push every ounce of speed out of these horses. Prepare yourself, for we may find the roads are no longer safe." He strode over and mounted his horse, then walked it over so that he could offer Aidah an arm up. She climbed up to sit in her usual spot behind him. As soon as Tavish and Kendrick had remounted, they spurred their horses on towards Freemont. Apparently there would be no swimming lessons for her before they reached the river.

By the time they reached the outskirts of Freemont, the sun had set. They were forced to rely on Jardan and Kendrick to light the way with small balls of fire, revealing the potholes and other dangers of the road that could trip a horse. Freemont was little more than a guard post with the industrial dregs that couldn't fit within Landaran's walls. It was poor and gritty, and it stank of smoke and refuse.

Again they headed directly for the guard post. Aidah had expected it to be as busy as the one in Geraine, if not busier, but it was nearly deserted. Gabriel flagged down one of the stablehands as he dismounted. Aidah dismounted as well, happy to even have a moment or two on the ground.

The stablehand, a boy of perhaps twelve, ran up to Gabriel and gave a quick bow. "Sir Mage?"

Gabriel waved aside his greeting. "Where is everyone? We need fresh horses. It's vital that we reach Landaran before dawn."

The boy grew wide-eyed and pale. "They're all off to the city, milord! Landaran's under attack!" He scratched his head, looking at the stables. "I'll have to ask the stablemaster what horses we might have. We're pretty much cleaned out right now." He ran off, shouting for the stablemaster. Aidah looked nervously over at her brother. Their horses could go no further tonight. Would they have to walk? Ride plough horses?

"Take a moment to eat," Gabriel urged them all, pulling out travel bread from his pouch. They each took a piece as they waited. In the distance, Aidah could hear thunder rumbling.

Tavish ate his the quickest and rubbed his hands on his trousers to brush off the crumbs. "They're not actually fighting each other yet, are they? I mean, in the dark and all." He glanced eastwards, but other than the occasional flash of lightning, it was difficult to tell what was happening. Aidah thought that battle must be noisy. They weren't that far away. Surely they would know if things were happening?

"Most likely not," Gabriel assured them. "The burning of the fields is standard practice for them. They destroy what they can outside the walls of the city to rattle the inhabitants. They're probably setting up camp tonight." He paused at the sound of feet running towards them through the empty stables. "That's why I want us to get there before dawn. By dawn, they may be ready to attack."

They all fell silent as the boy returned, followed by a brawny middle-aged man with a barrel chest and a full beard and mustache. He looked out of breath, his face sweat-covered and red. He made a quick bow to Gabriel and Jardan. "Barry here tells me you've need of horses? Tis late, you know."

Gabriel gave him a nod, letting the man catch his breath. "I understand that Empire troops have reached Landaran. We have to get inside the city before the fighting begins, but our horses are tired. We've ridden since dawn and we'll ride until the next dawn." He sighed. "We'll also need men to give their energy for us to continue."

He frowned, rubbing his large hands together. His apron was soiled with dirt and horsehair but despite his physical appearance he *felt* clean to Aidah—wholesome, honest. She smiled tentatively and he smiled back at her.

He gave a nod and slapped his thighs. "Right. If I have to pull some plough horses off the fields, I'll have steeds for you. Perhaps the two boys can ride together? I'll see what I can do." With that, he strode off, leaving the stable boy staring at them in confusion

Again, the five of them were left to wait. Tavish began pacing, fingering the dagger at his belt. "Plough horses? How are we going to ride plough horses into battle? Gods, I wish I had Buck again!" He clenched his fists in frustration, but Aidah could feel the real emotion coming off of him in waves. It was nice to know she wasn't the only one feeling afraid right now.

Before long, they heard footsteps again—too many for one man. The stable master emerged with two women in aprons, farmer's wives perhaps. One of the women held the hand of a young girl of no more than seven. The women curtsied before the mages, looking flustered.

The stablemaster spoke first. "Master Mages, we've found a few steeds, but you might have better luck in just stealing from them to enhance your own," he indicated the horses they had ridden, now frothing at the mouth and shaking with fatigue.

Gabriel said nothing, and the man flushed, hurrying to continue. "Two mules, one plow horse and a couple goats, Sirs.

That's the best we could manage on short notice." He glanced at the two women before looking at Gabriel again, uncertainly. "And we're here if you need, you know. That thing you Spirit Mages do."

This was the first time Aidah had seen real fear directed at Gabriel or Jardan. Sure, there had been the superstitious glances from the Gedar. But it dawned on her what kind of power Gabriel wielded, to be able to steal life force. The same power she possessed.

Gabriel's face betrayed no emotion, but he nodded. His voice was gentle. "We need five individuals. I would not want to pull too much from any one person." He stretched a little, joints popping. "I can make do with pulling from the animals as well. I think you are right in that we should keep our steeds."

The stablemaster nodded, and glanced at the boy who had greeted them. "You can use my son there as well." He looked nervous but determined.

Gabriel's brows furrowed in concern. "And what of running the stables? I know there are other troops headed this way." Aidah had to admit that for all the power he wielded, Gabriel didn't toss it around thoughtlessly. There was none of the arrogance that she had seen in Rangwar.

The stable master seemed prepared for such a question. "I'll get word to my brother. He's a blacksmith. He should be able to keep it running."

Again, Gabriel nodded. "I'll be sure to leave you enough strength to get home." He looked back at their horses. "Tavish, bring me the horses. Aidah—watch and analyze. You may need to do this on your own."

Aidah hurried to do as he asked, taking the reins of two of the horses and leading them over as Gabriel approached the first plough horse. When she reached him, he took the reins from her, keeping his hand close to the horse's chin, touching the animal there. His other hand he stretched out to touch the plough horse.

A blue glow began to shine from his fingertips where he touched the plough horse. As Aidah watched, the glow spread down his arm, across his chest, over to the horse who had been their steed for the past day. The horse's eyes widened and it stomped a foot in agitation. Something about the glow beckoned Aidah. As with the glowing amulet Evanson had shown her when first testing for her Talent, she could sense the animal's spirit. Everything about that light said 'horse' to her. It drew her. She blinked, taking a step back.

After a moment, the glow faded away. Gabriel released hold of the animals and directed Aidah to take their steed back to tie it up again, as he moved to the next one. The process was repeated, and this time Aidah watched her brother and Jarden, trying to determine if they could see the same glow that she saw. Neither of them were even watching. Tavish's attention was on the eastward sky.

"What do you see?" she asked him.

Tavish frowned, staring, then shrugged. "I dunno. Weird fluctuations in temperature in the skies. It's not natural." He glanced over at Gabriel and sighed. "Is he, you know? Doing what you did to me on that mountain?"

So he couldn't see the glow. She nodded. "He's moving the energy—the life force," she told him, then turned back to watch the transfer again. She almost reached out to touch Gabriel, touch the glow, but he hissed at her. 'Don't touch, Aidah. I know it draws you, but I don't need you interfering with the energies." She clenched her fist to make sure it stayed by her side, feeling a twinge of fear. Why did it draw her? And why was Gabriel acting so strangely. He acted like a dog standing over a particularly juicy bone.

After he'd finished the second transfer, he took a deep breath and looked at her apologetically. "I should have had you stand further away, with your brother, perhaps. I know the energy is enticing, but I don't want you helping with the animals just yet. You'll be drawn to explore their minds, and you mustn't do that. Never merge your consciousness with an animal's. You'll sink to their lesser intelligence, and then you won't remember who you are or how to pull yourself out. I'll have you help me when we move to the humans." He handed her the reins of the second horse and indicated for her to fetch the next one.

It was strange. She could see he was sweating with exertion, but there was a light in his eyes that hadn't been there when they'd first dismounted. Disquieted, she handed the reins of the steed to Jardan and brought Kendrick's horse over, thinking about what her parents had said so long ago. Angels or demons. She hadn't wanted to explore the horse's minds. She'd wanted to steal their energy for herself.

It didn't take long for Gabriel to finish with the horses. Aidah kept a little distance so that she wouldn't be tempted, but it was difficult. Even when she wasn't actually looking at the energy, some part of her sensed it. Instead of focusing on the animals, or for that matter on the steady mix of fear and anticipation that Tavish and Kendrick exuded, she concentrated on the stablemaster and his family, who waited anxiously for their turns to be drained. She remembered how poorly she had felt after giving Tavish strength, Would it be similar for them?

Gabriel's voice broke her out of her thoughts. "Aidah, I'd like your help on the next part." He sounded bone weary, and ancient. She turned to him in surprise. She'd forgotten—he was ancient! Ninety plus years and still riding around the countryside. Quickly, she went to his side, and he took her hand. She could feel the pulse in his veins, the calluses, the wrinkles. Yet his eyes were full of fire. "Bring the children first. They have more energy. You and I need to replenish, and then we can work on the others."

Aidah walked over to the little girl and the stable boy. "It'll be all right," she assured them, and took the girl's hands, leading her to Gabriel, who took her other hand and then Barry's, making a circle of them.

This time when Gabriel pulled the energy, she felt his mind joining with hers, as he had when teaching her in the wagon, and on the horse. Through his eyes she saw how he was able to pull, felt how to 'handle' the energies with her unseen hands. He needed her as backup strength because he was exhausted. He also wanted her to understand how to do this in case something happened to him. His thoughts, his knowledge flowed into her as easily as the strength, as naturally as taking in air when breathing.

She gasped, amazed at the sensation of handling the energies. Aidah remembered on the mountaintop how awful it had felt when she'd given Tavish her strength. This was just the opposite. Elation, power…it was incredible, the life energy that she felt flowing into Gabriel. It was his turn first, she thought or he thought—it didn't matter. She couldn't fully taste it yet. And she mustn't be seduced— that was Gabriel's word—by the power. Like Rangwar was. That was definitely Gabriel, because she hadn't know that. But it made sense. Just touching the energy was rapture.

All too soon it seemed the little girl's energy was drained, and Gabriel was letting go of her hand to let the girl stumble a bit and sit down on the soft hay-strewn earthen floor. He maintained the link with the stable boy, and with a delicate shift, began to feed that energy into Aidah. She knew his intent as surely as if it was her own intent. After the boy gave his strength to help abate her fatigue, they would take the two women next, and give their energy to Tavish and Kendrick. Gabriel wanted her help for Tavish in particular, because of their close bond.

Then her awareness of Gabriel, her brother, and anything outside faded away, as the energy poured into Aidah. It was indescribable; it was sunlight, it was youth, it was laughter. She took a deep breath, shaking with the intensity of it. As soon as Aidah lost herself to the surge, however, it was over, and she was being forced away from the sweet energy. She made a sound of protest before Gabriel took her physically by the hand and pried her fingers off the stableboy's hand. Aidah opened her eyes in surprise.

Gabriel's eyes held hers in understanding. "Now you know why it is so easy to abuse our abilities. Do not concern yourself with your lack of control. We will teach you control." This time she had a feeling that it was a different kind of control he was referring to. The self-control to not drain a person to death because it felt so good.

Aidah called her brother and took his hand, as Gabriel led one of the women over. Once again they joined hands. This time it was easy; she had given Tavish energy before. The only difference this time was that she could pull it from outside herself and not be drained. Gabriel allowed her to lead, but he was there the whole time inside her head, guiding her, letting her know when it was time to stop. The woman needed to be able to walk back to her house, after all.

From there, Gabriel dismissed Aidah to handle Jardan and Kendrick on his own. She hardly felt like she had mastered the skill, but at least she understood the basics of how to transfer strength and energy now. It would do in a pinch. At Jardan's suggestion, she and her brother mounted their steeds so that as soon as Gabriel was finished, they could ride.

It only took a few moments, and then the stable master and his wife staggered over to the side to sit down with their children. They looked about as exhausted as Aidah had felt before the energy. She noted, however, that they weren't in any danger. They would have the strength to walk home to a nice comfortable bed. Jardan and Kendrick took the reins of their horses, looking refreshed.

Before everyone could mount up, Gabriel held up his hand. "I can't have us giving ourselves away with the balls of light—Rangwar may have set up an ambush. I know the Sun Talents can see in the dark. I'm going to temporarily give that ability to the horses and to Aidah and myself."

Aidah blinked, looking to Gabriel in surprise. He could do that? She didn't have much time to ponder it; he strode up and placed his hand over her eyelids, covering her eyes. She sent him the question mentally, knowing he would hear. *How could he do this?*

The answer came not in words but in pictures. While Sun Mages could see rays of light that others couldn't see, Life mages could temporarily change things in their bodies. This lay far beyond her training. But what he was doing in effect was giving her the eyesight of a wolf. Wolves hunted by night and could see their prey. As the wolf saw, so would she.

Why not cats? Aidah couldn't help the thought even as it went through her head. Cats could see in the dark even better than wolves, couldn't they? The answer, however was simple.

Too difficult to maintain their irises—canine eyes are more similar to a human's. She pictured the slits of a feline's eyes in bright light, and had to agree.

Satisfied, she relaxed and let him work his Talent. She felt the energies entering her. This time there were no thoughts or feelings, but she could sense the changes to her body, just as she'd sensed the illness in the infant in Lothe . No sense of wrongness came with the change, but it did feel strange. She wanted to open her eyes but she was afraid of what she would see. *If* she would be able to see, in fact.

"Go ahead. Slowly," Gabriel said in a low voice, stepping back. Her altered eyes felt too large in their sockets. Blinking back tears at the strange sensation, Aidah cautiously opened her eyes. Color had left the world, which frightened her. But beyond the light of the stables, she could clearly see the road stretching on towards Landaran. She swallowed nervously.

"You'll change this as soon as we're there?" she asked. Everything felt strange, surreal. The loss of color was the strangest to get used to. She glanced at her brother and he blanched, looking away. "What?" she asked him.

"That's just not right. Your eyes…" he moved his horse a bit closer and took a second look. He wrinkled his nose in disgust.

"They're gold-ish, for one thing. And they're really big. I don't like it."

Aidah felt thankful she had no mirrors to see for herself. Gabriel's Talent stirred again, as he made adjustments to the horses' eyes as well—this time the change was quicker, and she agreed with Tavish. Wolf eyes did not belong on things other than wolves.

"We need to hurry," Gabriel stated as he mounted, allowing Aidah to scoot back in the saddle behind him. "I don't know what the Emperor's plans are this evening, but we have assume he is not idle. He may try to check in on us again." Aidah shivered.

With that, Gabriel spurred his horse forward, and the others followed, refreshed and ready for a run in the darkness.

24

Trapped

Tavish had never felt so alive. Or so scared. The energy was familiar. He'd felt like this the first time Aidah had given him energy, and he was thankful they were riding at full speed because his heart was pounding with the rush of it. He'd started off using the heat vision that had served him at the Gedar camp where they'd found Nera, but he'd then switched over to something different that Kendrick had suggested. It was like leftover sunlight, which colored everything in blue and violet.

Despite the new moons that hung overhead, the landscape sparkled in this altered vision, and Tavish could see clearly. The stars shone brightly in the cold air. It wasn't as cold as it had been in the mountains, or even in the hills. A steady wind blew from the east with the scent of salt from the Krimean Sea. He couldn't see the smoke from the city ahead of them, because he wasn't focused on the heat that had produced. Nor did he need to focus to know it was still there. Distant shouts and screams carried on the night air. Battle sounds? Or perhaps the cries of despairing farmers watching their crops burn?

As they gained in speed, leaving the village of Freemont, the wind of their passage drowned out the distant cries. Tavish could almost taste the tension in the air; nobody spoke, each person in their small party intent on tiny lights in the distance—fires in the watch towers. They formed a single file to navigate the road, though it was wide. Gabriel led in front, then Jardan, then Tavish and finally Kendrick. The life energy surged through Tavish, making him feel wide awake, but he was aware of distant aches in his legs, hints that once they were past danger, he'd be feeling the toils of the journey.

Time stuttered with the beat of hooves, a never-ending drum beat. Without the moons to reveal the passing hours, Tavish only had the changes in landscape to guide him. They passed by bits of light here and there—a mill, a dock, a house, some farms. Most seemed deserted.

The tiny lights in the distance which had seemed close together when they set off began to spread as they rode. With the strange bluish sight, Tavish could make out the pointed rooftops of towers, set at regular intervals on what must be the outer wall of the city. They were still rather far, at least three or four hours ride, he estimated, but already he could tell it was a great city, second only in size to the monstrosity of Geraine that they had passed before.

He couldn't dwell on the distance. Even with his abilities and the special sight that Gabriel had given their steeds, Tavish had to keep an eye on the road. Wagon tracks featured prominently on the packed dirt, and every now and then they passed by debris left behind by other travelers—a ripped and muddy cloak, a bucket, even a broken sword. They veered around each one, the horses' sides heaving at the hard pace. As the hours passed, they encountered not a single soul on the road, and this made Tavish wonder. Where were the fleeing peasants, if the fields were being burned? The soldiers? Would they only find ruins when they finally reached the city?

Tavish thought about shouting out a question, figuring they were making enough noise with the galloping hooves, but just as he opened his mouth, Gabriel raised up a hand and pulled back on his reins, slowing his horse to a walk. They all struggled to contain the animals. It seemed they burned with the same energy to act that he was experiencing.

In a hushed voice, Gabriel explained the sudden change of pace. "I sense people up ahead—a checkpoint, perhaps." They couldn't see anything, but the land had started to rise, so it was possible their sight of the checkpoint was blocked. Tavish adjusted his sword to be sure he could draw it easily if needed.

They rode forward at a walk until they had crested the small hill, and then Tavish could see it clearly. The river turned here, moving from their right side over to their left, with a large bridge as the only way across it. At the far end of the bridge he saw several torches planted into the ground, a campfire to one side, and about twenty men. Some stood beside the torches, presumably to check travelers, while others milled around the campfire.

Gabriel steered his horse over to Jardan and leaned to confer with him. Tavish couldn't hear any of the words, but by the looks on their faces, they weren't too happy with this situation. During the day this road had probably been full of traffic, including soldiers and refugees. At the moment, however, they were alone. Vulnerable targets.

Tavish nudged his horse over to Kendrick's and leaned over. "Do you think we can go around them?" he whispered, nodding his head in the direction of the checkpoint. Kendrick shook his head, his night vision making eyes glow faintly in the dark.

"If they have a Sun or Spirit Mage with them, they already know we're here, same as we know they're there. Plus it's difficult to swim across here. It's marshy on the other side of the bridge. No way we're getting our horses through that undetected." He grimaced. "We'll have to go through. Hopefully they're on our side."

At that moment the conference between their elders ended. Tavish straightened in his saddle as Jardan rode over to speak with them. He looked angry. He waved a hand at the two of them. "Mage Gabriel is going to take off the vision enhancements for himself and Aidah. We travel by firelight again. Don't draw your weapons, but be prepared for an ambush."

Tavish chewed his lip, his brows drawing together. "Can't he sense if they mean us harm? Are they even our soldiers?"

"They're from the Doane, according to Mage Gabriel," Jardan confirmed, but he didn't specify how or why the Spirit Mage had told him that. Tavish had the feeling that Jardan wasn't telling them everything. "They're focused on watching the road and warning away innocent travelers. Gabriel said that was about as much as he was getting from them at this distance."

Kendrick blew out a breath, gripping his reins tightly. "It doesn't matter, I suppose. If it's a trap, it's still the only way to the city, right? So we just have to be ready for a fight. Twenty's better than two thousand, anyways."

Jardan slapped him on the shoulder. "Good way to think about it. Now stay close." He returned to where Gabriel had his hand over Aidah's eyes, presumably to turn them back normal again. Tavish thought it was a bit of a waste, but on the other hand, he hadn't liked seeing her that way. The light of predawn would soon paint the sky purple. Even without light, he could see the road fairly well. Landaran couldn't be more than five miles away.

At Jardan's nod, Tavish and Kendrick produced small balls of fire to light their way. He noted that Gabriel didn't bother changing the horses' eyes back; they weren't that different looking to begin with, and he doubted the mage would want to change things again. Just as holding a continuously burning flame could be taxing, Tavish imagined it must be draining to change a living part of a person or animal.

That settled, Jardan clicked his tongue and urged his horse to a brisk trot. They kept to that pace as they neared the checkpoint, though Tavish longed to give his horse a swift kick and roar past them at full speed. Why hadn't there been guards in Freemont? He didn't like the feel of this. When he glanced at his sister, he noted that while she was holding on tightly to Gabriel with her left arm, her right hand she kept near the front of her, as if waiting. He wondered at that until he remembered the dagger he had given her, that he had insisted she wear. Good, he thought. It was gratifying to know that she was ready as well.

The closer they came, the more details Tavish could make out, and the tighter his gut seemed to clench. The men wore uniforms of dark blue over their leather jerkins, the color of the Doane Republic. Their hair was cut short and their faces were shaved. No pistols— cannons were sometimes used on the ramparts, Tavish had learned, but only if there was a Fire Talent nearby to protect the gunpowder from enemy mages. They did have swords, however, as well as crossbows. He didn't fancy trying to outrun a bolt shot from one of those

As one of the guards hailed them, Tavish found his fingers cramping up with the tight grip on the reins. He forced himself to loosen his hold, breathing slowly and deeply. Inside his head, he heard Gabriel's voice, *"Easy, young man. No need to alert them that we suspect anything. See if you can relax a little and smile."*

It wouldn't do to send them any warnings. Tavish agreed, so he tried to think happy thoughts as they drew near. They were going to be with Grandess, safe within the city in a matter of hours. They would find a way past the army. They'd be trained and protected.

"Halt! What business do you have, traveling at this early hour?"

The guard's crisp tone carried well in the still of pre-dawn. Tavish kept the smile but couldn't help glancing between the two men who stepped forward to block their way.

Even as the guard stepped in front of them, two more guards closed in from the side, converging on Gabriel and Aidah.

They didn't even give Gabriel a chance to answer.

The lead guard blocking them drew his sword, and the two men near Aidah grabbed at her, no doubt intending to pull her off the horse and spirit her away. Tavish raised a hand to flame them, but something—he wasn't sure what—seemed to cloud his vision. He blinked, his mind stuttering, trying to figure out what was happening, Too slow…it was as if something were battling in his brain, and he noted an expression of pain on Gabriel's face, as if he'd been struck.

Then suddenly time resumed its frantic pace. The guard who had been reaching up for Aidah fell back, clutching at his throat, blood flowing over his hands. She had stabbed him, with the knife hidden up her sleeve, Tavish realized, but there wasn't time to ponder that. The other guard pulled Gabriel off the horse and struggled with him. Gabriel seemed distracted, grimacing as he tried to break free.

Out of the corner of his eye, Tavish caught sight of a familiar face he'd hoped not to see again—Alaric Holt, Gabriel's son. No wonder Gabriel looked like he was under attack!

"Run, Aidah! Tavish—go with her!" Jardan cried, as Alaric neared Aidah.

Both Tavish and his sister seemed to come awake at that. Tavish saw Aidah give her horse a clumsy kick, but it was enough; the animal charged forward, nearly running over the two guards standing in their way. He spurred his own mount forward, determined not to leave her alone.

As he passed by the guards he pulled his sword out, and just barely managed to parry a blow one of them tried to aim at him. He didn't want to think what might have happened if it had connected. From behind he heard the sounds of fighting and the whistle of a bolt being shot from a crossbow; he ducked, and it flew past. He hoped Kendrick and Jardan could keep the guards from following.

Tavish caught up with Aidah and together they galloped past the torch lit checkpoint back into the violet shadows of the early predawn. It occurred to him that she might not have the wolf's vision any longer, but her horse still did, and it was a good thing. She threw him a frantic look as they left behind their friends, their protectors.

"What do we do?" she shouted and Tavish didn't know if she used her Talent to help him hear her words in his head or not, but he clearly heard her over the din of the galloping hooves. He looked ahead. They had only a few miles to reach the city. A mile or two before they came upon the hostile army. The road was not their friend any longer; they would be expected from that direction.

He remembered Gabriel had mentioned something about the northwest tower. "That way!" he shouted back to his sister. He slowed his horse down to a light canter, not trusting the ground beyond the road. Hopefully they were past the wet marshes. "We can't take the road," he said in a lower tone, once she had slowed her horse as well.

"Good idea," she agreed, as they left the road and started heading for the riverbank. She glanced behind them and Tavish looked as well, but he couldn't make out any pursuit, friend or foe. There seemed to be a great deal of heat back at the bridge, probably the result of Jardan and Kendrick using their powers in battle. "Do you think they'll catch up? Gabriel was supposed to teach me how to swim. The entrance is under water, at the northwest tower."

They fell silent and concentrated on riding. The eastern sky lightened, and even without his Talent, Tavish could start to see the walls of the city. He also could see rows upon rows of tents…and cannons…and cavalry. The men were scattered, probably still either sleeping or tending to their camps and animals, but it was obvious that this wasn't a little border raid. There had to be thousands of enemy soldiers, a mere mile or two away.

"This is nuts," Tavis said at last, bringing his horse to a halt as the enormity of their task hit him. He couldn't see any way they could sneak past so many enemies, especially while on horseback.

"We should probably walk," Aidah said, and perhaps she was reading his thoughts, or perhaps they were just on the same wavelength, just as they'd always been on their past adventures. She dismounted, and he followed, grimacing as his boots sunk an inch or two in the marshy earth. She chewed her lip as she often did when nervous, looking first towards the tower, then back the way they had come. "I don't want to leave the horses, but maybe if we do it will help Gabriel find us. They might also fall into the wrong hands, though."

Tavish nodded. "I don't think we can do anything about it. We're almost there. We can walk the rest, and we can't exactly sneak in with them. Grab whatever you think you need from the packs. I can use my Talent to make us less visible." He'd save the real invisibility for when they needed it most, but even so, he could make it harder for soldiers to spot them. He was about to reach into the saddle bags when Aidah grabbed his arm.

"I can make us less noticeable too. I can make people not want to notice us, or think about us." Tavish stared at her, confused, and she continued. "I did it back at the house, when I didn't want Grandpa to watch over me that day we found the wyrret nest."

Tavish suddenly remembered. Grandpa had come into the kitchen without a clue why he'd left. If she could repeat that, together with his visual cloaking, they might actually make it. "Do that." He pulled out only what he might need for the next twenty-four hours and then stepped away from the horse, taking his sister's hand, bending the light around them. "Let's do this."

Aidah gave a short nod, her hand firmly holding his. A cold wind blew from the east, scented with wood smoke and something else—the sea, Tavish guessed. He saw the campfires of the army like little beacons, too close for comfort.

Concentrating on making the light go mostly around them, Tavish began walking, crouching down a little just in case their tricks didn't work. They had to continue holding hands but that didn't matter; the closer they came to the city, the firmer the ground became. He felt terribly exposed, walking out in the open like this. They could see the men moving about their tasks with the approach of dawn. At any moment, Tavish expected a soldier to look their way and give a shout. He concentrated harder, against the sharp pins of a developing headache.

His sister's hand was cold, but the grip was firm, painfully so. He heard her breath whistling through her teeth as they drew closer and closer to the tents. If he messed up now, they would be captured. Several hundred yards beyond the tents, Tavish saw the walls of the city towering over them, solid and impenetrable. Along the ramparts he could make out the shapes of men—archers, he realized. What if they attacked? Would they be shot down and die with the enemy?

"I'm afraid too," his sister whispered, giving his hand a squeeze. He glanced at her and found her staring at him. "But you need to focus. I think we're starting to become visible." She pointed at their feet. Where before they had been almost translucent, they seemed a bit more solid. Tavish hastened to push away more of the light beams telling them to *go around.*

It worked; as he glanced down at his feet, he saw them fade a bit, blending into the ground. It was something like the ghostly image that Rangwar had presented when he'd appeared for them, but not as consistent, with some parts blending more than others.

He focused on his illusion as they crept closer, moving along the backside of the tents and campfires to head for the river. Their plan was to keep to the riverbank until they reached the city wall and the tower. From there, Tavish wasn't sure what they'd do. He'd never swum before, and apparently Aidah's lesson had been interrupted. He only hoped that someone on their side, anyone, would catch up to guide them.

As they crept past a particularly large tent, Tavish had time to feel a hot shiver go through him, like a premonition, and then suddenly a group of men rounded the corner, heading straight for them. Tavish tugged hard on Aidah's hand, mind going blank with panic.

His illusion faltered—it had to—but then Tavish felt an odd calmness sweep over him, blanking out his thoughts, making his eyelids droop. Too early. Too early to be up and about. Better to be sleeping right now. He blinked, uncertain of where the idea was coming from, fighting the sudden fatigue. In a sort of glaze, he noticed one of the men yawning as they passed by within feet of the twins. The men never stopped, but continued on past, heading south along the line of tents. The wave of sleepiness passed. Aidah let out a deep breath. "It worked."

Realization hit Tavish. She'd done *that?* She must have. It was the only explanation for why they hadn't been caught. She tugged on his hand, and he saw tension lining her face, belying the calm of her words. They dared not try that trick again. 'Let's keep moving."

They hurried forward, but they'd only gone another hundred yards or so past another large tent when a figure stepped out in front of them. His face was in shadow, but Tavish would know that silhouette anywhere. He gulped, wishing they'd waited for Gabriel and the others. The figure stepped forward, until Tavish could see the handsome face, the engraved armor and the crushed velvet cape.

Unlike the other times, this figure was solid. Real. He clutched at his sister's hand, forgetting every lesson on firestarting that he'd ever learned.

Rangwar's voice was warm with pleasure, not hollow or tinny as he had sounded in his ghostly form. "Well how very sweet of both of you. I'm glad to see that you saw the wisdom of turning yourselves over to me. You may have even prevented a war." He chuckled.

"No," Aidah said. Tavish felt a shock go through him at the sheer heat in her voice, a barely restrained fury. She looked at their enemy like she wanted to kill him. Tavish had known that she hated him because of what had happened to their family. But he'd never seen such rage in her before.

Rangwar chuckled, unfazed. "I appreciate your fire, dear, I truly do. But look around you. Hundreds of my soldiers. No one from the Doane here to support you. And me, of course. Come, let's put an end to all this silliness." He reached out a gloved hand, looking more like a benevolent uncle than the Emperor of a tyrannical nation.

Her hand flashed out almost faster than Tavish could see. Just as she had defended herself at the bridge against the men trying to remove her from her horse, Aidah defended herself, this time slashing with her little dagger at the outstretched hand. It clinked uselessly against the armor, but sliced through the leather glove, drawing blood across Rangwar's palm. He snarled, drawing his hand away and closing it into a fist.

Tavish would have expected his sister to cower back in fear. Instead, her eyes blazed. She looked ready to attack again. Tavish knew that he should help, do as he'd dreamed and flame the man. But somehow he seemed unable to focus, unable to act. He raised a hand half-heartedly, straining against his fear.

Rangwar never gave either of them the chance. Pain exploded in Tavish's head and down his spine. He doubled over, limbs curling up, unable to even think and barely able to breathe. It seemed to go on and on, and then just like that, it was gone, leaving him panting and blinking at the shock of it.

One glance over at his sister confirmed that she too had been struck by the pain. She lay on her back, clutching at her head. Their eyes met, and Tavish saw fear and awe that mirrored his own.

"You stupid fools," Rangwar said in a condescending tone. Even the words hurt Tavish's head, but he forced himself to roll to his side to look up at their enemy. They needed to get out of here, Tavish thought, but his muscles didn't seem to be obeying him at the moment. And where were they going to run to? This was it. They had failed.

Tavish glared up at Rangwar, determined to fight to the end if that's what he had to do. So he wouldn't be able to attack the man, so he might die in agony. He didn't care. He felt Aidah taking his hand in hers, a strong grasp that told him she felt the same way. He *knew* it, through that special link they shared. They'd die before the let the Emperor take them.

Rangwar saw the look. Tavish knew he did, because the pain assailed him again; Rangwar was going to teach them a lesson, Tavish figured, but he just didn't care. He screamed, body convulsing on the cold ground, wishing somebody, *anybody* would help them.

And then the pain stopped.

Tavish blinked his eyes, his vision a little fuzzy. A ghostly figure stood—or perhaps hovered—between Aidah and Rangwar, dressed in glowing white robes, with long, almost iridescent white hair almost floating about her without so much as a breeze. "Who—" he croaked out, forcing his body to move, sitting up. Aidah acted ahead of him, pulling him up to a standing position. She looked elated.

"Grandess," Aidah said, her voice full of hope.

25

The Protector

"Foolish girl," Rangwar said with a sneer, as Grandess Korva held off the pain, allowing Aidah to stand up and pull her brother up as well. Aidah knew Korva couldn't possibly fight Rangwar out of body. She'd experienced the differences in power between being there only in spirit and actually physically being there. She also knew she herself was no match for him.

"One day you'll stop calling me that," Korva grated under her breath. Aidah blinked. He wasn't talking to her? She pulled at her brother's hand, hard. "Go!" she hissed at him, trying to stay quiet, trying to use Korva's distraction. It had to be a distraction. Korva stood still, pain showing on her ghostly face as she held up one hand, a warning or an unconscious mirroring of what she was mentally doing, Aidah supposed, holding back Rangwar's mental attack.

A cold prickle stung the back of Aidah's neck. She heard Gabriel's voice in her head, *Where are you? We're coming. Don't stop moving—head for the tower.* Aidah glanced at Tavish to see if Gabriel had sent him the message as well.

A flash of understanding passed over Tavish's face. Aidah saw him, and then suddenly she couldn't see him, nor herself either. He was pulling that invisibility trick again, only full strength this time. She did her part to put up her mental shield over the two of them. It probably wouldn't be enough to hide them from a Spirit Mage of Rangwar's ability, but with Korva acting as a distraction, it just might give them enough time. Time to run to the river. Time to allow Gabriel and the others to rejoin them.

They ducked and scrambled; a few soldiers had drawn close to watch their Emperor torturing small children, but the twins were used to evading adult capture. Aidah crawled between two men and Tavish followed right after. The men never saw them, cloaked by Sun and Spirit. Even better, Rangwar also missed their exit, as he tried to reach out for Korva's ethereal form. She slipped out of the way, but just barely.

Aidah didn't have time to see more. She ran, pulling her brother along with her, furiously shielding her thoughts and emotions. The sun broke the horizon to the east. A crackle of thunder surprised her, almost causing her to trip over a tent rope. From the ramparts of the city walls, she heard shouts, and then arrows rained down, not close enough to strike the tents, but close enough to hit a few unsuspecting soldiers straying too near to the city. Korva must have ordered the attack. Another distraction.

Almost at the same time, Aidah heard Rangwar's shout, heard the fury and disbelief as he yelled for his men to *find the children*. She heard Korva cry out but she dared not look. She could see the river and the tower. The only problem was that she and Tavish would have to draw in close to the city, to reach the tower. Within the range of those arrows.

Another crack of thunder and a bright explosion—lightning— hit one of the tents, setting it aflame. This time Aidah did turn around, and what she saw made her pause. Illuminated by the light of fire, she caught sight of Jardan and Kendrick, their swords drawn, engaging with Empire soldiers. She caught a glimpse of Gabriel who seemed to be in a standoff with Rangwar.

Tavish turned and looked as well. "They caught up! Should we wait for them or keep moving?" He had that look on his face that told Aidah he was using his Talent too much again and was earning himself a bad headache for it. She couldn't worry about that.

She shook her head. "Reach the tower." She doubted that Gabriel had planned for them to be separated, but now that they were, she couldn't risk falling back into Rangwar's hands. She only hoped they didn't all sacrifice themselves for her in vain.

Even as she said that, Aidah caught sight of Rangwar's face turning in her direction, eyes searching for them. She felt *something* pass over them, like an invisible shadow. "Go," she whispered, afraid of even moving under that hawk-like stare. "I think he senses us."

The shadow became like a hard fist—she felt it hammer against her shields, the force of it actually causing her to stagger. "Run!" she screamed, knowing she couldn't hold up her part of their cloak for long. They ran, heedless of soldiers or arrows or anything else, dodging between groups of soldiers running back towards their commander. She tried not to think about Gabriel, about Jardan and Kendrick and what would probably happen to them. Lightning flashed again, but this time it struck the city ramparts. A man screamed and fell off the walls to land with a sickening crunch on the hard earth. Aidah focused on their destination, determined not to let anything else distract her. They couldn't be more than a thousand feet away now.

Chaos reigned on the battlefield as men scrambled to assemble. An arrow struck close by Aidah's foot, but she kept running. Surely Korva had told the city defences they were down here, hadn't she? Would they risk killing her to guarantee that Rangwar didn't take her?

Just as she thought that, the hammer of Rangwar's mind struck her again. This time the force caused her to stumble and fall, completely jarring her senses. She lost grip of Tavish but dimly she knew he was near, searching for her, still invisible. Dimly she felt his hand pulling at hers, trying to help, but she couldn't seem to move.

Come to me. Aidah heard Rangwar as clearly as if he were standing next to her. She stood up before she even knew what she was doing and began walking back towards him. An arrow struck the ground two paces from her. She didn't care. A figure stood in front of her, blocking her, pushing at her, but still she didn't care. She was going to him. That was all that was important.

The blurry vision of the figure before her faded, replaced by a much more active scene. She saw Gabriel fighting off three soldiers while Jardan traded small balls of fire with an enemy mage dressed in red leather armor. Kendrick fought nearby as well, using a sword wreathed in blue fire which cut a wide circle of destruction around him. Somehow Aidah knew that she was seeing out of Rangwar's eyes. Far away, she stumbled but regained her balance. *That's right. Come to me.*

Aidah started to reply that yes, of course she would come; it was unthinkable not to obey. But then Gabriel charged her—or Rangwar, rather—swinging a blade right at his face. A searing pain, and then she was herself again. Tavish had begun dragging her, his arms clasped tight around her shoulders. The urge to return to

Rangwar vanished. She grabbed Tavish's hands and stood on her own.

"I'm all right now," she said, but her voice shook.

Any response from Tavish was drowned out by a simultaneous blast of thunder overhead and the white flash of lightning striking far too close—close enough to smell it. She couldn't see Tavish through the illusion, but she felt his tug. Together they ran again, wondering if the next strike would hit them instead of the earth. Her ears rang, and the shouts of soldiers sounded muffled and distant.

The ground grew rocky and uneven as they neared the wall. They'd left the enemy soldiers behind, but they were in the open, hidden only by Tavish's powers. At any second Aidah expected to feel an attack of some kind—lightning, an arrow, perhaps even hot oil dropped from the high ramparts where she could hear men shouting.

She nearly stumbled and fell as the ground sloped towards the embankment of the river, turning to mud before the slowly moving water. The river here was both wide and deep, moving steadily towards the Krimean Sea. At the edge of the water, Aidah blew out a breath in frustration. The northwest tower actually stood a good twenty yards into the river, making that side of the city virtually unscalable. How were they to reach the secret chamber and trap door that was supposedly beneath the water?

Panic began to constrict her chest, making it hard to breathe. Tavish reached down to touch the water and groaned. "It's freezing," he moaned, glancing back the way they had come. "I guess we'd better try for it. Do you know where we're going?"

"Just that it's under the water," Aidah replied in a faint voice. She wasn't about to go back there and just give up, not after everything they'd been through. She pulled off her backpack. "We want to sink, but not to the bottom. Take off anything you can part with." They had to hurry. Any moment now Rangwar could beat Gabriel, or send his men here to fetch them. What would they do then?

She removed her stockings and cloak, leaving only the breeches and shirt she'd worn for riding. She pared a yearning look at her pack. Inside was the woolen dress she'd bought in Thornton. There would be others, she supposed.

No time to hesitate; she could hear the shouts of men back

near the enemy tents, shouting out orders to capture the twins. With a grimace, Aidah stepped into the water, breathing hard against the cold shock of it. Tavish was already waist deep. His focus was back towards the battlefield. "If they come, I'm raising my best fire storm."

She'd have to guide him, Aidah thought, fighting back the terror. Part of her wanted to curl up in to a ball right now, just shut out the world, the crash of thunder and the sounds of battle. For a brief second, death almost looked inviting. But she wasn't ready to die. She took a firm hold of Tavish's hand and made ready to dive into the water, with the vague notion of feeling her way down the tower wall.

Before she could do so, however, a flash of light appered behind her, streaking past her to form into a ghostly figure hovering over the water. Relief poured through her. "Korva!" The woman looked faded and tired, much as Rangwar had seemed at the end of some of his out of body encounters. But she was here.

"Hurry! The Emperor's men will be here soon," Korva warned them, but Aidah shook her head, holding out the hand not holding her brother's.

Tavish said it before she could. "We don't know how to swim!"

"And we don't know exactly where the entrance is," Aidah added, trying not to sound panicked. Her feet had gone numb already.

"I will show you," Korva said in a firm voice that immediately calmed Aidah's nerves. The elderly woman reached out a hand. Aidah glanced at Tavish, to see if he could see the spirit form of their Grandess as well, or if she would have to explain. By the look of rapt awe, she knew no words were needed.

Aidah wasted no more time, but reached out her hand. She expected it to pass right through, but instead she felt an electric shock as her hand came into contact with something that was not flesh, but not mere air either.

A vast awareness, a vast *knowing* intertwined with her own perspective, as delicately and as strongly as a braided rope. Where Rangwar's mind had felt overpowering, Korva's seemed more supportive, even though Aidah knew their power was nearly the same. More; Aidah felt her brother's mind as well, carried along like a child on piggyback, held protected from the vast experience of their

Grandess.

All the knowledge of how to swim lay right within reach; Aidah waded forward into the river until the water was chest high, allowing herself to get used to the cold. Tavish followed beside her; they linked hands, as they had already linked minds. Aidah felt/saw/heard the approach of guards. They needed to hurry.

Together they took several small quick breaths, then sucked in a great gulp of air and kicked downwards. They no longer held hands but they didn't need to—the link still existed in their minds. Aidah kept her physical eyes shut but saw through Korva's 'eyes' in her ethereal form, not that it mattered. The water was dark and murky with mud.

Deeper and deeper they kicked and pushed at the water. Korva told them to blow out most of their air to make themselves heavier and sink deeper. Aidah tried not to think about how they might not be able to get back to the surface for another breath. Her lungs burned, her ears hurt, and it seemed the weight of the entire river pressed down on her, threatening to make her black out.

She reached out, scrabbling for something, anything to tell her if she was even headed in the right direction. *"Can't breathe!"* she cried inside her head, hoping that Korva heard.

"Deeper!" Korva replied, in a stern tone that allowed no argument. Aidah felt like she couldn't possible kick any harder, that she'd let out every bubble of air inside. Cruel irony that they were both going to die, so close to safety.

Her hand brushed against something dark and slimy, and very solid—the stones of the tower, covered with algae. Aidah felt a mental tug from Korva to follow the stones and kick forward now, rather than down. In her mind's eye she saw a diagram of the tower. Under the water, the round tower hid a small chamber, sticking out from the structure like the stub of a branch from a tree. On the bottom of this little chamber would be a wooden trap door. The chamber was entirely under the surface of the river, invisible from above. She had to hurry before they both passed out.

"Kick!" She screamed inside her head at her brother. She kicked as hard as she could as well, feeling dizzy, feeling like at any second she would reflexively take in a breath, and that would be it. She felt along the edge of the tower to the chamber, felt how it protruded out several feet. Against all her instincts, she went beneath it, hoping to

feel wood rather than stone.

She didn't feel wood. Instead, she saw light.

A square of watery light, to be exact, denoting a surface somehow this deep under the water. Lungs ready to burst, Aidah swam towards it, and when her head broke the surface she coughed and drew in a grateful gulp of air. Before she could even take another breath, hands grabbed her arms and pulled her out, setting her down on hard cold stone. She wiped the water from her eyes to find herself in a small square chamber lit by candlelight with no windows. Three guards crouched over a trap door in the floor which was open to reveal the dark water of the river.

A second head popped up—Tavish. They pulled him out as well to lay down beside her, dripping wet. He couldn't seem to catch his breath and was coughing hard; she was light-headed and dizzy, but otherwise fine.

One of the guards knelt down before her, looking her over. He opened his mouth to speak, but then a glow suffused the room which was not from the candles. Korva rose through the floor, and Aidah knew she must have made herself visible, for everyone stared. The guards stood and snapped to attention. The one before Aidah spoke in a hushed voice. "Are the others coming?"

Korva looked troubled. "They're trying to fight their way out of the battlefield. I'm returning to help them. Close the trap door until I return and give you the signal." Her demeanor was firm, confident, used to leadership. Aidah almost felt the force of the woman's charisma like a physical thing. Not unlike the awe she had felt when she'd first met Rangwar, she thought with sudden clarity.

The guard nodded, and Korva turned to address the two guards by the trap door. "One of you, go up to the ramparts. Tell them to center all their attacks on the large northern tent. We need to pressure them into falling back."

The second guard nodded, and exited through a heavy iron door leading into the main tower stairwell. Korva nodded and addressed the remaining guards. "Once he returns and these two are dry, send them up to Captain Draych. He'll be in charge of them until either myself or Mage Holt are available."

"Yes, Protector," their guard said again. By the tone of Korva's voice, an underlying message was clear. *Protect these two at all costs.*

Korva nodded, and then she rose straight up through the

ceiling in a flash, leaving Aidah feeling dizzy and disorientated, their connection gone. She shivered, and gratefully took a blanket from the guard to wrap around herself. He looked kind, somewhere around the age of her parents, with a touch of gray in the temples and dark brown eyes. Once she and her brother both had blankets, he motioned for them to stand.

"Dry off. We're moving the two of you to a secure location. We have dry clothing for you as well." Even as he spoke, Aidah heard a far off explosion, and felt a slight vibration in the stone wall at her back.

They made short work of drying themselves. When it came to dressing in the clothes provided, however, Aidah almost balked. The red velvet gown was finer than anything she'd ever seen before. She had to have help in lacing up the bodice, though she was grateful for the modesty of a linen shift beneath the dress. Tavish looked almost as awkward as her in a tan leather jerkin and soft doeskin leggings. Once they were dressed, their guard motioned for them to follow. They left behind the remaining guard to watch over the secret entrance. Aidah hoped that their friends would find a way to escape and rejoin them.

Climbing the spiraling stairs was grueling work; they were both panting once they reached the circular chamber at the top of the tower. Twice on the way Aidah heard the crash of thunder, loud enough to shake the foundation. She could only imagine what was happening outside. She couldn't accept things. Was she really safe from Rangwar now?

They passed by a sturdy wooden door which led to the ramparts of the curtain wall. "I wish we could see what's happening" Tavish muttered, but the guard shook his head.

"Too dangerous. You'll be able to see a little from the top. There are arrow slits, though some will be manned." He guided them forward with a light touch.

At the top they found another trap door, this one with a ladder and a guard standing at attention. They made a hand signal to each other, a pass code, Aidah, presumed, and the second guard motioned for them to go on up. Feeling self-conscious about all the security, Aidah climbed.

She emerged in a small chamber with only a few pieces of furniture and a flat stone ceiling. As her guard had said, three archers stood at small slits in the walls with arrows nocked, looking towards the river and the battlefield to the west of the city.

What dominated the room, however, was a bed in the center, richly draped with a velvet coverlett and rich cotton sheets. Upon the bed laid an all too familiar figure: Korva. Her eyes were closed in deep sleep, her hands crossed over her heart. She wore full battle gear including some kind of light chain mail of a strange metal, not iron. Her silvery hair had been tied back into a long braid. In her ghostly form, she had worn white robes, Aidah recalled, and wondered at the difference. She hadn't thought of Grandess as a warrior before. But apparently, she was.

Aidah glanced at her brother and saw awe on his face. Somehow that made her own feelings more real, less confusing. *I'm overwhelmed by all this*, she thought, and double checked her aura to see if she was broadcasting. She wasn't. Gabriel had taught her well.

Slowly the two of them drew closer to the bed, past a guard standing with a hand on his sword, at the ready. Before they could come too close, however, the man spoke in a deep voice that matched his large frame. "Don't touch her. It could disrupt the spell."

Aidah pulled back her hand at once, feeling a chill go through her. She remembered when her mother had passed through the ghostly image of Rangwar, and how that had broken the spell. It must take an incredible amount of concentration to leave one's body and travel by spirit. Frowning, she looked at the arrow slits. Curiosity burned at her. 'Can we look to see what is happening?" The thunder was more distant now, but she could hear shouts of men calling for water to put out fires. Was the city burning? Or the tent where Gabriel and the others had been fighting?

One of the guards nodded to her and stepped aside. Feeling a cold prickle of anticipation, Aidah looked out the narrow opening. It didn't give her much of a view of the field below, but it gave her the instant impression of chaos. Smoke curled up from multiple fires around the tents, and soldiers seemed to be recklessly throwing themselves at the walls, trying to scale it. She couldn't see any sign of the place where Rangwar had confronted her, nor could she see any sign of Jardan or Kendrick's Talents. She looked away, disheartened, and allowed Tavish to get a look.

Just as she turned away, she heard a loud explosion, seemingly right outside the walls. Tavish jumped back, startled, but eagerly returned to watch. "That was a fireball! Do you suppose that was Jardan and Kendrick?" He stood on tiptoe, but then growled in frustration. "I wish I knew what was happening out there!"

Aidah started to answer, and then an explosion of another kind interrupted her. This seemed like an explosion of darkness, but of the mind rather than the eyes. Hopelessness and despair assailed her; she stumbled and fell to her knees. Around her, the guards staggered as well, which ironically comforted her. If Rangwar was attacking with his Spirit magic, at least he wasn't targeting just her.

She had to do something; she couldn't just stand here, inside this tower, and let everyone fight for her. Slamming her shields into place, Aidah found she was able to stand up. She crossed the room to her brother and extended the shield to him, as she had when concealing the two of them on the battlefield. He blinked, as if awakening from a dream and looked up at her. "Let's see what's happening outside," she said, offering him her hand.

Together they ran back over to the trap door in the floor. Aidah climbed down the ladder first, past the guard curled up on the floor. *This is what I could do to people if I were fully trained.* It was a sobering thought. Tavish followed, nimbly stepping past the inert form on the floor.

It wasn't far to the door leading to the ramparts. With a shove, Aidah opened it. Before her, she found soldiers all along the narrow top of the wall on their knees, struggling to get up, struggling against the unseen attack. She stepped out, feeling small and vulnerable, and looked down on the field where only a short time ago she and Tavish had been trying to stay invisible.

Aidah quickly spotted the thickest concentration of fighting, not far from where Rangwar had nearly captured her. From her vantage point, she could see only a cluster of armed soldiers but also black-robed men—mages, perhaps? In the midst of this furor she spotted orange—Jardan. Fire flashed around him in an arc, driving men back, but he was hopelessly outnumbered. Around them the earth was scorched, either from fire or lightning strikes.

She assumed that Gabriel and Korva in her ethereal form must be down there as well, and Rangwar, of course. Yet if Rangwar was attacking the entire curtain wall with his wave of emotion, did that mean Gabriel was dead? She searched frantically for him, this time using senses other than her eyes.

She wasn't sure what exactly she felt, but suddenly she knew he was over by the river, and he was in desperate trouble, trying to defend himself against both Rangwar and Alaric. Korva fought alongside him, but she was weakening. Aidah also remembered how limited Rangwar had seemed out of body; Korva must be the same. If they couldn't somehow distract Rangwar, then none of her friends would make it inside the city.

"What do we do?" Tavish hissed in her ear, looking down at the chaos below. Rangwar's men were taking advantage of their Emperor's spell, charging the walls with grappling hooks and ropes. All too soon they would be scaling the ramparts and overtaking this side of the city.

Aidah thought quickly. "Korva's going to have to come back to help break it, I'd imagine—which means she'll have to leave Gabriel to himself." She didn't want Gabriel to be killed or taken. He'd been kind to her, even when she'd vented her anger at him. She was a Spirit Mage, like him. But she was one person, small and untrained. What could she possibly do?

Gabriel was too far for any of her Talent to reach; the furthest she'd ever been able to extend it before had only been twenty feet or so. She looked at Tavish, remembering that here they had not just one mage, but two. He could possibly throw a fireball, but would it travel so far?

She gripped his arm. She couldn't take the time for words now; things were moving far too quickly. Instead, she dipped into his head and knew that he could never make it last that far. Aidah considered giving him more strength, as they had earlier, but he silently told her even that would do no good. They needed something that could be affected by muscle strength, not the strength or training of their Talents.

An arrow!

She remembered how the arrows had been striking all around them as they fled. It might be possible, with perfect control and aim, to get just enough distance to strike Rangwar, or at least distract him from the spell. Letting go Tavish's hand, Aidah raced over to one of the archers lying down along the narrow walkway of the parapet. She shook him awake, recalling how Gabriel had shown her to enhance abilities without sending too much.

She sent strength, and felt Tavish's presence beside her, supporting her, ready to assist. The archer came awake with a start and leapt up, looking at the two of them in confusion. She pointed over the wall. "No time to ask questions! Send an arrow into that group there—the one furthest back, do you see? Aim for the one in the red cloak!"

"Aye," the archer said, picking up his bow and reaching back to his quiver for an arrow. He nocked it, but before he could let it fly, Tavish reached out with a gleam in his eyes. "Let's really get him." The arrow began to burn with a low red flame near the tip. The archer pulled back the bow, blinking at the show of Talent.

Aidah dipped into his head, as she had with Tavish, and showed him where to aim, concentrating on his vision and muscle control, enhancing them. He let the arrow fly, and they watched as the flame grew with the speed of the wind.

It struck true, right into the break of armor where Rangwar's breastplate met his shoulder guard, under the arm. Not a lethal shot, but it was enough.

The blanket of despair vanished as the distant figure of the Emperor doubled over in pain. Men rose to their feet, dazed, and then began shouting orders. Aidah watched as the tiny figures of Gabriel, Jardan, and Kendrick made a run for the river, followed by a streak of light which could only be Korva.

She wanted to watch more, but a shout from the tower reminded her that she'd left their guardians behind. "You two! Back in the tower now!"

Tavish sighed and groaned. "At least we got to see what was happening." A rumble of thunder reminded Aidah that it probably wasn't safe standing on the parapet. She rolled her eyes at him, and ran back over to the doorway where their guard awaited.

As they climbed the ladder back up into the top chamber of the tower, Aidah heard voices echoing up the circular staircase. Hope stirred within her; they were opening the secret door to the river. That could only mean that soon their friends would be joining them. A guard pulled her up into the tower room and set her down with a stern look. She barely glanced at him; all her attention focused on Korva's sleeping form.

Outside, the sounds of the battle quieted. The sound of thunder grew distant, less furious. Aidah wondered if wounding

Rangwar meant they'd called off the attack. A rustle by the bed halted her thoughts. Stepping closer, she watched as a wrinkled hand brushed aside the covers.

Korva's eyes opened.

26

Welcome to Landaran

Aidah's heart stilled as Korva...Grandess...the Great Protector, blinked a few times and sat up. Just as Aidah had felt the difference between the spirit of Rangwar in her dreams and the real life version, Aidah felt awash with the power Korva radiated. She didn't care what Korva's age or appearance was; the woman exuded strength and beauty. Korva stood, and that regal bearing Aidah had seen earlier with the guards settled over the woman like a comfortable robe. She smiled and offered Aidah her hand. "Pleased to finally meet you, child. In the flesh."

For a second Aidah feared her mental privacy would be invaded yet again as she reached out to clasp hands, but Korva merely gave her hand a shake. A guard stepped forward to drape a light blue cloak over Korva's shoulders. She strode across the room to where Tavish stood with an uncertain look in his face, and gave him a nod. "I saw your handiwork—very nice. I expect Sun Mage Omar will be pleased to add you to the ranks."

"Yes, Ma'am—Grandess. Protector," Tavish stammered, blushing bright red.

Korva then tilted her head, cracking her neck, something Aidah would never have expected. "I detest staying out of body so long. Come. Gabriel and the others should be up here soon. Everyone is waiting for us at the Citadel. Rangwar has been wounded, but it won't take him long to recover. I'd wager that we have a week, perhaps two, before the next attack. Until things stabilize, you'll be staying inside my Keep." She smirked. "It's a fortress within a fortress. No one will be able to harm you there."

Aidah let out a breath she didn't realize she'd been holding. She was safe for now, but they'd attack again? "Has the Emperor ever managed to invade the city?" She recalled there had been a war before she was born. Grandpa had fought in it, but never spoke of it. He hadn't allowed Uncle Brenton to join the Guard because of it.

Korva shrugged. "Once, when I was young. I've built up the city defenses considerably since then. I've also made sure he cannot starve us out with a long siege; we have access to wells and fisheries. He can make things uncomfortable, however."

At the sound of the trap door opening, Korva broke off their talk, turning expectantly.

Aidah felt Tavish's anticipation as he stood beside her, and when he saw who it was, he gave a whoop of joy and hurried over to help Kendrick up the ladder into the room. "We didn't think you all were going to make it! How did you manage to get away?"

Kendrick grinned, looking damp from the river but unharmed. He opened his mouth to answer, then noticed Korva's presence. Eyes widening, he abruptly stopped and bowed. "Madame Protector!" He stiffened and gave an awkward salute.

Korva dismissed him with a nod, striding past him to where Jardan was helping Gabriel into the room. Gabriel looked far worse for wear, favoring his right leg and holding a bandage to his left shoulder. At once two guards hurried over to assist him on either side, guiding him to sit on the bed. Jardan also limped, but Aidah couldn't see any marks on him. His clothing looked a little singed, even though it was wet.

As Tavish and Kendrick drew aside, Aidah hesitated, wondering whether to listen to Kendrick's tale, or stay with the adults. What was to become of her now? Would Gabriel continue to train her, or would Korva be her mentor, as he'd hinted earlier?

She decided to listen to Kendrick. It was likely that she and Tavish would be separated and sent to their mentors for training. She didn't know when they would be able to see each other again. Behind her, she heard the adults speaking quietly as Kendrick wrapped a blanket tighter around himself, against the chill air. He began, "We almost didn't make it. They surrounded us. We heated up weapons and armor, sent fireballs—anything we could do to keep the soldiers off. We were lucky because their Sun Mages weren't there. I think the Protector distracted them somehow, or maybe she had another Spirit

Mage doing that. But wow. Gabriel and Rangwar drew swords, and they started sparring. We became cut off from them but we couldn't do much about it. And then that spell! Did you guys feel it? The sadness nearly knocked me over, it was so strong."

Tavish glanced at Aidah. She felt both fear and gratitude from him "Yeah, we did—but Aidah shielded herself and me after it hit. That's how we were able to help you." He practically danced on his heels, and Aidah realized how important it had been to Tavish that Kendrick had made it through.

Kendrick nodded. "I don't know what exactly you guys did. But suddenly the guards all passed out around us, and Gabriel and the Protector were there. They told us to run. We did."

"It was Aidah. She roused one of the archers—gave him strength, maybe? And then I set his arrow to ignite as it neared its target." Tavish looked at Aidah. "Is that right? Did you control the archer as well?" She heard a warring between pride and concern in his voice, and wondered at it. A troubling future suddenly yawned before her, one where she would grow and grow in power, and grow more distant from everyone she knew. Even her brother.

Aidah shook her head. "I just shielded him from Rangwar and gave him strength." It had been just a little use of her Talent, and yet it had made a huge impact. She wanted to ask about what had happened at the checkpoint with Alaric, but their talk was interrupted as Jardan walked over to them. Korva had bent to examine Gabriel's wound, and Aidah could feel an electric charge in the air. She realized it wasn't actually an electrical charge. Korva was healing Gabriel.

Jardan let out a breath, hands on his hips as he looked Aidah and Tavish over. "That could have gone better. Korva gave us both a lashing that we should have approached the city via the river—*under water*. Rangwar wouldn't have even known we'd slipped past that way." He shook his head. "I am deeply sorry, for leaving the two of you like that. What a mess."

Aidah flushed, feeling uncomfortable, but Korva saved her from having to speak. "They're here now, and that's the important thing. We need to head down into the city, before my generals start to worry." She straightened and stepped back to allow Gabriel to stand. He looked exhausted. As the rush of excitement started to dwindle, Aidah realized she was exhausted as well. They all were.

Gabriel noticed Aidah staring at him. "I'm all right. The

Emperor is a better swordsman. He can also use his Talent and fight at the same time, which I cannot." He smiled encouragingly. "Are you ready to meet the citizens of Landaran, Aidah?"

She felt her stomach flutter again. The way people were treating her, Aidah was beginning to feel like royalty. It was surreal. "I guess so," she said, aware of how small her voice sounded.

"With me, then," Korva commanded in a tone that allowed no argument. The guards opened up the trap door and assisted the elderly Protector in descending the ladder. The time for catching up was past, for now at least.

Aidah threw on last look at Kendrick and Jardan. "Hopefully you all can visit me? I'd like to hear the rest of what happened." Already she was having visions of another tower like this, of being locked away. Wouldn't that be safer for all?

Jardan looked confident, which helped settle her nerves. "Don't fear, Aidah. You'll have plenty of time to catch up with your brother and Kendrick." He nodded towards the trap door. "Go on, then. They've all been waiting for you."

Aidah took a deep breath. She felt two presences both monitoring and containing her emotions, ensuring that her Talent did not run loose and affect others. Gabriel's presence felt warm and concerned. She wished Korva's felt the same, but it seemed cold and aloof to her. She saw a frightening intensity of purpose in the woman. It dawned on her that the one her family called "Grandess" would kill without qualms anyone who threatened the Doane, including Aidah, if it ever came to that.

No wonder she was called the Protector.

"I'm ready," Aidah said in a soft voice. She followed Korva down the ladder, to the door she had passed through earlier leading to the ramparts. The others followed close behind, as they stepped out into the sunlight of breaking dawn.

The light blinded Aidah momentarily; she paused as her eyes adjusted, and heard the sound of armor slapping armor in a rythmic beat. The archers manning the wall stood in a line, snapping to attention as Korva emerged from the tower, right hand over breast, heads rigidly held upright. Aidah glanced at them curiously, wondered at the silence of the city. From far away she could hear voices, but they were too low to understand. Those sounds came from the battlefield far below them, she realized.

Korva gave the archers barely a glance, but strode along the ramparts to a stone staircase descending into the city proper. In her focus to repel Rangwar's attack and help Gabriel and Jardan, Aidah hadn't even looked at the city itself. It stretched out before them, tall gleaming towers of marble and stone, around which were packed hundreds, maybe thousands of tiny red-tiled roofs, narrow streets where buildings climbed three and even four stories high. Directly below their section of wall, Aidah saw a large fortress of some kind, teeming with military.

Last, in the center of the city upon a hill stood a second fortress, a castle with its own towers and walls. Hexagonal in shape, the walls were yet another layer of defense should the enemy ever get inside the city. A single tower rose from the main hall with a spired tip. Korva's castle? Aidah wondered.

All this Aidah took in as she walked down the stone steps, following in the wake of Korva's passage. Korva's armor caught the morning light in a dazzling sparkle, and a light cloak of blue wool covered her shoulders, flapping with the salty breeze from the sea. On the ground, rows upon rows of soldiers had lined up to watch. A cheer arose as they reached the first landing and began descending the final steps.

"Hail the Protector!" they shouted, once Korva and Aidah reached the courtyard. She saw both men and women dressed in armor, some carrying swords and others armed with crossbows. All stared at Aidah in open curiosity. Korva continued to walk past the lines of soldiers, towards a group dressed more finely than the rest. Aidah had to assume they were the commanders of the city's military might.

Out of the corner of her eye, Aidah saw her brother walking close by Kendrick, a look of nervous admiration on his face. She felt thankful for the rich fabrics Korva had provided for them, though it seemed odd to be wearing a gown in this crowd. She would have felt more comfortable in leggings or armor, even as Korva wore.

They halted in front of four individuals. One woman with graying red hair in full armor smiled and nodded at them, holding a finely crafted steel helmet in under one arm. Next to her stood a man with long white hair but no wrinkles, wearing only pieces of armor over blue robes, including chest plate, vambraces, and mailed gloves. A Storm Mage, Aidah realized. The third fellow had olive skin and a full beard and wore light chainmail with an orange cloak—Sun Mage, she guessed. And the last person wore no armor at all, but instead a light blue velvet cloak over a white satin doublet, a man with deep set eyes and thin lips. His cloak bore the mark of the Doane, a triangle with three spheres. Mayor, perhaps? Or possibly President of the Republic.

Korva stopped before them and motioned for Aidah and Tavish to stand beside her. "Aidah and Tavish Dernholt—meet the heads of our City Council. Head of City Defenses, General Tania Goring, Head of the Storm Mage College, Grant Gail, Head of Sun Mage College, Malik Omar, and Mayor Ian Haldane. Of course the two of you already met the Head of the Spirit Mage College, Gabriel Holt." She looked at Aidah expentantly, and Aidah realized it was time to show manners. She made a hasty curtsy, and Tavish followed with a clumsy bow.

"Very pleased to meet you," Mayor Haldane responded, with a nod. The others nodded as well, and General Goring looked at them appraisingly. Malik smiled at Korva.

"So finally, eh?" he asked, and there was no formality to his voice, leaving Aidah to wonder how these different leaders worked with each other. She had the sinking feeling that this would all be part of her studies very soon.

Korva put a hand on Aidah's shoulder, and Aidah jumped a little, startled by the contact. In Korva's voice she heard more warmth than she'd ever heard before. "Yes. Finally."

Aidah stared at Korva, as the soldiers around her tapped at their swords in unison, almost a sort of applause. It surprised her that Korva smiled. "What?" Aidah asked.

With a deep breath, Korva straightened, the lines of age on her face somehow appearing less engrained, losing some of the weariness she had shown since rising from the bed in the tower. A light of hope shined in her eyes. "You. My heir. I formally name myself your Mentor, and appoint you as Protector Apprentice. When I am gone, you will assume my duties to keep the Doane safe."

Aidah felt the ground sway a little and had to reach out for her brother's hand to steady herself. She'd known it, and yet it was something altogether different to have it announced publically.

Beyond the Citadel and the troops, she saw runners heading out into the city, carrying the word. The distant sounds of cheers carried on the morning air.

She'd reached safety. But before her loomed the prospect of trying to learn two hundred years' worth of knowledge.

And a war to be fought and won.

ABOUT THE AUTHOR

Judy Goodwin developed a passion for writing at a young age, creating picture books from the time she could read and write. She continued this passion throughout her schooling, earning her BA degree in Creative Writing from the University of Arizona. In her day job, she works as a technical writer in the healthcare field. She enjoys sharing her love of books and fantasy with her daughter and partner. They live in Gilbert, Arizona, with two Shiba Inu (Japanese) dogs, one wiener dog, and four black cats.

Ms. Goodwin has published short stories in small press and online magazines including *Space and Time, Dreams and Nightmares, Alienskin,* and *Beyond Centauri.* With the advent of eBooks and indie publishing, she decided to move into the brave new world of publishing with the debut of her first novel, *Heart of the Witch.*
Journey to Landaran is her second full length novel, the first installment of the *Spirit Mage Saga.*

You can find more titles by Judy Goodwin at Amazon, Barnes and Noble, and other online retailers. She loves to hear from fans either at her facebook https://www.facebook.com/judy.goodwin.9026 or at her blog, judygoodwin.wordpress.com.

Sign up for sneak peeks, upcoming releases, freebies and more at her mailing list: diamondprintpress.com .

www.ingramcontent.com/pod-product-compliance
Lightning Source LLC
Chambersburg PA
CBHW031546240626
47153CB00002B/396